DIANE D
And The Other Personality
Volume 3

by
Doris Miller

Published by:

Hill Publications
Queens, New York

DIANE D
And The Other Personality
Volume 3

by
Doris Miller

DIANE D
And The Other Personality
Volume 3
First written in **2016**

Book production by

Hill Publications

1.   Title. 2. Author

Library of Congress Catalog Card Number XXXXXXXXXX

ISBN No. **978-0-9662055-6-5** Softcover

DIANE D
And The Other Personality
Volume 3

Synopsis

DIANE D And The Other Personality is the third book of the series **DIANE D**. The **DIANE D** series is about a family owned Charity and Entertainment Organization called The Diaz-Davidson Organization. The Diaz-Davidson Organization would perform shows and concerts in clubs, theaters and arenas around the country and around the world to raise money for charity.

The **DIANE D** series involves 3 generations of the Diaz-Davidson and Brown families. The lead character of the series is the young, gorgeous, attractive, Dominican female named Diane Denise Brown known as Diane D. Diane D's grandparents Margarita and Tomas own and run the The Diaz-Davidson Organization which Diane D performs for.

Diane D, her older brother Nicolas, her younger brother Mickey, her mom Mary, Mary's parents Margarita and Tomas, Mary's older brother Tonio, Mary's younger sister Marilyn, Diane D's cousin Nancy and her other cousin Charlotte were all born in the Dominican Republic. They speak both Spanish and English. They now live in a mansion in Northern Westchester, New York.

Diane D's dad Barry Brown and his side of the family were all born in St. Thomas, Virgin Islands. Diane D's dad Barry who does not speak any Spanish also lives in Northern Westchester with her, her mom Mary, her grandparents Margarita and Tomas and the rest of Mary's family while his side of the family lives in Queens, New York. Diane D's handsome African-American husband Michael also lives with her family in Northern Westchester.

Diane D is a performer who sings and dances on stage with six beautiful female back-up singers and dancers called the Dianettes which includes her two cousins Nancy and Charlotte and four other young ladies named Miranda, Bernice, Lonna and Kelly. Diane D and the Dianettes are also gymnasts who sometimes do flips during their dance performance routines. Diane D also has extreme background skills in the martial arts and has extreme skills in meditation.

DIANE D And The Other Personality involves the 9-year old chubby black boy Marcus whose older brother Richard sent Diane D and her family a hoax letter a few years prior about a little three-year old boy that goes to Marcus' school who is dying of leukemia. After Diane D and her family received the letter, Diane D made a plan to go to the school to sing and perform for the children there and search for the child who has leukemia.

After Marcus tells Diane D the truth that the child she came all the way to the school for never existed, that she and her family had been tricked into coming to the school, she became shocked by the news that the child she became attached to, grew to love, bought toys and gifts for never existed. She became hurt by the betrayal. She became sad by it. She then became angry by it. She then went crazy and brutally attacked Marcus right inside the school hallway half killing him, then chased him down the back stairwell of the school! It was later discovered that Diane D does not remember attacking Marcus and claims she never attacked him!

Three years has now gone by. Marcus claims to have gotten nightmares since that night Diane D attacked him and claims that he continues to constantly have nightmares of that fateful night Diane D beat and attacked him on that third floor school hallway then chased him down the back stairwell of the school.

This story also involves Diane D's cousin Nancy accidentally encountering Diane D's other personality late one night inside the family's mansion in the upstairs hallway outside the bedrooms. After Nancy's eerie encounter with Diane D's other personality, Diane D goes inside her bedroom and shuts the door. Nancy becomes frightened by Diane D's strange behavior. She turns and goes to alarm the rest of the family banging on all their bedroom doors!

Later, Diane D's family rush to her bedroom door! They call out to her and bang on her bedroom door, but Diane D does not respond. Her family try to open her bedroom door, but it is locked, they cannot get in. After Diane D's grandfather Tomas goes and gets the master key, he unlocks her bedroom door. Diane D's family bursts into her bedroom and surround her as she lays face down on the bed. They grab her and sit her up on the bed. They question her, wanting to know what is going on with her.

Several days later, two doctors, Dr. Stone and Dr. Kahn, have Diane D under hypnosis inside a large hypnosis room at a hospital as she lays on her back on a psychiatrist couch with her hands folded over her chest and her eyes completely shut. The doctors then have Diane D's family enter the room. Diane D's family including her parents Mary and Barry, her grandparents Margarita and Tomas, her older brother Nicolas, her husband Michael, her cousin Nancy, her other cousin Charlotte, her aunt Marilyn and her uncle Tonio quietly sit in the side and middle of the large room. Diane D is totally unaware that her family is sitting in the room as she lays under hypnosis. Doctors then bring out Diane D's original personality as her family watches. The doctors speak to Diane D's original personality. After the doctors finish speaking with Diane D's original personality, they bring her family out into the hallway. They tell Diane D's family that they're going to try to bring out her other personality, the one that her cousin Nancy had an encounter with. The doctors tell Diane D's family that before they try to bring her other personality out, they want to protect themselves from her other personality due to her other personality's violent history. They tell Diane D's family that they would need their permission to have Diane D's physical body wrapped in chains and have her physical body chained to the psychiatrist couch to be on the safe side, just in case her other personality becomes out of control like it has done several times in the past. Diane D's family would not hear of it! They claim they do not want to see or have her physical body wrapped in chains and chained to the couch! The doctors tell Diane D's family that they will refuse to bring her other personality out to the surface unless her physical body is wrapped in chains and chained to the couch. After a while, Diane D's family gives in. When Diane D's family re-enters the room, they are shocked and devastated seeing her physical body wrapped in chains and chained to the couch with shackles around her feet.

This story also involves Diane D's grandmother Margarita having her own eerie encounter with Diane D's other personality late one night inside Diane D's hospital room.

Table of Contents

Chapter 1

The Flashback!

FLASHBACK: Three years earlier

One Friday night, Diane D is inside an elementary school cafeteria which is crowded with parents and children. Diane D approaches all the parents who have little boys who appear around 3-years old searching for the child who has leukemia. Diane D does not find the child. Later on that night, she goes to perform inside the school auditorium for the children and their parents. After Diane D's performance inside the auditorium is over, she signs autographs for the children and their parents. Marcus, a chubby 9-year old black boy, approaches Diane D. He tells her that he wants to talk to her in private. Diane D tells Marcus to meet her in the upstairs hallway outside the principal's office.

Later on, Marcus meets up with Diane D, her husband Michael, her uncle Tonio and her aunt Marilyn in the dark dimly lit third floor school hallway outside the principal's office. Marcus is nervous. He tells Diane D that he wants to talk to her alone. After Diane D's husband Michael, her uncle Tonio and her aunt Marilyn go into the principal's office to wait for her, Marcus takes Diane D around two corners to the other side of the building where no one else could see or hear them. He takes Diane D halfway down the other hallway to the side, that's when he confesses the truth to her and tells her that there is no little boy in the school who has leukemia, that there never was a little boy in the school who has leukemia. After Marcus finishes confessing the truth to Diane D, she becomes shocked by the news. She refuses to believe what Marcus just told her. Marcus convinces to Diane D that he is telling the truth that there is no little boy who goes to his school who has leukemia, that it was all a hoax planned by him and his brother just to get her to come to his school to perform. Diane

7

D continues to remain shocked. She starts to back away from Marcus. Marcus apologizes to Diane D for the hoax. Diane D backs all the way to the corner of the hallway and stands there not saying a word as she angrily stares down the hallway at Marcus.

Marcus decides to leave the area and get back to where the principal's office is. As he is about to go past Diane D to get back to where the principal's office is, Diane D goes right in front of him blocking his path! She's refusing to let him go by her to get back to where the principal's office is. Marcus becomes shocked at what Diane D is doing! He makes a few attempts to go past her to get back to where the principal's office is, but she keeps blocking his path refusing to let him go by her. On Marcus' final attempt to get past Diane D, she goes crazy! She jumps, spins her entire body around and gives Marcus a kung fu kick breaking his arm and wrist! Marcus' arm and wrist are broken and bent backwards out of shape! He is shocked at what Diane D just did! He can't believe what she had just done! He then turns and runs from her! Diane D then chases Marcus down the dimly lit school hallway! Then she jumps and drop kicks him so hard that she causes his little body to fly two feet in the air! Marcus' body lands hard on the floor!

After a while, Marcus reaches for his cell phone inside his pocket. When he tries to make a call, Diane D charges at him and gives him more kung fu kicks, breaking more of his bones and knocks his cell phone right out of his hand! Marcus' cell phone lands several yards away from him! He lays helpless, injured and bleeding on the floor crying and screaming for help, but no one sees him or hears his cries for help! He lays there helpless for hours trapped alone with Diane D inside that isolated dark school hallway. He suddenly hears Diane D's cell phone ringing, but she does not answer it. She stands there in a state of trance staring at Marcus as she ignores her cell phone while it is ringing inside her pocket. When Marcus gets the strength to stand up, he starts to back away from Diane D! He gets closer to the end of the hallway where the large window and exit sign are. The eerie sounds of the crickets coming from outside the window become louder as Marcus gets closer to the end of the hallway. He quickly turns his head back forward and looks back at Diane D who is standing way down the hallway staring at him as she ignores her cell phone.

Marcus gets further away from Diane D. He suddenly hears Diane D's cell phone stop ringing. He stops right in his tracks and anxiously looks towards Diane D's cell phone again. He frighteningly looks at Diane D again as he slowly starts to back away from her again. Suddenly, he hears his cell phone ringing which is still laying on the floor in the distance not too far from Diane D. Marcus stops right in his tracks again. He anxiously looks at his cell phone! He frighteningly looks back at Diane D.

Diane D continues to stand there in the dark school hallway in a trance like state looking down the hallway at Marcus giving him a cold stare with half dead puffy and swollen eyes as her face remains pale, bruised and bleeding.

Marcus cell phone continues to ring. He anxiously looks at his cell phone again as it lays all the way down the hallway. He trembles as he frighteningly looks at Diane D again! He anxiously looks back at his cell phone. He painfully tries to ease towards his cell phone. Diane D suddenly moves and is about to charge Marcus! Marcus quickly stops and steps back as he cries! Diane D stops right in her tracks and stands there in a trance continuing to give a cold hard stare down the hallway at Marcus.

Marcus slowly backs away as he cries and frighteningly looks at Diane D! His cell phone continues to ring as it lays on the floor down the hallway. He painfully tries to ease towards his cell phone again. Diane D moves and is about to charge Marcus again! Marcus quickly stops and steps backs again! Diane D stops right in her tracks again as she continues to give a cold hard stare at Marcus.

Marcus' cell phone is still ringing as it lays on the floor. He sadly looks at his cell phone and cries as he slowly backs away. He frighteningly looks at Diane D again. He turns his head around again and looks towards the end of the hallway again as he continues to back away.

Marcus is closer to the end of the hallway where the large window and exit sign are. The eerie sounds of the crickets coming from outside the window continue to become louder as Marcus gets closer to the end of the hallway. Marcus quickly turns his head back forward and frighteningly looks back at Diane D. He suddenly stops right in his tracks and freezes with fear as he stares down the hall at Diane D! He sees that Diane D has moved closer to him!

Diane D still appears to be in a state of trance as she stands there completely still, not moving at all with the bruises, swelling and the blood still on her eerily pale face as her half dead swollen eyes remain fixed on Marcus! Suddenly, she moves, kicks one the objects on the floor out of her way as she slowly starts to walk down the hallway towards Marcus.

Marcus remains frozen in fear as he watches Diane D coming down the hallway towards him.

Suddenly, Diane D starts to run towards Marcus!

Marcus stands there frozen in fear watching Diane D running towards him! He finally breaks loose, quickly turns around and makes a quick painful dash for the back stairwell doors! Marcus pushes the stairwell doors open. He quickly runs into the stairwell as the stairwell doors close behind him!

Marcus cries and screams as he frighteningly and painfully runs down the flight of stairs practically rolling down the stairwell with his body still bent forward in pain! He frighteningly looks up and screams then hears heavy footsteps jumping and charging down the top flight of stairs after him! He screams even more!

Marcus reaches the first floor landing as he continues to cry and scream! He quickly runs to the first floor stairwell doors as his body remains bent forward shouting, "Aaaaaahh! Help me! Somebody help me please! Aaaaaahh!"

Later on that night while Diane D wakes up inside her family's van as they are riding back home. She feels intense pain all over her body not knowing where it's coming from. It is later discovered that she has no memory of her attack on Marcus! She has no memory of chasing after him down the hallway or down the back stairwell of the school and claims she never attacked him! Doctors then discover that Diane D suffers from Split Personality Disorder. She is sent away to a state mental hospital for a while for what she did to Marcus.

Chapter 2

Marcus' Nightmare!

It is now three years later. Marcus, who is now around 12-years old, is laying in his bed tossing and turning. He is having a nightmare!

NIGHTMARE:

Marcus finds himself right back in the same area in the dark dim isolated school hallway. He is frightened, scared, bleeding and injured as he steps backwards towards the end of the hallway looking back towards the end of the hallway as he continues to cry with his body bent forward in pain. He is getting closer to the end of the hallway where the large window and exit sign are. The eerie sounds of the crickets coming from outside the window become louder as Marcus gets closer to the end of the hallway. Marcus quickly turns his head back forward and looks back at Diane D.

Diane D is standing way down the dark school hallway staring at Marcus. She is in a trance like state looking down the hallway at Marcus giving him a cold stare with half dead puffy and swollen eyes with her face pale, bruised and bleeding.

Marcus continues to back away as he cries and frighteningly looks at Diane D. He turns his head around again and looks back towards the end of the hallway again as he continues to back away. He is closer to the end of the hallway. He quickly turns his head back forward. He suddenly stops right in his tracks and freezes with fear! He sees that Diane D has moved closer to him! Suddenly, Diane D moves and slowly starts to walk towards Marcus. She then runs towards him!

Marcus stands there frozen in fear! He finally breaks loose, quickly turns around and makes a quick painful dash for the back stairwell doors! He pushes the stairwell doors open and quickly runs into the stairwell as the stairwell doors close behind him!

Marcus cries and screams as he frighteningly and painfully runs down the staircase practically rolling down the staircase with his body still bent forward in pain! He hears heavy footsteps jumping and charging down the top flight of stairs after him! He screams even more! He quickly runs to the first floor stairwell doors as his body remains bent forward shouting, "Aaaaaahh! Help me! Somebody help me please! Aaaaaahh!"

PRESENT:

"Aaaaaahhh!" Marcus wakes up screaming as he sits up on his bed! His slim mother Jessica and slim grandmother Vanessa rush right into his bedroom!
They rush right to him and shout, "Marcus!" They bend to him and grab him as Vanessa shouts, "Marcus, it's okay! It's us!"
"Aaaahhh, help me, help me!" Marcus screams. "She's still after me! She keeps coming after me in the back stairwell of the school! She keeps trying to kill me! We have to call the cops!"
"Call the cops?!" Jessica shouts.
"Yes! I want her arrested!"
"Arrested?!" Jessica and Vanessa shout.
"Yes!"
"Oh Marcus!" Vanessa shouts. "You're having another nightmare about Diane D! You can't have her arrested, because she hasn't done anything to you lately! She hasn't been anywhere near or around you since a few years ago that night inside that school hallway!"
"I don't caaare! I still want her arrested because she keeps coming into my dreams and nightmares!"
"Marcus the police can't arrest Diane D for that!" Jessica shouts. "She has no control over your dreams and nightmares!"
"She just might! I still want her arrested! We have to call the police on her!"
"No Marcus!" Vanessa shouts. "We cannot call the police just because you see someone in your dreams and nightmares! They cannot control your dreams and nightmares! It's your own subconscious doing that to you!"
"So what are you saying Grandma?! Are you saying that you're not going to call the police on Diane D?!"
"Yes that's what I'm saying Marcus! The police cannot stop you from dreaming or having a nightmare about somebody!"
"Okay then! If you won't call the police on Diane D, there is only one way to stop her from coming into my dreams and nightmares."

"Oh yeah?! And what is that Marcus?!"

"Kill myself!"

"What!" Vanessa and Jessica shout. "Kill yourself?!"

"Tell us you didn't say that Marcus," Jessica shouts. "Tell us you didn't say that!"

"I did say that Mom! And I mean it too!"

"No Marcus nooooooo!!"

The next day, Officer Henley, a stocky white male police officer with dark hair around his mid 40's and Officer Grey, a slim black male police officer around his early 40's are standing outside the Diaz-Davidson Charity Organization's front door. Alex, a tall white/Hispanic male with dark hair who is one of the employees, opens the front door. He sees the police officers and says, "Hi. May I help you?"

"Yes," Officer Henley says. "I'm Officer Henley and this is Officer Grey. We would like to speak to someone in charge of the Diaz-Davidson Organization."

"You mean Margarita and Tomas Diaz-Davidson?"

"Yes them."

"Oh they're not here right now. They're out of town."

"They're out of town?"

"Yes."

"Where?"

"They went back to their home country to the Dominican Republic."

"They're in the Dominican Republic now?"

"Yes."

"How long have they been there?"

"Oh they've been there for the past few months."

"They have?"

"Yes."

"Do you know when they're returning?"

"They should be back in another few months."

"Another few months?"

"Yes."

"Is Diane D with them? Is she in the Dominican Republic too?"

"Yes Diane is with them in the Dominican Republic also."

"She is? How long has she been there?"

"Oh she left the same time they left which was a few months ago."

"Has she been back and forth here since a few months ago?"

"No Diane hasn't been coming back and forth. She hasn't left the Dominican Republic since she's gone there with her family a few months ago. Why? Is there a problem?"

"Well, not with Diane D or anybody in her family."

"No? So what's the problem then?"

"Well, it's about that kid Marcus who claimed that Diane D beat him up inside that isolated school hallway that night a few years ago, then chased after him in the back stairwell of that school. You remember that case right?"

"Of course I do. Everybody remembers that case. What about it?"

"Well that kid Marcus is still having nightmares about Diane D coming after him in that isolated school hallway and in the back stairwell of that school."

"Yeah I heard that kid is still having nightmares about Diane even though a few years already went by."

"Yeah. He claims that Diane D is trying to kill him and he keeps calling the police department claiming that he wants Diane D arrested."

"What! He still wants Diane arrested?! Listen, Diane has nothing to do with that kid's nightmares! She has no control over what he's dreaming about!"

"Try telling that to him."

"She has not been anywhere near that kid since that night she appeared at his school a few years ago, she's in the Caribbean! So you cannot come here and arrest her for something she has no control over!"

"No sir, you're misunderstanding! We're not here to arrest Diane D!"

"You're not?"

"No."

"So what are you here for then?"

"We just want to see if we can talk to her. We want to know if she and her family can try to talk to this kid Marcus just one more time and tell that kid that she forgives him for the hoax that he and his brother pulled on her and her family years ago! Maybe if he finally accepts her forgiveness, his nightmares of her would stop and he would stop calling us telling us that he wants her arrested!"

"Look, Diane has tried many times since that incident to tell that kid that she forgives him, especially when she heard about the nightmares he keeps having about her, but every time she gets on the phone and tries to talk to him, all that kid does is scream at the top of his lungs and runs away from the phone, shouting that Diane is a monster!"

"We know he does that, but we just want to try and see if Diane D can try just one more time to talk to him."

"That's right," Officer Grey says, "because this kid keeps calling the precinct with these false accusations of Diane D. We want this kid to stop calling the precinct because of his nightmares. We cannot stop this kid's nightmares. That's why we want to know if Diane D can try one more time to tell the kid that she forgives him and hopefully his nightmares of her coming after him will stop because he's talking about taking his own life again!"

"What!" Alex shouts. "Oh no! He is?!"

"Yes! He might have to be on a suicide watch again!"

"My God! I'm sorry he's going through that, but what else can

Diane do about it if the kid refuses to come to the phone and accept her forgiveness?!"

"Try to talk to him just one more time. If the kid still refuses to come to the phone to talk to Diane D and accept her forgiveness, then it is out of our hands. It's in his and his doctors' hands."

"Well I'll give Diane and her family the message when they return in another few months."

"Okay, thank you sir."

"You're welcome."

"How is Diane D by the way," Officer Henley asks. "Is she okay?"

"Yeah she's fine. She's enjoying herself in the Caribbean with her family and relatives."

"She is?"

"Yes. I think that kid Marcus is the last thing that's on her mind right now."

"I'm sure it is. Well thank you sir. Tell them to give me a call when they return?"

"Sure, no problem Officer."

"Okay. Thank you."

"You're welcome."

"Take care."

"You too."

Officer Henley and Officer Grey turn and walk away.

Chapter 3

Diane D And Her Family Are In The Caribbean

Diane D who is now around 27-years old and her family and relatives are sitting on a large boat in the Caribbean. Diane D and her cousin Dana of **(DANGEROUS DANA)** who is now around 28-years old are both dressed in scuba diving gear with each of them having their hair back in long thick braids. Diane D's older brother Nicolas and Dana's two older brothers Sammy and Thomas are also dressed in scuba diving gear. Their uncles Uncle Tonio and Uncle Willie are dressed in scuba diving gear also. Diane D and Dana then sit on the edge of the boat. They are about to go into the water. They put their scuba diving masks on as their family and relatives stand and surround them. Diane D and Dana finish fixing their scuba diving gear. Uncle Willie then counts, "One .. two .. three .. go!" Diane D and Dana fall back and dive into the ocean as their family and relatives scream and cheer.

IN THE WATER:

Diane D and Dana go deep into the ocean. Diane D then dives down to the bottom of the ocean as her long braid flows in the water like a tail behind her head. She then sees something on the ocean floor. She looks up through her gear and gestures for Dana to come to her.

Dana dives down to the bottom of the water to Diane D as her long braid also flows in the water like a tail behind her head.

Dana approaches Diane D as Diane D shows her something buried partially in the sand. They both try to dig it up. Nicolas, Sammy, Thomas, Uncle Tonio and Uncle Willie suddenly dive to the bottom of the water to Diane D and Dana. Diane D shows them the object in the water. Nicolas, Sammy, Thomas, Uncle Tonio and Uncle Willie try to dig up the object. Dana then gestures something to Diane D. She then swims up and goes around to the other side of the men. Diane D then swims up and follows Dana.

BACK ON THE BOAT:

Ten minutes later, Dana, Nicolas, Sammy, Thomas, Uncle Tonio and Uncle Willie are back on the boat. They and the rest of the family are surrounding Diane D's grandfather Tomas, a handsome Dominican man with a lighter fairer skin tone and black hair which is slightly gray who resembles Diane D, her paternal grandfather Mike, a handsome Island man with a lighter fairer skin tone and black hair also slightly gray who resembles Dana, and Diane D's dad Barry as they try to open a silver box.

Diane D is sitting on the other end of the boat as she takes her scuba mask off. Her beautiful long black wavy hair is all damp and shining from the sun as she puts her mask to the side and starts to take her flippers off. Her other two cousins Nancy and Charlotte who are her back singers and dancers approach her as Nancy says, "Hey Diane! How was the water?"
"It was nice," Diane D says.
"Y'all caught a silver box down there?"
"Yeah."
"Oh wow," Charlotte says. "That means y'all dove all the way to the bottom again?"
"Yeah."
"Wow! Where is the box?"
"Grandpa has it. They're over there at the other end looking at it."
"Oh boy! Let's go look at it! You coming Diane?"
"Yeah I'll be there. I just want to take these flippers off."
"Okay. We'll meet you in the front."
"Okay Charlotte." Diane D continues to take off her flippers as Charlotte and Nancy turn and hurry towards the other end of the boat.

Chapter 4

Diane D And Her Family Are Back From The Caribbean

It is a few months later. Margarita, a beautiful youthful Dominican woman with tanned skin who is a former Dominican Beauty Queen dressed in a black pants suit with her long straight black hair hanging around her front, sides and back, and Tomas are angrily walking inside the police station towards one of the back rooms as Diane D, her husband Michael, her mom Mary, her dad Barry and her brother Nicolas walk behind them.

Margarita and Tomas enter the back room of the police station as Diane D, Michael, Mary, Barry and Nicolas enter in behind them. Officer Henley approaches them and says, "Hey Diaz-Davidson family! I'm Officer Henley!" Officer Henley then looks at Diane D and says, "Diane D! How are you?" Officer Henley looks back at the rest of the family and says, "Would you all like to have a seat?"

"No we don't want a seat Officer!" Tomas angrily shouts in a Dominican accent. "Our employee Alex gave us the message! What's this we hear about that kid Marcus wanting Diane arrested?! He's still going around with this bull crap?!"

"That's right!" Margarita shouts in her Dominican accent. "We just come back into this country after several months of being away and THIS is what we have to hear and put up with?!"

"I can't believe that kid is saying that he wants Diane arrested because of HIS nightmares?!" Mary shouts.

"I'm sorry Diaz-Davidson family," Officer Henley says. "But that kid Marcus keeps calling the police department telling us that he keeps having nightmares about Diane D coming after him inside the back stairwell of that school trying to kill him and he wants her arrested! We just want to know, if Diane D can try just one more time to talk to that kid and hope he finally accepts her forgiveness and hopefully, his nightmares of her coming after him trying to kill him will stop once and for all."

"Listen Officer," Diane D says as she slowly approaches Officer Henley. "I've had it up to here with that kid keep calling the police on me, saying that I'm trying to kill him when I'm not even thinking ab0ut him! I can't believe that he's still calling the police on me even while I'm out of the country! You know what I should do? I should file harrassment charges against HIM, that's what I should do! I mean I can't even enjoy being back in my home country in peace with my family with this kid calling the cops on me saying that he wants me arrested and I haven't been anywhere near that kid since I last saw him inside that school hallway three years ago! I do not go around trying to harm children, especially trying to kill them! Of course I was angry at first when I learned that kid and his brother pulled that hoax on me and my family, but I'm not angry at him anymore. I have forgiven him and moved on with my life. But as soon as I come back into this country after staying several months in my home country, I have to hear this bullshit that he wants me arrested because of HIS nightmares about me trying to kill him! I mean he is really making my image look bad!"

"I'm sorry Diane D. I know you're frustrated with this whole situation, so is the police department because we're the ones who have to deal with this kid constantly calling us. I just want to know, if you can please try just one more time to tell that kid Marcus over the phone that you forgive him for the hoax that he and his brother pulled on you and your family? It's for all of our sake and his sake too because he's talking about suicide again!"

"Yeah that's what Alex told us."

"Yes! He's gonna have to be on a suicide watch again! Could you try to talk to that kid Marcus just one more time Diane D and tell him that you forgive him? Please?"

Diane D stares at Officer Henley. She then says, "Okay call him up."

"You'll do that Diane D?!"

"Sure. Just call him up."

"Thanks!"

"But I promise you Officer. This is the last time I'm going to try to talk to that kid on the phone to tell him that I forgive him. If he still refuses to come to the phone and I hear him screaming all over the other end of the phone calling me a monster and everything, I am done with that kid, I am finished!"

"I cosign with you Diane D. If he still refuses to accept your forgiveness, then it is out of all of our hands. There's nothing else any of us can do for him. He will have to be at the mercy of his doctors. I'll call his family up." Officer Henley goes to the side of the room as Diane D and her family quietly turn to each other.

Officer Henley reaches for the phone at the desk. He dials a number. He then puts the phone to his ear and listens. He then whispers, "Hey Mrs. Whitley? This is Officer Henley."

"Oh Officer Henley," Vanessa says from the other end of the phone. "How are you?!"

"I'm okay and yourself?"

"I'm trying to hang in there as much as I can, but I don't know how long I can take this!"

"I know. I just want to tell you, that Diane D is here at the police department."

"What! Diane D is there?! I mean is she there right now?!"

"Yes! She's standing in the room with her family!"

"Her family is there too?!"

"Yes!"

"Oh my God!"

"They came here when they heard about Marcus still wanting to have Diane D arrested."

"Wow. I bet they're upset about that."

"Of course they are. I told Diane D and her family that if she can just try one more time to tell Marcus that she forgives him for the hoax that he and his brother pulled on her and her family, then maybe his nightmares about her coming after him trying to kill him will hopefully stop. Well she's willing to get on the phone to try one more time to tell Marcus that she forgives him."

"What! She's willing to try one more time?!"

"Yes, because she doesn't like the fact that Marcus keeps having these nightmares about her! Plus she says it's making her image look bad."

"I understand."

"So could you bring Marcus to the phone to tell him someone wants to talk to him? Just don't tell him that it's Diane D because he will never come to the phone."

"I don't ususally tell him it's her, but he still wants to know who it is on the phone! He refuses to even come on the phone if I don't tell him who it is! One time I had to lie to him who it was on the phone just to get him on the phone! As soon as he heard Diane D's voice, he threw the phone down screaming all over the place saying that she's a demon, shouting that he does not want to talk to the devil!"

"I understand Mrs. Whitley, but this might be the only way to help Marcus and stop his nightmares after all, if he would just accept her forgiveness."

"Okay, I'll bring him to the phone. Let's just keep our fingers crossed."

Vanessa looks down the hallway inside her apartment and shouts, "Marcus! Marcus!"

"What is it Grandma?" Marcus says from down the end of the hallway.

"It's your doctors. They want to talk to you."

"They want to talk to me?"

"Yes."

"About what?"

"About your nightmares, just get on the phone and talk to them."

"Are you sure it's the doctors Grandma? Because one time you had me come on the phone and I heard Diane D's voice on the other end!"

"I know, but it's not her this time Marcus. It's your doctors. They said they want to update your perscriptions."

"They want to update my perscriptions?"

"Yes."

"Well why can't they tell YOU about my perscriptions Grandma?"

"I don't know, but for God's sake Marcus could you just get on the phone and talk to your doctors so they can help you with your nightmare condition?"

Marcus suspiciously looks at Vanessa. He then walks towards Vanessa. He approaches Vanessa and suspiciously looks at the phone. He then takes the phone from Vanessa. He nervously puts the phone to his ear and tries to listen for any strange sounds.

Vanessa puzzled looks at Marcus. She then says, "Well go ahead and say something Marcus!"

Marucs hesitates. He nervously says, "Hello?"

"Hello Marcus," Diane D says. "It's me......"

"Oh noooooo! It's HER!" Marcus throws the phone across the room! He then looks at Vanessa and shouts, "It's HER Grandma! You lied to me, you lied to me! Aaaaahh!" Marcus screams as he turns and runs down the hallway!

"Marcus please!"

Marcus turns to Vanessa and shouts, "I can't talk to her Grandma!"

"Why not?!"

"Because she's a monster!" Marcus then cries, "She's a monster she's a monster she's a monster!"

Back at the precinct, the speaker phone is on the desk as Diane D, her family and Officer Henley hear Marcus' voice through the speaker phones crying, "She's a monster she's a monster she's a monster! ...Hhhhh ..... she's a monster she's a monster she's a monster ..... Hhhh .... She's a monster she's a monster she's a monster! ...." Diane D and her family stare at the speaker phone. Officer Henley hangs up the phone. Diane D turns and angrily looks at Officer Henley as her family holds on to her worriedly looking at her.

"I'm sorry Diane D," Officer Henley says. "Sorry you had to hear that. Well what do you have to say?"

"I'll tell you what I have to say," Diane D says. "What I have to say, is that this kid really hurt my feelings. I get on the phone to try and save his life when you told me he's on a suicide watch and this is what I have to hear? Him calling me a monster?! That, I did not have to hear again. See what I have to put up with every time I try to talk to that kid?! I am done! I am out of here!"

"I understand Diane D. Thanks anyway for trying. But before you go, can I just ask you one thing?"

"Sure Officer. What is it?"

"Even though you say you're not angry at that kid Marcus anymore and that you have forgiven him and moved on with your life, I just want to know that is it possible, that deep deep down in the back of your subconscious, that you still might be angry at that kid Marcus, but you yourself might not even be aware of it? I mean the hoax letter that he and his brother sent you and your family about the little three-year old boy who was dying of leukemia did cause you to be emotionally attached to the little three-year old boy when you thought he existed. So is it possible, that you still might be angry at that kid Marcus for causing you to be attached to the little three-year old boy, but you might not be aware of it?"

"No I'm not angry at him anymore, I've moved on. Even if I was still angry at him, I still will have no control over his or anybody else's dreams or nightmares. I don't have the power to enter anybody's dreams or nightmares even if I wanted to."

"Okay. I just wanted to ask, that's all."

"It's okay. Now I think my family and I should get out of here right now because our time here was a waste."

"A waste? You really think so Diane D?"

"I know so. Nothing was accomplished! The only thing I got out of this whole thing, was hearing this kid calling me a monster like he's done many times before!"

"I'm sorry Diane D. I just thought that maybe we can try to save this kid from his torment and hopefully save his life! I don't think trying to save someone's life especially a child's life is a waste. You did your part and tried to talk to him, I really appreciate that. Now he has to do his part by seeing his psychiatrists. I'm sorry this didn't work out. I'm sorry you had to hear the name he was calling you in the background."

"It's okay, I'm not worried about it."

"You're not?"

"No."

"Oh that's good."

"Now, if you would excuse us Officer, my family and I are going to go back home so we can get ready to go out for dinner tonight."

"You all are going out for dinner?"

"Yes we are." Diane D puts her cap on her head, fixes it and says, "Have a nice day." She looks towards her family and says, "Ready guys?" She then turns around and walks away towards the doorway. Her family turns and follows her towards the doorway. Officer Henley sadly looks on at them.

The next day, Diane D and Michael are walking down the street. A few reporters anxiously approach them as a white male reporter shouts, "Hey Diane D! Hey Michael!" Diane D and Michael stop right in their tracks. They turn and puzzled look at the reporters as the white male reporter says, "So Diane D, how do you feel about what that kid Marcus is going through? How do you feel about him having constant nightmares about you coming after him trying to kill him inside that school hallway?" The reporter holds the microphone to Diane D's mouth.

Diane D angrily grabs the microphone out of the reporter's hand and shouts, "Listen everybody! I'm sick and I'm tired of hearing about this damn Marcus kid, alright! I'm not thinking about him! I have no control over his constant nightmares about me! If anything, he needs to see a psychiatrist about his constant nightmares about me because I think it's that kid's own subconscious that's controlling his dreams and nightmares, not me!"

"He is seeing a psychiatrist about the constant nightmares he keeps having about you Diane D, but it's not helping him! His doctors feel that the only way for Marcus to overcome the constant nightmares he keeps having about you, is that maybe you can talk to him and tell him yourself that you're not angry at him anymore and that you forgive him. Please Diane D, that kid needs help! He's on a suicide watch! He tried to jump out of a window last year, but his family stopped him in time! Now he's thinking of killing himself again! Could you please try to talk to Marcus and tell him that you're not angry and upset with him anymore? Please Diane D!"

"Look! I offered to talk to that kid on the phone at the police station to tell him that I'm not mad or angry with him anymore, but he's still afraid of me and refuses to talk to me on the phone! If he doesn't want to talk to me, then fine it's on him! I am not going to push myself on him or anybody! From now on, I don't want to hear anymore questions about Marcus, you all got that?! I don't even want to hear his name anymore! I swear if I EVER hear that kid's name mentioned to me one more time, I'm going to REALLY let off some steam, you all got that?!" The reporters nervously look at Diane D. Diane D then says, "Good! Have a nice day!" Diane D angrily shoves the microphone right back into the reporter's hand. She then turns turns to Michael and says, "Come on Michael let's go." Diane D turns and walks away as Michael turns and follows her.

The reporters nervously stare at Diane D. The reporter turns to the others and says, "Wow, we're sure lucky she didn't kung fu kick us or else we would be going through the same thing that kid Marcus and that storage room door at the hospital went through."

"You got that right," a second reporter says.

Chapter 5

Diane D And The Dianettes Get Interviewed On TV

It is two weeks later. Diane D and the Dianettes, which includes six young beautiful tan and dark Latin/Caribbean females with waist length hair which includes her two cousins Nancy and Charlotte, Miranda, Bernice, Lonna and Kelly, are at a TV Station sitting on stools with Diane D in the middle. Roxanne Jackson, a middle aged black female TV reporter with a very short hair cut speaks to the camera and says, "Good evening ladies and gentlemen, I'm Roxanne Jackson. Here we have the lovely Diane D and the lovely Dianettes promoting their upcoming tour." Roxanne Jackson turns to Diane D and the Dianettes and says, "So hello ladies. How is everything?"

"Okay," the Dianettes say.

"Good. So Diane D, I hear you and your family's organization are doing an upcoming show in England right?"

"Yes we are," Diane D says.

"That's good. Now tell us about your show. What's going to happen in your show?"

"We are going to do a dance performance routine with some male dancers."

"You're going to perform with male dancers?"

"Yes."

"That's good. I hear you're going to do some gymnastic routines in your performance too. Is that true?"

"Yes."

"How long have you all been doing gymnastics?"

"Since we were all small."

"Since you were all small?"

"Yes."

"Where did you learn gymnastics?"

"At the dance school we all went to."

"Really?"

"Yes."

"That's good. Now Diane D, I hear you're going to be doing some other routines during your show. What other routines are you planning to do during your performance?"

"We're going to do some ballet moves."

"Ballet moves?"

"Yes, and I'm also going to do a martial arts routine with a female opponent."

"Martial arts?! You're going to do a martial arts routine?!"

"Yes."

"With a female opponent?!"

"Yes."

"Wow, that's fantastic! I love martial arts! I'm a huge fan of it! So who's the female opponent going to be? One of these ladies?"

"No," Nancy says. "We don't do martial arts."

"You don't?"

"No," Charlotte says. "Just Diane does that."

"Just Diane?"

"Yeah."

"Wow I see. Diane D you've been doing martial arts for a long time since you were small, haven't you?"

"Yes," Diane D says.

"And where did you learn and practice that skill?"

"In Asia when my family's organization traveled there."

"In Asia? Really?"

"Yes."

"Who taught you martial arts?"

"The teachers and instructors in Asia."

"The teachers and instructors there? Really?"

"Yes."

"Wow, fascinating! And Asia is where you also learned meditation, right?"

"Yes."

"So you started meditating there?"

"Yes."

"Interesting! Who taught you meditation while you were in Asia?"

"The teachers and instructors there."

"The teachers and instructors again?"

"Yes."

"Wow that's fascinating too! Do you like meditating?"

"Yes I love meditating.

"Do you meditate a lot?"

"When I can."

"What do you mean 'when you can'?"

"My family don't really like for me to meditate."

"They don't?"

"No."

"Why not?"

"They just don't."

"Well how does meditation make you feel?"

"It makes me feel very good and very relaxed."

"It does?"

"Yes. I usually feel free as a bird right after I meditate."

"You do?"

"Yes. Meditation usually gives me a peace of mind."

"It does?"

"Yes."

"I see." Roxanne Jackson looks at the Dianettes and says, "What about the rest of you ladies? Do any of you ladies medidate?"

"No they're not into meditation."

"They're not?"

"No. They don't want to get involved with it. I try to get them involved with meditation, but they refuse to get involved with it."

"They refuse? How come?" Roxanne Jackson looks at the Dianettes and says, "How come you ladies don't get involved in meditation like Diane D does?"

"I guess we're sort of afraid of it," Miranda says.

"Afraid of it? Why?"

"We just are."

"Really?"

"Yes they are," Diane D says. "They be trying to get me to stop meditating."

"They be trying to get you to stop meditating?" Roxanne Jackson looks at the Dianettes and says, "You girls be trying to get Diane D to stop meditating?"

"Yes," the Dianettes say.

"Why do you try to get Diane D to stop meditating?"

"Because we're afraid of it like Miranda says," Lonna says.

"Really?"

"Yes."

Roxanne Jackson puzzled looks back at Diane D and says, "Well Diane D, maybe there's a reason why the Dianettes are afraid of meditation and be trying to get you to stop meditating. I hear that some people who work for your family's organization have complained to your grandparents that every time you meditate, odd things seem to happen with you or around you after you meditate."

"Odd things seem to happen with me or around me aftere I meditate?" Diane D asks.

"Yes, odd things that you yourself might not even be aware of."

"Odd things like what?"

"Something supernatural."

"Something supernatural?"

"Yes, like these weird state of trances I hear you be getting into then not remembering them! And having these superhuman strengths that you yourself are not even aware of! Could that be the reason why the Dianettes are afraid to get involved with meditation and be trying to get you to stop meditating because what they see happen with you?"

"No that's not the reason why they're afraid of it, because odd things do not happen with me or around me after I meditate."

"They don't?"

"Not that I know of."

"See? There you go."

"Look. People tend to exaggerate a lot of things. People seem to get information blown out of proportion. Nothing peculiar happens after I meditate. The only odd things that happen after I meditate, is when I start to feel very relaxed and very refreshed. That's the only odd thing that happens after I meditate."

"But feeling very relaxed and very refreshed doesn't happen on its own? It only happens after you meditate?"

"Don't get me wrong, it can happen on its own, but most of the time, meditation helps. It's like the icing on the cake for me."

"The icing on the cake for you?"

"Yeah."

"Well what do your grandparents say or do, when people who work for them complain to them about the strange occurrences that happen after you meditate?"

"They would tell me to stop meditating."

"Your grandparents would tell you to stop meditating?"

"Yes."

"How do you feel about that?"

"I feel that the employees who work for them are raining on my parade. I feel that they're trying to sabotage what I'm doing. I feel that they're trying to take something that I love and adore away from me. I don't mean any harm whenever I meditate, I'm not trying to harm anyone. I meditate for my own purpose, my own gain and my own self worth, what's wrong with that?"

"Nothing is wrong with that, but is there anywhere else you can meditate if you can't meditate at your family's organization?"

"I used to meditate at home, but my grandparents banned me from meditating there too."

"They did?"

"Yes, that's why I started meditating at the organization in the first place, until I got banned from meditating there too."

"So where can you meditate at?"

"No where. My family strictly forbid me to meditate period."

"They did?"

"Yes they did."

"How come?"

"Because people keep complaining to them about it, that's why!"

"Wow, sorry to hear about that Diane D, because I know you love meditating."

"I do."

"Are you sure you weren't hurting anyone by meditating?"

"No I wasn't hurting anyone!"

"So why would anybody complain about you meditating, if they weren't getting hurt by it?"

"I don't know why! I do not force meditation on anyone! If anybody wants to meditate with me, fine they're welcome to. If they don't, that's fine too."

"I see. Sorry your family banned you from it. Well I'm glad one good thing comes out of it. Is that you feel very relaxed and very refreshed afterwards. I'm glad that part comes out of it for your sake. Now let's change the subject. By the way, where do you live or stay at now?"

"I still live and stay with my family."

"Your grandparents, right?"

"Yes."

"Where?"

"In Westchester."

"In Westchester?"

"Yeah."

"What part of Westchester does your family live in?"

"Northern Westchester."

"Northern Westchester?"

"Yes."

"That's where you stay?"

"Well I go back and forth between Westchester, Queens, the Dominican Republic and Jamaica."

"Westchester, Queens, the Dominican Republic and Jamaica?"

"Yeah. Sometimes I stay at my maternal grandparents' house in Westchester, sometimes I stay at my paternal grandparents' house in Queens, sometimes I stay with my great-grandparents in the Dominican Republic."

"Your great-grandparents?"

"Yes."

"In the Dominican Republic?!"

"Yeah, and sometimes I stay with my uncle David's family in Jamaica."

"Your uncle David's family in Jamaica?"

"Yeah."

"Wow, you seem to travel a lot and get around! But the Dominican Republic is where you're originally from, right?"

"Correct."

"Were you three born in the Dominican Republic, you and your two cousins right here Nancy and Charlotte? Were you three born in the Dominican Republic?"

"Yeah."

"That's nice." Roxanne Jackson looks at Miranda and Bernice and says, "What about the rest of you Dianettes? Where were you two born?"

"In Brazil?" Bernice says.

"What! You were born in Brazil?!"

"Yes."

"My goodness! I didn't know that! What about your cousin Miranda? Where were you born Miranda?"

"I was born in Brazil too," Miranda says.

"You were born in Brazil too?!"

"Yes."

"Really?! So you're Brazilians! I didn't know that! Do you two speak Brazil's native language Portuguese?"

"A little bit, but we came to America when we were very small."

"You did?"

"Yes."

"I see!" Roxanne Jackson looks at Lonna and Kelly and says, "What about you two? Where were you two born?"

"We were born in Trinidad," Lonna says.

"You two were born in Trinidad?!"

"Yes."

"Wow! Oh my goodness! I didn't know that either! I didn't know that the rest of you Dianettes were born in other countries! I knew that Diane D and her two cousins Nancy and Charlotte and the rest of their family were born in the Dominican Republic, but I didn't know that the rest of you Dianettes were born in Brazil and Trinidad! No wonder why you all look so exotic! You all are from three beautiful exotic countries! Do you all have your citizenship papers?"

"Yeah we all have our citizenship papers," Diane D says. "We're all legal here."

"I was just teasing Diane D," Roxanne Jackson smiles. "So there are three sets of cousins amongst yourselves, right?"

"Yes."

"I see. Now Diane D, what part of this country did your family first moved to when they first came to this country?"

"They moved here to New York.

"What part of New York?"

"Washington Heights."

"Washington Heights?"

"Yeah."

"Wow, that's a big Dominican community! So that's where you all stayed when you first came to this country?"

"Yes."

"How did your family wind up moving from Washington Heights to Westchester?"

"Well after my family left Washington Heights, we moved to the lower part of Westchester several miles from the Bronx. Then when my family left the lower part of Westchester, we moved to the Northern part of Westchester and have been there since."

"Wow, that is so interesting! So which family members live in your maternal grandparents' house in Northern Westchester?"

"My two cousins here Nancy and Charlotte."

"Nancy and Charlotte live there?"

"Yes."

"Who else lives there?"

"My husband lives there with us, my parents live there."

"Your husband and your parents too?"

"Yes."

"Who else lives there?"

"My two brothers live there, my aunt and uncle and other relatives."

"Your aunt, uncle and other relatives? Wow you have so many family members living with you Diane D! That is so nice! Who does most of the housework there? I mean who does all the cooking, cleaning and everything?"

"Who does most of the housework?"

"Yes."

"Why? Does it matter? One thing I do not like, is when people ask me what goes on inside my family's household."

"You don't like it?"

"No."

"Why not?"

"Because first of all, it's none of anybody's business. Second of all, people don't need to know what goes on in anybody else's household. But just in case anybody out there is interested in knowing, we do have a maid and a housekeeper, and that's all anybody needs to know. So let's change the subject."

"Yeah you're certainly right about that Diane D. So, I see that you all are still performing together and you all have been performing together for such a long time, right?"

"Yes," the Dianettes say.

"You all met each other in this country when you all went to dance school when you were all small, right?"

"Yes."

"How is it like working together?"

"Fun."

"We have a good time working together," Lonna says.

"You do?" Roxanne Jackson asks.

"Yes."

"That's good. How do you all get along with each other? Do you all get along well?"

"Yes we do," Miranda says.

"Really?"

"Yeah we get along very well," Bernice says.

"Seriously, how do you all really get along?"

"We get along okay! You don't believe us?"

"Well I would really like to know is, how do you all get along with Diane D?"

"What?" the Dianettes say.

"How do they all get along with me?" Diane D puzzled says. "Wait a minute, just hold up!" Diane D turns to the Dianettes and says, "I got this girls." She turns back to Roxanne Jackson and says, "Here's another thing I don't like. I really don't like when people ask individuals in a group 'how do they get along with other individuals in the group'. I really resent that question."

"You do?" Roxanne Jackson asks.

"Yes I do."

"How come?"

"Because how do you think we all get along with each other and why are you asking that question in the first place? Why are you putting us on the spot? Are you trying to dig up some dirt or something?"

"Trying to dig up some dirt? No I'm not trying to dig up any dirt Diane D. It's just a curious question."

"A curious question?"

"Yes, I didn't mean anything by it."

"Listen, our relationship of how we get along is no different from anybody else out there's relationship. We get along just fine. Of course we have our ups and downs just like everybody else, we're no different! But we still pull through and that's all you need to know."

"You're right Diane D. That's all I need to know."

"Now next question please."

"Okay. So when is your family's upcoming show in England?"

"April thirteenth."

"April thirteenth? That's good. Where will your family's organization perform next?"

"In Miranda and Bernice's home country, Brazil."

"Brazil?! Your family's organization is going to Brazil?! Wow, that is awesome! I would love to go to Brazil, someday! Wow! Well that's all the questions I have for you. Thank you ladies." Roxanne Jackson turns to the camera and says, "So there you have it ladies and gentlemen, if you happen to be in England on April thirteenth or in Brazil later on in the future, come see Diane D and the Dianettes perform their show." Roxanne Jackson turns back to Diane D and the Dianettes and says, "Thanks ladies."

Chapter 6

Diane D And Dana Get Put On Probation

It is Friday 12:00 noon. Inside Diane D's paternal grandparents Gracy and Mike's house in Queens, NY, Diane D, Dana and their Aunt Celeste are in the kitchen. Diane D turns to Aunt Celeste and says, "Aunt Celeste, can't we just go to the sporting good store real quick to buy some helmets?"

"No way Diane," Aunt Celeste says.

"But the store is gonna close soon. It's gonna close early today because of the holiday. It's gonna close at twelve noon."

"Listen, you two can't go out there riding motorcycles without any helmets on your heads! Are you crazy?! It's not safe for you to ride your motorcycles without any helmets on! If the police catch you two riding your motorcycles without any helmets on, they're gonna stop you and give you both fines! If you two want to go buy helmets real quick, then you're just gonna have to call a cab or take the bus."

"Aunt Celeste, the sporting good store is gonna close in twenty minutes," Dana says. "We're not gonna make it there in time if we wait for the bus or wait for a cab."

"Then don't ride the bikes then! You're just gonna have to wait until your brothers bring your helmets back."

"We don't know what time they're gonna come back with the helmets Aunt Celeste. They might not come back until tonight. The motorcycle club is gonna leave in around an hour."

"That's too bad! You two are just gonna have to miss out on it, that's all!"

"But Aunt Celeste," Diane D says.

"No buts about it Diane! You two better not go out there riding motorcycles without any helmets on your heads, because if I find out you two went riding out there without any helmets on your heads, you don't have to worry about the police coming after you, you're gonna have to worry about me coming after you! Don't ride out there without any helmets on! Now I have to go to the pharmacy real quick. I'll be back in about half an hour. When I get back, I expect to see both of your motorcycles still out there in front of the house, okay?! See you." Aunt Celeste turns and heads out the kitchen. Diane D and Dana lean on the counter and stare at the kitchen entry way.

Diane D turns to Dana and says, "I don't see why we can't just go to the sporting good store real quick. If we go there real quick, we'll be back here just in time before Aunt Celeste gets back."

"Aunt Celeste is right Diane," Dana says. "We shouldn't take a chance."

"Dana, if we don't get the helmets now, we're gonna miss out on the motorcycle events. We can go get the helmets real quick and come right back. Aunt Celeste will never know we were gone."

"What time is it?"

"Almost a quarter to twelve. The store is gonna close in about fifteen minutes!"

"Damn, that's right. Come on let's go." Dana leans off the counter and heads for the kitchen entry way as Diane D follows right behind her.

Dana and Diane D walk through the living room. They see their grandfather Mike in the den talking on the cell phone so they slow down as Dana pulls Diane D behind her back. They stare at their grandfather Mike as they walk slowly towards the front door.

Dana and Diane D reach the front door. Dana opens the front door and leaves out of it holding and pulling on Diane D's hand as they leave out the house. The front door shuts behind them.

Dana and Diane D reach the front gate and open it. Dana leaves out of the gate still holding and pulling on Diane D's hand as Diane D leaves the gate. Dana and Diane D head for two motorcycles that are parked in the street.

They each hop on a motorcycle. They turn on the engines. They look around. They then look back forward and make a run for it! They start to speed the motorcycles down the street as the motorcycles roar loudly.

Aunt Celeste is chatting with a female friend around the corner. She and the friend hear loud motorcycles speeding past the street. They both turn to look. When they look, Aunt Celeste gets shocked to see both Dana and Diane D speeding down the streets on the motorcycles, not wearing any helmets on their heads! Aunt Celeste starts to scream! She starts to run and scream towards the street corner! She reaches the corner and shouts, "Dana! Diane! Both of you get back here!"

Dana and Diane D continue to speed their motorcycles down the street, not hearing Aunt Celeste!

Aunt Celeste hysterically gets on her cell phone and dials up a number! She puts the cell phone to her ear. She then speaks into her cell and shouts, "Hey Mary! I need you and Christine to get over here right away! Hurry!" Aunt Celeste hysterically continues to look down the street!

Diane D and Dana head down a local street a few blocks away. They approach and stop where two guys and around 10 motorcycles are. Diane D says to them, "Y'all ready to leave soon, right?"

"Yeah," Larry, one of the guys says.

"We have to go to the sporting good store real quick to buy some helmets. Our brothers took our helmets."

"They did?" asks Ricky.

"Yeah," Dana says. "We don't know what time they're coming back and we don't have time to wait for them."

"Okay then," Larry says. "We'll wait for you two while y'all go to the sporting good store."

"Okay, thanks," Diane D says. "We'll be right back."

"Alright. Be careful."

"We will." Diane D and Dana start to speed their motorcycles down the street.

A few blocks away, a car pulls up and stops in front of Aunt Celeste. Aunt Celeste hysterically gets into the back door of the car behind the front passenger seat and closes the door. The car starts to speed down the street!

Aunt Celeste is inside the car with Mary who's also in the back seat. Dana's mom Christine from Jamaica is in the front passenger seat and a Hispanic friend Pedro is driving the car. Christine turns to Celeste and says, "Celeste? Are you sure they're riding their motorcycles without any helmets on?"

"Yeah, I saw them!" Aunt Celeste shouts. "They went right behind my back and went riding without any helmets on their heads, right after I told them not to!"

"Don't worry Celeste," Mary says. "We're gonna take care of those two. They both ought to know better."

"They know it's dangerous to ride motorcycles without any helmets on their heads!" Christine shouts. "They know the police will come after them!"

"Maybe they want to take a chance real quick," Pedro says.

"Taking a chance is not worth it Pedro!" Aunt Celeste shouts. She then looks towards the window and says, "Hey, there goes Ricky and Larry! They might know where Diane and Dana are!"

"Okay everybody," Mary says. "We don't want to get these guys suspicious." The car starts to pull to the side.

The car pulls up to Ricky and Larry. Aunt Celeste opens the back window and says, "Hi fellows."

"Hi Celeste," Larry says. "Hi everybody."

"Hi. We're looking for Diane and Dana. You happen to see them or know where they are?"

"They just left here," Ricky says.

"They did?"

"Yeah."

"You know where they went?"

"Yeah. They went to the sporting good store real quick to buy some helmets. They said they'll be right back."

"Okay guys. Thanks a lot."

"You're welcome."

The car starts to pull off and head down the street.

Everyone inside the car is worried and hysterical. As the car continues to head down the street, Celeste and the rest of them suddenly spot Diane D and Dana way in the distance. "There they go!" Aunt Celeste shouts. "That's them!" Everyone in the car looks forward. They all see Diane D and Dana way in the distance on their motorcycles, riding slow.

"Yeah I see them too, not wearing any helmets!" Mary shouts. "They have a lot of guts to do that!"

"They sure do!" Christine shouts. "Let's get them! Speed up the car Pedro!" Pedro steps on the gas and starts to speed the car down the street towards Diane D and Dana. All of a sudden they see Diane D and Dana heading right towards the ramp of the highway! "Oh no!" Christine shouts. "They're going straight for the highway!" Everyone in the car then sees Diane D and Dana go down the ramp.

"My God, they're going down the ramp!" Aunt Celeste shouts. "We gotta stop them!" Pedro speeds the car more as they go after Diane D and Dana.

Diane D and Dana are cruising their motorcycles down the highway. Dana is on the left and Diane D is on the right. All of a sudden they both hear a police siren behind them. They turn their heads around to look.

Inside of the car Mary shouts, "Oh no the police are after them!"

"See!" Aunt Celeste shouts. "I knew this would happen! This is exactly what I was afraid of!" Aunt Celeste, Mary and Christine all become hysterical watching from inside the car.

Diane D and Dana continue to cruise their motorcycles down the highway as they hear police siren behind themselves. Suddenly, they hear a voice on the police speaker shout, "Pull over to the right!" Diane D and Dana look at each other. They look towards the front again. "I said pull over to the right! Both of you!" the voice on the police speaker shouts again. Diane D and Dana turn their heads around and look back at the police car. Then they look back at each other again. Diane D shouts to Dana, "You wanna make a run for it?!"

"I don't know Diane!" Dana shouts. "I'm still on probation!"

"That's why you should make a run for it! If they catch you, you'll be in more trouble!"

"Oh yeah?!"

"Yes!"

"Okay! Let's do it!"

"Okay then, hit it!" Diane D and Dana start to speed their motorcycles down the highway! The police car starts to give chase!

Inside of the car Christine shouts, "My God what the hell are they doing?!"

"They're running from the police!" Aunt Celeste shouts. They all see the police car chasing after Diane D and Dana! Pedro steps on the gas and speeds the car down the highway chasing after Diane D, Dana and the police car! As everyone in the car continues to look, they see the police car continuing to speed in the distance, but they do not see any sign of Diane D or Dana anywhere on the highway! "Where are they?" Pedro asks. "I don't see them anywhere!"

"Me neither!" Christine shouts. Everyone in the car continues to look.

Mary suddenly spots Diane D and Dana. "There they go!" Mary shouts. "I see them!" Everyone in the car continues to look!

"I see them too!" Aunt Celeste shouts. Everyone sees Diane D and Dana way in the distance with the police car still pursuing them. They suddenly see another police car going after Diane D and Dana! They see Diane D and Dana speeding way up ahead of the police cars, refusing to give up to the police as they continue to speed their motorcycles down the highway!

Diane D and Dana continue to speed their motorcycles down the highway. They suddenly head towards an exit on the highway! They speed up the exit ramp and leave the highway!

Diane D and Dana approach a local street and speed their motorcycles down the street! They reach a corner and make a quick turn, making a quick getaway!

Back on the highway, the police cars suddenly head towards the same exit! They speed up the exit ramp and leave the highway!

The police car approach the local street and speed down the street!

They reach the corner and stop.

Inside of the police cars, two white male police officers look around. They do not know which way Diane D's and Dana's motorcycles went. "Where the hell they went?" the first officer says.

"Beats me!" the second officer says. The officers continue to look their heads around for Diane D and Dana.

The first officer gets on the police radio and speaks into it saying, "Be on the lookout for two females riding their motorcycles without any helmets on their heads."

Inside of the car, Aunt Celeste says, "Where are they? I don't see them anymore!"

"Me neither!" Mary shouts.

"Well the police cars went off of that exit right there," Pedro says. "Maybe Diane and Dana went off that exit too, because that's the way to the sporting good store! We got to go to the sporting good store, maybe we can find Diane and Dana there!"

"Okay Pedro," Mary says.

Diane D and Dana are inside a sporting good store. They are at the cashier. Dana pays for two helmets as Diane D looks back towards the front door. The cashier hands Dana back her change and says to her, "Thank you Ma'am." Dana takes her change and quickly puts it away in her pocket. Then she quickly grabs both helmets off the counter and hands one of the helmets to Diane D. Diane D quickly takes the helmet as she and Dana turn away from the counter and start to head for the front door.

Diane D then turns to Dana and says, "You think the police are still after us Dana?"

"I don't know," Dana says. "They might be. We gotta be careful." Dana and Diane D stop at the front door. Dana leans against the glass door, peeking out of it as Diane D leans behind and against her, peeking out the glass door also. They both look towards the street. They don't see any signs of any police cars. Dana opens the door and leave out of it as Diane D follows out behind her.

Diane D and Dana walk in the parking lot towards their motorcycles. They reach the motorcycles and put the helmets on their heads. They sit on the motorcycles and turn the engines on. They head towards the parking lot exit.

Diane D and Dana reach the street and make a run for it, speeding their motorcycles down the street!

The car Aunt Celeste, Mary and Christine are riding in suddenly turns around the corner.

Inside the car, Aunt Celeste shouts, "There they go!" Everyone in the car sees Diane D and Dana speeding their motorcycles down the street!

Mary then shouts, "Catch up to them Pedro!" Pedro speeds the car up! He tries to catch up with Diane D and Dana, but there are several cars in front of the car blocking the car's way.

The traffic light ahead becomes red. All the cars come to a stop as Diane D and Dana speed their motorcycles way up ahead, stopping their motorcycles in front of the cars! Diane D and Dana sit on their motorcycles waiting at the red light. They turn their heads towards each other and start to talk to each other as they wait at the red light.

Inside the car, Christine shouts, "They stopped at the light! Beep the horn Pedro! Let's try to get their attention!" Pedro beeps the horn. Everyone in the car looks towards Diane D and Dana. They do not see Diane D and Dana responding to the horn. They see Diane D and Dana remaining at the red light still talking to each other. Pedro beeps the horn again a few times. Everyone in the car sees Diane D and Dana still not responding to the horn. Pedro beeps the horn a few more times. They suddenly see Diane D and Dana turn their heads around to look. The light suddenly turns green. Diane D and Dana turn their heads back forward. They start to speed their motorcycles down the next street!

"Oh no!" Aunt Celeste shouts, "they're too far ahead now! We're never gonna catch up to them!"

"Maybe they're gonna go back to Ricky and Larry, Celeste," Christine says. "Pedro drive back to where Ricky and Larry were and see if Dana and Diane are gonna head back over there."

"Okay Christine," Pedro says. Pedro drives the car down the street.

A few miles away, Ricky and Larry are still out on the street with several motorcycles around them. The car pulls up to them again as they turn to look.

Inside the car, Aunt Celeste opens the rear window again. She looks out the rear window and says, "Hi fellows! We're back!"

"Did you find Diane and Dana?" Larry asks. "They just left here."

"They did?"

"Yeah. They came and left outta here so fast. They said they were gonna go back home real quick and come back."

"Why are they going back home?"

"They didn't say. They just said they had to go home real quick and come back in a little while."

"Oh yeah? Okay, fellas thanks."

"You're welcome. Take care."

Pedro starts to pull off and head the car down the street.

Inside the car, Aunt Celeste says, "I know why they're going back home."

"Oh yeah?" Mary says. "Why Celeste?"

"Because I told those two not to go riding motorcycles without any helmets on their heads! I told them if I find out they went riding out there without any helmets on their heads, they're gonna have to worry about me coming after them! I told them I was gonna go to the pharmacy and that I'll be back in about half an hour. I told them when I get back, I expect to see both of their motorcycles still out there in front of the house, so that's what I think they went to do, wait at the house until I get there, so I can see them and the motorcycles and not think that they went out there riding the motorcycles without their helmets on! I think they're both trying to play me for a fool!"

"Really? Well we'll see about that Celeste! We're gonna go straight to the house and get to the bottom of this!"

"I'm sure they're both waiting right at the house for me."

Mary turns to Pedro and says, "Take us to the house Pedro. Let's see if Diane and Dana are there."

"Alright," Pedro says. Pedro continues to drive the car.

A few miles away, the car pulls up in front of the house. They all look and see two motorcycles on the street right in front of the house.

"Well what do you know," Christine says. "There goes their motorcycles, just like you said Celeste."

"See what I mean?" Aunt Celeste says.

"Come on everybody," Mary says. "Let's go inside the house and have a talk with those two."

"I'll wait right here," Pedro says.

"Okay Pedro, we'll be right back." Mary, Christine and Aunt Celeste get out of the car.

Mary, Christine and Aunt Celeste approach the front of the house. Celeste unlocks the front door and goes inside the house followed by Mary and Christine.

Aunt Celeste, Mary and Christine enter the livingroom. They all look around for Diane D and Dana. "Diane!" Aunt Celeste shouts. "Dana!" They do not see Diane D or Dana anywhere. They go up the stairs.

Mary, Christine and Aunt Celeste check the bedrooms and bathroom. "Dana!" Aunt Celeste shouts. "Diane!" Aunt Celeste, Mary and Christine still do not see any sign of Diane D or Dana.

One of the bedroom doors open. Gracy quickly comes out of the bedroom. She is hysterical. She then shouts, "You're not gonna find Diane or Dana here!" Aunt Celeste, Mary and Christine turn around to look. They see Gracy all upset and hysterical! They rush to her.

"What's the matter Ma?" Aunt Celeste asks. "What's going on? What happened?"

"I just got home a few minutes ago! Then your father called me on the phone and told me that Diane and Dana had gotten arrested!"

"What!" Aunt Celeste, Mary and Christine shout. "Arrested!"

"What do you mean they got arrested Ma?" Christine says. "What are you talking about?"

"Ma!" Mary shouts. "Don't tell us that Diane and Dana got arrested for not wearing their helmets or refusing to pull over on the highway and running away from the police when the police were chasing after them!"

"Yes that's exactly what I was about to tell you all!" Gracy shouts. "How did you know about it?"

"We saw them Ma!"

"You saw them?"

"That's right Ma!" Christine says. "We were following them! Celeste called up me and Mary and told us that Diane and Dana were riding the motorcycles without wearing any helmets on their heads! So we all got worried! Then Mary and I asked Pedro if he could take us to pick up Celeste and take us all to look for Dana and Diane and he did!"

"We went looking for them Ma!" Aunt Celeste says. "Then we spotted them! They were riding their motorcycles without any helmets on, then we saw them going straight into the highway, so we started to follow them, but they didn't see us! Then we saw the police going right after them on the highway, but Diane and Dana didn't stop. They started to run from the police, so the police started to chase after them!"

"What!" Gracy shouts.

"Yeah! Then Pedro sped up the car and tried to follow Diane, Dana and the police, but they were all way up ahead! We couldn't catch up with them! We lost them, so we rode to the sporting good store and figured that's where they went, that's when we spotted them again, speeding away, but this time, we saw them wearing helmets which they obviously just bought!"

"Oh really?"

"Yeah!" Mary says. "They sped away so fast, we lost them again! So we rode back to the motorcycle club and spoke to Ricky and Larry again! They said Dana and Diane just left from over there and were on their way over here, that's why we came here! We figured they were here, especially when we saw the motorcycles parked right on the street!"

"Well Dana and Diane WERE outside of the house, but your father said as soon as they parked the motorcycles and got off of them, the police pulled up right in front of them and arrested them both right on the spot!"

"What!" Aunt Celeste, Mary and Christine shout.

"Yeah! Your father said the police were on a look-out for two females on motorcycles! I guess the police finally found Diane and Dana and came right over here and got them! They're both at the police station right now! Your father is with them now! I'm getting ready to head over there myself!"

"We'll go with you Ma!" Christine shouts. "Come on, let's go everybody!" They all turn away and quickly go down the staircase.

Gracy, Aunt Celeste, Mary and Christine arrive at the police station. They walk into the lobby. Christine rushes to a white male police officer and says to him, "Hello officer!" The officer turns to Christine as Christine says, "I'm looking for my daughter Dana and my niece Diane! I understand that they're both here!"

"Oh yeah?" the officers says. "Why would your daughter and niece be here? What's the problem?"

"Well officer," Mary says. "Our daughters were riding their motorcycles on the highway without any helmets on their heads! We learned they got arrested and were brought over here!"

"Oh, those are your daughters Diane D and her cousin Dana!" the officer says. "I reckognized those two! Well your daughters got arrested for not wearing any helmets on their heads and for refusing to pull over on the highway when the police told them to! Well they're both in the back right now."

"Well what's happening to them officer?" Gracy asks. They all of a sudden hear a commotion coming from the back of the police station. They all look towards the back of the station. They see Diane D and Dana walking with their heads down as Grandpa Mike and a few police officers surround them, leading Diane D and Dana down a hallway with Grandpa Mike scolding both Diane D and Dana. Aunt Celeste then shouts, "Dad!"

Grandpa Mike, Diane D, Dana and the officers turn to look.

Aunt Celeste, Christine, Mary and Gracy rush to Grandpa Mike, Diane D and Dana. "What's going on?!" Aunt Celeste shouts. "Are you all alright?!"

"Diane, Dana what the hell is going on?!" Mary shouts.

"They have to pay a heavy fine!" Grandpa Mike shouts. "That's what's going on!"

"A heavy fine?!" Christine shouts.

"That's right!"

"We were about to throw them both in jail!" one of the officers shouts. "But luckily for them, their grandfather came to their rescue!"

"Now you two no better!" Mary shouts. "How can you two risk something like this riding bikes with no helmets, you know that's dangerous!"

"Mom, we were riding to the store to purchase the helmets," Diane D says.

"Oh don't hand me that Diane! You know you shouldn't have been

41

riding bikes without any helmets on!"

"That's right!" Christine shouts. "You two could have been seriously injured! But I'm glad both of you are alright. But don't ever do that again, you got that?!"

"Yes Mom," Dana says.

"Good!"

Grandpa Mike turns to Diane D and Dana and says, "Now since you two have to pay a heavy fine, we got work for you two to do."

"Work for us?" Diane D says. "What kind of work Grandpa?"

"You two have to do community service."

"Community service?!"

"Yes. You got three months of community service to do."

"Three months of community service?!" Dana shouts

"Yes!"

"Doing what?!"

"We'll show you!"

"Show us?!" Diane D shouts. "I don't know if I can do community service Grandpa, we have a show coming up! I have to perform!"

"Really! Then why didn't you think about that before you decided to pull this stunt Diane?! You will get to perform in the show as long as you do your community service! Now either you two do the community service or head to jail and you won't be able to perform at all because you'll be locked up! Now which one do you two want to do, community service, or jail time?!" Diane D and Dana stare at their grandfather not knowing what to say. "I thought so," Grandpa Mike says. "Let's go girls!" Grandpa Mike and the police officers turn and lead Diane D and Dana away as Christine, Mary, Aunt Celeste and Gracy turn and follow.

The next morning at Grandma Gracy and Grandpa Mike's house, Grandpa Mike is in the kitchen talking on his smartphone as he says, "Yes Reeve Exterminating Service? This is Mike Brown."

"Yes I was expecting your call," a white male says from the other end of the phone. "I understand you have two employees who will work for this exterminating company?"

"Yes I do."

"Okay. Well who do you have?"

"My two granddaughters, Diane and Dana."

"Diane and Dana? You mean Diane D and her cousin Dana?!"

"Yes those two. They're on probation right now and have to do community service."

"Yes I heard."

"They will work for your exterminating company for three months. They will work for free."

"For free?"

"Yes. The pay that is owed to them will go straight to the heavy fine they have to pay."

"Oh I see."

"So what will you have them do?"

"They will do on the job training with the exterminating company. We will go to different hotels and exterminate them because I hear a lot of hotels are having roach issues and bedbug problems. Then we will go to some apartments that have mice problems. I will have them exterminate the mice."

"Okay. So when can they start?"

"They can start next week."

"Good. I'll make sure they'll be there."

"Thank you Mr. Brown."

"No problem. Take care." Grandpa Mike hangs up his phone.

The following week inside one of the hotel rooms, a white male guest with dark hair around his late thirties is inside the room. Suddenly there is a loud knock on the door. The man hurries to the door. He opens the door. He then looks out the door and says, "Diane D?"

"You have to get out the room sir," Diane D's voice says. "We have to get in there and exterminate the place."

"You have to do exterminating?"

"Yeah. So get out the room."

"Okay. Could you hold on for a minute? My girlfriend is in the bathroom. Thanks." The man stares out the door. He then closes the door and heads back into the room.

Diane D and Dana are standing outside the room inside a hotel hallway wearing matching white short sleeved polo shirts and matching navy blue mini-skirt uniforms, matching navy blue stockings and thick black sneakers as they stand facing a male Hispanic employee from the exterminating company with Diane D standing with her feet apart and arms folded, and Dana standing with one foot on the equipment with her hand leaning on a wall beam. The male employee says to them, "Now you two remember what I trained you yesterday, right? We're going to go into each of these rooms an exterminate the bedbugs and roaches."

Inside the hotel room, a white female with dark hair also around her late thirties comes out of the bathroom as the man says to her, "We have to leave the room. The exterminator company wants to get in here."

"The exterminator company?" the woman asks.

"Yes. And you will not believe who the exterminators are."

"Oh yeah? Who?"

"Diane D and her cousin Dana!"

"What! Diane D is out there?! And her cousin Dana?!"

"Yeah!"

"Oh my God! Are they staying at this hotel?!"

"No, they're not staying at this hotel! They're not guests."

"They're not?"

"No. They're working here!"

"Working here? Diane D and her cousin Dana are working here?"

"Yes!"

"Doing what?"

"Exterminating!"

"Exterminating?!"

"Yes!"

"What the heck are they doing exterminating?!"

"Didn't you hear that Diane D and her cousin Dana got put on probation and have to do community service for the heavy fine they have to pay for riding motorcycles without wearing any helmets?"

"Yeah I heard about that."

"Well guess who's the one that banged on the door a little while ago and said we have to get out? It was Diane D herself!"

"Really?!"

"Yeah!"

"She told you, you have to get out the room?"

"Yeah."

"I don't believe that she's out there! Let me go take a look!" The woman rushes to the door.

The woman reaches the door and opens it. She then looks out the hallway.

Diane D and Dana continue to stand in the hallway with the Hispanic male as they turn their heads and look at the woman. The woman becomes excited and shouts, "Oh my God! It's Diane Di! Hi Diane D!"

Diane D and Dana continue to stand there with their heads turned back looking at the woman.

The woman then says, "I understand that you all want to get in here!"

"Yes we do Ma'am!" the Hispanic male says to the woman. "We have to exterminate your room!"

"Okay. We'll be right out of your way!" The woman excitingly looks back at Diane D. She then closes the door.

Back inside the room, the woman rushes to the man and says, "You're right! That IS Diane D out there!"

"See?" the man says. "I told you!"

"You know, maybe I should get her autograph and take a picture with her!"

"Get her autograph and take a picture with her?"

"Yeah!"

"I don't think Diane D is here to sign any autographs or take any pictures with anybody. She's here to do work. By the way she banged on that door earlier and the look I saw on her face, it doesn't seem like she really wants to be here. I don't think she's in the mood to be bothered with fans."

"No?"

"No. When I said her name, she never even bothered to say hello."

"She didn't?"

"No. She just said 'You have to get out the room sir. We have to get in there and exterminate the place'. Then I said to her 'You have to do exterminating?' and then she said 'Yeah. So get out the room'."

"My. How unfriendly she sounds."

"She sure did sound unfriendly. She doesn't want to be here. She's only here because her and her cousin Dana's grandfather made them do work with the exterminating company."

"Wow."

"Let's hurry and leave the room before she bangs on the door again."

"Okay."

"And don't ask her for any autographs or pictures. Maybe some other time when she appears to be in a better mood."

"You got it." The woman and the man grab their belongings. They turn and head for the front door.

The woman and man come out the hotel room door into the hallway. "Leave your door open please," the Hispanic male says .

"Okay," the woman says. She and her boyfriend leave the door open as Diane D and Dana start to pick up the equipment. The woman and her boyfriend look at Diane D and Dana. The woman becomes excited again. She approaches Diane D and says, "Diane D! Wow it's so nice to see you here!" Diane D annoyingly looks at the woman as the woman says, "How are you?! I've always wanted to meet you! If you don't mind, is it alright if I get your autograph or maybe take a picture with you?"

"Not now lady!" Diane D rudely shouts. "I'm not here for that! I have work to do!" Diane D turns to the Hispanic male and says, "I'm gonna get started in there."

"Okay Diane," the Hispanic male says.

Diane D walks away from the woman and goes right into the woman and the woman's boyfriend's hotel room as Dana goes past them. Dana goes into the room also as the Hispanic male follows in after them. The woman and the man stare towards their hotel room door. The man then turns to the woman and mimics, "'Not now lady!'?" He then says, "It looks like she just gave you the brush-off! That was rude!"

"Well she's working right now. I mean her and her cousin Dana are busy trying to exterminate this place."

"In mini-skirts? And in stockings? That don't seem like the type of attire people do exterminating work in. With that rude behavior of Diane D's, we shouldn't even go to see her family's upcoming show if we take a vacation to England."

"Well maybe she has things on her mind. After all, she is on probation."

"Well who's fault is that?! No one told her and her cousin Dana to be riding motorcycles without wearing any helmets!"

"I know."

"Come on. Let's get out of here." The man and his girlfriend turn and walk away.

Chapter 7

It's Showtime

It is one week later. Diane D and the Dianettes are at Miranda's apartment inside Miranda's bedroom. They are all on the bed in a complete circle being on their knees. They each have a wireless microphone in their hands as Diane D says to them, "Come on girls we got to get this song right. We got to keep practicing."

"Oh Diane," Charlotte says. "Can we get a little break?"

"Not yet Charlotte. We gotta keep rehearsing."

"Why Diane?" Nancy says. "Are we even able to do the show with you being on probation and having to do community service?"

"If I keep up with my community service, we will be able to perform."

"Why do you have to do community service in the first place Diane?" Miranda's brother Marty asks. "I hear you were riding on a motorcycle without wearing a helmet. Is that true?"

"Yes it is."

"Why did you take a risk like that? The helmet is for your own safety."

"I know. It was a mistake Marty, but I learned from it."

"That's good. Are you ready for me to turn the music on?"

"Yes we're ready Marty, hit it."

Marty gets behind the computer and DJ equipment. He starts to play the music. Diane D and the Dianettes start to sway to the beats. Diane D then shouts, "Ready girls?! Hit it!" Miranda starts to hum to the beats as Diane D follows. Bernice then hums to the beat as Diane D follows again. They start to sing a song as music plays from the speakers.

ENGLAND:

It is two months later. The hotel room is crowded with Margarita, Tomas, Mary, Barry, Tonio, Marilyn, Nicolas, Mickey, Diane D, Michael and the Dianettes. Margarita starts to shout to everyone, "Okay everybody, listen up!" The entire crowd turns to Margarita as Margarita shouts, "We have to leave for the show at the theater now! Is everyone ready?!"

"Yeah!" everyone shouts.

"Okay let's get going!"

Everyone in the room turns and heads towards the doorway.

THEATER:

Inside the theater, the audience is packed full of excited people. The stage is very large. A white male announcer around his early 40's comes on the stage with a microphone in his hand. He speaks into the microphone and shouts, "Ladies and gentlemen, The Diaz-Davidson Organization is here!" The crowd starts to cheer! The announcer then says, "Their first performance is ready to come out! Ladies and gentlemen, here are Nicolas and Mickey the Diaz-Davidson Brothers!" The crowd screams and cheers.

Nicolas and Mickey come out on the stage with a guitar in each of their hands. They wave to the crowd as they walk to the center of the stage with their guitars. They sit on two stools that are on the stage. Nicolas and Mickey start to play the guitars and sing some tunes.

After three minutes, Nicolas and Mickey finish their act. The crowd cheers and applauds. Nicolas and Mickey turn and wave to the crowd as they leave the stage. The announcer comes back on stage. He speaks into the microphone and shouts, "Let's give it up one more time for Nicolas and Mickey The Diaz-Davidson Brothers!" The crowd cheers again. The announcer then shouts, "Okay ladies and gentleman, we have another wonderful performance! Ladies and gentlemen, here performing are Diane D and The Dianettes!" The crowd screams and cheers as music starts to play. One of the women in the crowd turns to the others and says, "Oh oh, Diane D is about to come out. Is she going to levitate like she did in her performance in Germany?"

"I sure hope not," another woman in the crowd says. "Because if she starts that levitation stuff, I'm running right out of here!"

"I'm right behind you." The women turn and look back at the stage as Diane D and the Dianettes come out on stage. Diane D and the Dianettes start to sing and dance with Diane D being in the lead.

After three minutes, Diane D and The Dianettes finish their performance. The crowd cheers. Diane D and The Dianettes turn and leave the stage. The announcer comes back on stage. He speaks into the microphone and says, "Wow what a great performance! Let's hear it for Diane D and The Dianettes!" The crowd cheers and applauds again! The announcer then says, "Okay ladies and gentlemen! We have another wonderful performance! Ladies and gentlemen, The Diaz-Davidson Organization presents Michael and The Diaz-Davidson Band!" The crowd cheers.

Michael and six male band members come out on the stage. They wave to the crowd. They start to play the instruments.

After three minutes, Michael and The Diaz-Davidson Band finish their performance. The crowd cheers. Michael and The Diaz-Davidson Band turn and wave to the crowd as they leave the stage. The announcer comes back on stage. He speaks into the microphone and says, "Wow what a fantastic performance! Let's give it up again for Michael and The Diaz-Davidson Band!" The crowd cheers and applauds again! The announcer then says, "Okay ladies and gentlemen! We have another wonderful performance! Ladies and gentlemen, here again are Diane D and The Dianettes!" The crowd cheers. Ballet/jazz music starts to play. Bernice, Charlotte and two male dancers twirl out on the stage. They then do ballet routines. Bernice, Charlotte and the two male dancers twirl around the stage. One of the male dancers lifts and twirls Bernice high up in the air as the other male dancer lifts and twirls Charlotte high up in the air!

After three minutes, Bernice, Charlotte and the two male dancers finish their performance. They then twirl off the stage. Different ballet/jazz music starts to play. Miranda, Lonna and two male dancers twirl out on the stage. They then do ballet routines. Miranda, Lonna and the two male dancers twirl around the stage. One of the male dancers lifts and twirls Miranda high up in the air as the other male dancer lifts and twirls Lonna high up in the air!

After three minutes, Miranda, Lonna and the two male dancers finish their performance. They then twirl off the stage. Different ballet/jazz music starts to play. Nancy, Kelly and two male dancers twirl out on the stage. They then do ballet routines. Nancy, Kelly and the two male dancers twirl around the stage. One of the male dancers lifts and twirls Nancy high up in the air as the other male dancer lifts and twirls Kelly high up in the air!

After three minutes, Nancy, Kelly and the two male dancers finish their performance. They then twirl off the stage. Music fron India starts to play. Diane D and one male East Indian dancer twirl out on the stage. They then do Indian dance moves. Diane D and the male Indian dancer twirl around the stage. The Indian dancer then lifts and twirls Diane D high up in the air! He then brings Diane D down to the floor and spins her around the stage floor as she starts to do break dance moves, kicking her feet high up in the air!

After three minutes, Diane D and the Indian dancer finish their performance. They then twirl off the stage as the crowd screams and cheers. The announcer comes back on stage. He speaks into the microphone and says, "Wow what a fantastic performance that was! Let's give it up again for Diane D, The Dianettes and their male dancers!" The crowd cheers and applauds again! The announcer then says, "Okay ladies and gentlemen! We have another wonderful performance! Ladies and gentlemen, The Diaz-Davidson Organization presents The Alpha Dancers!" The crowd cheers. The Alpha Dancers, four black women and four black men come out on the stage. They start to perform a tap dance routine.

After three minutes, the Alpha Dancers finish their performance. The crowd cheers. The Alpha Dancers turn and leave the stage. The announcer comes back on stage. He speaks into the microphone and says, "What a wonderful performance! Let's give it up for the Alpha Dancers!" The crowd cheers and applauds again! The announcer then says, "Okay ladies and gentlemen! We have another wonderful performance! Ladies and gentlemen, whatever you do, don't try this at home! But here again is Diane D and coming out for the first time, is Lynn Cho as she and Diane D do a martial arts performance!"

The crowd cheers as one of the men in the crowd excitingly turns to the others and says, "Martial arts? Diane D is going to perform martial arts?! This, I got to see!"

"Me too!" a woman in the crowd says. They turn and look back at the stage.

Diane D and an Asian female Lynn Cho who is around the same height as Diane D twirl out from opposite sides of the stage dressed in black body suits with long sticks in each of their hands as the crowd cheers. Diane D and Lynn Cho face each other from opposite sides of the stage. Music starts to play. Diane D and Lynn Cho start to run towards each other with the long sticks in their hand! They start to do a martial arts routines. Lynn Cho swings her stick and tries to hit Diane D with the stick as Diane D ducks from the blows! In return, Diane D spins her body around, swings her stick and tries to hit Lynn Cho with the stick as Lynn Cho ducks from the blows! Lynn Cho spins her body around, swings her stick and tries to hit Diane D with the stick again, but Diane D throws her stick aside and starts to do forward flips towards the side of the stage avoiding being hit with the stick as Lynn Cho follows her trying to hit her with the stick! The crowd cheers!

Diane D stops forward flipping as Lynn Cho continues to try hitting her with the stick! She starts to back flip towards her stick and quickly grabs her stick off the floor! Diane D and Lynn Cho face each other again as Lynn Cho tries to hit Diane D with the stick again, but every time, Diane D manages to avoid the blows as she ducks and bends from the stick! Diane D spins her body around again and tries to hit Lynn Cho with the stick again, but every time, Lynn Cho manages to avoid the blows also as she ducks and bends from Diane D's stick! Lynn Cho then spins her body and swings the stick at Diane D again! She knocks Diane D's stick right out of Diane D's hand! Diane D's stick lands on the stage floor! Lynn Cho spins her body around again and swings the stick at Diane D again as Diane D does back flips towards the side of the stage avoiding the blows! Diane D reaches the end of the stage as excited audience members try to touch her shoulders and shout, "Diane D!" Diane D manages to do flips right back towards the middle of the stage as Lynn Cho continues to swing her stick at her! Diane D suddenly does the split! Lynn Cho is about to swing the stick right on the top of Diane D's head as the crowd screams, but Diane D quickly throws her arm and hand high up in the air breaking the stick! "Woooohh!" the audience shout as Diane D and Lynn Cho start to do martial arts without the sticks! They do side kicks and fantastic back flips! They do martial stunts trying to kick each other as the crowd screams and cheers!

After three minutes, Diane D and Lynn Cho finish their performance. The crowd stands, scream and cheer very loud! Diane D and Lynn Cho face each other. They then head towards each other. They approach each other and bow to each other. They then hug each other. They then hold each other's hand as they turn and face the crowd. They smile to the crowd and wave their other hand to the crowd as the crowd continues to stand and cheer. Diane D and Lynn Cho then let go of each other's hand. They then twirl off towards opposite sides of the stage. They then disappear off the stage as the crowd continues to scream and cheer.

Chapter 8

The Double Exposure

Inside Gracy and Mike's house in Queens, NY, Grandpa Mike and the rest of the family are sitting at the kitchen table eating breakfast. Diane D is leaning against the kitchen counter drinking a glass of orange juice. Gracy approaches Diane D and says, "You're suppose to do a photo shoot at the studio today, aren't you Diane?"

"Yeah Grandma," Diane D says.

"Well you better hurry up and get going before you wind up missing it, then they'll have to cancel it and reschedule."

"Okay Grandma. I gotta go up stairs and get something."

"Okay hurry up now."

"Okay Grandma." Diane D turns away from Gracy and heads out the kitchen.

Thirty minutes later, Nicolas and Uncle Willie come into the kitchen. Nicolas then says, "Hey Grandma, where's Diane? She hasn't come to the car yet. We're still waiting for her."

"She said she had to go upstairs to get something," Gracy says. "She should have been back down by now."

"Well if she doesn't hurry up, she's going to miss her photo shoot," Uncle Willie says.

"Let me go upstairs to see what's keeping her."

"I'll go with you Ma."

"Okay." Gracy starts to head to the kitchen entry way as Uncle Willie and Nicolas turn and follow her.

Gracy, Uncle Willie and Nicolas are walking in the upstairs hallway. Most of the bedroom doors are open as Gracy, Uncle Willie and Nicolas peak their heads in all the bedrooms and the bathroom. They then walk to the bedroom at the end of the hallway that has the door closed. Gracy, Uncle Willie and Nicolas approach the bedroom door as Gracy turns to Uncle Willie and Nicolas and says, "I guess she's in here." Gracy turns back to the door and taps on it. There is no answer. "Diane," Gracy says. There is still no answer. She tries to open the door, but the door is locked. It won't open. Gracy knocks on the door again and shouts, "Diane!" There is still no answer. Gracy turns to Uncle Willie and says, "What's going on? She has to be in there. She never came back downstairs."

"I'll go get the master key," Uncle Willie says as he goes away.

Nicolas quietly pulls Gracy down the other end of the hallway.

Nicolas brings Gracy aside and whispers to her, "Try not to knock on the door again Grandma."

"Why not?" Gracy whispers.

"Because I think Diane is up to something."

"Up to something? Like what?"

"I have a strange feeling, that she's in there meditating."

"What? Meditating? You think so Nicolas?"

"I know so Grandma because that's what she does! Why do you think she has the door locked. I think she is secretly meditating in there."

"But your Grandma Margarita and Grandpa Tomas told her that she's not allowed to meditate anymore."

"Yeah but Grandma Margarita and Grandpa Tomas aren't here. That's why Diane's taking advantage of it right now. So let Uncle Willie get the master key so we can open the door and catch her in the act."

"Okay Nicolas."

"Here comes Uncle Willie with the master key," Nicolas says as he looks behind Gracy. Nicolas and Gracy turn towards Uncle Willie and start to walk towards him.

Nicolas and Gracy approach Uncle Willie as Uncle Willie whispers to them, "I got the master key. I'm going to open the door."

"Go ahead Willie," Gracy whispers. They all turn to the bedroom door. Uncle Willie approaches the bedroom door and taps on it. They still hear no answer. Uncle Willie puts the key in the keyhole and turns the lock. He unlocks the bedroom door and opens it. Uncle Willie, Gracy and Nicolas look in the room. They are shocked to see Diane D and Dana both sitting on the floor in a state of trance facing each other meditating with their legs folded and several litted candles on the floor surrounding them as they hold two lighted candles in each of their hands! "Diane, Dana!" Gracy and Uncle Willie shout!

Uncle Willie, Gracy and Nicolas rush into the bedroom to Diane D and Dana. They bend and carefully take the litted candles out of Diane D's and Dana's hands and blow the candles out! They bend again and pick the litted candles off the floor and blow them out too! Uncle

53

Willie, Gracy and Nicolas then look at Diane D and Dana. They shake Diane D and Dana by the shoulders trying to snap them out of their state of trance. Diane D and Dana suddenly snap out of their state of trance. They turn their heads and puzzledly look around. They then look up at Uncle Willie, Gracy and Nicolas as Uncle Willie shouts to them, "What the hell is going on here?!"

"What are you two doing?!" Gracy shouts. "Are you two trying to burn up the place?! And you're supposed to be on your way to a photo shoot right now Diane and THIS is what you and Dana are doing instead?! Lighting up the room with candles meditating?!" Diane D and Dana nervously look at Gracy not knowing what to say.

Around an hour later, Mary and some organization staff members are inside a studio room as they impatiently wait for Diane D to show up. Suddenly Diane D enters the studio and shouts, "I'm here everybody!" Everyone in the studio turns towards Diane D.

"Diane!" everyone shouts. Everyone approaches Diane D.

"Diane where have you been?!" Mary shouts. "You're late!"

"I'm sorry Mom," Diane D says, "but I got caught up in something."

"You got caught up in something?! Something like what?!"

"Mom, can we talk about it later?"

"Oh you bet we will talk about it later because time is money! You should have been here already! Now let's get this photo shoot going! Where's your brother and your Uncle Willie?"

"Oh they said they were going to the cafeteria to get some coffee."

"Okay." Mary turns to the side and shouts, "Make-up!" A Hispanic female make-up artist hurries to Diane D. She approaches Diane D with make-up in her hands. Diane D closes here eyes and holds her head up as the make-up artist quickly dabs a little make up on her face.

The female make-up artist finishes dabbing Diane D's face. She turns to Mary and says, "I'm done Miss Mary."

"Thank you," Mary says as the female make-up artist turns and hurries back. Mary turns to Diane D and says, "Now go get in front of the camera Diane."

"Okay Mom," Diane D says. She then turns and hurries to the middle of the room.

Diane D approaches the middle of the room where a middle aged Mid-Eastern male photographer with dark hair and a beard, his male assistant and a camera are. The photographer looks at Diane D and says, "Diane D! Wow it is so nice to see you again!"

"Thank you sir," Diane D says. "Sorry I'm late. How do you want me to pose?"

"Well I would really like you to hold the parrot while I take your photo."

"Parrot? What parrot?" Diane D looks to the side and sees a parrot. She starts to smile and says, "Wow, what a lovely parrot! You want me to take a photo shoot with it?"

"Yes."

"Okay. How do you want me to pose with the parrot?"

"I want you to hold the parrot slightly over your head, face your body sideways and have one leg up with your foot on the stool while you're looking into the camera, okay?"

"Got it."

The male assistant takes the parrot and brings it to Diane D. Diane D smiles at the parrot as the male assistant hands it to her. She holds the parrot. She admires the parrot. "Almost ready Diane D?" the photographer's voice says.

Diane D turns to the photograhper and says, "Yes, I'm ready."

"Okay."

Diane D faces sideways. She puts one leg up with her foot on the stool. She then holds the parrot slightly over her head as she turns her head and looks into the camera.

"Perfect," the photographer says. The photographer looks into the camera and is about to snap Diane D's photo. Diane D suddenly looks to the side of the camera. The photographer then says to her, "I need you to look directly into the camera Diane D. Try not to look to the side."

"Okay." Diane D continues to hold the parrot slightly over her head with one foot on the stool as she looks into the camera.

"Perfect," the photographer says again. The photographer looks into the camera and is about to snap Diane D's photo again. Diane D suddenly looks to the side of the camera again. The photographer then says to her, "Can you try not to look to the side Diane D? I need you to look directly into the camera."

"Sorry. I'll try again."

"Okay."

Diane D continues to hold the parrot slightly over her head as she looks into the camera.

"Perfect," the photographer says again. The photographer looks into the camera and is about to take Diane D's photo. Diane D annoyingly looks to the side of the camera. The photographer, Mary, the male assistant and everyone else in the room puzzled look at Diane D. They then turn their heads and look to the side to see what she's looking at. They do not see anything special. They look back at Diane D. Mary walks towards Diane D.

Mary approaches Diane D with her arms folded as Diane D lowers the parrot. She then says, "What's wrong Diane? Hm? Is everything alright?"

"Yeah everything is okay Mom," Diane D says.

"Are you sure?"

"Yes I'm sure."

"Then why aren't you looking into the camera like the photographer

55

asked?"

"I don't know Mom. Maybe my coordination is off."

"Your coordination?"

"Yeah."

"Come on Diane we got to get it together. We got to get this photo shoot right. Money is riding on this."

"Okay Mom. I'll try my hardest to keep my eye on the camera."

"Okay, we'll try it again." Mary turns away and heads towards the photographer.

Mary approaches the photographer and says, "Let's try this again."

"Okay," the photographer says.

Diane D holds the parrot slightly over her head again as she looks into the camera.

"Perfect," the photographer says again. The photographer looks into the camera and is about to snap Diane D's photo again. Diane D annoyingly looks off to the side of the camera again. The photographer and Mary become annoyed. They puzzled look back at Diane D. They then turn their heads and look to the side again to see what she's looking at. They still do not see anything special. They look back at Diane D again. The photographer then turns to Mary and says, "I don't think this is gonna work out. She keeps taking her eyes off the camera looking at something. What is she looking at?"

"I don't know," Mary says. "But let me go find out." Mary turns from the photographer and heads back towards Diane D.

Mary approaches Diane D and says, "Diane is everything okay? What's the matter baby? Is there something you want to talk about?"

"No Mom," Diane D says. "What is there to talk about?"

"Well first of all, you came to this photo shoot late, now you're not looking into the camera as the photographer is about to snap your picture. Is there anything you want to talk about?"

"No Mom. I'm fine."

"Are you sure?"

"Yeah I'm sure."

"Good. Since your eyes keep going off to the side of the camera, I think the photographer should change your pose and position. I'm going to see if he can have you looking at the parrot instead of looking at the camera."

"Okay Mom."

"Are you okay with that?"

"Yeah. I don't see why not."

"Okay. Hang on." Mary turns away from Diane D and walks back towards the photographer.

Mary approaches the photographer and starts talking to him as Diane D looks on at them.

Diane D then turns her head to the parrot and smiles at it as she continues to hold it. "Diane D!" the photographer's voice calls out. Diane D turns and looks at the photographer.

The photographer then says, "We're going to try to take a photo of you looking at the parrot instead of at the camera, how that sounds?!"

"That's sounds wonderful!" Diane D shouts.

"Are you sure you can handle that?"

"We can try! Let's go for it!"

"Okay! We're going to have your sideview and face facing the camera while your looking at the parrot, okay?"

"Got it." Diane D changes positions as she goes to the other side of the stool. She then holds the parrot slightly over her head as she looks at it with her sideview and face facing the camera.

"Perfect," the photographer says again. The photographer looks into the camera and is about to snap Diane D's photo. The photographer then snaps Diane D's photo. He snaps it a few times and shouts, "Perfect!"

Diane D looks at the photographer and shouts, "How was that?! Was that better?!"

"Much better Diane D! Thanks." The photographer takes the camera and looks down at it. He goes to the pictures of Diane D inside of it. He opens up the pictures. He and his assistant look down at the pictures. They find the pictures of Diane D with the parrot. They see two pictures of her posing with the parrot. They suddenly see a photo of Diane D with the parrot and a second image of Diane D standing right in front of herself with its back right up against the front of Diane D angrily staring directly into the camera! "What the..!" the photographer and his assistant shout as they see two different images of Diane D standing with each other in the same photo! Everyone in the room turn and puzzled look at the photographer and his assistant. They are stunned to see a look of shock on the photographer's and his assistant's faces as the photographer and his assistant stare at the camera.

"What happened?!" Mary shouts to them. The photographer and his assistant shockingly look up at everybody in the room. They then turn and shockingly look at Diane D!

Diane D puzzled looks at the photographer and says, "Why are you looking at me like that sir?"

"I just want to know," the photographer nervously says.

"You just want to know what?"

"Do you have an identical twin sister?!"

"What!" everyone shouts as they look at the photographer.

"Do I have an identical twin sister?" Diane D asks.

"Yeah," the photographer says.

"No, I don't have an identical twin sister."

"You don't have an identical twin sister?"

"No I don't. As a matter of fact, I don't have any sisters at all."

"No sisters at all?"

"No, just two brothers."

"Just two brothers?"

"Yes," Mary says. "She only has two brothers sir. She's my only girl."

"Your only girl?"

"That's right. She doesn't have a twin."

"Well was she born a twin? Did she ever had a twin sister who passed away at birth or something?"

"No, I never gave birth to twins."

"Never?"

"No, not at all! I had three pregnancies and they all resulted in single birth babies. There were no multiple births among my children."

"No multiple births at all?"

"No none at all. What's the problem?"

"The problem is, I saw two of her in one of these photos!"

"Two of her! Diane?"

"Yeah!"

"What? Let me take a look!" The photographer shows Mary the photos in the camera. Diane D approaches the photographer. She looks at the camera as the photographer shows the pictures to Mary and everyone else. Everyone looks at the pictures. They see all the photos of Diane D holding the parrot, but they do not see anyone else in the photo. Mary then says, "What are you talking about, there's no one else in these pictures."

"You don't see a double image of Diane D?"

"No I don't."

"It's strange because I don't see it now either."

"You mean whatever you saw in the picture is gone?"

"I don't see it now. But it WAS there!"

"It was!" the male assistant shouts. "I saw it too!"

"You said you saw two of Diane inside the picture," Mary asks.

"Yeah we did!" the photographer says.

"Well maybe it was a double exposure of Diane. I mean she had plenty of photos taking of herself. Maybe that is an old image inside the camera."

"Miss Mary this camera is brand new. It has never been used before."

"It hasn't?"

"No! But if it was used before, Diane D was no where around it!"

"What did you see inside the picture with Diane?"

"I saw a second image of her."

"You saw a second image of her?"

"Yes."

"Well if you saw a second image of her, maybe the picture somehow duplicated itself! I mean you did snap a few photos of her. Maybe the camera double clicked or something."

"No it couldn't have double clicked Miss Mary because the second image of Diane D was posing in a different way!"

"What do you mean it was posing in a different way?"

"It was looking directly into the camera while the regular image of Diane D was looking at the parrot!"

"What!" everybody shouts. "Looking into the camera?!"

"Yeah!"

"How did the image look like while it was looking at the camera?" Mary asks.

"Mean!"

"Mean?!"

"Yeah!" the camera assistant says. "It looked like Diane D's twin looking right at the camera giving us a mean stare!"

"What!" everybody shouts.

"Looking at the camera giving you a mean stare?" Mary asks.

"Yeah! And now it's not there!"

"Wow," Alex says. "That sounds pretty creepy."

"It certainly does," Stephanie, a black female staff member, says.

"Are you sure that the image looked like Diane?" Mary asks.

"Yes it looked just like her!" the photographer shouts. The photographer looks back at Diane D and says, "Was that a ghost of your twin Diane D?"

"Didn't you hear what my mom just told you?" Diane D says. "I don't have a twin and never had one. If I ever was born a twin, my mom would be the first to know. Didn't you have me look right into the camera when you first tried to snap a photo of me?"

"Yeah."

"Well there you go!"

"But when I had you look directly into the camera, I never got the chance to snap the photo of you because your eyes kept going off camera, which made me not snap the photo of you! Maybe that's why your eyes kept going off the camera and looking to the side when I first tried to snap your photo. You were probably looking at something the rest of us couldn't see, were you?"

"What the hell would I be looking at, that the rest of you can't see?"

"Well the direction your eyes kept looking towards when I first tried to snap a photo of you, was the exact same spot I saw that second image of you standing! Your eyes kept looking to the side at that same exact spot like you were annoyed by something. Was there something next to you that you were annoyed by Diane D? Something the rest of us couldn't see?"

"Yes as a matter of fact, there was something next to me that I was annoyed by."

"There was?"

"Yeah."

"Well what was it?!"

"A tiny fly that kept flying right in front of my face."

"A tiny fly?"

"Yeah. I was very annoyed by that fly, that's what I kept looking at. Of course none of you were able to see the fly because it was too tiny and small for any of you to see or notice it."

"Really? So you're blaming a fly for your eyes going off camera?"

"Yes I am. We all know flies can be real pests."

"I haven't seen any flies around here lately Diane D."

"Well maybe it could have been Mary in the picture," Stephanie says. "Maybe that second image of Diane was actually Mary! After all, Mary and Diane do look alike. They favor each other a lot. They can pass for twins themselves. Maybe it could have been Mary in the double exposure."

"Miss Mary was never in front of the camera while I was snapping the photo of Diane D. So it can't be her."

"Are you sure there is no camera reverse switch that can turn the camera lens around and snap a picture of Mary at the same time you snapped a photo of Diane?" Alex asks. "I mean Mary was standing behind the camera at the same time you were snapping the photo of Diane."

"This camera lens can only face one direction at a time. It cannot turn around. Plus Mary is not wearing the same clothes Diane D is wearing. The second image I saw of Diane D was wearing the exact same thing she's wearing right now." The photographer puzzled looks at Diane D again.

Diane D annoyingly says, "You're still looking at me like that?! Well while you're looking at me, I'm going to go out for lunch." Diane D turns to Mary and says, "Mom, I'll be outside."

"Okay baby," Mary says as Diane D leaves and heads out the door.

Around two hours later, Margarita, Tomas, Mary, Barry, Marilyn and Tonio are at the organization inside Margarita's office surrounding Margarita as she sits behind her desk wearing a black pants suit with her long black hair hanging all around her sides and back. Mary paces back and forth with her arms folded as Barry turns to her and says, "You didn't see the double image of Diane in the picture Mary?"

"No," Mary says as she stops pacing. "But the photographer and his assistant swore it was there!"

"And no one else saw this double image of Diane but the photographer and his assistant?" Tomas asks.

"Yeah Dad, no one else saw it."

"Wow, that's strange," Margarita says.

Suddenly the door opens. Nicolas and Uncle Willie enter the office. "Hey everybody," Nicolas says.

"Hey Nicolas, hey Willie," the family says.

"How was Diane's photo shoot today?" Uncle Willie asks "Did she get to have her photo taking in time? I hope she didn't miss it."

"She almost missed it Willie," Margarita says. "The photographer was about to cancel her photo shoot because she came there late! But Mary wind up convincing him to wait a little while longer!"

"Oh. Sorry we got her there late Mary."

"Willie," Barry says. "Since you and Nicolas drove Diane to the photo shoot, why did y'all bring her there late?"

"We had to wait for her to come out the house. We couldn't leave without her."

"So what took her so long to come out the house?"

"I'll tell you the reason what took her so long."

"What's the reason?"

"She was upstairs meditating."

"What!" Barry, Mary, Magarita and Tomas shout. "Meditating?!"

"She was meditating?!" Mary shouts. "Seriously?!"

"Yeah!" Uncle Willie says. "She was meditating right inside the bedroom upstairs!"

"She was meditating again?!" Margarita shouts.

"Yeah! Mom, Nicolas and I caught her! That's what took her so long to come out the house!"

"My God I don't believe this!"

"I even asked Diane why she came to the photo shoot late, and she didn't want to tell me right away!" Mary shouts.

"Well that's why she didn't want to tell you!" Uncle Willie shouts. "She was upstairs in the room meditating!"

"How did you catch her meditating Willie?!"

"When Diane took a while to come out the house, Nicolas and I went back in the house to see what's keeping her. That's when Mom told us that Diane went back upstairs. So we found out, that Diane went upstairs, but never came back down. So we went upstairs to check on her. All the bedroom doors were open except for the last bedroom door so we went to it! We called out to Diane, but she never answered. We tapped on the door, but there was still no answer! We tried to open the door, but it was locked. We couldn't open it, so I decided to get the master key. I came back with the master key and unlocked the door. When I opened the door, there she was sitting there on the floor meditating."

"Tomas and I strictly told Diane she's not allowed to meditate anymore?!" Margarita shouts.

"Well that's what she was doing, meditating! Her and Dana!"

"What!" Barry, Mary, Magarita and Tomas shout. "Dana too?!"

"Yes! Both Diane and Dana were sitting on the floor in a state of trance meditating with litted candles surrounding them!"

"What!"

"They were both in a state of trance?!" Margarita shouts.

"With litted candles surrounding them?!" Tomas shouts.

"Yeah," Uncle Willie says. "So we went into the room, picked the candles up off the floor and blew them all out! Then we woke Diane and Dana up from their state of trance! That's why Diane was late to the photo shoot because she was busy meditating!"

"Why that sneaky woman!" Mary shouts.

"No wonder why this strange thing happened with the photo shoot!" Margarita shouts.

"What happened with the photo shoot?" Nicolas asks.

"The photographer told Mary and everyone else inside the studio that he saw two different images of Diane right in the same photo on his camera!"

"He saw two different images of Diane?!"

"Yeah, he and his assistant did! They thought they were looking at a pair of twins in the photo!"

"A pair of twins?!"

"Yes! No wonder why that strange thing happened at her photo shoot, because she was meditating before she got there!"

"You think the double image of Diane on the photo has something to do with her meditating?" Tomas asks.

"Most likely! Every time she meditates, strange things seem to follow her! But yet she tells everyone in the room the reason why she kept looking off camera to the side is because of a fly flying around her face?! She knew there was no fly in that room! She was just trying to cover herself because she knew what was going on! Wait till I see her again! I'm going to have a word with her about meditating behind our backs and trying to cover it up!" Margarita presses a button on her desk phone. She then shouts into the phone, "Evette, can you tell Diane to come into my office?! Tell her that her family wants to see her, nooow!"

"She's still rehearsing inside the Banquet Room Miss Margarita," Evette's voice says.

"She is?"

"Yes."

"Nevermind, we'll come to her!"

"Okay."

"Thanks Evette!" Margarita presses the button again.

Fifteen minutes later, Diane D's family is scolding her inside the Banquet room as Diane D shouts to them, "I only meditated for a few minutes!"

"But your grandparents told you that you're not allowed to meditate at all!" Barry shouts.

"I know they told me that Dad!"

"So why are you still doing it?!"

"I needed it to help boost my energy!"

"To help boost your energy?!" Mary shouts. "You need meditation to help boost your energy?!"

"Yeah."

"Look Diane," Margarita says. "I'm only going to say this one more time! No more meditating, you got that?!"

"But Grandma, I was meditating at Grandma Gracy's!"

"Ohhh so you think that makes it okay to meditate behind our backs because you did that over there?! No it doesn't!"

"Look Diane!" Tomas shouts. "It doesn't matter where it is you meditate at! We don't care if it's in the grocery store, we don't care if it's in the movie theater, we don't care if it's in here at the organization and we certainly don't care WHOSE HOUSE it's in! No more meditation for you! Do you understand?!"

"But Grandpa...!" Diane D shouts.

"No more meditating!"

"But Grandpa...!"

"No more meditating Diane! Do you understand?!"

Diane D sadly looks at Tomas. She then says, "Yes Grandpa."

"Good! Now we're gonna have you work upstairs in the office!"

"Work upstairs?"

"Yes, starting right now!"

"So let's get going Diane!" Margarita shouts. "Move it!"

Diane D sadly looks at Margarita. She turns and grabs her belongs. She then heads towards the doorway as Margarita, Tomas, Barry and Mary follow her.

Chapter 9

Marcus Has Another Nightmare!

Marcus is laying in his bed tossing and turning. He is having another nightmare!

NIGHTMARE:

Marcus finds himself right back in the same area in the dark dim isolated school hallway. He is frightened, scared, bleeding and injured as he steps backwards towards the end of the hallway looking back towards the end of the hallway as he continues to cry with his body bent forward in pain. He is getting closer to the end of the hallway where the large window and exit sign are. The eerie sounds of the crickets coming from outside the window become louder as Marcus gets closer to the end of the hallway. Marcus quickly turns his head back forward and looks back at Diane D.

Diane D is standing way down the dark school hallway staring at Marcus. She is in a trance like state looking down the hallway at Marcus giving him a cold stare with half dead puffy and swollen eyes with her face pale, bruised and bleeding.

Marcus continues to back away as he cries and frighteningly looks at Diane D. He turns his head around again and looks back towards the end of the hallway again as he continues to back away. He is closer to the end of the hallway. He quickly turns his head back forward and looks in the distance at Diane D again. He suddenly stops right in his tracks and freezes with fear! He sees that Diane D has moved closer to him! Suddenly, Diane D moves and slowly starts to walk down the hallway towards Marcus. She starts to run towards Marcus!

Marcus stands there frozen in fear! He finally breaks loose, quickly turns around and makes a quick painful dash for the back stairwell doors! Marcus pushes the stairwell doors open! He quickly runs into the stairwell as the stairwell doors close behind him!

Marcus cries and screams as he frighteningly and painfully runs down the first flight of stairs practically rolling down the stairwell with his body still bent forward in pain! He then runs and rolls down the second flight of stairs as he frighteningly looks up and screams! He hears heavy footsteps jumping and charging down the stairs after him!

Marcus reaches the first floor landing as he continues to cry and scream! He quickly runs to the first floor stairwell doors as his body remains bent forward shouting, "Aaaaaahh! Help me! Somebody help me please! Aaaaaahh!"

PRESENT:

"Aaaaaahhh!" Marcus wakes up screaming again as he sits up on his bed! Jessica and Vanessa rush into his bedroom again!

Jessica and Vanessa rush to Marcus as Jessica shouts, "Marcus!" They bend to him and grab him!

"Marcus Marcus Marcus!" Vanessa shouts. "It's okay baby! It's us!"

"Help me, help me!" Marcus screams and shouts. "She still keeps coming after me! She still keeps chasing after me in the back stairwell of the school! We have to call the cops on her again!"

"Call the cops again Marcus?!" Jessica shouts!

"Yes!"

"You know this is ridiculous!" Vanessa shouts. "You know what I'm gonna do first thing in the morning Marcus?! I'm going to call your psychiatrist up and get to the bottom of this whole thing because this can't keep going on!"

Three days later, Jessica and Vanessa have Marcus sitting inside a psychiatrist office as he shouts to the psychiatrist, "I want Diane D arrested! As long as she keeps entering my dreams and nightmares, I want her arrested! I told my mom and grandma to call the police on her, but they refuse to do it!"

"Marcus what do you want the police to do?" Dr. Turk, a middle aged white male with dark hair, says.

"What do you mean what do I want the police to do?! I want them to arrest Diane D that's what I want them to do!"

"The police can't arrest Diane D because of your dreams and nightmares Marcus! The only thing I can probably do right now is speak to Diane D's doctors again and see if they can get to the bottom of this and speak to Diane D herself!"

"Speak to Diane D about what Doctor Turk?" Vanessa asks.

"To see if her own subconscious could have something to do with Marcus' nightmares! I doubt it does, but this has been going on for the past three years! Getting Diane D's doctors to go deep into her subconsciousness might be the only thing we can do right now."

Vanessa, Jessica and Marcus worriedly look at Dr. Turk.

Two days later, Dr. Turk, Diane D's doctors Dr. Stone, a white male doctor who is now around his mid 50's with slightly salt and pepper hair who had put Diane D under hypnosis before, and Dr. Kahn, a taller white male with darker hair around his mid 50's now also, are standing inside Dr. Turk's office as they surround Marcus who is sitting on a chair with Jessica and Vanessa standing on the side. Marcus has just finished telling Dr. Stone and Dr. Kahn about his constant nightmares of Diane D. Dr. Stone then says to Marcus, "Thanks for telling us all that information Marcus. I'm sorry you're going through this. I'm sorry you have been going through this horrific ordeal for three years!"

"You have to do something about Diane D, or whatever it was that took over her inside that school hallway that night!" Marcus shouts.

"You really think something took over Diane that night Marcus?" Dr. Kahn asks.

"I don't think so, I know so! I don't know what it was, but I felt the presence of an evil vicious soul, spirit and entity that took over her body that night and I feel that same evil vicious soul, spirit and entity is coming into my dreams and nightmares scaring me to death!"

"So what's going to happen now Doctor Stone?!" Vanessa shouts. "Diane D is YOUR patient! What are you going to do about her?!"

"Well the only thing I can do about Diane, is try to get deep inside her subconscious again like Doctor Turk says," Dr. Stone says. "I have to find out if deep down inside her subcounsious, she's still angry at Marcus for the hoax that he and Richard pulled on her and her family!"

"Try to get deep inside her subconscious again?!" Jessica shouts. "You said you and Doctor Kahn tried to get inside Diane D's subconscious before when she FIRST beat up Marcus, but it didn't work!"

"Well I guess we're just going to have to try again Miss Whitley!" Dr. Stone turns to Dr. Turk and says, "I'll see if I can speak to Diane's family and have her come into my office."

"Thank you Doctor Stone," Dr. Turk says, "because getting inside Diane D's subconscious might be the only way we can stop Marcus' horrific nightmares about her coming after him!"

"I'll see what I can do. Okay, we're going to get going." Dr. Stone looks at Marcus and says, "Take care Marcus. Try to get some rest." Marcus sadly looks at Dr. Stone as Dr. Stone sadly looks back at him. Dr. stone then turns to Jessica and Vanessa and says, "I'll talk to you later. I'll see what I can do about Diane." Jessica and Vanessa sadly look at Dr. Stone as he sadly looks back at them. Dr. Stone turns and approaches Dr. Kahn. They then turn and head towards the doorway. They then leave the room as Jessica, Vanessa and Marcus sadly look at them.

Chapter 10

Nancy's Close Encounter With The Other Personality

It is around 1:30 in the morning. It is dark and windy outside. Inside Margarita and Tomas' mansion in Northern Westchester, Nicolas and Mickey are in Diane D and Michael's bedroom chit-chatting with Diane D and Michael, as Diane D sits up on her bed fully dressed with her back and head leaned against the headboard. The eerie sounds of the wind comes through the bedroom. Nicolas looks towards the bedroom window as the curtains blow in the wind. He then says, "I think the storm is coming. It's too late to go out there now." He then turns to Mickey, Michael and Diane D and says, "Well, we might as well go to my room and watch the Sports Channel."

"Okay," Mickey says.

"Y'all gonna watch the Sports Channel now?" Diane D asks.

"Yeah," Michael says. "You coming?"

"No I'm gonna stay here and get some rest."

"Okay. See you later Diane."

"Okay."

Michael, Nicolas and Mickey start to head towards the bedroom doorway. They then leave the room. Diane D continues to sit up on the bed. Suddenly there is a loud wind sound. Diane D looks towards the bedroom window. She stares at the bedroom window and sees the curtains blowing in the wind. She then looks at the unlit candles that are laying on the floor in the front corner of the room. She stares at the candles. She then looks towards the bedroom doorway. She then gets up off the bed and goes towards the bedroom door. She looks out the bedroom door into the upstairs hallway. It is dark and dimly lit in the upstairs hallway. Diane D doesn't see anyone around in the upstairs hallway. She quickly closes the bedroom door and leaves it slightly opened. She turns and hurries to the unlit candles laying on the floor. She takes several candles and quickly puts them into several different candle holders. She bends to the floor and stand the candles up on the floor near the side of her bed. She then sits on the floor. She folds her legs and places the candles halfway around her body surrounding the front and sides of her body. She then takes a lighter and starts to light all the candles. Once all the candles are lit, Diane D takes her left hand and grab one of the litted candles as she takes her right hand and grabs another candle. She has a litted candle in each hand. She holds the litted candles. She then puts both arms and hands out to the sides and gets into a meditation mode. The wind sounds become louder as Diane D closes her eyes and holds her head up in the air. She starts to secretly meditate.

It is now around 2:00 in the morning. Nancy and Charlotte are inside the dimly lit upstairs hallway outside the bedrooms. They hear the eerie sounds of the wind coming through the hallway as they stand there looking down the hallway towards Diane D's bedroom door. They see that Diane D's bedroom door is slightly opened with the dim candle lights shining through it. Charlotte then turns to Nancy and whispers, "Is Diane meditating in there? It kind of looks like candle lights are shining through the doorway in her room."

"Yeah I think she is meditating Charlotte," Nancy whispers.

"Oh yeah? I thought Grandma and Grandpa banned her from meditating anymore."

"They did. That's why she's not allowed to have her door shut tight anymore. But obviously she's trying to take advantage of the situation while she thinks no one is watching."

"So where's Michael?"

"He's in the other room watching sports with Nicolas and Mickey."

"Oh."

"I want to go check on Diane, but I'm afraid to look. I don't like seeing her in these weird state of trances that she be getting into."

"I don't like seeing her in these state of trances either. It scares me."

"It scares me too. You still got those close-up pictures of her eyes that you and your mom took of her before when she was in a state of trance?"

"Yeah but Grandpa have those close-up pictures of her eyes locked away in the closet somewhere?"

"He does? Why?"

"He says those close-up pictures of her eyes being in a state of trance scares little kids whenever they come to the house and wind up coming across them. He doesn't want little kids to get scared, so he locked those pictures away."

"I don't blame him. Well let's go back in our room and chill out in there and wait there for Diane until she finishes meditating."

"Okay." Charlotte and Nancy turn and go the opposite direction towards their room as they look back towards Diane D's bedroom door.

Around forty-five minutes later, it is still windy outside. Diane D, Nancy and Charlotte are in Nancy and Charlotte's bedroom laughing and chit-chatting. Charlotte sits on the side of one of the double beds facing the other double bed as Nancy sits on the side of the other double bed facing Charlotte with Diane D standing between the foot of both double beds with a bottled water in her hand as she faces Nancy and Charlotte. Suddenly, there is a loud thunder sound! Nancy and Charlotte frighteningly jump as they and Diane D look towards the window. "Wow," Charlotte frighteningly says. "Did y'all hear that?"

"We sure did," Nancy frighteningly says.

"My God." Charlotte, Nancy and Diane D continue to stare at the window at the thunder and eerie wind sounds. They then turn towards each other as Charlotte says to Diane D, "So Diane, how did your meditation go?" Then she puzzled says, "How do you feel now that you just finished?"

"Why?" Diane D asks. "You saw me?"

"No I didn't see you, but I could tell that you had a candle light burning in your room because I could see the candle light shining through the doorway."

"You could see it?"

"Yeah. So how was your meditation?"

Diane D takes a quick drink of some bottled water and says, "You know something Charlotte, I feel so relaxed and so refreshed."

"You do?"

"Yeah. I feel free as a bird again."

"You do?"

"I sure do. You two should try it sometimes."

"Try it sometimes?" Nancy says. "No that's okay Diane. I think I'll pass."

"Yeah me too," Charlotte says. "Besides Diane, didn't Grandma and Grandpa forbid you from meditating anymore because of these weird state of trances you be getting into?"

"Yeah they did," Diane D says. "But I figured if I meditate real quick, they won't catch me or know about it."

"So you're gonna sneak behind their backs doing it anyway like you did before?"

"Yeah, but I don't want to. It's something I need to do for myself. I don't know what everybody is so afraid of, meditation is good for you."

"Yeah but we don't think it's good for YOU Diane," Nancy says.

"No? Why not? It doesn't bother me at all."

"It doesn't?" Charlotte asks.

"No."

"I don't know about that Diane. I mean you DO go off into these weird state of trances every time you meditate. And odd things or occurrences do seem to follow you after you meditate! That's why Grandma and Grandpa banned you from meditating anymore."

"I don't remember being in any state of trance Charlotte. And I

70

don't see any odd things or occurrences following me after I meditate!"

"That's because you're not aware of it Diane! That little boy Marcus did claim that you went into a weird state of trance up in that school hallway that night!"

"I don't care what that little boy said! I was never in a state of trance in that school hallway! I was never in a state of trance inside that school at all and I'm sick of him going around telling everybody that!"

"Maybe because it's true Diane," Nancy says. "I don't think he would make that story up! I mean what is he going to get out of it?! We have witnessed you being in a state of trance ourselves plenty of times."

"Oh really."

"Yes really."

"Well, am I in a state of trance right now?"

"No. Not now."

"What do you mean 'not now'? Was I in a state of trance a little while ago when I left my room?"

"No."

"Was I in a state of trance while I was in my room?"

"I don't know Diane. I was afraid to look in your room to find out."

"Yeah me too," Charlotte says.

"Oh come on now you two," Diane D says. "Y'all are being silly right now, I'm fine. There's nothing wrong with me. I'm not in any doggone state of trance right now, I feel good. As a matter of fact, I feel great. Right now I'm in such a good mood and spirit. Since I'm not in this doggone state of trance I be hearing everybody talking about, I think we should celebrate."

"Celebrate? How? By having a picture taking of you? No thanks Diane. I don't want to see or witness that ghostly image of your look-alike soul, spirit or personality being right next to you inside a picture!"

"Me neither," Nancy says.

"What are you talking about!" Diane D shouts. "I don't have a look-alike soul, spirit or personality being next to me inside a picture!"

"We heard that's what happened at your photo shoot!"

"Well I never saw it!"

"Well Aunt Mary said the photographer saw it and told everyone else in the room about it!"

"Well he's full of shit! I never saw the photo!"

"So you think he was lying when he claim he saw a double image of you in the photo?"

"Not lying, maybe exaggerating."

"Exaggerating?! You think the man was exaggerating about seeing two different images of you inside the same photo?"

"Yes I do! Most likely it could have been an old picture of me that got caught up inside his camera and that old picture of me got mixed up with the current picture of me! Who knows?! But I wasn't talking about celebrating by having a picture taking of me. I was talking about celebrating by having a small drink."

"You want to have a small drink?"

"Yeah. How 'bout it."

"Well, since you're not in a state of trance Diane, maybe we could celebrate. I think I'll have a drink too." Nancy turns to Charlotte and says, "How about you Charlotte? You want to celebrate Diane's non-state of trance and have a drink too?"

"I'll drink to that!" Charlotte says. "Why not? Let's celebrate Diane's non-state of trance."

"Alriiiight," Diane D says. "So what do you two want to drink? Now you two know I'm not down for any of you drinking hard liquor, but I'll let y'all slide tonight since we're celebrating."

"Why thank you Diane."

"No problem Charlotte. So what do y'all want to drink?"

"I want some Vodka and Martini. How about you guys, are y'all down for that?"

"Yeah I'll take some Vodka, Martini and Bacardi," Nancy says.

"Bacardi too?" Diane D says. "Okay Vodka, Martini and Bacardi coming right up. I'll go downstairs and make the Martini and get the rest of the liquor and cups out of the bar and bring them right up."

"Okay Diane."

"I'll be back." Diane D turns away and walks towards the bedroom door. She opens the door and leaves the room closing the door behind herself.

Forty-five minutes later, it is now raining, thundering and lightning outside. Nancy and Charlotte are sitting on the bed looking towards the window at the rain, thunder and lightning outside. Charlotte then looks towards the bedroom door. She then turns to Nancy and says, "Wow, Diane is taking a while to come back upstairs with the Vodka, Martini and Bacardi. What's keeping her?"

"I don't know Charlotte," Nancy says. "She's probably still making the Martini."

"Well she should have been back by now."

"I know. I hope she didn't go off and meditate again."

"I hope not either. Maybe we should check on her just in case she decided to meditate again and is in a state of trance right now."

"You think so."

"Could be."

"I'll go check on her, you stay here. I'll be back."

"Okay Nancy."

Nancy gets up off the bed. She turns and heads towards the bedroom door. She opens the bedroom door and steps out the room closing the door behind herself.

Nancy steps into the dimly lit upstairs hallway. She can still hear the rain, thunder and lightning outside. Nancy is about to walk towards the stairs. She looks to the side and suddenly sees Diane D across the upstairs hallway slowly heading towards the opposite direction towards her bedroom empty handed. Nancy puzzledly looks at Diane D. She then calls out to her, "Hey Diane!" Diane D stops in her tracks with her back towards Nancy. She stands there, but does not turn around. Nancy puzzledly looks at Diane D again. She calls out to her again, "Diane!" Diane D continues to stand there with her back towards Nancy. She still does not turn around. Nancy slowly approaches Diane D. She calls out to Diane D again, "Diane?" Diane D slowly turns around towards Nancy. Her face has an eerie pale unearthly appearance to it and her eyes are very puffy, swollen and appear half dead as she suspiciously looks at Nancy. Nancy stops right in her tracks! She becomes shocked and stunned seeing Diane D's strange facial appearance. She then shouts, "Diane are you okay?! What happened to you?! You look sort of different! Your face looks pale, almost like a dead person! And your eyes look very swollen! It kind of looks like you were just in a fight or boxing match or something! You look like a dead person!" Diane D continues to suspiciously stare at Nancy. Nancy then says, "Are you okay? What took you so long to come back to the room? You weren't meditating again, were you?" Diane D suspiciously stares at Nancy with the eerie pale face and puffy and swollen eyes. Nancy then says, "Did you get the Vodka, Martini and Bacardi?" Diane D puzzled stares at Nancy giving Nancy a confused look. Nancy then says, "Diane you seem kind of out of it. You look sort of confused or something. Are you alright? Where's the Vodka, Martini and Bacardi?" Diane D continues to puzzled stare at Nancy. Nancy then says, "Diane what's wrong, didn't you hear me? Where's the Vodka, Martini and Bacardi?"

"What Vodka, Martini and Bacardi?" Diane D puzzled says.

Nancy puzzled stares at Diane D and says, "'What Vodka, Martini and Bacardi'? What do you mean 'What Vodka, Martini and Bacardi'? The Vodka, Martini and Bacardi you were supposed to bring up here to me and Charlotte so we all can have a drink together. You forgot already?" Diane D continues to puzzled stare at Nancy giving Nancy a confused dazed look. Nancy then says, "Don't tell me that you drunk all the Vodka, Martini and Bacardi for yourself and got sort of drunk and don't remember that you were supposed to bring the Vodka, Martini and Bacardi up here to me and Charlotte. Is that what took you so long to come back up? You drank the Vodka, Martini and Bacardi for yourself and got a little drunk?"

"I don't know what you're talking about," Diane D says as she continues to give Nancy a confused dazed look.

"'You don't know what I'm talking about? What do you mean 'you don't know what I'm talking about' Diane? I'm talking about the drinks you said you were in the mood for a little while ago then said you were going to go downstairs to the bar and make the Martini and bring the

73

Martini, Vodka, Bacardi and cups up here to me and Charlotte, but I don't see the Martini, Vodka, Bacardi or cups anywhere on you. Where are the Martini, Vodka, Bacardi and cups?"

"I don't have it."

"Yeah I can see that. Why didn't you bring the Martini, Vodka, Bacardi and cups up here like you said you were going to do? Did you drink up all that stuff Diane? Did you? Come on and say something Diane! Did you drink up all that stuff?!"

"Look, Diane is not here right now."

Nancy puzzled stares at Diane D. She then says, "What .... did you just say?"

"I said Diane is not here right now."

"Diane is not here right now? What the hell are you talking about? What do you mean 'Diane is not here right now'. You're Diane. And you're standing right there."

Diane D hesitates. She stares at Nancy and says, "I'm not Diane."

Nancy puzzled stares at Diane D again. She then says, "What .... did you just say? What do you mean 'You're not Diane'?"

"I'm not Diane. She isn't here right now."

"What?"

"I said she isn't here right now."

"She isn't here right now? Who isn't here right now?"

"Diane. She isn't here right now."

"She isn't?"

"No she isn't."

"What the hell are you talking about? What do you mean 'Diane is not here right now'. I'm looking right at you."

"I told you, I'm not Diane."

"You're not?"

"No I'm not."

"Okay come on now Diane, enough with the joke alright? Because you're really starting to scare me."

"I'm not joking. I'm not Diane."

"You're not?"

"No I'm not. But don't worry, Diane is okay. She'll be back."

"What? Diane will be back? What do you mean 'Diane will be back?'"

"She'll be back."

"She'll be back? Back from where? Where is she?"

"She's wandering the universe for right now."

"She's wandering the universe? What do you mean 'she's wandering the universe'?"

"Like I said, she's wandering the universe."

Nancy hesitates. She puzzled looks up in the air listening to the thunder and lightning outside. Then she puzzled stares at Diane D again. She then says, "How come she's wandering the universe?"

"I can't tell you?"

"You can't tell me?"

"No."

"Well why not?"

"I just can't."

"What? My God. So, if you're not Diane, then who are you?"

"I can't tell you."

"You can't?"

"No."

"Why not?"

"I just can't."

"Oh my God. Do you have a name?"

"No I don't."

"You don't have a name?"

"No. Now if you would excuse me, I have to leave Diane's body so she can come back."

"What? You have to leave Diane's body so she can come back?"

"Yes."

"But where're you gonna go?"

"I can't tell you."

"You can't tell me?"

"No I can't."

"Why not?"

"I just can't."

"Why not?"

"I just can't." Diane D gives Nancy a cold stare. Nancy puzzledly and frighteningly looks at Diane D. Diane D then turns away from Nancy and continues to head towards her bedroom.

"Wait a minute!" Nancy suddenly shouts. Diane D stops and turns around towards Nancy. Nancy then says, "So if you're not Diane, then how do you know that's her room over there?"

"I just know."

"You just know? How do you know?"

Diane D hesitates and stares at Nancy again with a cold stare. She then says, "It's not my first time being inside this house."

"What? It's not your first time being inside this house? What do you mean 'It's not your first time being inside this house?' You've been inside this house before?"

"Yes, plenty of times."

"Plenty of times? How?"

"Whenever Diane meditates and leaves her body, I come into her body and take her place until she comes back."

"What? You come into her body and take her place whenever she meditates?"

"Yes I do."

"Why?"

"I just do." Diane D gives Nancy another cold stare as Nancy frighteningly looks at her. "Like I said, don't worry, Diane is okay.

She'll be back." Diane D continues to give Nancy a cold stare. She then turns away from Nancy and continues to head to her bedroom. Nancy puzzledly and frighteningly stares at Diane D.

Diane D reaches her bedroom door. She opens the bedroom door and goes inside the bedroom closing the door behind herself. The door is then heard being locked.

Nancy puzzledly and frighteningly stands there shaking not knowing what to do as she puzzled stares at Diane D's bedroom door. She frighteningly backs up. She then turns and runs towards the other bedroom doors. She starts to scream and bang on all the bedroom doors.

A minute later, Margarita, Tomas, Barry, Mary and Tonio rush down the hall to Diane D's bedroom door as Marilyn, Nicolas, Mickey, Michael, Nancy and Charlotte hurry behind them.

Margarita, Tomas, Barry, Mary and Tonio approach Diane D's bedroom door. They start to bang on Diane D's bedroom door and shout, "Diane! Diane! Diane, are you okay?! Diane! Are you okay?!" Diane D does not answer. Margarita, Barry and Tomas try to open Diane D's bedroom door, but they cannot open it. It is locked. Tomas turns to his family and shouts, "I'm gonna get the Master Key!" Tomas turns and rushes off.

"Hurry Tomas!" Margarita shouts as she, Mary and Barry continue to bang and try to open the bedroom door.

Barry then shouts through the door, "Diane are you okay baby! Open up!" Diane D still does not respond. Barry turns to Nancy and shouts, "Nancy are you sure that's what she said to you, that 'Diane's not here right now'?!"

"Yes that's exactally what she said to me out here!" Nancy shouts.

Mary turns to Nancy and shouts, "And are you sure that she said to you, that 'she's not Diane'?!"

"Yes that's exactally what she told me out here too!"

Tomas quickly approaches them with the Master key and shouts, "I got the Master key! Step aside everybody!" Everyone steps aside as Tomas goes to the door and puts the key into the keyhole. He turns the lock and unlocks Diane D's bedroom door. The door opens and they all anxiously rush into Diane D's bedroom.

Diane D's family rush into her room and see her lying face down on the bed. "Diane!" they shout as they rush to her. Diane D's family reach her and grab her as they shout to her, "Diane! Wake up baby!" They tug and pull on her trying to wake her up. They then turn her face up on the bed. Diane D suddenly wakes up as her family shouts, "Diane!" Diane D becomes startled. Her face is less pale, her eyes are less puffy and less swollen as her family shouts, "Diane! Are you okay?" Diane D is confused. She puzzled looks at her family as her family sit her up on the bed. Her family then holds and hugs on to her tight as she puzzled looks around the room. Mary shouts, "Diane what happened to you?! Are you okay?!" Diane D puzzled looks at Mary then at the rest of her family.

"Diane are you alright?!" Barry shouts. "Is everything okay?!" Diane D puzzled looks at Barry.

Diane D's family puzzled looks at her as Tomas shouts, "Diane what happened?! Are you okay?! Nancy had rushed to all of us and said that you were out of it! Is that true?!"

Diane D puzzled looks at Tomas. She then puzzled looks at Nancy then the rest of her family. She then says, "I don't know."

"You don't know?!" Margarita shouts. "You don't know whether or not you were out of it?!"

"No Grandma, I don't. All I know, is that I was in the other room with Nancy and Charlotte. I told them that I was gonna go downstairs to the bar, make the Martini and bring up the Martini, Vodka, Bacardi and some cups, so I went downstairs to get it."

"You did?"

"Yeah."

"Then what happened while you were down there?"

"I made the Martini and took a few sips of it to taste it. Then I opened up some other drinks, poured just a teeny weeny bit in a cup and took a few sips. The next thing I know is that I felt dizzy."

"You felt dizzy?"

"Yeah. It felt like I was about to pass out."

"You felt like you were about to pass out?" Barry asks.

"Yeah."

"From the Martini and the other drinks?"

"I don't think so because I only took a few sips. It wouldn't cause me to feel dizzy or feel faint that fast."

"So what happened then?"

"I started holding my head. Then the next thing I know, is that I was feeling woozy, then I was falling."

"You were falling?" Michael asks.

"Yeah. But I don't remember hitting or landing on the floor."

"You don't remember landing?"

"No. Then the next thing I know, is that my soul or spirit was out there in space wandering the universe."

"Your soul or spirit was out there in space, wandering the universe again Diane?" Mary asks.

"Yeah Mom. It wasn't my intention though. While my soul or spirit was out there wandering the universe, the next thing I know is that I hear you all calling my name."

"You heard us calling your name while your soul or spirit was out there in the universe?" Margarita asks.

"Yeah. The next thing I know, is that I feel you all tugging and pulling me."

"You felt us all tugging and pulling you?" Barry asks.

"Yeah. Then the next thing I know, is that I'm waking up here laying right on this bed with you all surrounding me. And I don't even know or remember how I got up here."

"What!" the family shouts.

"You don't know or remember how you got up here Diane?" Charlotte asks.

"No," Diane D says.

"You don't know or remember coming up the stairs running into Nancy when she approached you out in the hallway?" Barry asks.

"No Dad I don't remember." Diane D puzzled looks at Nancy and asks, "You approached me in the hallway Nancy?"

"Yeah," Nancy says. "Don't you remember?"

"No I don't. Nancy, wasn't I in the other room with you and Charlotte, and we were all talking about celebrating and I said I wanted to have a small drink before I go to bed? Then we all said we want some, Vodka, Martini and Bacardi. Then I told you and Charlotte that I was going to go downstairs and get the Vodka, Martini, Bacardi and cups out of the bar and bring them right up, then I left the room to go downstairs to get the Vodka, Martini, Bacardi and cups and bring it right up? Did that really happened, or was that a dream I had?"

"No Diane it wasn't a dream you had, it really happened! You were in the other room with me and Charlotte talking about celebrating with a drink! You went downstairs and took a while to come back up! Charlotte and I were wondering what was taking you so long to come back up to the room with the Vodka, Martini and Bacardi. So I told Charlotte that I was gonna go check on you. So I stepped out the other room and went right out into the hallway. That's when I saw you. You were walking towards this room instead of coming back to the other room where Charlotte and I were and you had no Vodka, Martini, Bacardi or cups in your hand. So I called out to you and said 'Hey Diane!' Then you stopped. But you didn't turn around towards me right away."

"I didn't?"

"No you didn't. So I called out to you again and said 'Diane!' You still didn't turn around! Then I walked towards you and called out to you again and said 'Diane?' That's when you turned around and looked right at me. I noticed your face was kind of pale and your eyes were puffy and very swollen so I stopped!"

"My face was pale and my eyes were puffy and very swollen?"

"Yeah, out in the hallway! I was shocked to see your face looking like that, so I asked you 'were you okay' 'what happened to you' 'you look sort of different! Then I told you that 'your face looks pale and that 'your eyes look very swollen that 'it kind of looks like you were just in a fight or boxing match or something' but you didn't say anything. You just stared at me giving me a suspicious look!"

"A suspicious look?"

"Yeah! I figured maybe that's why you didn't turn around towards me right away when I first called out to you, because you didn't want me to see or notice your face looking different. But your face don't look different now Diane! Your face don't look pale and your eyes don't look puffy or swollen now!"

"It doesn't?"

"No! It's back to normal!"

"Back to normal?"

"Yes!"

"My God Nancy. I don't know how my face would get pale or my eyes would all of a sudden get puffy or swollen that quick! I only took a few teeny weeny sips of some Martini and other liquor at the bar and it was only a few teeny weeny sips! That's not enough to cause anybody's face to get pale or their eyes to get puffy or swollen at all!"

"But your face was pale and your eyes were puffy and swollen out in the hallway Diane! I saw it!" Diane D puzzled looks at Nancy. Nancy then says, "Then I asked you 'what took you so long to come back to the room? Then I asked you 'did you get the Vodka, Martini and Bacardi' and you just stared at me like you didn't know what I was talking about?!"

"I did?"

"Yeah! I said 'Diane you seem kind of out of it, you look sort of confused or something. Then I asked you 'were you alright', 'where's the Vodka, Martini and Bacardi' and you still didn't seem to know what I was talking about! Then I asked you 'what's wrong, didn't you hear me?', 'where's the Vodka, Martini and Bacardi', then you asked me 'what Vodka, Martini and Bacardi'!"

"I said that?"

"Yes! Then I told you the Vodka, Martini and Bacardi that you were supposed to bring up here to me and Charlotte so we all can have a drink together! I thought that you drank all the Vodka, Martini and Bacardi for yourself and got sort of drunk and don't remember that you were supposed to bring the Vodka, Martini and Bacardi up here to me and Charlotte. I thought that's what took you so long to come back upstairs!"

"No. Like I said, I only took a few teeny weeny sips of Martini and some other liquor at the bar. That's not enough to cause anybody to get drunk!"

"Well I didn't see the Vodka, Martini, Bacardi or cups anywhere on you when you came back upstairs. So I thought that you drank all the Vodka, Martini and Bacardi for yourself, that's why I asked you 'where are the Vodka, Martini, Bacardi and cups'. You said you didn't have it! Then I asked you 'why didn't you bring the Vodka, Martini, Bacardi and cups up here like you said you were going to do'. Then I asked you 'did you drink up all that stuff Diane'. Then I said 'Come on and say something Diane! Did you drink up all that stuff?'. Then do you know what you said to me?"

Diane D puzzled looks at Nancy and says, "No. What did I say to you?"

"You said 'look, Diane is not here right now'."

Diane D looks at Nancy stunned. She then says, "What did you just say?"

"You said to me, 'Diane is not here right now'."

"I said that to you?"

"Yes you did!"

"You got to be kidding me Nancy."

"No I'm not kidding Diane! You said that to me!"

"I did?"

"Yes you did!"

"I don't remember saying that!"

"You don't?"

"No! Why would I say that to you Nancy?!"

"That's what we're all trying to find out Diane!" Tomas shouts. "That why would you say that to Nancy! Why would you refer to yourself in the third person!"

"Refer to myself in the third person?"

"Yes!"

"I don't remember saying that to her Grandpa!"

Nancy puzzled stares at Diane D and says, "You don't remember saying that Diane?"

"No I don't remember saying 'Diane is not here right now'. Why would I say that about myself Nancy? Why would I refer to myself in the third person?"

"I don't know Diane, but you did! Then I asked you 'what the hell are you talking about, what do you mean 'Diane is not here right now' I told you that you're standing right there'! Then do you know what the next thing you said to me?"

Diane D puzzled looks at Nancy again and says, "No. What did I say?"

"You said to me, 'I'm not Diane'."

Diane D looks at Nancy stunned. She then says, "Repeat that."

"You said to me 'I'm not Diane'."

"I said to you 'I'm not Diane'?"

"Yes you did!"

"You're joking."

"No I'm not joking Diane! That's what you said to me!"

"I did?"

"Yes you did! I thought that YOU were joking!"

"You thought that I was joking?"

"Yeah!"

"I guess I wasn't joking Nancy, because I don't remember saying that either!"

"You don't?!"

"No! Why would I say that 'I'm not Diane'?!"

"I don't know! You tell me!"

"I can't tell you Nancy, because I don't remember saying that to you!"

Nancy puzzled stares at Diane D and says, "You don't remember saying that at all?"

"No I don't. Why would I say 'I'm not myself?'"

"I don't know Diane, you did! So I asked you 'what do you mean 'You're not Diane'. Then you just said 'you're not'. Then I told you enough with the joke because you're starting to scare me. Then you told me that you weren't joking, 'you're not Diane'. Then I asked 'you're not' then you told me 'no you're not. Then I could see it in your eyes, that you weren't joking. Then you told me 'but not to worry, Diane is okay. She'll be back."

"What? I said 'not to worry, Diane will be back'?"

"Yes that's what you said. Then I said 'what do you mean 'Diane will be back, back from where, where is she', then you said 'she's wandering the universe for right now."

Diane D looks at Nancy stunned. She then says, "What did you just say I said?"

"You said to me, 'Diane's wandering the universe for right now'."

"I said that to you?"

"Yes you did!"

"Now that part I DO remember!"

"What?! You remember saying that to me?!"

"No I don't remember saying that to you. I remember my soul or spirit wandering the universe, like I just told you all a little while ago!"

Nancy hesitates again and shockingly stares at Diane D again. She then says, "So are you saying, that you, or WHOEVER you were out there in the hallway, was right about you wandering the universe?"

"I guess so, because that's the only part I remember doing, after I fell out downstairs!"

"My God," the family says.

"How come your soul or spirit was wandering the universe again Diane?" Barry asks.

"I don't know Dad," Diane D says.

Barry turns to Nancy and says, "Nancy did you ask Diane, or whoever she was out there in the hallway, why she was wandering the universe?"

"Yes I did ask 'why'," Nancy says. "She said she can't tell me, then I asked 'why not' then she said she just can't. Then I said to her 'so if you're not Diane, then who are you?"

"You asked her that?" Margarita says.

"Yes I did."

"Then what did I say?" Diane D asked.

"You said you can't tell me that either! Then I asked 'why not' then you said you just can't! Then you gave this cold stare."

"I did?"

"Yes you did! Then I asked you, or whoever you were out there in the hallway, 'do you have a name'"

"You asked me that?"

"Yes I did."

"What did I say?"

"You just said 'no you don't'."

"I told you 'I don't have a name'?"

"Yeah! Then you said to me 'now if you would excuse me, I have to leave Diane's body so she can come back'."

"What!" the family shouts.

"She said 'now if you would excuse her, she have to leave Diane's body so she can come back?" Mickey asks.

"Yes that's what she said!" Nancy says. "Then I asked her where is she gonna go and she said she can't tell me?"

"I told you that?" Diane D asks.

"Yeah, then I asked you 'why not' and you said 'you just can't. Then you gave this cold stare again. Then you turned away from me and continued to head towards this room! Then I said said to you 'wait a minute'. Then you turned around to me and I asked you 'so if you're not Diane, then how do you know that this is her room'. Then do you know what you said to me?"

"No. What did I say to you?"

"You said to me that this is not your first time being inside this house."

"What!" the family shouts.

"She said this is not her first time being inside this house?" Nicolas asks.

"Yeah!" Nancy shouts.

"What did she mean by that 'It's not her first time being inside this house?'" Marilyn asks.

"Diane, or whoever she was out there in the hallway, said she's been inside this house before, plenty of times!"

"Plenty of times?!" the family shouts.

"Yes!"

"How?!" Mary asks.

"Whoever she was out there in the hallway, said whenever Diane meditates and leaves her body, they would come into her body and take her place until she comes back."

"What!" the family shouts.

"Whoever she was out there in the hallway, said they would 'come into Diane's body and take her place whenever she meditates?" Margarita asks.

"Yes that's what she said!" Nancy says. "Then I asked 'why'. She said 'she just do'! Then she said to me again 'not to worry, Diane is okay. She'll be back'. That's when Diane, or whoever she was out there in the hallway, turned away from me and continued to head to this room! Then she came to this bedroom door, opened the door, came inside this room and closed the door behind herself locking it. I just

82

stood there shaking, I didn't know what to do! That's when I backed up, turned and ran away towards your rooms banging on everybody's doors! That's when you all came and rushed right in here."

"My God!" the family shouts.

Tomas turns to Charlotte and says, "Charlotte did you see or hear any of this?!"

"No I didn't see anything because I never left the bedroom when Diane came back up the stairs!" Charlotte says.

"You didn't?"

"No! I only heard Diane and Nancy talking out in the hallway."

"You heard them talking?"

"Yeah, but I couldn't make out the words they were saying to each other."

"You couldn't?"

"No. I only heard their voices."

"Wow," the family says.

Nancy looks at Diane D and says, "Boy Diane, you really gave me a good scare!"

"And you just gave me a good scare Nancy!" Diane D says, "hearing this story, because I don't remember any of those things you just said I said to you!"

"You don't remember anything at all what Nancy just told you Diane?" Tonio asks.

"No, not a thing! I have no recollection of any of that at all!"

"Even though this all happened only a minute or two ago, you still don't remember any of it?"

"No I remember none of it!"

"So the only thing you DO remember during that point in time when you and Nancy were out in the hallway, was seeing your soul or spirit wandering the universe?" Margarita asks.

"Yes that's the only thing I remember Grandma."

"My God it's happening again! While Diane's soul or spirit was out there in space wandering the universe, that other soul, spirit or personality came into her body and took over her body again!"

"What!" the family shouts.

"Yes!" Margarita looks at Nancy and shouts, "My God Nancy! I think you just had an encounter with Diane's other personality!"

"What!" Nancy and the rest of the family frighteningly shouts. "Her other personality?!"

"An encounter with her other personality?!" Nancy shouts.

"Yes!" Margarita shouts.

"You mean, her other personality that attacked all those people in the past, like the security guards, the police officers and that little boy Marcus in the school hallway?!"

"Yes I think so!"

"Oh no la abuela!" Nancy turns around and shouts. She turns back towards Margarita and shouts, "Qué vamos a hacer!"

"I know one thing we're gonna do! Being that Diane fell out downstairs in the living room, we're going to take her to the hospital emergency right now for her physical health! And being that she wasn't herself out there in the hallway, we're going to call up Doctor Stone and make an appointment with him again for her mental health!" Margarita looks back at Diane D and says, "Diane, you weren't meditating before you went downstairs to get the liquor, were you?"

"Uum," Diane D nervously looks at Margarita with a look of guilt on her face. She then says, "Yeah Grandma, I was."

"What!" the family shouts. "Oh my God!"

"You were meditating?!" Margarita shouts.

"Yeah Grandma," Diane D says. "I had just got through meditating when I was talking with Nancy and Charlotte in the other room and told them I feel very good from the meditation. I told them I felt free as a bird."

"You told them you felt free as a bird?!"

"Yeah."

"And several minutes after that, that's when you went downstairs to the bar, made Martini, took a few sips of liquor then felt dizzy then felt like you were about to pass out, then find your soul or spirit wandering the universe, right?!"

"Exactly. And while my soul or spirit was wandering the universe, that's when I heard you all calling my name, tugging and pulling on me, then I woke up here finding myself laying on the bed with you all surrounding me."

"Diane, I thought we all told you to give up on this meditating stuff!" Tomas shouts. "Didn't we tell you to give up on it?! Because every time you meditate, situations like THIS happens with that other soul, spirit or personality coming into your body, taking over your body scaring the crap out of people and you don't even be aware of it! Now it just caused your own cousin to get scared right out of her wits coming into contact with that other soul, spirit or personality in the hallway having an encounter with it!"

Diane D worriedly looks at Tomas. She then looks at Nancy and says, "I'm sorry Nancy. I didn't mean for that to happen. I didn't mean for any of it to happen at all! All I wanted to do was get a few small drinks after my meditation was finished. I was just in a mood for a few drinks, that's all. I'm sorry that happened to you." Diane D then looks at the rest of her family and says, "I didn't mean to cause all of this."

"Well you did cause all of this by meditating when we strictly told you not to do it anymore!"

"That's right Diane!" Margarita shouts. "Now that we all know you had meditated behind our backs when we strictly told you not to do it anymore, then you do it anyway when no one is looking and wind up practically scaring your cousin when this other soul, spirit or personality took over your body in the hallway, do you know what this means?!"

"No Grandma," Diane D nervously says. "I don't."

"That means we have to keep a strict eye on you girl! You're not allowed to be alone anymore young lady!"

"Not allowed to be alone anymore? What do you mean?"

"You're gonna have to either move back into our bedroom with us, or some of us have to move back in here with you and Michael!"

"That's right Diane!" Tomas shouts. "Not only that, we're gonna have to change the alarm system in this house to make sure that whenever this other soul, spirit or personality comes into your body and takes over your body while we're all asleep, you won't wind up leaving the house and go out there into the street and wind up doing something crazy and not be aware of it!"

"That's right Diane!" Barry shouts. "It's a good thing that this other soul, spirit or personality decided to come upstairs and bring your physical body up to this room instead of having your physical body go out the front door into the street and do something wild and crazy or something vicious and you not be aware of it!"

"Yeah Diane," Nancy says. "Even though that whole incident that happened in the hallway was very creepy, I'm glad your original soul and spirit came back." Nancy goes and grabs Diane D giving her a big hug and holds onto her very tightly with tears flowing from her eyes as Diane D hugs her back. Nancy then cries, "And please Diane, don't ever leave us again." Nancy and Diane D continue to hug and hold each other with tears in their eyes as everyone else sadly hugs and holds them.

Three hours later, Diane D is laying face up on a bed inside the hospital emergency room with her eyes closed as her family and relatives surround her. Dr. Kern, a male white doctor around his early 60's approach Michael, Mary, Margarita, Barry and Tomas and pulls them to the side as the rest of Diane D's family remain around her.

Dr. Kern then says to Michael, Mary, Margarita, Barry and Tomas, "She's going to be alright."

"She is Doctor?" Michael asks.

"Yes. Her physical health seems to be okay. She didn't seem to suffer any physical damage."

"She didn't?"

"No."

"Thank God," Michael, Mary, Margarita, Barry and Tomas say.

"We just want her to stay in the hospital overnight for observation."

"For observation?" Mary asks.

"Yes. We might want to keep her here for one or two nights just to make sure."

"Okay Doctor," Margarita says.

"Good. When are you going to call up Doctor Stone and make another appointment for her mental health?"

"Oh we're going to call him up as soon as his office opens this morning," Margarita says.

"As soon as his office opens?"

"That's right," Barry says.

"Okay good. Let me go check on her again."

"Okay Doctor."

Dr. Kern turns and heads towards Diane D as Barry, Margarita, Michael, Mary, Tomas turn and follow him.

That same afternoon Diane D is sleeping face up in the bed inside the hospital room as her family members surround her talking with each other as they smile at her admiring her. Nicolas approaches Mary and Barry and says, "Mom, Dad what time is visiting hours over?"

"Well we still have a few hours to go Nicolas," Barry says. "Why?"

"Well because Dana is on her way here and she's bringing the rest of the family too."

"Oh yeah?" Mary asks.

"Yeah. They should be here in ten minutes. I'm gonna meet them downstairs."

"Okay Nicolas. Vamos a estar aqui y mantener un ojo en Diane."

"Bien Mama." Nicolas turns and leaves the area.

Chapter 11

Diane D's Family Take Her To See Dr. Stone Again

It is four days later around 1:00 in the afternoon. Diane D, who is wearing a navy button collar shirt with sleeves rolled to her elbows, navy pants and thick black sneakers, is sitting inside a waiting area of a doctor's office surrounded by all her loved ones as she sits between Nancy and Charlotte with Nancy and Charlotte holding tightly onto her sadly resting their heads against the front of Diane D's shoulders with their eyes closed. Diane D also has her eyes closed as she rests her face on top of Nancy's head. The office door to the doctor's office opens. Dr. Stone comes out of the office door. He approaches Diane D and her family and says, "Hey, how're you all doing now?"

"We're okay for now Doctor Stone," Margarita says.

"Good." Dr. Stone looks at Diane D and says, "Hey Diane." Diane D, Nancy and Charlotte open their eyes and look at Dr. Stone. Dr. Stone then says to Diane D, "So how are you feeling now Diane?"

Diane D, Nancy and Charlotte lift their heads up as Diane D says, "I feel great Doctor."

"You do?"

"Yes I do. I feel fantastic."

"You feel fantastic?"

"Oh yeah."

"That's good. Is it okay if I speak to some of your family members alone in another room, while some of your family members stay in here with you?"

"Sure Doctor."

"Okay." Dr. Stone turns to Margarita, Tomas and the rest of the family and says, "I want to talk to you all in another room."

"Sure Doctor," Margarita says.

"I would need Nancy to come also, since she's the one who actually witnessed and encountered this incident and I would also need Charlotte to come since she's the one who heard Diane and Nancy talking."

"Okay."

"No!" Nancy shouts as she and Charlotte hug tightly onto Diane D's torso each pulling her torso towards their own direction. "We don't want to leave Diane!"

"That's right!" Charlotte shouts. "We don't want her soul or spirit to be snatched or pulled out of her body again!"

"Yeah! We don't want her soul or spirit to leave us again!"

Everybody puzzled looks at Nancy and Charlotte as Dr. Stone says, "So you think holding on to her so tight is gonna stop it?"

"I don't know, but I hope it does!"

"I'm not gonna go anywhere Nancy and Charlotte," Diane D says. "It's okay girls, I'm gonna still be here. You two go ahead." Nancy and Charlotte worriedly look at Diane D. They then let go of her as she tells them, "Go with Dr. Stone and the rest of the family. I'll be here."

Nancy tearfully looks at Diane D and says, "Are you sure?"

"Yeah I'm sure."

"You promise?" Charlotte tearfully asks. "You promise you won't go wandering the universe while we're gone?"

"I promise I'll still be here when you all come back."

"Okay Diane. We love you."

"I love you too." Diane D and Charlotte give each other loving kisses on the cheeks. Diane D smiles at Charlotte and gently squeezes Charlotte's cheek. She then turns the other way to Nancy. She and Nancy give each other loving kisses on the cheeks.

"Okay Diane," Nancy says. "We'll be back."

"Okay Nancy."

Nancy and Charlotte get up from their seats. Tomas turns to Gracy, Grandpa Mike, Aunt Celeste, Michael, Nicolas and Mickey and says, "You all wait in here and keep and eye on Diane while the rest of us go speak with Dr. Stone."

"Okay Tomas," Grandpa Mike says. "We got her."

"Thanks Mike." Tomas and Grandpa Mike hug and tap each other on the shoulder. Tomas then turns to Diane D and says, "Estaremos de vuelta Diane."

"Okay Grandpa Tomas," Diane D says.

Tomas turns to leave the office with Margarita, Nancy, Charlotte and the rest of the family.

Thirty minutes later, Dr. Stone is sitting on a chair inside another room with a clipboard and pen in his hands taking notes and speaking with the other members of Diane D's family as they sit on a long bench in front of him. Nancy has just finished telling Dr. Stone everything that happened the night she had the encounter with Diane D's other personality inside their family's home as Dr. Stone puzzled says to her, "Diane said all that stuff to you?"

"Yes," Nancy says.

"Wow. When I spoke to Diane privately inside the other room yesterday, she told me the same thing that she told you all, that she went downstairs to the bar to make and get the liquor to bring the liquor upstairs to you and Charlotte, then felt herself passing out, then finds her soul or spirit wandering the universe, then finds herself upstairs lying on her bed being awakened by her family. She says she has no recollection nor any memory of coming back up the stairs. She says she has no recollection nor any memory of running into you in the upstairs hallway. She says she has no recollection nor any memory of seeing you in the upstairs hallway nor talking to you at all."

"See what I mean? All I know, is that she went downstairs as Diane, then came back upstairs a completely different person."

"Wow. This other personality of hers is known for being very aggressive towards other people in the past, like beating up and attacking them, breaking their bones and everything by giving them kung fu kicks. What I want to know, if it is the same spirit or personality, who attacked and beat up that kid Marcus inside the school hallway."

"What!" the family shouts

"You want to know if it's the same spirit or personality that attacked Marcus?" Margarita asks.

"Yes I need to know," Dr. Stone says. "I want to know if it's the same spirit or personality who attacked all the other people that Diane has attacked and beat up in the past." Dr. Stone looks back at Nancy and says, "Now Nancy, I need to know in your opinion, how was this other personality behaving towards YOU when you encountered it inside your family's house that night. We're going to forget about Diane's original personality for now, we're going to put her original personality on the back burner. Right now, we're just going to focus on the personality that you encountered inside your family's upstairs hallway that night, okay?"

"Okay," Nancy nervously says.

"Good. So now Nancy, how was this other personality behaving towards YOU inside your family's house? Was it agressive towards YOU in any kind of way?"

"No, not that I could remember."

"It wasn't? It wasn't aggressive towards you at all?"

"No it wasn't."

"It never seemed like it wanted to harm you or attack you in any kind of way?"

"No, not that I remember."

"That's good. When did you first notice something odd or peculiar, about your cousin Diane's appearance that night?"

"When I called out to her across the upstairs hallway and she turned around and looked at me. I noticed that her face was sort of pale and both of her eyes appeared very puffy and swollen."

"Her face was sort of pale and both of her eyes appeared very puffy and swollen?"

"Yeah. Her face was not pale and her eyes were not swollen when she first left the bedroom to go downstairs to get the liquor."

"They weren't?"

"No."

"I see. What did you think of her facial appearance when you first saw it like that?"

"Her face had sort of an unearthly appearance to it."

"An unearthly appearance?"

"Yeah."

"What do you mean by 'an unearthly appearance'?"

"It was like something out of this world."

"Something out of this world?"

"Yes. Her face sort of had that ghostly appearance to it because it was pale. She almost had the face of a dead person."

"The face of a dead person?!"

"Yeah, sort of like a beautiful corpse."

"A beautiful corpse."

"Yeah."

"Wow. How did you feel when you saw her face like that?"

"Shocked, startled, scared."

"You were shocked, startled and scared?"

"Yeah."

"Wow, I can imagine. When did you first notice something odd or peculiar, about your cousin Diane's behavior that night, besides her taking a long time to come back upstairs with the liquor?"

"When I saw her walking the other direction across the hallway empty handed, instead of her coming back to the bedroom where Charlotte and I was, when she was supposed to come back to the bedroom where Charlotte and I was with the liquor."

"But instead, you saw her going the opposite direction empty handed."

"Right."

"I see. What else did you notice was odd or peculiar about your cousin Diane's behavior that night?"

"When I first called out to her across the upstairs hallway and she stopped, but didn't turn around towards me right away."

"When she stopped but didn't turn around towards you right away?"

"Yeah."

"Do you know why she didn't turn around towards you right away when you first called out to her?"

"No. Not until I called out to her the third time and walked towards her, that's when she turned around towards me and I saw her face. Then I knew that's the reason why she didn't turn around towards me right away because she probably didn't want me to see or notice that her face was different."

"She probably didn't want you to see or notice that her face was different, because maybe she wanted to protect YOU from seeing or noticing that her face was different."

"Protect me?"

"Yes protect you. You said you were shocked, startled and scared when you saw her face. That's probably why she didn't turn around towards you right away. She knew her face was different and she knew you would notice it. She knew. So she probably decided to finally turn around towards you when you called out to her the third time, because she knew, that if she didn't turn around towards you the third time you called out to her, you would have most likely gotten suspicious and start to wonder why she's not turning around towards you, right?"

"Right."

"That's probably why she decided to turn around towards you to keep you from getting suspicious, even though she knows that you would see her face. What else did you notice was odd or peculiar about your cousin Diane's behavior that night?"

"When she started referring to herself in the third person."

"When she started referring to herself in the third person?"

"Yeah, by saying things like 'Diane's not here right now' when I'm looking right at her. Then saying that 'she's not Diane'. Then saying things like 'Diane is okay' that 'Diane is wandering the universe' and saying that 'Diane will be back'. It was very creepy."

"It sounds creepy, I can imagine. How did the other personality speak to you? Did the other personality speak to you very aggressive?"

"No not really."

"It didn't?"

"No."

"So how do you think it spoke to you?"

"It spoke to me very firm, like in a very firm serious voice."

"A very firm serious voice?"

"Yeah, like it wasn't joking or kidding around, because after a while, I could see it in Diane's eyes that she or this other personality wasn't joking."

"You could see it in her eyes?"

"Yeah."

"Wow. How do you think this other personality's voice sound to you. Did it sound like Diane's normal voice, or did the voice sound different from Diane's normal voice?"

"It sounded the same as Diane's normal voice, deep."

"It did?"

"Yeah. The only difference was the way it spoke."

"The way it spoke?"

"Yeah almost like a firm pattern to it."

"A firm pattern?"

"Yeah."

"I see." Dr. Stone then looks at Charlotte and says, "Now

Charlotte, you didn't see or witness any of this conversation between your two cousins Diane and Nancy outside the upstairs bedrooms, did you?"

"No I didn't see or witness what was going on at all," Charlotte says. "I only heard Diane and Nancy talking out in the upstairs hallway outside the bedrooms."

"You only heard them talking?"

"Yeah."

"Do you remember what you heard?"

"I remember hearing their voices talking, but I couldn't hear the exact words they were saying to each other."

"You couldn't hear the exact words at all?"

"No because I never left the room."

"I see. What did you think, when you heard Nancy's and Diane's voices talking with each other out in the hallway? Did their tone of conversation sound normal to you?"

"Yes it did. It sounded like they were just having a normal conversation. It sounded like Nancy was just trying to find out what happened to Diane, wanting to know why it took Diane so long to come back upstairs, so I didn't think anything of it. I didn't hear or notice anything out of the ordinary, so I just remained inside the other room, until I heard Nancy hollering and screaming banging on everyone else's bedroom door, that's when I ran out there in the hallway to find out what happened. When Nancy told the rest of my family what Diane said to her, that's when we all ran to Diane's bedroom door, but it was locked. That's when my grandfather ran off to get the Master key. Then he came back and unlocked Diane's bedroom door then we all bursted in there and saw her lying face down on her bed sleeping."

"She was sleeping?"

"Yeah. My family went and grabbed her to wake her up. That's when she told my family what happened that she fell out downstairs. Then Nancy told Diane and the rest of my family what Diane said to her in the hallway and we all realized that Diane has no recollection of coming back up the stairs and that she has no recollection of running into Nancy in the hallway and she has no recollection of what she said to Nancy out in the hallway. That's when I realized what had happened out in the hallway."

"Wow. So you never really encountered Diane's other personality like Nancy did. You only heard the other personality's voice out in the hallway which you assumed, was Diane's voice, right."

"Right."

"I see." Dr. Stone then looks back at Nancy and says, "So Nancy, when your family went into Diane's room and woke her up, was her odd appearance still the same as when you saw her out in the hallway and spoke to her? I mean did her face still look pale and did her eyes still appear swollen?"

"No they didn't?" Nancy says.

"They didn't?"

"No. By the time my family went to wake her up and I saw her face again, the paleness in her face and the swellness in her eyes were gone. They seemed to completely disappear."

"They did?"

"Yeah."

"So the rest of your family never saw Diane's face appearing pale nor her eyes appearing swollen. You were the only one in the house that night who saw and witnessed Diane's face appearing pale and her eyes appearing swollen, right?"

"Yes."

"And Charlotte never saw Diane's face looking pale nor her eyes appearing swollen because she never left the room, but would have seen it and encountered Diane's other personality as well, if she had left the room also, right?"

"Right."

"I see. Okay. So what we're going to do today, is try and see if we can hypnotize Diane again like we did years ago to bring out this other personality and talk to it."

"What!" the family shouts.

"Hypnotize Diane again to bring out this other personality and talk to it?" Tomas asks.

"Yes," Dr. Stone says.

"Doctor Stone, you tried to bring that other personality out of Diane when you hypnotized her before," Margarita says. "It didn't work!"

"That doesn't mean we shouldn't try it again. What might not work the first time might work the second or third time. I want to try to see if I can find out why the other personality entered Diane's body that night and find out what its intentions were."

"That personality already told Nancy, that whenever Diane meditates, they would come into Diane's physical body and enter it."

"I still want to talk to it and find out, if it's the same vicious personality that beat up that kid Marcus inside the school hallway that night and attacked all the other people in the past like the police officers and security guards."

"But would it be safe to bring that other personality out of Diane Doctor Stone?" Marilyn asks.

"I don't know, but we still have to try. What Dr. Kahn and I want to do is record the hypnotizing process, if you all don't mind."

"Record it?" Barry asks.

"Yes."

"Why?" Mary asks.

"So Diane can look back at the video and see the hypnotizing process for herself. She's not going to see, hear or be aware of what's going on, so she needs to look back at the video and see her behavior on it herself. Once the hypnotizing process is finished, the video is yours to keep. You will own the rights to the video as Diane's family."

"Okay Doctor Stone. You can record the hypnotizing process for Diane to see when the video is played back for her."

"Okay. You can all see Diane one more time before we put her under hypnosis."

"Okay Doctor Stone."

"You're welcome. Come this way." Dr. Stone gets up from his chair as Diane D's family get up from their seats. Dr. Stone turns and heads towards the doorway as Diane D's family turn and follow him.

Chapter 12

Dr. Stone And Dr. Kahn Put Diane D Under Hypnosis

Fifteen minutes later, Diane D is laying up on a dark brown leather psychiatrist couch that has metal bars beneath the sides inside a large room as her family, Dr. Stone and Dr. Kahn surround her. Dr. Stone then turns to Diane D's family and says, "You all can wait outside now."

"Okay," Margarita says. Margarita turns to Diane D and says, "Diane, vamos a estar e el pasillo."

"Okay Grandma," Diane D says.

"We'll be right back baby," Barry says.

"Okay Dad."

"Nos vemos luego," Mary says.

Diane D waves her hand to her family as her family take one last look at her. Diane D's family then turn and walk towards the doorway.

Forty-five minutes later, Diane D's family is sitting out in the hallway. Dr. Stone's Indian female nurse approaches them and says to them, "Doctor Stone now has Diane under hypnosis."

"He does?" Tomas asks.

"Yes. He said not every family member can come inside the room. He said only up to ten family members can come in."

"Only ten family members?" Margarita asks.

"Yes, the ten family members who were actually inside the house the night Diane's other personality came out. He especially wants the two cousins who heard and witnessed Diane's other personality to be inside the room."

"The two cousins?" Barry asks. "You mean Nancy and Charlotte."

"Yes, those two."

"Okay." Barry turns towards Nancy and Charlotte and says. "Okay girls, let's go." Nancy, Charlotte, Barry, Margarita, Tomas, Mary, Tonio, Marilyn, Nicolas and Michael stand up from their seats as Gracy, Grandpa Mike, Mickey, Aunt Celeste and Aunt Laura remain in their seats.

Gracy turns to Margarita and Tomas and says, "We'll wait right here Margarita and Tomas."

"Thanks Gracy and Mike," Margarita and Tomas says. The nurse turns away and leads Margarita, Tomas, Mary, Barry, Tonio, Marilyn, Nicolas, Michael, Nancy and Charlotte down the hallway.

As the nurse leads Margarita, Tomas, Mary, Barry, Tonio, Marilyn, Nicolas, Michael, Nancy and Charlotte down the hallway, she turns to them all and says, "You all can come into the room now to watch and listen. Dr. Stone said for me to quietly bring you into the room again, because he doesn't want Diane to know that you all are inside the room. He wants to make sure that Diane is not influenced into saying just anything out of the ordinary, if she knows that her family is inside the room watching and listening. So when I bring you all inside the room, please come in as quiet as possible. We can't let Diane know that you all are inside the room. And before we go inside the room, all cell phones must be turned off. There cannot be any disturbances during the hypnosis process."

"No problem nurse," Margarita says.

"Okay. Follow me." The nurse turns around and walks down the hallway as Margarita, Tomas, Mary, Barry, Tonio, Marilyn, Nicolas, Michael, Nancy and Charlotte turn off all their cell phones and continue to follow her.

The nurse reaches outside the room door and stops as Margarita, Tomas, Mary, Barry, Tonio, Marilyn, Nicolas, Michael, Nancy and Charlotte come behind her and stop. The nurse turns to them and whispers, "I'm going to quietly bring you guys back inside the room. When we go inside, this time, I'm going to quietly bring you all to the middle of the room."

"The middle of the room?" Margarita whispers.

"Yes. Dr. Stone wants you all closer to Diane this time."

"Oh yeah?" Tomas aks. "Why?"

"To make sure you all are able to hear the hypnosis process. Plus there will be a microphone pointing at Diane and the doctors so the sound can come out of the speakers so you all can hear the hypnosis better."

"Okay."

"Now remember everybody, all cell phones off." The nurse turns around and quietly opens the room door. She then heads into the room as Margarita, Tomas, Mary, Barry, Tonio, Marilyn, Nicolas, Michael, Nancy and Charlotte follow her.

The nurse quietly brings Margarita, Tomas, Mary, Barry, Tonio, Marilyn, Nicolas, Michael, Nancy and Charlotte back into the large room. Margarita, Tomas, Mary, Barry, Tonio, Marilyn, Nicolas,

Michael, Nancy and Charlotte quickly turn their heads towards the front of the room. They see Diane D in the front of the room this time lying flat on her back on the psychiatrist couch under hypnosis with her head back and eyes closed with her face pointing high up towards the ceiling. There is a microphone pointing towards her face. There are two video cameras on tripods with the video cameras pointing towards her. There is a thick white sheet laid beneath her back and buttocks making her back and buttocks raised higher off the couch. There are pillows laid beneath her knees making her knees raised higher off the couch. There is a small blanket laid out on top of her waist and hips as her arms and hands rest on top of her abdomin.

Diane D's family then turn their heads back forward and follow the nurse as the nurse quietly leads them towards the middle and side of the room where it is dimly lit and several chairs and speakers are.

Five minutes later, Margarita, Tomas, Mary, Barry, Tonio, Marilyn, Nicolas, Michael, Nancy and Charlotte are quietly sitting in the middle of the room anxiously watching the front of the office at Diane D.

Dr. Stone sits in a chair next to the couch on the right side of Diane D's head as he is slightly leaned towards Diane D with a clipboard and pen in his hands. Dr. Kahn sits in a chair next to the couch on the opposite side of Diane D's head as he is slightly leaned towards Diane D with a clipboard and pen in his hands. Dr. Stone and Dr. Kahn have been talking to Diane D's subconscious for a few minutes taking notes. Dr. Stone continues to speak to Diane D's subconscious as he looks down at her and asks, "Is there a soul, spirit or personality there inside this physical body?" Dr. Stone and Dr. Kahn stare at Diane D. Diane D does not respond. Her physical body continues to lay on the couch as her eyes remain closed.

Margarita, Tomas, Mary, Barry, Tonio, Marilyn, Nicolas, Michael, Nancy and Charlotte continue to sit quietly in the middle of the room puzzled looking at Diane D.

Dr. Stone continues to look at Diane D and says, "Is there a soul, spirit or personality inside this physical body now? If there is a soul, spirit or personality inside this physical body now, we need you to come out and talk to us. We need to talk to Diane's original soul, spirit and personality first. Is Diane's original soul, spirit or personality in there now? Reveal yourself. Come out and speak to us. Is Diane's original soul, spirit or personality in there now?" Dr. Stone and Dr. Kahn continue to stare at Diane D. Diane D's physical body continues to lay on the couch not responding as her eyes remain closed.

Margarita, Tomas, Mary, Barry, Tonio, Marilyn, Nicolas, Michael,

Nancy and Charlotte continue to puzzled look at Diane D.

Dr. Stone then says, "If Diane's original soul, spirit or personality is inside this physical body now, please reveal yourself to us and talk to us." Suddenly, Diane D starts to breathe hard. Dr. Stone and Dr. Kahn anxiously look at Diane D as her chest starts to rise and eyeballs seem to roll towards the top of her head underneath her closed eyelids.

Margarita, Tomas, Mary, Barry, Tonio, Marilyn, Nicolas, Michael, Nancy and Charlotte anxiously look at Diane D.

Dr. Stone and Dr. Kahn anxiously look at each other, then back at Diane D. Diane D continues to breathe hard as her eyes remain closed. Suddenly her breathing slows down, her chest lowers back down. Dr. Stone then asks, "Was that a soul, spirit or personality trying to come out? Is there a soul, spirit or personality inside this physical body now? If there is a soul, spirit or personality inside this physical body now, respond yes by waving your fingers three times when I ask again. Now is there a soul, spirit or personality inside this physical body now?" Diane D continues to lay on the couch as her eyes remain closed. Suddenly her fingers wave once, twice, then three times.

Margarita, Tomas, Mary, Barry, Tonio, Marilyn, Nicolas, Michael, Nancy and Charlotte become excited and nervous as Nicolas turns to them and whispers, "Did y'all see that? She waved her fingers three times!" Nicolas, Margarita, Tomas, Mary, Barry, Tonio, Marilyn, Michael, Nancy and Charlotte continue to anxiously look at Diane D.

Dr. Stone continues to speak to Diane D's subconscious as he looks down at her and says, "Okay good. Now is this Diane's original soul, spirit or personality in there now? Is Diane's original soul, spirit or personality inside this physical body now? If Diane's original soul, spirit or personality is the one inside this physical body now, respond 'Yes' by waving your fingers three times when I ask. If Diane's original soul, spirit or personality is NOT the one inside this physical body now, respond 'No' by waving your fingers twice. Now is Diane's original soul, spirit or personality inside this physical body now? 'Yes' or 'no'?" Diane D continues to lay on the couch as her eyes remain closed. Suddenly her fingers wave once, twice, then three times.

Margarita, Tomas, Mary, Barry, Tonio, Marilyn, Nicolas, Michael, Nancy and Charlotte become anxious and nervous again as Barry turns to them and whispers, "It's her!" Barry, Nicolas, Margarita, Tomas, Mary, Tonio, Marilyn, Michael, Nancy and Charlotte continue to sit quietly in the middle of the room anxiously looking at Diane D.

Dr. Stone continues to look at Diane and says, "This IS Diane's original soul, spirit or personality in there?" Diane D continues to lay on the couch as her eyes remain closed. Her fingers wave once, twice, then three times again. "Okay good," Dr. Stone says. "So Diane, we need to talk to you. We need to find out what happened the night you and your two cousins Nancy and Charlotte were up around two o'clock in the morning chit-chatting inside one of the bedrooms inside your family's home, then you went downstairs to make Martini at the bar and bring the Martini, Vodka and Bacardi back upstairs to the room where your cousins Nancy and Charlotte were waiting for you. Are you able to talk about it now? Do you want to talk about it now? If you are able to talk about it now or willing to talk about it now, respond by saying 'yes' when I ask again. If you are NOT able to talk about it now or NOT willing to talk about it, respond by saying 'no' or wave your fingers twice when I ask again. Now are you able to talk about it now or are you willing to talk about it now? 'Yes' or 'no'?"

Diane D continues to lay on the couch as her eyes remain closed. She suddenly says, "Yes."

Margarita, Tomas, Mary, Barry, Tonio, Marilyn, Nicolas, Michael, Nancy and Charlotte become anxious and nervous again as Marilyn turns to them and whispers, "She spoke! She said 'yes'!" Marilyn, Margarita, Tomas, Mary, Barry, Tonio, Nicolas, Michael, Nancy and Charlotte continue to sit quietly in the middle of the room anxiously looking at Diane D.

Dr. Stone then says, "So you're willing to talk about it now?"

"Yes," Diane D says as her eyes remain closed.

"Good."

Dr. Kahn then says, "Okay Diane, this is Dr. Kahn speaking now, okay? What I'm gonna do right now is talk to you and I need you to answer some questions, alright? What I need for you to do right now is, state your name?"

"State my name?" Diane D asks.

"Yes. I need to hear you say who you are, okay? So who are you or what is your name?"

"Diane."

"You're Diane?"

"Yes."

"Good. Now Diane do you speak or understand a specific language?"

"Yes."

"Okay. And what specific language is that? What specific language can you speak and understand?"

"English."

"You can speak and understand English."

"Yes."

"Okay, good. Can you speak and understand any other language?

What other language can you speak and understand besides English?"

"Spanish."

"You can speak and understand Spanish?"

"Yes."

"Okay, good. Can you speak and understand any other languages besides English and Spanish? What other languages can you speak and understand besides English and Spanish?"

"Some French."

"You can speak and understand some French?"

"Yes."

"Wow, that's incredible. Can you speak and understand any other languages besides English, Spanish and some French? What other language can you speak and understand besides English, Spanish and some French?"

"That's it."

"That's it? You cannot speak or understand any other language?"

"No."

"So you can mainly speak and understand English, Spanish and some French."

"Yes."

"And nothing else."

"No."

"Okay. Well since we mainly speak English, we're going to continue to communicate to you in English. So Diane, tell us what happened when you and your two cousins Nancy and Charlotte were up one night in the wee ours of the morning. Tell us what happened when you were all inside one of the upstairs bedrooms inside your family's home."

"Nancy, Charlotte and I were laughing and chit-chatting."

"You, Nancy and Charlotte were laughing and chit-chatting?"

"Yes."

"Then what happened?"

"Charlotte asked me 'how did my meditation go' and asked me 'how did I feel now that I just finished'."

"Your cousin Charlotte wanted to know how did your meditation go and wanted to know how you felt after you just finished?"

"Yes."

"What did you tell her?"

"I told her that I felt so relaxed and so refreshed that I felt free as a bird."

"You told her that you felt relaxed and refreshed that you felt free as a bird?"

"Yes."

"I see. Your cousin Charlotte said she mentioned to you that your grandparents had forbid you from meditating anymore because of these weird state of trances you be getting into. I heard that your grandparents had forbid you from meditating anymore because they claim that these weird state of trances that you be getting into sometimes become violent.   Did your grandparents forbid you from meditating anymore?"

"Yes they did."

"They did?"

"Yes."

"Then why did you continue to meditate after your grandparents forbid from meditating anymore?"

"Because it's something I needed to do for myself."

"Something you needed to do for yourself?"

"Yes."

"I see. As a matter of fact, you felt good after you meditated, right?"

"Yes."

"You felt great after you meditated, right?"

"Yes."

"I heard you were in such a good mood and spirit that night, that you wanted to celebrate by having a small drink before you went to bed, right?"

"Right."

"Then your two cousins Nancy and Charlotte decided to join you and have small drinks too, right?"

"Right."

"You three decided to have some Vodka, Bacardi and Martini, right?"

"Right."

"You decided to go downstairs to the family's bar in the living room to make the Martini and get the rest of the liquor and cups out of the bar to bring them right up to the bedroom. Then you turn away from Nancy and Charlotte, walk out the bedroom and leave the room closing the door behind yourself, right?"

"Right."

"What happened when you went downstairs inside your family's home that night?"

"I went to the bar to make the Martini and get the other drinks."

"You went to the bar to make the Martini and get the other drinks?"

"Yes."

DIANE D'S FLASHBACK:

It is near 3:00 in the morning. The downstairs living room of Margarita and Tomas' mansion is dark and dimly lit. It is raining, thundering and lightning outside. Diane D comes down the stairs. She goes into the living room and looks around. Then she goes to her left and walks several yards to where the bar is. She goes to the bar, grabs some glasses and starts to make the Martini.

Diane D finishes making the Martini and pours some in a glass. Suddenly, there is a loud thunder sound! Diane D quickly turns towards the window and looks up through the window at the rain, thunder and lightning outside. She turns back forward and puts the glass to her mouth and takes a few sips of the Martini tasting it. She enjoys the taste. Then she opens up some other liquor. She pours a teeny bit of liquor in the glass and takes a few sips. She enjoys the taste of the other liquor. There is another loud thunder sound! Suddenly Diane D puzzled looks up in the air. She starts to feel faint. She then starts to feel dizzy. She looks in a mirror at her reflection. She closes her eyes and almost loses her balance as if she's about to pass out. She takes her hand and painfully holds onto her forehead as she starts to lose her balance. She opens her eyes again and gets woozy. She then turns her head and looks towards the stairs. She reaches her arm and hand out towards the stairs for someone in her family to help as she shouts, "Help! Mom, Dad!" Diane D continues to reach her arm and hand out towards the stairs and shouts, "Grandma, Grandpa!" She then closes her eyes again as she continues to hold her forehead. She starts to fall. She suddenly passes out and collapse on the floor making sort of a thud sound. She lays chest up on the floor near the bar motionless with her head back facing sideways, eyes half closed and eyeballs disappearing behind her half-closed eyelids as it continues to rain, thunder and lightning outside.

BACK TO THE PRESENT:

"You fell out?" Dr. Kahn asks.
"Yes," Diane D says.
"But before you fell out, you were reaching your arm and hand out towards the stairs calling out to your family for help?"
"Yes."
"But no one heard you."
"No."

Margarita, Tomas, Mary, Barry, Tonio, Marilyn, Nicolas, Michael, Nancy and Charlotte turn and sadly look at each other. They then turn their heads back forward and continue to sadly listen to Dr. Kahn and Diane D.

"Then what happened after you reached your arm and hand out towards the stairs calling out to your family for help?" Dr. Kahn asks.
"It seemed like the floor was coming up towards me," Diane D says.
"It seemed like the floor was coming up towards you?"
"Yeah, but I don't remember hitting or landing on the floor."
"You don't remember hitting or landing on the floor?"
"No."
"So what happened after it felt like the floor was coming up towards you? What did you experience?"
"The next thing I know, is that my grandparents' house was gone."

"Your grandparents' house was gone?"

"Yeah."

"What do you mean 'your grandparents' house was gone'?"

"It wasn't there. I didn't see it anymore."

"You didn't see your grandparents' house anymore?"

"No."

"Well where did it go?"

"It disappeared."

"It disappeared?"

"Yes."

"To where?"

"I don't know, I just didn't see it anymore."

"I see. Then what happened after you saw your grandparents' house disappear?"

"I found my soul or spirit out there in space wandering the universe."

"You found your soul or spirit out there in space wandering the universe again?"

"Yes."

"Isn't that exactly what happened to you before, when you had that incident on the third floor school hallway with that kid Marcus three years ago after you got upset with him when you first learned that he and his brother lied to you and your family and tricked you all about a little three year old boy who have leukemia, just to get you to come to his school? When you were standing at the edge of the school hallway angrily staring at him, you saw the school hallway disappear at that time too, right?"

"Yes. It's like the same thing happening again."

"The same thing happening again?"

"Yes."

"But this time, instead of you seeing the school hallway disappear, you saw your grandparents' house disappear the night you went downstairs to make and get the liquor, right?"

"Right."

"Why was your soul or spirit out there in space wandering the universe this time?"

"I don't know, I didn't plan it."

"You didn't plan it?"

"No. It was beyond my control."

"It was? You mean you had no control over it?"

"No."

"No control over it at all?"

"No, no control over it."

"I see. Since you didn't plan to have your soul or spirit out there in space wandering the universe nor had any control over it, do you know who or what put your soul or spirit out there in space wandering the universe?"

"No I have no idea who or what put my soul or spirit out there."

"You don't know?"

"No. All I know, is that I was out there, I don't know who or what put me out there or why."

"I see. Then what happened while your soul or spirit was out there in space wandering the universe?"

"I suddenly heard my family calling my name."

"You heard your family calling your name while your soul or spirit was still out there in space wandering the universe?"

"Yeah."

"Then what happened after you heard your family calling your name?"

"I could feel them tugging and pulling me."

"You felt your family tugging and pulling you?"

"Yeah."

"Then what happened after that?"

"I woke up and found myself lying on my bed with my family members surrounding me tugging and pulling me."

"You woke up and found yourself lying on your bed with your family surrounding you?"

"Yes."

"Did your family know, that your soul or spirit was out there in space wandering the universe when they woke you up?"

"No, not until I told them."

"I see. Since your family found you upstairs in the bedroom on the bed, did they know that you were laying down there on the living room floor passed out?"

"No, nobody knew."

"Nobody? No one else was downstairs in the house when you were at the bar, making the Martini then passed out on the floor?"

"No, no one else was down in the living room when I was at the bar?"

"You were all alone when you were in the living room?"

"Yes."

"So therefore, no one witnessed you falling passing out on the floor."

"No."

"I see. Do you know how long your physical body was laid out on the living room floor passed out?"

"No, I have no idea."

"No idea at all?"

"No."

"I see. After you passed out on the living room floor, do you know how you got upstairs to your bedroom?"

"No, I have no idea."

"You have no idea how you got to your bedroom?"

"No I don't."

"You don't remember how you got from the living room floor to your bedroom at all?"

"No. When my family woke me up on the bed, at first I thought maybe they found me on the living room floor downstairs, then carried me upstairs to my room then laid me on the bed."

"You thought your family found you on the living room floor downstairs, then carried you upstairs to your room then laid you on the bed?"

"Yes."

"But your family didn't find you laying on the living room floor downstairs Diane. When they found you, you were already laying upstairs on your bed. Now if your family didn't put you upstairs on your bed and you don't remember putting yourself upstairs on your bed, the big question is 'Who put you there?'."

Margarita, Tomas, Mary, Barry, Tonio, Marilyn, Nicolas, Michael, Nancy and Charlotte turn and frighteningly look at each other. They then turn their heads back forward and continue to anxiously listen to Dr. Kahn and Diane D.

"Do you remember coming up the stairs running into your cousin Nancy in the upstairs hallway when she called out to you and approached you then she and you started talking with one another?" Dr. Kahn asks.

"No, I don't remember that," Diane D says.

"You don't remember that at all?"

"No."

"But before you went downstairs to the bar, you remember being in one of the upstairs bedroom with your two cousins Nancy and Charlotte, then going downstairs to the bar to get the drinks then pass out and find your soul or spirit wandering the universe, then find yourself on your bed surrounded by your family, right?"

"Right."

"So if you found yourself falling towards the floor downstairs, but don't remember landing on the floor, most likely, your physical body did land and lay on the floor for a while before your physical body was found on the bed upstairs. And you say you don't know how long your physical body was lying on the floor downstairs, before it was somehow placed upstairs on the bed, right?"

"Right."

"Okay now Diane, being that we had just mentioned about that kid Marcus, I would like to ask you, how do you feel about him now?"

"How do I feel about Marcus?"

"Yes."

"How am I suppose to feel about him?"

"I mean are you still angry with him from the night you learned that he and his brother tricked you and your family into coming to his school? Are you still angry with him when he confessed to you that the little three-year old boy who's dying of leukemia didn't exist?"

"Yeah I was angry with him at first, but I'm not angry about that anymore."

"You're not?"

"No. Why?"

"Well he feels that deep down inside of you, you're still angry with him."

"He does?"

"Yes."

"Why does he feel I'm still angry at him?"

"Because he claims that he's constantly having nightmares about you still coming after him in the back stairwell of that school, trying to kill him. Have you heard about the nightmares he keeps having about you coming after him in the back stairwell of that school, trying to kill him?"

"Yes I've heard about it."

"You have?"

"Yes I have."

"Well how do you feel about that? Because Marcus claims that the nightmares about you coming after him trying to kill him in that back stairwell of the school happens to him almost every night. It's unusual to have the same dreams or nightmares constantly repeated. The nightmares he has about you coming after him in that back stairwell of the school keeps happening to him that he's thinking of suicide just to get away from it. He already tried to jump out of a high story window, but his family stopped him just in time. He's constantly on a suicide watch. So if you're not angry with Marcus anymore, do you know why he is constantly having nightmares about you coming after him in the back stairwell of the school?"

"No I have no idea why he's still having nightmares of me coming after him, I'm not even thinking about him! I already mentally forgave that kid and moved on with my life."

"You mentally forgave?"

"Yes I did. I have been willing to forgive him in person, but he's not willing to accept my forgiveness. He doesn't even want to come near me nor be in the same space as me. He doesn't even want to talk to me on the phone, what else am I suppose to do? I can't make him accept my forgiveness if he doesn't want to. The only thing I can do, is move on with my life, he should too."

"But he can't move on with his life Diane because he keeps having constant nightmares about you coming after him trying to kill him in the back stairwell of that school."

"I have no control over that! I'm not capable of entering anybody's dreams or nightmares!"

"I know you're not capable of that."

"I'm not! I don't have the power to do that!"

"I know you don't have the power to do that Diane. I just needed to know and find out how YOU still felt about Marcus, that way he and his family can hopefully get his nightmares to stop, and they can hopefully get some closure and hopefully get some rest. We know you're not capable of entering anybody's dreams or nightmares and we know you don't have the power to do that, we just needed to hear it from YOU. We needed to hear it coming from you yourself. And thank you so much for your answer. Okay Diane, that's all I want to ask you and say to you about Marcus. Thanks."

"Okay Now Diane," Dr. Stone says. "Now Diane, there are some people right here in this very room that I want you to identify, okay? When I count to three, I want you to open your eyes." Diane D continues to lay on the couch with her eyes closed. Dr. Stone then says, "One ..... two ..... three! Open your eyes." Diane D slowly opens her eyes.

Margarita, Tomas, Mary, Barry, Tonio, Marilyn, Nicolas, Michael, Nancy and Charlotte quietly sit in the middle of the room anxiously watching Diane D.

Diane D looks her eyes around. She then looks at Dr. Stone as she continues to lay on the couch. Dr. Stone smiles at Diane D and says to her, "Hi there Diane. Are you feeling okay?"

Diane D puzzled looks at Dr. Stone. She then says, "Yeah."

"You do?"

"Yeah."

"That's great."

Dr. Kahn looks at Diane D. He also smiles at her and says to her, "Hey Diane." Diane D puzzled looks at Dr. Kahn. He then says, "How are you feeling today?"

"Okay," Diane D says.

"You do?"

"Yeah."

"That's good."

"Now Diane, I need you to sit up for a minute," Dr. Stone says. "I need you to sit up so you can identify some people that are in this room, okay?"

"Okay," Diane D says.

"Good. You may sit up now."

Diane D slowly starts to sit up.

Margarita, Tomas, Mary, Barry, Tonio, Marilyn, Nicolas, Michael, Nancy and Charlotte continue to quietly sit in the middle of the room anxiously watching Diane D.

Diane D sits up and looks forward. She then looks a little to her right and sees her family sitting in the middle of the room several yards away from her watching her. She becomes shocked and surprised seeing them sitting there.

Margarita, Tomas, Mary, Barry, Tonio, Marilyn, Nicolas, Michael, Nancy and Charlotte anxiously smile at Diane D. They wave their hands to her.

Diane D smiles and waves back to her family and says, "Hey. What are y'all doing here?"

Dr. Stone looks at Diane D and says to her, "Now Diane, do you know who those people are over there?" as he points to her family.

Diane D turns her head to her right and puzzled looks at Dr. Stone. She then says, "Do I know who those people are?"

"Yes."

"Of course I know who they are! They're my family!"

"They are?"

"Yes! You know that!"

"Okay, good. Could you identify for me each family member?"

Diane D puzzled looks at Dr. Stone again. She then asks, "Identify for you each family member?"

"Yes."

"You want me to identify my own family?"

"Yes I do."

"Why? I already know who they are."

"I know you already know who they are."

"So why do you want me to identify them?"

"Because I need to HEAR YOU say it, for the record."

"For the record?"

"Yes."

"What record?"

"The reports I'm making about your status."

"The reports you're making?"

"Yes."

"Oh. Okay." Diane D looks at her family again. She then looks at Margarita who is sitting on the far right and says, "That's my grandma Margarita." She then looks at Tomas who is sitting next to Margarita and says, "That's my grandpa Tomas." She then looks at Mary and says, "That's my mom." She then looks at Barry and says, "That's my dad." She then looks at Tonio and says, "That's my uncle Tonio, my mom's brother." She then looks at Marilyn and says, "That's my Aunt Marilyn, my mom's sister." She then looks at Nicolas and says, "That's my older brother Nicolas." She then looks at Michael and says, "That's my husband Michael." She then looks at Nancy and says, "That's my cousin Nancy." She then smiles at Charlotte and says, "And that's my cousin Charlotte." Diane D turns back to Dr. Stone and says, "There. You got that?"

"Yes I got it," Dr. Stone smiles and says. "Thanks Diane. Now that you identified each of your family members correctly, I'm going to send you away temporary. I'm going to put you back to sleep, okay? Now lay back down." Diane D looks back at her family.

Margarita, Tomas, Mary, Barry, Tonio, Marilyn, Nicolas, Michael, Nancy and Charlotte anxiously smile at Diane D again. They wave their hands to her again and whisper, "See you later."

Diane D smiles at her family and waves back to them. She then lays back down on the psychiatrist couch. Dr. Stone then says to her, "Now Diane when I count to three, I want you to close your eyes and go back to sleep, okay?" Diane D continues to lay on the couch with her eyes opened looking at Dr. Stone. Dr. Stone then says, "Now one ..... two ..... three! Go back to sleep!" Diane D's eyes slowly closes. Her eyes are now completely shut. Dr. Stone and Dr. Kahn continue to sit near Diane D and watch her as she goes back to sleep. Diane D continues to lay on the couch with her eyes closed. She quickly goes back into a deep sleep. She is now back into a state of hypnosis.

Margarita, Tomas, Mary, Barry, Tonio, Marilyn, Nicolas, Michael, Nancy and Charlotte puzzled look at each other as Nicolas whispers, "Is she back to sleep?"
"I think so," Barry says. Barry, Nicolas, Margarita, Tomas, Mary, Tonio, Marilyn, Michael, Nancy and Charlotte turn back forward and puzzled look at Diane D again.

Dr. Stone and Dr. Kahn continue to watch Diane D as she sleeps. They then turn their heads and look towards Diane D's family. They get up from their chairs and walk towards Diane D's family.

Dr. Stone and Dr. Kahn approach Diane D's family as Diane D's family stand from their seats. Dr. Stone whispers to them, "She's back to sleep."
"Yeah we can see that?" Margarita whispers, "but that quick?"
"Yes. She's still under hypnosis."
"She is?"
"Yes."
"Wow," Diane D's family says as they puzzled stare at her.
"Can we talk to you all outside the room for a minute?"
"Sure Doctor," Margarita says.
"Okay." Dr. Stone and Dr. Kahn turn and quietly lead Diane D's family towards the back door. Diane D's family turn their heads towards her and amazingly stare at her quickly being back into a deep sleep as she continues to lay on the couch under hypnosis with her eyes closed.

Two minutes later, Dr. Stone and Dr. Kahn bring Diane D's family out in the hallway. They bring Diane D's family way down the hallway.

Dr. Stone and Dr. Kahn bring Diane D's family to the side as Dr. Stone says to them, "Well what do you all think?"

"Well the hypnosis itself was amazing!" Margarita says.

"You think so?"

"Yes! But it was terrible to find out that she had passed out downstairs in the living room and was lying there on the floor all alone without any of us knowing about it!"

"I know."

"Doctor Stone, what was that all about?" Barry asks. "Why did you have Diane sit up and look at all of us, then have her identify all of us when she already knows who we all are? Why do you need that for the record?"

"Because I wanted us all to make sure, that it was her ORIGINAL soul, spirit or personality that was there inside her physical body, because if I have her sit up and see you all and she knows who you all are, that means it's her ORIGINAL soul, spirit or personality there inside her physical body. But if I have her sit up and see you all and she DOES NOT know who you all are or doesn't seem to reckognize any of you, that means it's NOT her original soul, spirit or personality there inside her physical body, but someone else." Diane D's family shockingly and nervously look at Dr. Stone.

Dr. Kahn then says to Diane D's family, "Now Dr. Stone and I are gonna try to see if we can bring out, the OTHER personality."

"What!" Diane D's family shouts. "Bring out the other personality?!"

"You're gonna try to see if you can bring out the other personality?" Michael asks.

"Yes," Dr. Kahn then says. "But before we do that, we would need your permission to strap Diane's physical body down to the couch with handcuffs, just in case the other personality emerges to the surface and starts to get out of control."

"What!" the family shout.

"Strap her physical body down to the couch with handcuffs, just in case the other personality emerges and starts to get out of control?!" Barry shouts.

"Yes," Dr. Kahn says.

"You think if this other personality emerges to the surface, it might get out of control?" Michael asks.

"Well it happened before when Diane attacked all those people in the past that she herself wasn't aware of."

"So you feel you need to strap her physical body down with handcuffs, just in case?!" Mary shouts.

"Yeah for our safety, because this other soul, spirit or personality that emerges out of her don't play. It is known for being very violent and very vicious and having superhuman strength, which is not normal for the average person. That other soul, spirit or personality already attacked some security guards and some police officers in the past landing several them in the hospital with permanent injuries! They had to leave the police force because of their injuries! Dr. Stone and I don't want to be Diane's or this other soul, spirit or personality's next victims, then we both wind up laying right here in this very hospital with broken bones and permanent injuries ourselves! Diane already tried to attack those correction officers who were trying to keep her inside that jail cell! Those correction officers said they had a very tough time trying to keep Diane inside that jail cell because they said she had the strength of a wild animal or beast! They said her superhuman strength was no match for them, even though she was only one woman against five or six men!"

"And two male hospital employees at the other hospital who worked the night shift already witnessed Diane's superhuman strength when she spinned her entire body around and kung fu kicked a stuck storage room door wide open, knocking the storage room door right off its hinges, then going inside the storage room damaging the storage room by lifting and turning heavy furniture upside down like if she was the Incredible Hulk!" Dr. Stone says. "The storage room door and the storage room were damaged beyond repair and she's wasn't even aware of herself doing that! The only thing she knew, is that she felt pain in her leg and foot after her original soul, spirit or personality came back and she didn't even know where the pain in her leg and foot came from! She didn't know or realize, that the pain in her leg and foot came from her kung fu kicking that stuck storage room door wide open! The very same door that the two male hospital employees tried to open themselves, but couldn't. Then she a female comes along and kung fu kicks the storage room door wide open, even though there was heavy office furniture leaning behind it! Those two male hospital employees were so traumatized by what they had witnessed, that they had to transfer to another hospital to work! They claim they couldn't deal with the memory of what they had witnessed inside that clinic hallway."

"And that kid Marcus already claimed that it was Diane herself who attacked him on that third floor school hallway that night by kung fu kicking him a couple of feet in the air, breaking his ribs and everything else and she's wasn't even aware of herself doing that to him! The only thing she knew, is that she felt pain all over her body after her original soul, spirit or personality returned and she didn't even know where the pain all over her body came from! She didn't know or realize, that the pain in her body came from Marcus throwing those objects at her inside that school hallway! Marcus was also traumatized by what he had went through inside that school hallway with Diane that he had to transfer to another school. He claimed he couldn't deal with the memory of what Diane did to him inside that school hallway! She already bashed in the dashboard of your family's van with her bare fists after you all were driving away from the school after that incident with her and Marcus, and she wasn't even aware of herself doing that either!"

"And whenever Diane gets out of control and several people try to hold her and pull her back, she just literally starts dragging them all at once! I mean WHO does that?!"

"No one else. So in order for Dr. Stone and I to protect ourselves from that other personality's wrath or fury, we need your signed permission to strap Diane's physical body down to the couch with handcuffs to hold her physical body in place just in case the other personality emerges and becomes out of control again."

"Well if you feel that you have to strap Diane's physical body down doctor, maybe it is best, not to try and bring this other personality out to the surface," Marilyn says.

"But we need to talk to the other personality to find out if it's the same personality that Nancy encountered inside your family's home that night," Dr. Stone says. "And we need to know, if it's the same personality who kung fu kicked that stuck storage room door wide open at the other hospital, and we need to know, if it's the same personality who attacked and harm that kid Marcus in the school hallway and attacked other people in the past!"

"You don't think it's the same personality that Nancy encountered Doctor?" Margarita asks.

"We don't know, that's what we want to find out. And we need to know, if it's the same personality who is tormenting Marcus by coming into his dreams and nightmares every night practically scaring him to death!"

"Coming into his dreams and nightmares every night?!" Mary shouts. "So you think Diane is responsible for that kid's nightmares?! You heard her said she's not thinking about that kid!"

"Yes I did hear her say that Miss Mary. Dr. Kahn and I just wanted to know if she was still angry with him because we were wondering, that if she still had any anger issues towards Marcus at all, maybe her anger issues towards him might somehow get into his dreams or nightmares."

"Her anger issues towards him might somehow get into his dreams or nightmares? She has no control over what he's dreaming about! You heard her say it yourself that she's not capable of entering anybody's dreams or nightmares! She just said that she doesn't have the power to do that!"

"That's right Doctor Stone!" Barry shouts. "People don't have the power to enter other people's dreams or nightmares! The only people who ARE capable of entering other people's dreams and nightmares, are deceased people! THEY"RE the ones who have the power to come into other people's dreams or nightmares, not the Living! Diane is not deceased! She's still alive so she cannot enter other people's dreams or nightmares even if she wanted to!"

"That's right Doctor Stone!" Nicolas shouts. "Diane hasn't been anywhere near that kid Marcus since that incident happened inside that school hallway that night! So I don't want that kid Marcus, blaming my sister for his nightmares which she has absolutely nothing to do with nor any control over! If that kid keeps seeing my sister in his nightmares every night coming after him in that back stairwell of the school trying to kill him, then it's on him, she has absolutely nothing to do with it! If it wasn't for that false letter that he and his brother sent to our family's organization about some little boy dying of leukemia, he would not be going through his nightmares right now!"

"That's right!" Mary shouts. "Let that kid's doctors take care of him! Let them put him under hypnosis to get rid of his nightmares or let THEM put him on some doggone medication or something!"

"They already tried all of that," Dr. Stone says. "It's not working!"

"Sorry, but Diane has nothing to do with it!"

"Okay. We'll contact Marcus' doctors about it again. We just needed to find out how Diane still felt about him, that's all. We needed to hear it from HER. We already got our answer from her. But if we succeed in bringing this other soul, spirit or personality out to the service, we will have to see and find out how the other soul, spirit or personality feels about Marcus?"

"What!" Diane D's family shout.

"See and find out how the other soul, spirit or personality feels about Marcus?" Tomas asks.

"That's right," Dr. Kahn says. "Why do you think I was asking Diane all those questions about Marcus in the first place? To see how SHE really feels about him because of the constant nightmares he keeps having about her. We needed to know where her state of mind stand. We just heard from her original soul, spirit or personality that she's not angry at Marcus anymore, that she's not thinking about him and that she's moved on with her life. That's what her ORIGINAL soul, spirit or personality was saying. We don't know how THE OTHER soul, spirit or personality might feel about Marcus, yet."

"What!" Diane D's family shout.

"So you think that this other soul, spirit or personality might have something to do with Marcus' nightmares?" Margarita asks.

"We think so," Dr. Stone says. "If it's not Diane's original soul, spirit or personality causing Marcus' nightmares, we think it's definitely the other soul, spirit or personality entering his dreams causing his nightmares."

"What!" Diane D's family shout.

"But that kid Marcus is claiming that he sees Diane in his nightmares!" Michael shouts, "not some soul, spirit or personality!"

"We know," Dr. Stone says. "Most likely this other soul, spirit or personality is making itself up into the form of Diane so Marcus can see it and think that it is Diane he's seeing in his nightmares, even though it's not her! Even though Diane's original soul, spirit or personality might have forgiven Marcus, this other soul, spirit or personality might

NOT have." Diane D's family worriedly look at Dr. Stone. Dr. Stone then says, "But in the mean time, can we get your signed permission to strap Diane's physical body to the couch with handcuffs to hold her physical body in place just in case the other personality emerges and becomes out of control?"

"Well it depends on how you cuff her to the couch Doctor," Tomas says.

"That's right," Tonio says. "And just how would you cuff my niece to the couch?"

"We would have a long chain attached to each of her handcuffs while she's still under hypnosis," Dr. Stone says.

"What!" Diane D's family shouts. "Long chains?!"

"Attached to each of her handcuffs?!" Mary shouts.

"While she's still under hypnosis?!" Tonio shouts.

"Yes," Dr. Stone says. "Each chain from her handcuffs would be hooked to the metal bars beneath each side of the couch where her arms are."

"What!" Diane D's family shouts.

"Each chain from her handcuffs would be hooked to the metal bars beneath each side of the couch where her arms are?!" Tomas shouts.

"Yes," Dr. Stone says. "We would also have a chain wrapped around each of her upper arms."

"What!" Diane D's family shouts.

"A chain wrapped around her upper arms?!" Margarita shouts.

"You're gonna have a chain wrapped around her upper arms?!" Nicolas shouts.

"Yes," Dr. Stone says. "Each chain wrapped around her upper arms would be hooked to the metal bars beneath each side of the couch where her shoulders are. We would also have a chain going over and around her shoulders."

"What!" Diane D's family shouts.

"A chain going over and around her shoulders?!" Mary shouts.

"Yes," Dr. Stone says. "Each chain going over and around her shoulders would have one end hooked to the metal bar where her head is and the other end hooked to each chain wrapped around her upper arms."

"What!" Diane D's family shouts.

"Now this is ridiculous!" Tomas shouts. "Each chain going over and around her shoulders would have one end hooked to the metal bar where her head is and the other end hooked to each chain wrapped around her upper arms?!"

"Yes," Dr. Stone says.

"And you're going to have chains wrapped around her upper arms hooked to the metal bars beneath each side of the couch where her shoulders are?!"

"Yes. We would also have a chain wrapped around each of her legs."

"What!" Diane D's family shouts.

"Chains wrapped around her legs?!" Margarita shouts.

"Yes," Dr. Stone says. "Each chain wrapped around her legs would be hooked to the metal bars beneath each side of the couch where her legs are. Last but not least, we would also have a long chain attached to each of her shackles."

"Shackles?!" Diane D's family shouts.

"You want shackles on her too?!" Mary shouts.

"With chains attached to each of her shackles?!" Nicolas shouts.

"Yes," Dr. Stone says. "Each chain from her shackles would be hooked to the metal bars beneath each side of the couch where her feet are."

"What!" Diane D's family shouts.

"Yes. We would have a set of keys for the cuffs, chains and shackles for emergency and you will also have a set of keys too."

"What!"

"We will have a set of keys too?!" Barry shouts.

"Yes," Dr. Stone says.

"Whoa wait a minute now Doctor Stone!" Margarita shouts. "I'm not feeling this! I'm not sure if I want to see or have my own grandchild cuffed and hooked to the couch, especially with chains and shackles on her feet! If you're talking about hooking a chain to each of her handcuffs and having a chain wrapped around each of her upper arms and having a chain going over and around each of her shoulders and having a chain wrapped around each of her legs and having a long chain attached to each of her shackles, that's two chains for each body part! That means you're going to have ten chains hooked to my grandchild Doctor Stone! Ten! Plus handcuffs and shackles!"

"That's right Doctor!" Nicolas shouts. "I don't want my sister cuffed, chained and shackled like she's some wild animal or something!"

"But that IS the way your sister behaved before when she attacked all those people in the past and wasn't even aware of it!" Dr. Stone says.

"We still don't want to see her cuffed, chained and shackled like she's some wild animal or beast!" Michael shouts.

"That's right!" Barry shouts. "And why do you feel my child needs to be cuffed, chained up and shackled Doctor? You think she's crazy don't you?"

"Of course they think she's crazy Dad!" Nicolas shouts. "Why do you think they want to cuff, chain and shackle her up in the first place?! Because that's what they sometimes do to mental patients, is chain them up!"

"No that is not true!" Dr. Kahn shouts. "If that's the case, then why didn't we consider having Diane's physical body cuffed, chained up and shackled a little while ago while her ORIGINAL soul, spirit or personality was there? It's THE OTHER soul, spirit or personality we think is crazy, not Diane!"

"Saying that the THE OTHER soul, spirit or personality is crazy IS like saying that my child is crazy too!" Mary shouts.

"Miss Mary, why do you think we had your daughter commited before in the first place?" Dr. Stone says. "We didn't have your daughter commited for nothing! She viciously attacked and harmed people in the past and was not aware of it!"

"But it wasn't Diane's original soul, spirit or personality who attacked and harmed those people Doctor Stone!" Margarita shouts. "It was that OTHER soul, spirit or personality who did that!"

"Why do you think we want to cuff, chain up and shackle that OTHER soul, spirit or personality in the first place Miss Margarita?!"

"Yeah but if you cuff, chain up and shackle that OTHER soul, spirit or personality, you're actually cuffing, chaining up and shackling Diane!"

"So what are we suppose to do Miss Margarita, go after the OTHER soul, spirit or personality alone without going after Diane, and just have the other soul, spirit or personality commited and be locked up, but not Diane?! That is NOT possible! That other soul, spirit or personality have no physical body, they're using Diane's physical body temporary! So how would we even find or get to that other soul, spirit or personality without going through Diane's physical body?! Going through Diane's physical body is the only way to get to that other soul, spirit or personality! That other soul, spirit or personality and Diane's original soul, spirit or personality DO come inside the same package, which is Diane's physical body! When we had the other soul, spirit or personality commited, unfortunately Diane's physical body had to go along with it."

"I still don't want my grandchild cuffed, chained and shackled!"

"Okay, okay. We understand how you all feel. Listen, if it makes you all feel better, we won't have the security officer put the cuffs, chains and shackles on Diane's physical body. We don't want to have you all feeling uncomfortable. But if we don't have the cuffs, chains and shackles on Diane's physical body, we are not going to try to bring out the OTHER personality."

"What!" Diane D's family shouts.

"Seriously?!" Michael shouts. "You're not gonna try to bring out the other personality if the cuffs, chains and shackles aren't on Diane's physical body?!"

"No we're not! As long as those cuffs, chains and shackles aren't gonna be on Diane's physical body, Dr. Kahn and I are not going to take the risk! I mean Diane is known for having deadly kung fu kicks that she did to other people and that storage room door at the other hospital! That's why we want to make sure we cuff, chain and shackle her legs and feet down just in case that other personality emerges and tries to kung fu kick us! Dr. Kahn and I don't want to be on the receiving end of Diane's or that other personality's kung fu kicks! We would like to leave out of this hospital and make it back home in one piece!" Diane D's family angrily looks at Dr. Stone. He then says, "You understand, don't you?" Diane D's family then worriedly look at Dr. Stone. They then turn and sadly look at each other. They then turn and look back at Dr. Stone. Dr. Stone then says to them, "It's up to you. If you all let us continue with the hypnosis on Diane and try to bring out the other personality, we'll have to have the cuffs, chains and shackles on her physical body to hold that other personality down, for our safety. Once the hypnosis is all done and over with, we'll have the cuffs, chains and shackles removed from off Diane's physical body before we snap her out of hypnosis. She'll wake back up and won't even know that the cuffs, chains and shackles were ever there."

"I don't know," Margarita says. "I'm still not feeling it!"

"Me neither!" Mary shouts.

"We understand how you all feel," Dr. Kahn says. "Believe me, we do. But it's the only way to possibly be safe from that other soul, spirit or personality's wrath if that other soul, spirit or personality emerges and suddenly gets out of control! Plus we'll have a priest on stand by."

"What!" Diane D's family shouts. "A priest?!"

Margarita puzzled looks at Dr. Kahn and shouts, "You're gonna have a priest on stand by?!"

"Yeah," Dr. Kahn says. "Just in case."

"Just in case?!" Barry shouts. "Just in case what?!"

"Just in case the other soul, spirit or personality turns out to be some evil vicious entity that the little boy Marcus claimed to have felt inside the school hallway that night."

"What!" Diane D's family shouts. "Some evil vicious entity?!"

"Oh boy!" Mary shouts. "Here we go with that Marcus kid again and his 'evil vicious entity' stories! So you feel you need a priest for what that kid said about my child inside that school hallway, like she's possessed or something?!"

"Just in case," Dr. Kahn says.

"Just in case?! Oh I get it! First you think my child is crazy that you want to cuff, chain and shackle her up! Then you think she's possessed that you want to have a priest on stand by! So now you want to have cuffs, chains, shackles and a priest go up against my child, don't you?!"

"No it's not true Miss Mary! We don't want to have cuffs, chains, shackles and a priest go up against Diane! Remember, it's the OTHER personality that we want to cuff, chain up, shackle and have a priest for, not Diane! We have absolutely nothing against Diane! It's not her ORIGINAL PERSONALITY that we're worried about! It's that violent, aggressive personality with the superhuman strength that we're afraid of!"

"But that violent, aggressive personality with the superhuman strength wasn't violent or aggressive towards Nancy when Nancy had an encounter with it inside our family's home in the upstairs hallway!"

"Well that's Nancy! Nancy is part of Diane's family! That other personality most likely know that Nancy is part of Diane's family! That's probably why the other personality was never violent or aggressive towards her!"

"So are you saying that's why Nancy was spared from that other personality's violent rages and vicious assaults?" Margarita asks.

"Yes that's exactly what I'm saying. But Dr. Stone and I are a different story, we're NOT members of Diane's family. WE'RE the ones who have to watch our backs, not YOU guys."

Diane D's family worriedly look at Dr. Kahn. They then look at each other. They turn back to Dr. Kahn as Barry says to him, "Okay Doctor, let's do it."

"Let's do it? Are you sure?"

"Yes we're sure. Let's just get this whole thing over with! As long as we're there in the room with Diane and we have our own set of keys for the cuffs, chains and shackles, let's do this."

"You got it. But before we go in there now, we only need a few of you inside the room while the security officer hooks the cuffs, chains and shackles on Diane's physical body."

"What!" Diane D's family shouts.

"Only need a few of us inside the room, while the security officer hooks the cuffs, chains and shackles on her?" Michael asks.

"Yes," Dr. Kahn says.

"Why only a few of us?"

"Because you might all change your minds while you all are standing there watching the security officer cuff, chain and shackle Diane's physical body up."

"We might change our minds?" Tomas asks. "Why, is it that bad?"

"You will have to see for yourself while the security officer is cuffing, chaining and shackling her."

Diane D's family worriedly look at each other. Barry says to them, "I'm gonna go in there and be there while the security officer is cuffing, chaining and shackling her."

"So will I!" Michael shouts.

"I'm gonna go in there too!" Mary shouts. "No way they're gonna cuff, chain and shackle up my child while I'm not in there!"

"I'm going in there too!" Margarita shouts.

"So am I!" Nicolas shouts. "That's my sister!"

"I'm going in there too!" Tonio shouts. "That's my niece!"

Tomas turns to Marilyn and says, "Marilyn, Nancy y Charlotte esperar aquí hasta la hipnosis obtiene listo para empezar de nuevo. Voy a ir allí también."

"Bien papá," Marilyn says.

"Let's go step back inside the room," Dr. Stone says. Dr. Stone and Dr. Kahn turn and lead Barry, Michael, Mary, Nicolas, Margarita, Tonio and Tomas back down the hallway towards the room as Marilyn, Nancy and Charlotte stay behind nervously looking on.

Forty-five minutes later back inside the large room, Diane D continues to lay flat on her back on the psychiatrist couch motionless still under hypnosis with her head back, face up towards the ceiling and eyes closed. Her face has an eerie pale unearthly beauty to it again with a firm serious expression on it as her eyes appear very puffy and swollen again as she lays there with her eyes closed with her eyeballs appearing to be at the top of her head underneath her closed eyelids. The blanket is completely off of her making her body viewable as her hands are on top of her chest with thick handcuffs and chains wrapped around each of her wrists. Her body is wrapped in chains and chained to the psychiatrist couch! Her legs and feet are spread apart with chains wrapped around each of her legs and shackles wrapped around each of her ankles. Each chain wrapped around her legs is hooked to the metal bars beneath each side of the couch where her legs are. There is a long chain attached to each of her shackles. Each chain from her shackles is hooked to the metal bars beneath each side of the couch where her feet are. There is a long chain attached to each of her handcuffs. Each chain from her handcuffs is hooked to the metal bars beneath each side of the couch where her arms are. There is a chain wrapped around each of her upper arms. Each chain wrapped around her upper arms is hooked to the metal bars beneath each side of the couch where her shoulders are. There is a chain going over and around each of her shoulders. Each chain going over and around her shoulders have one end hooked to the metal bar where her head is and the other end hooked to a chain wrapped around her upper arms. Diane D is totally unaware of the cuffs and chains wrapped around her body and shackles on her feet as she lays motionless on the couch under hypnosis. She is completely surrounded by velvet ropes hooked to poles that are several yards away from all sides of her with the doctors' chairs near the velvet ropes.

Barry, Mary, Margarita, Tomas, Michael, Nicolas, Tonio, Dr. Stone, Dr. Kahn, the Indian nurse, a security officer, a priest and Marilyn stand behind part of the velvet ropes that are on Diane D's right side as they sadly stare across the floor at her. Nancy and Charlotte nervously stand beside and behind their family holding each other as they sadly stare across the floor at Diane D. "Wooow," Tonio whispers. He then turns to Dr. Stone and Dr. Kahn and whispers, "You guys are really afraid of that other personality aren't you?"

"Aren't you?" Dr. Stone says. "We rather be safe than sorry."

Margarita then whispers to the doctors, "I don't like all those cuffs and chains wrapped around her and those shackles on her feet!"

"Me neither!" Tomas whispers. "Remove those cuffs, chains and shackles from off our granddaughter immediately!"

"But you said it was okay at first," Dr. Kahn whispers.

"Yeah but we changed our minds," Mary whispers.

"I don't like it at all!" Margarita whispers. "Are those cuffs, chains and shackles tight on her?!"

"No they're not tight on her at all Miss Margarita," Dr. Kahn whispers. "We're not putting your granddaughter through some torture experience or anything. The chains are loose enough for her to move around, but not loose enough for her to break free from just in case the other personality emerges to the surface and gets out of control. We have to get prepared for that other personality's fury! Believe me, we want to try and make your granddaughter as comfortable as possible."

"But it's not only the cuffs, chains and shackles that bothers me!"

"Not only the cuffs, chains and shackles?"

"No!"

"Then what else is it?"

"I don't like the way she looks laying like that! She looks like a corpse laying completely still like that!"

"You think she looks like a corpse?"

"Yes, with her face all pale and her eyes all puffy! She looks like a dead person!"

"She's not dead Miss Margarita," Dr. Stone whispers. "She's still under hypnosis. Can't you see her breathing?"

Diane D's family puzzled look at her across the floor. Margarita then whispers, "Yeah a little bit."

"Her heart rate is just a little slow right now."

"It is?" Barry whispers. "Well I think we should get a little closer to her and check on her to make sure she's breathing." Barry starts to unhook the velvet rope that is in front of him.

Dr. Stone and Dr. Kahn stop him as Dr. Stone whispers, "No you all can't go close to her. You'll disturb and interupt her being under hypnosis then we won't be able to finish helping her." Diane D's family worriedly look at Dr. Stone. He then says, "You can go around the rope to check on her, but don't go past the rope or make any noises, okay?"

"Okay Doctor," Barry whispers. Barry and the rest of the family start to walk around the velvet ropes. They slowly walk several yards away from the top of Diane D's head. They stop and stare down at Diane D as she remains under hypnosis with her eyes closed. They then look at the cuffs and thick chains wrapped around her body. They sadly stare at Diane D. Mary starts to cry, "Ohh, my poor baby!" The rest of the family sadly turn to Mary and try to comfort her. They turn back and sadly stare at Diane D again with tears in their eyes.

"Can you see her breathing Aunt Mary?" Nancy tearfully asks.

"Yes she's breathing Nancy," Nicolas says. "I can see it."

"I can see it too," Michael says. "She's just breathing slow right now." The family continues to sadly stare at Diane D.

"Diane!" Marilyn suddenly calls out as the family quickly turns to her then look back at Diane D. They do not see Diane D responding. She continues to lay under hypnosis with her eyes closed.

"I don't think she can hear you Aunt Marilyn," Nicolas says. The family continues to sadly stare at Diane D.

Margarita starts to cry, "I can't take this." The family turns to

Margarita and tries to comfort her. Margarita then looks towards Dr. Stone.

Dr. Stone approaches the family and whispers, "Are you alright Miss Margarita?"

Diane D's family turns to Dr. Stone as Margarita whispers, "No I'm not alright Doctor Stone, seeing my grandbaby cuffed, chained and shackled like this!"

"I understand Miss Margarita. I understand how you feel. Listen, if it's that important to you not to have Diane cuffed, chained and shackled, we can remove the cuffs, chains and shackles off her right now if you want."

"Yes I want the cuffs, chains and shackles removed from off my granddaughter now!"

"Okay, but if we remove the cuffs, chains and shackles from off her, then we're not going to try to bring out the other personality."

"Good! Let that other personality stay wherever it's at! Just give us back Diane!"

"Okay, no problem." Dr. Stone turns towards the security officer and whispers, "Security?" The security officer approaches Dr. Stone as Dr. Stone tells him, "The family is not comfortable with the cuffs, chains and shackles on Diane. So remove the cuffs, chains and shackles from off her now."

"Sure, no problem," the security officer whispers. The security officer turns towards the velvet rope and starts to unhook the part of the rope from in front of himself.

"Wait a minute," Dr. Kahn whispers as he approaches Diane D's family. The security officer stops as he and everyone else turn and look at Dr. Kahn. Dr. Kahn then looks at Margarita and whispers, "Miss Margarita, what if we release some of the chains from off Diane. Will it be alright for us to continue the hypnosis process?"

"Release some of the chains?" Margarita whispers.

"Yeah. We still want to continue with the hypnosis on Diane, but we want to still feel safe doing so. Can we release just some of the chains off her and still go through the hypnosis process?"

Margarita and the rest of Diane D's family look at Dr. Kahn. They then look at Diane D. They then turn and look at each other. Margarita then whispers, "What do you all say?"

"I guess we can have some of the chains release from off Diane Mom," Barry whispers.

"Oh yeah? Which ones?"

"I don't know." Barry turns to Dr. Stone and whispers, "What do you say Doctor Stone? If we do allow you to release some of the chains off Diane, which chains would YOU feel safe having released from off her?"

"The ones farthest away from me and Dr. Kahn," Dr. Stone says. "That's for sure."

"Oh yeah? Which chains are they?"

Dr. Stone and Diane D's family look back at the chains wrapped around Diane D. Dr. Stone then looks back at Barry and whispers, "I guess the chains that are wrapped around her upper arms."

"The chains wrapped around her upper arms?"

"Yeah."

"The chains wrapped around her upper arms are pretty close to you Doctor Stone. What about the chains attached to the shackles? You don't want to release those?"

"I'm not sure if I feel safe if the chains attached to her shackles are released. If that other personality emerges to the surface, it might just lift one of her legs high up in the air and give Doctor Kahn and I kung fu kicks right to the head!"

"Give you kung fu kicks to the head?"

"That's right."

"There's nothing to worry about Doctor Stone. All you have to do, is be careful and not have your heads close to her feet."

"That's right Doctor Stone," Nicolas whispers. "You think it's possible for her to give you a kung fu kick to the head while you're far away from her feet?"

"It didn't stop her before when she gave an officer in Germany a kung fu kick to the head while he was far away from her feet!" Dr. Stone whispers.

"What?" Diane D's family says.

"What are you talking about Doctor Stone?" Margarita whispers.

"You guys never actually witnessed what happened on that stage in Germany when she had supposedly levitated off the stage, then landed on the stage floor," Dr. Stone whispers. "I heard and read what happened in Germany. I heard while Diane was laying face up on the stage floor after she supposedly levitated, one of the officers ran over to her, bend down to the floor close to her head to check on her. And while he was bent to the floor checking on her, I heard that she suddenly raised her knee all the way up to her chest then raised her foot high up in the air and kicked that officer right in the head and he wasn't even near her feet when that happened and she didn't even know or realize that she kicked him! So I don't feel safe if those chains attached to her shackles are released. I would feel more safe if her feet stay grounded to the couch for now."

"So which chains would you feel safe to have released from off her Doctor Stone?"

"Well actually none of them!"

"None of them?"

"That's right, none of them! I'm sorry I don't feel safe if any of the chains are released from off of her."

"Miss Margarita," Dr. Kahn whispers. "If we can hurry and get this hypnosis done with, the sooner we can get those cuffs, chains and shackles released from off your granddaughter."

Margarita and the rest of Diane D's family look at Dr. Kahn. They then turn and look at each other. Margarita then whispers, "Well, what do y'all say?"

"I just want to hurry and get this hypnosis done with Mom," Barry whispers.

"Yeah so do I," Mary whispers.

"Okay." Barry turns to Dr. Stone and Dr. Kahn and whispers, "Okay Doctors, we're going to allow the cuffs, chains and shackles to stay, but if this hypnosis takes too long, or if we see Diane getting uncumfortable with the cuffs, chains and shackles in any kind of way, we want the cuffs, chains and shackles removed from off her right away, you got that?!"

"Sure," Dr. Stone whispers.

"Does that make you feel safe Doctor Stone?" Margarita whispers.

"I won't feel safe until this whole hypnosis process is over."

"And I won't feel better until ALL those cuffs, chains and shackles are removed from off my granddaughter."

"We'll have the cuffs, chains and shackles removed from off your granddaughter as soon as possible. Don't worry, she'll be alright."

Diane D's family sadly stare at Dr. Stone. They then continue to sadly stare at Diane D as she remains wrapped in chains under hypnosis. They slowly start to walk around the velvet rope again towards the left side of Diane D. They slowly walk several yards away from her left side. They stop and stare down at her. They look back at the cuffs, chains and shackles wrapped around her body. They sadly stare at Diane D again. They then turn and slowly start to walk several yards away from her feet. They stop and sadly stare down at her again.

Dr. Stone approaches them again and whispers, "Are you all ready to start the rest of the hypnosis now? We want to hurry and get this done with so we can release the cuffs, chains and shackles from off her then get her out of hypnosis."

"Okay Doctor Stone," Barry whispers. "Okay."

"Did you all finish signing the paper for your permission to have the cuffs, chains and shackles on her?"

"Yes Doctor we're finished. Michael has the paper."

"Yes it's right here," Michael whispers. He hands Dr. Stone back the clipboard with paper on it. He then hands Dr. Stone back his pen.

"Thank you," Dr. Stone whispers. "Now let me walk you all back to your chairs so we can continue and get this thing done with." Dr. Stone turns and head towards the middle of the room where the chairs are. Diane D's family turn back towards her and stand there sadly staring at her again.

Dr. Kahn turns towards the security officer and the priest and whispers, "Thank you."

"You're welcome," the security officer whispers.

Dr. Kahn, the security officer and the priest take another sad look at Diane D. Then they turn as the priest tells Dr. Kahn, "We'll be out in the hallway."

"Okay," Dr. Kahn says. The security officer and the priest take another look at Diane D. They then turn their heads and head towards the door.

Margarita and Tomas turn towards the security officer and the priest. Margarita then turns to Dr. Kahn and whispers, "Excuse me Doctor Kahn?"

Dr. Kahn turns towards Margarita as the security officer and the priest head out the door. Dr. Kahn walks towards Margarita as the door closes behind the security officer and the priest.

Dr. Kahn approaches Margarita and Tomas and says, "Yes Miss Margarita?"

"Where is that security officer going with the keys for the cuffs and chains? I don't want him to be too far, not with my granddaughter cuffed, chained and shackled like this!"

"Oh no Miss Margarita, the security officer is not going anywhere. He and the priest are going to be waiting right outside in the hallway while we're hypnotizing Diane because what is said inside this room, is suppose to be confidential between us doctors, the patient and the patient's family, which are you guys. That's why the security officer and the priest left the room. They're going to be on stand by just in case of an emergency, okay? Don't worry, your granddaughter will alright."

"Okay Doctor." Margarita, Tomas, Mary, Barry, Tonio, Marilyn, Nicolas and Michael turn and continue to sadly stare at Diane D again. They slowly start to walk away towards the middle of the room. Nancy and Charlotte do not move. They continue to stand there several yards away from Diane D holding each other nervously staring at Diane D with tears in their eyes.

Michael approaches Nancy and Charlotte and whispers, "Are you girls alright?"

"No," Nancy cries. "We don't like seeing her like this Michael!"

"I know Nancy. But the sooner we get this thing done, the sooner those cuffs, chains and shackles will be off of her. So let's not waste anymore time and get this thing over and done with, okay? I want those cuffs, chains and shackles off her myself." Michael, Nancy and Charlotte continue to stand there sadly staring at Diane D. They then turn and slowly start to walk away towards the middle of the room as they sadly stare at Diane D.

Diane D's family sits back down in the middle of the room several yards from her on her lower right again facing her. Dr. Stone stands in front of them and whispers, "Are you all okay?"

"No we're NOT okay Doctor Stone!" Barry whispers. "My daughter is laying over there wrapped in chains!"

"I know. We're going to get started right now. I can't wait to have those cuffs, chains and shackles removed from off her myself. Now we're going to get this thing started again, okay? This time, we're gonna try to bring out and meet, the OTHER personality." Diane D's family frighteningly stare at Dr. Stone. He then whispers to them, "So get ready. Wish us luck." Dr. Stone turns away and goes back towards the rope as Diane D's family nervously stare at him.

Dr. Stone, Dr. Kahn and the Indian nurse who is now holding the blanket go into the velvet rope that is surrounding Diane D. Dr. Stone and Dr. Kahn head towards the chairs and grab them as the nurse heads towards Diane D. As the nurse approaches Diane D's left side, she gently smiles at Diane D's face and gently strokes the top of Diane D's hair and forehead. Then she gently holds Diane D's left shoulder continuing to smile at her. She then turns and gently places the blanket back over Diane D just below her forearms covering Diane's lower half of the body. She then turns and walks away as she takes one last look at Diane D again. She then looks forward and heads towards the velvet rope. She leaves from the velvet rope and heads towards the front door. She then leaves the room and closes the door behind herself.

Chapter 13

Dr. Stone Brings Out Diane D's Other Personality

Fifteen minutes later Dr. Stone and Dr. Kahn are sitting near Diane D's head leaning towards her head again. Dr. Stone speaks to Diane D's subconscious again and says to her, "Is there another soul, spirit or personality in there using this physical body also? Is there another soul, spirit or personality in there? If there is another soul, spirit or personality in there using this physical body also, we need you to come out and talk to us. Is there another soul, spirit or personality in there?" Dr. Stone and Dr. Kahn stare at Diane D. Diane D continues to lay on the couch as her eyes remain closed with the cuffs and chains wrapped around her body and blanket on top of her.

Margarita, Tomas, Mary, Barry, Tonio, Marilyn, Nicolas, Michael, Nancy and Charlotte nervously hug and hold on to each other as they continue to sit quietly in the middle of the room puzzled looking at Diane D.

Dr. Stone speaks to Diane D's subconscious again as he looks down at her and says, "Is there another soul, spirit or personality inside this physical body now? If there is another soul, spirit or personality inside this physical body now, we need you to come out and talk to us. We need to talk to the soul, spirit and personality that Diane's cousin Nancy encountered inside their family's home in their upstairs hallway outside their bedrooms that night, NOT Diane's original soul, spirit or personality now, we already talked to her original soul, spirit and personality. We need to talk to the soul, spirit or personality that had an encounter with her cousin Nancy in their family's upstairs hallway, but before we do that, we want to make sure, that this is NOT Diane's original soul, spirit or personality anymore. Is the soul, spirit or personality that Diane's cousin Nancy encountered inside their family's home inside this physical body now? Reveal yourself. Come out and speak to us. Is the soul, spirit or personality that Diane's cousin Nancy encountered inside the family's home inside this physical body now?" Dr. Stone and Dr. Kahn stare at Diane D. Diane D does not respond. Her physical body continues to lay on the couch not responding as her eyes remain closed.

Margarita, Tomas, Mary, Barry, Tonio, Marilyn, Nicolas, Michael, Nancy and Charlotte continue to sit quietly puzzled looking at Diane D.

Dr. Stone continues to look at Diane and says, "Is there another soul, spirit or personality there inside this physical body?" Dr. Stone and Dr. Kahn continue to stare at Diane D. Diane D's physical body continues to lay on the couch not responding as her eyes remain closed.

Margarita, Tomas, Mary, Barry, Tonio, Marilyn, Nicolas, Michael, Nancy and Charlotte continue to puzzled look at Diane D.

Dr. Stone then says, "If the soul, spirit or personality that Diane's cousin Nancy encountered inside their family's home is inside this physical body now, please reveal yourself to us and talk to us." Suddenly, Diane D starts to breathe hard. Dr. Stone and Dr. Kahn anxiously look at Diane D as her chest starts to rise and eyeballs seem to roll towards the top of her head again underneath her closed eyelids.

Margarita, Tomas, Mary, Barry, Tonio, Marilyn, Nicolas, Michael, Nancy and Charlotte start to anxiously look at Diane D.

Dr. Stone and Dr. Kahn anxiously look at each other, then back at Diane D. Diane D continues to breathe hard as her eyes remain closed. Suddenly her breathing slows down, her chest lowers back down. Dr. Stone then says, "Is that a soul, spirit or personality trying to come out? Is there a soul, spirit or personality in there inside this physical body now? If there is a soul, spirit or personality inside this physical body now, respond yes by waving your fingers three times when I ask again. Now is there a soul, spirit or personality inside this physical body now?" Diane D continues to lay on the couch as her eyes remain closed. Suddenly her fingers wave once, twice, then three times.

Margarita, Tomas, Mary, Barry, Tonio, Marilyn, Nicolas, Michael, Nancy and Charlotte become excited and nervous as Michael turns to them and whispers, "She waved her fingers three times!" Michael, Nicolas, Margarita, Tomas, Mary, Barry, Tonio, Marilyn, Nancy and Charlotte continue to anxiously watch Diane D.

"Okay good," Dr. Stone says as he continues to speak to Diane D's subconscious. "Now we want to talk to the soul, spirit or personality that Diane's cousin Nancy encountered inside their family's home that night, NOT Diane's original soul, spirit or personality now. We want to talk to the soul, spirit or personality that had an encouter with her cousin Nancy, but before we do that, we want to make sure that this is NOT Diane's original soul, spirit or personality anymore. Now is this Diane's original soul, spirit or personality in there now? Is Diane's original soul, spirit or personality there inside this physical body now? If Diane's original soul, spirit or personality is inside this physical body now, respond 'Yes' by waving your fingers three times when I ask. If Diane's original soul, spirit or personality is NOT the one inside this physical body now, respond 'No' by waving your fingers twice. Now is Diane's original soul, spirit or personality inside this physical body now? 'Yes' or 'no'?" Diane D continues to lay on the couch as her eyes remain closed. Suddenly her fingers wave once then twice.

"What!" Margarita, Tomas, Mary, Barry, Tonio, Marilyn, Nicolas, Michael, Nancy and Charlotte whisper. They become shocked and more nervous as Tomas turns to them and whispers, "Oh oh! She only waved her fingers twice!" Tomas, Margarita, Mary, Barry, Tonio, Marilyn, Nicolas, Michael, Nancy and Charlotte continue to shockingly and nervously watch Diane D.

"Is this Diane's original soul, spirit or personality inside this physical body now?" Dr. Stone says. Diane D continues to lay on the couch as her eyes remain closed. Suddenly her fingers wave once then twice.

"What!" Margarita, Tomas, Mary, Barry, Tonio, Marilyn, Nicolas, Michael, Nancy and Charlotte whisper. They become shocked and more nervous as Mary turns to them and whispers, "My God! She only waved her fingers twice again!"
"Oh my God!" Margarita whispers. "That means it's not her!"
"Oh no!" the rest of the family whispers. They continue to shockingly and nervously watch Diane D.

"Are you saying, that this is another soul, spirit or personality inside this physical body now?" Dr. Stone says. Diane D continues to lay on the couch as her eyes remain closed. Suddenly her fingers wave once, twice, then three times.

"What!" Margarita, Tomas, Mary, Barry, Tonio, Marilyn, Nicolas, Michael, Nancy and Charlotte whisper. They become more shocked and nervous as Margarita turns to them and whispers, "It's the other personality!" Margarita, Tomas, Mary, Barry, Tonio, Marilyn, Nicolas, Michael, Nancy and Charlotte continue to shockingly and nervously watch Diane D.

"Is this the soul, spirit or personality that Diane's cousin Nancy encountered inside their family's home inside their upstairs hallway?" Dr. Stone says. Diane D continues to lay on the couch as her eyes remain closed. Suddenly her fingers wave once, twice, then three times.

"What!" Margarita, Tomas, Mary, Barry, Tonio, Marilyn, Nicolas, Michael, Nancy and Charlotte whisper.

"Are you saying, that YOU"RE the soul, spirit or personality that Diane's cousin Nancy encountered inside their family's upstairs hallway that night?" Dr. Stone asks. Diane D continues to lay on the couch as her eyes remain closed. Suddenly her fingers wave once, twice, then three times again.

"It IS the other personality!" Margarita frighteningly whispers.
Nancy frighteningly turns to her family and whispers, "I think I want to leave!"
"You want to leave?" Tomas asks.
"Yes! I don't want to stay here!"
"Why not?"
"Because I'm afraid to be here right now! I don't think I want to meet that other personality again!"
"You don't?"
"No! That was a bad experience I went through that night!"
"I want to leave too!" Charlotte whispers.
"You do?" Margarita whispers.
"Yeah. I'm afraid to be here too."
"Okay girls. Go out the back door, okay? But leave quietly."
"Okay Grandma."
"Aren't the rest of you coming too?" Nancy asks.
"No Nancy," Barry whispers. "Who's going to be here for Diane if we all leave?"
"But aren't you all afraid?"
"Yes, we're all afraid! We're all afraid for Diane, that's why we can't leave her! We're her family and some of us have to be here for her!"
"Okay. But I'm out." Nancy and Charlotte quietly get up from their seats. They turn around towards the back of the room avoiding looking back towards Diane D. Nancy grabs Charlotte's hand as they quickly but quietly head towards the back door.

Nancy and Charlotte reach the back door. They quietly open the back door and leave out of the room, not looking back towards Diane D. They quietly close the door behind themselves.

Dr. Stone and Dr. Kahn puzzled look towards the back door. They turn back to Diane D and continue to speak to her other personality as

Dr. Stone says, "Okay, we need to talk to you. We need to find out what happened the night you encountered Diane's cousin Nancy inside their family's home in the upstairs hallway outside the bedrooms. Are you able to talk about it now? Do you want to talk about it now? If you are able to talk about it now or are willing to talk about it now, respond by saying 'yes' when I ask again. Now are you able to talk about it now or are you willing to talk about it now?"

Diane D's physical body continues to lay on the couch as her eyes remain closed. Her other personality suddenly says, "Yes," as the cuffs and chains remain wrapped around her physical body.

"What!" Margarita, Tomas, Mary, Barry, Tonio, Marilyn, Nicolas and Michael whisper.

"You're willing to talk about it?" Dr. Stone asks.
"Yes," Diane D's other personality says.
"Good."
"Okay, hi," Dr. Kahn says to Diane D's other personality. "I'm Doctor Kahn. I'm gonna talk to you now and I need you to answer some questions, okay? What I need to know is, do you have a name?"
"No," Diane D's other personality says.

"What!" Margarita, Tomas, Mary, Barry, Tonio, Marilyn, Nicolas and Michael whisper.

"You don't have a name?" Dr. Kahn says.
"No," Diane D's other personality says.
"Oh. Well do you have a gender?"
"No."
"You don't have a gender?"
"No."
"Wow. Okay. Do you speak or understand a specific language?"
"No."
"No? What do you mean 'no'?"
"There is no specific language I speak or understand."
"There's no specific language you speak or understand? What do you mean by that?"
"I can speak and understand any language."
"What!" Dr. Kahn and Dr. Stone shout.
"You can speak and understand any language?!" Dr. Stone asks.
"Yes," Diane D's other personality says.
Dr. Stone and Dr. Kahn puzzled look at each other. Then they puzzled look back at Diane D's other personality. Dr. Stone then asks, "So you can speak and understand English."
"Yes."
"What about Spanish? Can you speak and understand Spanish?"
"Yes."

"Okay. Can you speak and understand French?"
"Yes."
"All French, or some French?"
"All French."

"What!" Margarita, Tomas, Mary, Barry, Tonio, Marilyn, Nicolas and Michael whisper. They shockingly look at each other. Then they shockingly look back at Diane D's other personality.

"All French?!" Dr. Stone shockingly asks. "You can speak and understand ALL French?!"
"Yes," Diane D's other personality says.

"What!" Margarita, Tomas, Mary, Barry, Tonio, Marilyn, Nicolas and Michael whisper. Margarita, Tomas, Mary, Barry, Tonio, Marilyn, Nicolas and Michael puzzled look at each other with their mouths wide open. Then they puzzled look back at Diane D's other personality.

"How did you get to speak and understand all languages?" Dr. Kahn asks.
"I can adapt to any language," Diane D's other personality says.
"You can adapt to any language?"
"Yes."
"Wow. Well can you speak and understand Dutch?"
"Yes."
"All Dutch or some of it?"
"All of it."
"Really? You can speak and understand ALL Dutch?"
"Yes."
"Wow. What about Arabic? Can you speak and understand Arabic?"
"Yes."
"All Arabic or some of it?"
"All of it."
"You can speak and understand ALL Arabic?"
"Yes."
"Wow. What about Japanese? Can you speak and understand Japanese?"
"Yes."
"All of it?"
"Yes."
"Wow. What about Hebrew? Can you speak and understand Hebrew?"
"Yes."
"All of it?"
"Yes."
"Wow. What about Swahili? Can you speak and understand

Swahili?"

"Yes."

"All of it?"

"Yes. I can speak and understand all languages on this planet."

"All languages on this planet?!"

"Yes."

"Wow. Fascinating! Okay. Well we mainly speak English, so we're going to continue to communicate to you in English, okay? Let me start by saying, that one night in the wee hours of the morning, Diane and her two cousins Nancy and Charlotte were in one of the upstairs bedrooms inside their family's home laughing and chit-chatting after Diane had just finished meditating. Diane told her cousins Nancy and Charlotte that she was in such a good mood and spirit that night or morning, that she wanted to celebrate by having a small drink before she goes to bed. Her two cousins Nancy and Charlotte decided to join her and have small drinks also. They decided to have some Vodka, Bacardi and Martini. Diane decided she was going to go downstairs to the family's bar inside the living room to make the Martini and get the rest of the liquor and cups out of the bar to bring them right up to the bedroom to her cousins Nancy and Charlotte. So while she's still upstairs in the bedroom with Nancy and Charlotte, she turns away from them, walks out the bedroom and leaves the bedroom closing the door behind herself. She goes downstairs to the family's bar to make the drinks, but something happened to her while she was downstairs at the bar that night. She took a few sips of the liquor. After that, she suddenly felt dizzy. She started calling out to her family for help, but no one in her family heard her. Then she suddenly passes out on the living room floor lying there. While her physical body was laying there on the floor alone, somehow, YOUR soul, spirit or personality winds up inside her physical body that night, right?"

"Yes."

"And your soul and spirit is inside her physical body right now."

"Yes."

Margarita, Tomas, Mary, Barry, Tonio, Marilyn, Nicolas and Michael become shocked and nervous as they continue to listen to Dr. Kahn and Diane D's other personality.

"Okay," Dr. Kahn then says. "How did your soul, spirit or personality wind up inside this physical body that night?"

"I saw this physical body just laying there on the floor passed out," Diane D's other personality says.

"You saw this physical body laying on the floor?"

"Yes."

"Where were you when you saw this physical body laying on the floor?"

"I was hovering over it."

132

"You were hovering over this physical body?"

"Yes."

"In other words, you were an invisible soul or spirit hovering over this physical body?"

"Yes."

"So if someone in Diane's family suddenly happen to come down the stairs that night and saw her laying on the floor, that family member would not have seen you or notice you hovering over her physical body, since you were an invisible soul or spirit there, right?"

"Yes."

"They would not have known you were there?"

"No."

"I see. Why were you hovering over Diane's physical body in the first place?"

"To guard her physical body."

"To guard her physical body?"

"Yes."

"Why?"

"To watch over it, to make sure her physical body was safe."

"To make sure her physical body was safe?"

"Yes."

"Why did you want to make sure, that her physical body was safe?"

"Because no one else was there. No one knew she had fell and passed out on the floor."

"No one knew?"

"No, no one. Her physical body was just laying there on the floor all alone unintended. I didn't want her physical body just laying right there on the floor all alone and unintended."

"You didn't?"

"No. Her physical body shouldn't be there on the floor. It should be upstairs in the bed."

"You felt Diane's physical body should be upstairs in the bed, instead of downstairs on the floor?"

"Yes. I wasn't going to allow her physical body to just remain there on the floor like that."

"You weren't?"

"No."

"So what happened? What did you do?"

"I decided I was going to take her physical body off the floor and place her physical body upstairs in the bed where it should be."

"You decided you were going to take Diane's physical body off the floor downstairs and place her physical body upstairs in the bed?"

"Yes."

"And how were you going to do that? How were you going to take Diane's physical body off the floor downstairs and put her physical body upstairs in the bed?"

"By entering her physical body."

"What!" Margarita, Tomas, Mary, Barry, Tonio, Marilyn, Nicolas and Michael whisper. They become shocked and look at each other. They look back and continue to listen to Dr, Kahn and Diane D's other personality.

"By entering her physical body?" Dr. Kahn asks.
"Yes," Diane D's other personality says.
"And how did you do that? How did you enter her physical body?"
"I just went to it and entered it."
"You just went to this physical body and entered it?"
"Yes."
"Wow. And once you entered into this physical body that night, what were your intentions?"
"My intentions was to walk this physical body up the stairs."
"Your intentions was to walk this physical body up the stairs?"
"Yes."
"Then what were your intentions once you got this physical body up the stairs?"
"To walk this physical body to Diane's bedroom."
"To walk this physical body to Diane's bedroom?"
"Yes."
"Then what were your intentions once you got this physical body to Diane's bedroom?"
"To place her physical body safely on her bed."
"To place her physical body safely on her bed?"
"Yes."
"Then what were your intentions once you got her physical body on the bed?"
"To leave her physical body."
"You were planning to leave this physical body once you got this physical body safely on the bed?"
"Yes."
"What made you want to bring this physical body upstairs and place this physical body safely on Diane's bed, instead of taking this physical body out of the house into the street?"
"Why would I take this physical body out of the house into the street?"
"Because Diane's family was worried, that her physical body could have gone out of the house into the street and do something wild, crazy or vicious without Diane herself being aware of it."
"I wouldn't do that to her physical body."
"You wouldn't?"
"No. My mission is not to enter into this physical body to bring this physical body out of the house into the street then do something wild, crazy or vicious with it and make Diane look like fool. I do not enter her physical body to make her look like a fool."

"You don't?"

"No, I wouldn't do that to her."

"Oh well that's good. But why were you planning to leave this physical body once you got this physical body safely on Diane's bed?"

"So she can come back into it. I wasn't planning to stay inside her physical body once I placed her physical body on the bed."

"You weren't?"

"No. My mission was to look out for her physical body and get her physical body off the floor downstairs and bring her physical body upstairs to her bed, that was it."

"I see. But on your way to walking this physical body to Diane's bedroom, you ran into someone in Diane's family when you got her physical body as far as the upstairs hallway. You ran into her cousin Nancy that night, didn't you?"

"Yes."

"Oh no!" Margarita, Tomas, Mary, Barry, Tonio, Marilyn, Nicolas and Michael whisper. They become shocked and look at each other. They then turn back and continue to listen to Dr. Kahn and Diane D's other personality.

"How did you feel about that?" Dr. Kahn asks. "How did you feel when you realized that you had ran into someone in Diane's family in the upstairs hallway?"

"I wasn't expecting to run into anybody in her family once I got her physical body upstairs," Diane D's other personality says.

"You weren't?"

"No. I just wanted to place her physical body on the bed, that was it."

"You didn't expect anything else?"

"No."

"I see. Now when you first saw Diane's physical body laying on the floor downstairs, walk us through from the time you first entered her physical body, to the time you left her physical body."

DIANE D'S OTHER PERSONALITY'S FLASHBACK:

It is close to 3:30 in the morning. It is raining, thundering and lightning outside. The living room of Margarita and Tomas' mansion is dark and dimly lit. Diane D's physical body is laying there on the floor passed out. The other soul, spirit or personality hovers over Diane D's physical body for a while looking at her physical body watching it. It slowly moves closer to Diane D's physical body. The other soul, spirit or personality then speeds towards Diane D's physical body and enters it! Diane D's physical body continues to remain motionless on the floor. Suddenly her physical body moves! Her physical body suddenly turns over! Her physical body then sits up. Her physical body then gets up off the floor and is bent down. Her physical body then straightens up and stands! Diane D's physical body staggers as it stands there in the darkness looking around. Her physical face has an eerie pale unearthly appearance to it with an angry expression on it as her physical eyes appear very puffy and swollen. Suddenly there is a loud thunder sound and lightning! Diane D's physical body looks towards the living room window at the rain, thunder and lightning outside. Her physical eyes then looks down at the rest of her physical body. Her physical body then looks back up then looks in the mirror behind the bar at its reflection. Diane D's physical body then looks around again. Her physical body continues to stand there in the darkness looking around. Her physical body then looks at the stairs. Her physical body stands there looking at the stairs. Her physical body then looks up the stairs. Her physical body stands there looking up the stairs. Her physical body then walks and staggers to the stairs. Her physical body then stops and stands there looking up the stairs as the rain, thunder and lightning continues! Her physical body then walks up the stairs.

Diane D's physical body enters the upstairs hallway. Her physical body stands there in the darkness looking around the upstairs hallway. Her physical face still has an eerie pale unearthly appearance to it with an angry expression on it and her physical eyes are still very puffy and swollen. Diane D's physical body continues to stand there in the darkness looking around. Her physical body then looks at the bedroom doors. It then looks at HER bedroom door. Her physical body then looks around again. It then looks back her bedroom door. It then walks towards HER bedroom door.

Diane D's physical body gets closer to her bedroom door. "Hey Diane!" Nancy's voice suddenly shouts. Diane D's physical body stops right in her tracks. Her physical body stands there not turning around. "Diane!" Nancy's voice shouts again. Diane D's physical body continues to stand there and closes its eyes in frustration, but still does not turn around. Nancy slowly approaches Diane D's physical body. "Diane?" she calls out again. Diane D's physical body opens its eyes and slowly turns around towards Nancy. Her physical face suspiciously looks at Nancy. Nancy becomes shocked and stunned seeing Diane D's strange facial appearance and stops. She then says, "Diane are you okay? What happened to you? You look sort of different! Your face looks pale and your eyes look very swollen. It kind of looks like you were just in a fight or boxing match or something!" Diane D's physical face suspiciously stares at Nancy with the eerie pale face and puffy and swollen eyes giving Nancy a suspicious look. Nancy then says, "What took you so long to come back to the room? You weren't meditating were you? Did you get the Vodka, Martini and Bacardi?" Diane D puzzled stares at Nancy giving Nancy a confused look. Nancy then says, "Diane you seem kind of out of it. You look sort of confused or

something. Are you alright? Where's the Vodka, Martini and Bacardi?"
Diane D's physical eyes continues to puzzled stare at Nancy. Nancy
then says, "Diane what's wrong, didn't you hear me? Where's the
Vodka, Martini and Bacardi?"

BACK TO THE PRESENT:

"Nancy asked you where's the Vodka, Martini and Bacardi?" Dr.
Kahn asks.
"Yes," Diane D's other personality says.
"Then what did you say to her?"
"I asked her 'what Vodka, Martini and Bacardi'."
"You asked Nancy 'what Vodka, Martini and Bacardi'?"
"Yes."
"Then what did she say to you?"
"She said 'what do I mean 'What Vodka, Martini and Bacardi'?
Then she told me the Vodka, Martini and Bacardi I was supposed to
bring up there to her and Charlotte so we all can have a drink together.
She thought Diane forgot."
"She thought Diane forgot?"
"Yes."
"But the fact is, it's not that Diane forgot, it was that Diane wasn't
there anymore, you were there instead, right?"
"Yes."
"And at that particular point, Nancy had no idea, that Diane's
original soul, spirit or personality wasn't there anymore and that it was
a different soul, spirit or personality there instead, right?"
"Yes."
"Then what happened?"

DIANE D'S OTHER PERSONALITY'S FLASHBACK:

Diane D's other personality continues to puzzled stare at Nancy
giving Nancy a confused dazed look. Nancy then says, "Don't tell me
that you drunk all the Vodka, Martini and Bacardi for yourself and got
sort of drunk and don't remember that you were supposed to bring the
Vodka, Martini and Bacardi up here to me and Charlotte. Is that what
took you so long to come back up? You drank the Vodka, Martini and
Bacardi for yourself and got a little drunk?"
"I don't know what you're talking about," Diane D's other
personality says as she continues to give Nancy a confused dazed look.
"'You don't know what I'm talking about? What do you mean 'you
don't know what I'm talking about' Diane? I'm talking about the drinks
you said you were in the mood for a little while ago then said you were
going to go downstairs to the bar and make the Martini and bring the
Martini, Vodka, Bacardi and cups up here to me and Charlotte, but I
don't see the Martini, Vodka, Bacardi or cups anywhere on you. Where

are the Martini, Vodka, Bacardi and cups?"

"I don't have it."

"Yeah I can see that. Why didn't you bring the Martini, Vodka, Bacardi and cups up here like you said you were going to do? Did you drink up all that stuff Diane? Did you? Come on and say something Diane! Did you drink up all that stuff?!"

"Look, Diane is not here right now."

Nancy puzzled stares at Diane D. She then says, "What .... did you just say?"

"I said Diane is not here right now."

"Diane is not here right now? What the hell are you talking about? What do you mean 'Diane is not here right now'. You're Diane. And you're standing right there."

Diane D's other personality hesitates. She stares at Nancy and says, "I'm not Diane."

Nancy puzzled stares at Diane D again. She then says, "What .... did you just say? What do you mean 'You're not Diane'?"

"I'm not Diane. She isn't here right now."

"What?"

"I said she isn't here right now."

"She isn't here right now? Who isn't here right now?"

"Diane. She isn't here right now."

"She isn't?"

"No she isn't."

"What the hell are you talking about? What do you mean 'Diane is not here right now'. I'm looking right at you."

"I told you, I'm not Diane."

"You're not?"

"No I'm not."

"Okay come on now Diane, enough with the joke alright? Because you're really starting to scare me."

"I'm not joking. I'm not Diane."

"You're not?"

"No I'm not."

BACK TO THE PRESENT:

"You said to Nancy that 'Diane is not here right now' and that 'you're not Diane'?" Dr. Kahn asks.

"Yes," Diane D's other personality says.

"Why did you tell her that?"

"Because she was asking me questions and I had no idea what she was talking about."

"You didn't know what she was talking about?"

"No."

"Then what made you tell her the truth, that you were not Diane?"

"Because she was getting suspicious."

"She was?"

"Yes."

"Well if you really wanted to, you could have just easily went along with Nancy and just allow her to think or believe that you were Diane's original soul, spirit or personality, she wouldn't have known the difference. She would have just thought that Diane was behaving different. Why did you tell Nancy the truth, that you were not Diane?"

"Because I didn't want to lie to her."

"You didn't?"

"No."

"Why not?"

"Because she's Diane's family."

"Because she's Diane's family?"

"Yes."

"That's why you didn't want to lie to her?"

"Yes."

"I see. Well Nancy became very shocked when you told her that you were not Diane. Then she said you told her 'not to worry, that Diane is okay, she'll be back'. Is that true?"

"Yes."

"Then what happened after that?"

DIANE D'S OTHER PERSONALITY'S FLASHBACK:

"What?" Nancy says. "Diane will be back? What do you mean 'Diane will be back?'"

"She'll be back," Diane D's other personality says.

"She'll be back? Back from where? Where is she?"

"She's wandering the universe for right now."

"She's wandering the universe? What do you mean 'she's wandering the universe'?"

"Like I said, she's wandering the universe."

Nancy hesitates. She puzzled looks up in the air listening to the thunder and lightning outside. Then she puzzled stares at Diane D again. She then says, "How come she's wandering the universe?"

"I can't tell you?"

"You can't tell me?"

"No."

"Well why not?"

"I just can't."

"What? My God. So, if you're not Diane, then who are you?"

"I can't tell you."

"You can't?"

"No."

"Why not?"

"I just can't."

"Oh my God. Do you have a name?"

"No I don't."

"You don't have a name?"

"No. Now if you would excuse me, I have to leave Diane's body so she can come back."

"What? You have to leave Diane's body so she can come back?"

"Yes."

"But where're you gonna go?"

"I can't tell you."

"You can't tell me?"

"No I can't."

"Why not?"

"I just can't."

"Why not?"

"I just can't." Diane D's other personality gives Nancy a cold stare. Nancy puzzledly and frighteningly looks at Diane D. Diane D's other personality then turns away from Nancy and continues to head towards her bedroom.

"Wait a minute!" Nancy suddenly shouts. Diane D's other personality stops and turns around towards Nancy. Nancy then says, "So if you're not Diane, then how do you know that's her room over there?"

"I just know."

"You just know? How do you know?"

Diane D's other personality hesitates and stares at Nancy again with a cold stare. Her other personality then says, "It's not my first time being inside this house."

"What? It's not your first time being inside this house? What do you mean 'It's not your first time being inside this house?' You've been inside this house before?"

"Yes, plenty of times."

"Plenty of times? How?"

"Whenever Diane meditates and leaves her body, I come into her body and take her place until she comes back."

"What? You come into her body and take her place whenever she meditates?"

"Yes I do."

"Why?"

"I just do." Diane D's other personality gives Nancy another cold stare as Nancy frighteningly looks at her.

BACK TO THE PRESENT:

"You told Nancy that it's not your first time being inside that house, that you've been inside their family's house before?" Dr. Kahn asks.

"Yes," Diane D's other personality says.

"And you told her that you come into this physical body and take over whenever Diane meditates?"

"Yes."

"Is that what brought your soul or spirit into their home that night, because Diane had meditated earlier while she was upstairs in her bedroom?"

"Yes."

"Really? So in other words, Diane herself brought you there into that house by meditating?"

"Yes."

"Did she know that she brought you there by her meditating?"

"No."

"She didn't know that she brought you there?"

"No."

"Did she know that you had took over her physical body that night while her soul or spirit was out there in space wandering the universe?"

"No."

"She didn't know?"

"No."

"She didn't know that you took over this physical body, brought this physical body upstairs then you wind up running into her cousin Nancy in the upstairs hallway having an encounter with her cousin Nancy?"

"No."

"She didn't know any of that stuff at all?"

"No."

"Wow. I see. Does Diane ALWAYS attract you there into that house every time she meditates?"

"Most of the time."

"Most of the time?"

"Yes."

"Does she KNOW that she attracts you there into that house every time she meditates?"

"Sometimes she knows."

"She knows sometimes?"

"Yes."

"Wow. Does Diane attract you to the house itself whenever she meditates, or does she attract you to herself?"

"She attracts me to herself."

"She attracts you to herself?"

"Yes."

"Wow. So it's not the house itself that you're attracted to whenever Diane meditates, it's Diane herself who happens to BE inside that house that you're attracted to?"

"Yes."

"So if Diane is inside her family's organization, and she decides to sit right there on the floor to meditate, you will get drawn to her there?"

"Most of the time."

"Even if she's inside her family's organization?"

"Yes."

"Wow. So if Diane was inside a grocery store and she decides to sit right there on the floor to meditate, you will get drawn to her?"

"Most of the time."

"Even if she's inside a grocery store?"

"Yes."

"Wow. What if Diane was inside a church and she decides to sit right there on the floor to meditate, you will get drawn to her right inside the church?"

"Most of the time."

"Oh yeah? What if she was inside a movie theater and she decides to sit right there on the floor to meditate, you will get drawn to her right inside the movie theater?"

"Most of the time."

"My God. What if she was inside a park or at the beach and she decides to sit right there on the grass or sand to meditate, you will get drawn to her right there at the park or at the beach?"

"Most of the time."

"Wow. So it wouldn't matter where Diane is whenever she meditates, your soul or spirit will get drawn to her?"

"Yes."

"Does she know that?"

"Most of the time."

"She does?"

"Yes."

"Wow. So what happened after you told Nancy that whenever Diane meditates and leaves her physical body, you come into her body and take her place?"

DIANE D'S OTHER PERSONALITY'S FLASHBACK:

Diane D's other personality continues to give Nancy a cold stare as Nancy frighteningly looks at her. Diane D's other personality then says, "Like I said, don't worry, Diane is okay. She'll be back." Diane D's other personality continues to give Nancy a cold stare. Her other personality then turns away from Nancy and continues to head to Diane D's bedroom.

Diane D's other personality reaches her bedroom door. Her other personality opens her bedroom door and goes inside her bedroom.

Diane D's other personality enters her bedroom closing the door behind itself. Her other personality turns towards the door and locks it. Diane D's other personality turns towards the inside of Diane D's room and looks around Diane D's room as the rain, thunder and lightning is heard outside the window. Diane D's other personality then looks at her bed. Her other personality then goes over to her bed.

Diane D's other personality gently lays on Diane D's bed face down. Her other personality then closes her eyes. Suddenly, there are banging sounds outside the bedroom door as Diane D's family's voices call out to her, "Diane! Diane! Diane, are you okay?!" Diane D's other personality quickly lifts her head up. "Diane! Are you okay?!" Diane D's family's voices shout from the other side of the door. Diane D's other personality does not answer. Her other personality angrily turns her head towards the bedroom door hearing the banging sounds of Diane D's family. Diane D's family is heard trying to open the bedroom door from the outside, but they cannot open it. It is locked. "I'm gonna get the Master Key!" Tomas' voice shouts. He is then heard rushing off.

"Hurry Tomas!" Margarita's voice shouts as she and the rest of the family continue to bang and try to open the bedroom door.

"Diane are you okay baby!" Barry's voice shouts through the door. "Open up!" Diane D's other personality still does not respond. Her other personality angrily stares at the bedroom door. "Nancy are you sure that's what she said to you?!" Barry's voice shouts to Nancy outside the door, "that 'Diane's not here right now'?!"

"Yes that's exactly what she said to me out here!" Nancy's voice shouts.

"And are you sure that she said to you, that 'she's not Diane'?!" Mary's voice shouts.

"Yes that's exactly what she told me out here too!"

"I got the Master key!" Tomas' voice shouts as he is heard quickly approaching the rest of Diane D's family outside the bedroom door. Diane D's other personality continues to angrily stare at the bedroom door. Tomas' voice then shouts, "Step aside everybody!" Everyone is heard stepping aside. The key is then heard going into the keyhole. Diane D's other personality angrily stares at the keyhole. The key is then heard turning the lock. Diane D's other personality angrily stares at the lock. The key is then heard unlocking the bedroom door! Diane D's other personality angrily and nervously stares at the bedroom door! Her other personality quickly turns her head away from the door! Her other personality lays her head back down and tightly shuts her eyes! The doorknob turns! Suddenly, Diane D's other personality leaves Diane D's physical body! It becomes a soul or spirit again as it hovers over Diane D's physical body. As the bedroom door swings open, the soul or spirit hovers higher in the air then quickly leaves Diane D's bedroom as Diane D's physical body becomes out of sight!

BACK TO THE PRESENT:

"Wow," Dr. Kahn says. "So your soul and spirit left this physical body just before Diane's family entered her bedroom?"

"Yes," Diane D's other personality says.

"In other words, you had left this physical body just in the nick of time! If you had stayed inside this physical body just a little bit longer, the rest of Diane's family would have had an encounter with you as well as her cousin Nancy did, right?

"Yes."

"So in other words, Diane's family just missed meeting you by an inch, didn't they?"

"Yes."

"Wow!" Margarita, Tomas, Mary, Barry, Tonio, Marilyn, Nicolas and Michael whisper. They become shocked and look at each other. They then turn back and continue to listen to Dr. Kahn and Diane D's other personality.

"Is there a reason, why you didn't wait to have an encounter with the rest of Diane's family?" Dr. Kahn asks.

"My purpose was not to be there to meet or have an encounter with anybody," Diane D's other personality says. "My purpose was to get this physical body from off the floor downstairs, bring it up to Diane's bedroom, place it on her bed then leave. Once my mission was accomplished, there was no longer a need for me to stay there."

"It wasn't?"

"No."

"So you just picked up and left this physical body once you got this physical body placed on the bed."

"Exactly."

"I see. Do you hover over Diane's physical body all the time?"

"No. Only when she meditates or gets angry."

"When she gets angry too?"

"Yes."

"May I ask why you come into this physical body and take over whenever Diane meditates or gets angry?"

"Because I look out for her."

"You look out for Diane?"

"Yes."

"What do you mean you look out for her?"

"I don't like anybody getting her angry."

"You don't like when anyone gets Diane angry?"

"No."

"Why not?"

"I just don't."

"Is that what happened inside that school hallway, when that little boy Marcus accused Diane of beating him up in there? Diane said she does not remember beating up that kid Marcus inside that school hallway and claims she had nothing to do with beating up Marcus and claims he's lying about it. He's saying one thing and Diane is saying another. What I need right now, is for you to answer this very important question that I'm about to ask you, okay? Since Diane's original soul, spirit and personality DOES NOT remember beating up or attacking that little boy Marcus inside that third floor school hallway, did your soul, spirit or personality have something to do with beating up Marcus inside that third floor school hallway that night Diane and her family came there? Did you use this physical body to beat up and attack that little boy Marcus with it?"

"Yes."

"What!" Margarita, Tomas, Mary, Barry, Tonio, Marilyn, Nicolas and Michael whisper. They turn and shockingly look at each other. They then turn their heads back forward and shockingly look a Diane D's other personality!

Dr. Kahn and Dr. Stone shockingly look at each other. They shockingly look back at Diane D's other personality as Dr. Kahn shouts, "It was YOU?! It was YOU who beat up that kid Marcus inside that school hallway?!"

"Yes," Diane D's other personality says.

"Oh my God! Why?!"

"Why did you beat up Marcus?!" Dr. Stone asks.

"Because he lied to Diane and upsetted her," Diane D's other personality says.

"He lied to Diane and upsetted her?"

"Yes."

"What did he lie to her about?"

"He confessed to Diane in that school hallway, that the little boy who has leukemia didn't exist. He told her that he and his brother made that whole story up just to get her and her family to come to his school."

"He told Diane that he and his brother made that whole story up just to get her and her family to come to his school?" Dr. Kahn asks.

"Yes."

"That's when Diane realized that she was lied to?"

"Yes."

"Then what happened when Diane realized that Marcus lied to her?"

"She became shocked."

"She became shocked?"

"Yes."

"Then what happened?"

"She got sad and started to cry.

"Diane got sad and started to cry?"

"Yes."

"Then what happened?"

"She started backing away from him."

"Diane started backing away from Marcus?"

"Yes."

"Then what happened?"

"She got upset."

"She got upset?"

"Yes. Then she got angry at him."

"She got angry at Marcus?"

"Yes."

"Then what happened?"

"She was getting angrier and angrier at that kid."

"She was?"

"Yes."

"Go on. Tell us what happened after that."

"She got so angry at that kid that she wanted to beat the hell out of him."

"Diane wanted to beat the hell out of Marcus?"

"Yes."

"Then what happened?"

"She didn't do it!"

"Diane didn't beat up Marcus?"

"No, she decided not to beat him."

"Diane decided not to beat Marcus?"

"Yes she decided that."

"Why did she decide not to beat Marcus?"

"Because he's a kid."

"Because he's a kid?"

"Yes. She didn't believe in beating up a kid."

"Diane didn't believe in beating up a kid?"

"No."

"But I don't understand. How in the world, did Diane believe in NOT hitting or beating Marcus because he's a kid, then he winds up getting beat up by her anyway?"

"Because I decided to take over."

"What? YOU?! YOU decided to take over?"

"Yes."

"What do you mean YOU decided to take over?" Dr. Stone asks.

"I said if she doesn't do something about that kid and beat the hell out of him, I'm gonna do it."

"What!" Margarita, Tomas, Mary, Barry, Tonio, Marilyn, Nicolas and Michael whisper. They turn and shockingly look at each other. They then turn their heads back forward and shockingly look back at Diane D's other personality.

"You said if Diane doesn't do something and beat the hell out of Marcus, you're gonna do it?!" Dr. Kahn asks.

"Exactly," Diane D's other personality says.

"How?! How did you wind up beating up Marcus?"

"By entering this physical body to do it!"

"What! You entered Diane's physical body while she was standing in the school hallway, just so that you can use her physical body to beat up and attack Marcus?!"

"Exactly."

"How did you do that?! How were you able to enter this physical body while Diane was standing inside that school hallway?"

"I approached her physical body and pulled her soul and spirit out of it."

"What!" Margarita, Tomas, Mary, Barry, Tonio, Marilyn, Nicolas and Michael whisper. They turn and shockingly look at each other. They then turn their heads back forward and shockingly look back at Diane D's other personality.

"You approached this physical body while Diane was standing inside the school hallway and just literally pulled her original soul and spirit out of it?!" Dr. Stone shouts. "Then she finds her soul and spirit wandering the universe and claims she didn't know why her soul or spirit was out there at the time and didn't know who or what put her soul or spirit there! It was YOU who did that to her?! It was YOU who pulled her original soul and spirit out of this physical body, then put her original soul or spirit out there in space wandering the universe?!"

"Yes," Diane D's other personality says.

"Why?! Why did you do that to Diane?"

"So I can use her physical body to beat the hell out of that kid!"

"What!" Dr. Kahn says. "So you can use her physical body to beat the hell out of Marcus?!"

"Yes."

"Why?!"

"Because she refused to do it!"

"Because she refused to do it?! So you made a decision to pull Diane's soul and spirit right out of her physical body to enter it and beat up Marcus, because she didn't do it?!"

"Exactly."

"How did you beat up Marcus?! By breaking his bones and everything?!"

"Exactly."

"How can you say that? How can you beat up Marcus, he's just a kid!"

"I don't care if he's just a kid!"

"You don't care if he's just a kid?"

"No!"

"But Diane cares that he's a kid! She claims she would never beat up or harm a child!"

"No she wouldn't beat up or harm a child! But I will!"

"You will?!"

"That's right!"

"You mean you would have the audacity to beat up a child?" Dr. Stone asks.

"If that child hurts Diane, yes!"

"But Marcus didn't mean to hurt Diane when he and his brother sent that false letter to her family's organization about the little boy who's dying of leukemia! It was just an innocent hoax that he and his brother pulled!"

"I don't caaare! He still hurted her!"

"Is that why Marcus keeps having nightmares about Diane coming after him in the back stairwell of that school? Marcus is claiming that he has nightmares about Diane coming after him in the back stairwell of that school almost every night! Now we already talked to Diane's orginal soul, spirit and personality about it. She claims she has nothing to do with Marcus' nightmares that she's not thinking about him and that she's moved on with her life. She says she has no control over what Marcus is dreaming about and says that she does not have the power to enter into his dreams or anybody's dreams or nightmares."

"She doesn't."

"She doesn't?"

"No. But I do."

"What!" Dr. Stone and Dr. Kahn shout.

"You have the power to do that?!" Dr. Kahn shouts. "You have the power to enter people's dream or nightmares?!"

"Yes I do," Diane D's other personality says.

"So you're entering Marcus's dreams and nightmares?!"

"Yes I am."

"Oh my God, how?! How are you able to do that?! Do you even have an appearance when you're not inside this physical body?!"

"No I don't."

"You don't have an appearance when you're NOT inside this physical body?"

"No."

"So if you don't have an appearance, why does Marcus see DIANE in his nightmares instead?!"

"Because I make myself up to look like her whenever I enter his dreams or nightmares."

"What!" Dr. Kahn and Dr. Stone shout.

"You make yourself up to look like Diane whenever you enter Marcus' dreams or nightmares?!" Dr. Stone shouts. "You mean you have the power to make yourself up into Diane's image whenever you enter Marcus' dreams or nightmares, so that he can think that it's Diane he's seeing?!"

"I can make myself look like anybody," Diane D's other personality says.

"What!" Dr. Kahn and Dr. Stone shout.

"You can?!" Dr. Stone shouts. "You have the power to do that?!"

"Yes I do," Diane D's other personality says.

"But when you enter Marcus' dreams and nightmares, you choose to make yourself look like Diane, right?!"

"That's right!"

"Why?! Why are you making yourself up to look like Diane?! If you're making yourself up to look like Diane so that Marcus can think that it's Diane he sees coming after him, he's gonna be afraid of HER forever! That's why he's afraid of her right now!"

"Too bad!"

"Why are you tormenting Marcus?!" Dr. Kahn shouts.

"He shouldn't have done what he did to Diane!"

"And what is that?!"

"He lied to her! He told her that there was a child dying of leukemia when he knew there wasn't, causing her to be attached to the child playing with her emotions! Then made her cry when he told her that the kid never existed!"

"We know what he did was wrong! But he's not bothering Diane anymore!"

"I don't caaare!"

"Diane has forgiven Marcus! Can't you forgive him too?"

"No! I will never forgive that kid for what he did to her!"

"Why not?!"

"Because he hurted her!"

"Yes he hurted Diane, but Diane isn't hurt anymore! She's moved on! Why can't you?!"

"I told you! Because he hurted her!"

"Is that why Diane kept blocking Marcus' path when he was trying to get back to where the principal's office is?" Dr. Stone asks. "Because Marcus claim that after he confessed to Diane that the little boy who's dying a leukemia didn't existed, she became sad and then backed away from him all the way down to the corner of that school hallway. Marcus said he started apologizing to Diane but she didn't say anything. He said that he notice Diane kept staring at him from down the corner of that dark school hallway! He said then he decided to go back to where the principal's office is. He said he got closer to the corner of the hallway to go around the corner to get back to where the principal's office is, but said in order for him to go around the corner to get back to where the pricipal's office is, he had to go past Diane to do so! He said he never made it around the corner to get back to where the principal's office is because Diane kept blocking his path when he was trying to get past her. That's when his nightmarish ordeal with her began. He said on his LAST ATTEMPT to try to get past Diane to get back to where the principal's office is, that's when she jumped, spun her entire body around and gave him a kung fu kick knocking him down breaking his arm and wrist! Diane claims she remembers none of that stuff! She claims she doesn't remember Marcus getting close to her while she was standing at the corner of the school hallway and said she does not remember blocking his path when he was trying to go past her to get back to where the principal's office is and says she does not remember giving him any kung fu kick at all and claims she wouldn't do that to a child! Since Diane claims not to remember any of that stuff, was it your soul, spirit or personality who was inside this physical body who kept blocking Marcus' path when he was trying to get back to where the principal's office is?"

"Yes."

"Oh no!" Margarita, Tomas, Mary, Barry, Tonio, Marilyn, Nicolas and Michael whisper. They turn and shockingly look at each other. They then turn their heads back forward and continue to shockingly listen to Diane D's other personality.

"It was YOU who did that?!" Dr. Kahn asks. "My God it was YOU who kept blocking Marcus' path when he was trying to get back to where the principal's office is?!"

"Yes it was me," Diane D's other personality says.

"My goodness! Was it YOU who spun this physical body around and gave Marcus a kung fu kick knocking him down breaking his arm and wrist?!"

"Yes."

"It was YOU who did that to him too?!"

"Yes!"

"My goodness! Marcus also claim, that while he was laying helpless and injured on that third floor school hallway floor, Diane was just standing there staring at him and was in a trance while she was standing there! Marcus claim that Diane never once took her eyes off him and that her eyes kept following him no matter where he moved to! Diane claims she doesn't remember any of that stuff either! Was it YOU who kept standing there staring at Marcus while he was laying on the third floor injured?"

"Yes that was me."

"That was YOU too?!"

"Yes."

"Was it YOU who was standing in the school hallway in a trance?!"

"No."

Dr. Kahn and Dr. Stone puzzled look at each other, then back at Diane D's other personality as Dr. Stone asks, "It wasn't you who was standing there in the school hallway in a trance?"

"No. I was never in a trance in that school hallway."

"What!" Dr. Stone and Dr. Kahn say.

"You were never in a trance in that school hallway?!" Dr. Kahn asks.

"No," Diane D's other personality says.

"That's strange, because that's the exact same thing Diane said, that she was never in a trance inside that school hallway, but yet Marcus claim he saw Diane standing there in a state of trance! If Diane's original soul and spirit wasn't the one inside of this physical body at the time of the state of trance, I thought your soul or spirit might have been the one inside of this physical body at the time of the trance. So if your soul or spirit wasn't the one inside of this physical body when this physical body was standing there in a state of trance and Diane's original soul or spirit wasn't the one inside of this physical body when this physical body was standing there in a state of trance, then who's soul or spirit WAS inside this physical body when this physical body was standing there in the hallway in a state of trance?"

"No one's soul or spirit was inside this physical body when this physical body was in a state of trance."

"No one's soul or spirit was inside this physical body when this physical body was in a state of trance? What do you mean?"

"There was no soul or spirit inside this physical body when this physical body was in a state of trance."

"What!" Dr. Kahn and Dr. Stone shout.

"There was no soul or spirit inside this physical body while this physical body was standing there in a state of trance?!" Dr. Stone asks.

"No there wasn't," Diane D's other personality says.

"Where was your soul or spirit when this physical body was in a state of trance?"

"I had left this physical body temporary."

"What!" Dr. Kahn and Dr. Stone shout.

"You left this physical body while it was standing there in the hallway staring at Marcus?" Dr. Kahn asks.

"Yes," Diane D's other personality says.

"When your soul or spirit left this physical body temporary, did Diane's original soul or spirit return and come back into this physical body?"

"No."

"No? So no soul or spirit not even Diane's original soul or spirit was inside this physical body while it was standing there in the school hallway in a state of trance?!"

"No."

"You're not saying that this physical body was left standing on its own, are you?"

"Yes that's exactly what I'm saying."

"What! Dr. Kahn and Dr. Stone says.

"This physical body was left standing on its own?!" Dr. Stone asks. "You mean this physical body was just standing there in the school hallway without a soul or spirit inside of it?!"

"At that moment, yes," Diane D's other personality says.

"My God, how?!"

"When I left this physical body temporary, that's when it became in a state of trance because there was no soul or spirit inside it at the moment."

"No?! How was this physical body able to stand there on its own without falling down if no soul or spirit was inside of it at the time?!"

"It just happened."

"It just happened?!"

"Yes."

"But I don't get it, because Marcus said Diane's eyes kept following him the whole entire time on that third floor school hallway and claim that she NEVER ONCE took her eyes off him! Now in order for her to do THAT, it had to be a soul or spirit inside this physical body by then! Was it your soul or spirit back inside this physical body, causing its eyes to follow Marcus?"

"No. I wasn't inside this physical body during that time either."

"You weren't?"

"No."

"Was it Diane's original soul or spirit back inside this physical body, causing its eyes to follow Marcus?"

"No. Her soul or spirit wasn't inside this physical body during that time either."

"It wasn't?"

"No."

"Well if your soul or spirit wasn't the one inside this physical body during the time this physical body's eyes kept following Marcus, and if Diane's original soul or spirit wasn't the one inside this physical body during the time this physical body's eyes kept following Marcus, then WHOSE soul or spirit WAS the one inside this physical body, causing its eyes to follow Marcus?!"

"No one's! There was no soul or spirit inside this physical body when the eyes of this physical body was following that kid."

"What!" Dr. Kahn and Dr. Stone shout.

"There was no soul or spirit inside this physical body, causing its eyes to follow Marcus?!" Dr. Stone asks.

"No," Diane D other personality says.

"How can that be?!" Dr. Kahn asks. "How can the eyes of this physical body follow Marcus if there's no soul or spirit in it?!"

"Because his body became a magnet to the eyes of this physical body while I was temporarily away from it."

"What!" Dr. Kahn and Dr. Stone shout.

"Marcus' body became a magnet to the eyes of this physical body while your soul or spirit was away from it?!" Dr. Kahn asks.

"Yes," Diane D's other personality says.

"Oh my God! How did Marcus' body become a magnet to the eyes of this physical body while there's no soul or spirit in it?!"

"It just happened."

"It just happened?"

"Yes."

"Did you made it happen?"

"No. It happened on it's own."

"It happened on it's own?!"

"Yes."

"You had nothing to do with it?"

"No."

"How did it happen on its own if you had nothing to do with it?!"

"It just did."

"Maybe Diane's original soul or spirit had something to do with it."

"Her soul or spirit had nothing to do with it either."

"It didn't?"

"No."

"Plus Diane claims she doesn't remember staring at Marcus or having her eyes following him," Dr. Stone says. "This is so strange."

"It is," Dr. Kahn says. "Wow." He then says to Diane D's other personality, "So while your soul or spirit was gone away from this physical body temporarily, that's when this physical body is left standing in the hallway on its own with no soul or spirit inside of it, causing it to be left in a state of trance having its eyes fixed on Marcus following him."

"Exactly," Diane D's other personality says.

"No wonder why Marcus claim that Diane's eyes looked blank and seemed to have had no life in it while she was standing there in a state of trance, because there was no soul or spirit inside this physical body! Why did Marcus' body become a magnet to the eyes of this physical body having the eyes of this physical body keep following him?"

"It just did."

"Wow, that is so scary!"

"It is!" Dr. Stone says. "It's like having the eyes of a dead person following you!"

"It sure is! I can imagine what Marcus must have been going through! That poor kid!" Dr. Kahn and Dr. Stone puzzled stare at each other. They then look back at Diane D's other personality as Dr. Kahn says to it, "But while this physical body was left standing there in the hallway in a state of trance, Marcus said that his cell phone was laying across the floor after Diane had kung fu kicked it right out of his hand. He said that his cell phone suddenly rang. He claim that when he tried to reach for his cell phone, that's when Diane suddenly sprung into action and was about to charge right at him like if she was about to attack him again, so Marcus said he had to quickly back up and stop reaching for his cell phone! He said when he stopped reaching for his cell phone, that's when Diane stopped charging at him and started staring at him again. So if YOUR soul or spirit wasn't the one inside this physical body when this physical body was left standing in the hallway in a state of trance and Diane's original soul or spirit wasn't the one inside this physical body, then WHOSE soul or spirit WAS inside this physical body causing it to charge at Marcus when he tried to reach for his cell phone?! It had to be a soul or spirit inside this physical body by then! I know this physical body didn't about to charge at Marcus on its own! Who's soul or spirit was inside this physical body causing it to charge at Marcus?!"

"It was me," Diane D's other personality says.

"It was YOU? It was your soul or spirit who was about to charge at Marcus?!"

"Yes."

"I thought you said your soul or spirit left this physical body temporarily which made this physical body become in a state of trance!"

"I did leave this physical body at first, then I came back into it when I realized that kid was trying to reach for his cell phone."

"What!" Dr. Kahn and Dr. Stone shout.

"You came back into this physical body when you realized that Marcus was trying to reach for his cell phone?" Dr. Stone asks.

"Yes," Diane D's other personality says.

"My God! Marcus said that while he continued to lay there on the floor helpless, Diane went right back into a state of trance again! If you came back into this physical body when Marcus was trying to reach for his cell phone, then how did this physical body wind up back into a state of trance again?"

"I left this physical body again."

"You left this physical body again?"

"Yes."

"That's why Diane seem to have went right back into a state of trance again?"

"Yes."

"But Marcus claim, that when he tried to reach for his cell phone again, Diane suddenly sprung into action again and was about to charge right at him again, so he had to quickly back up again and stop reaching for his cell phone! He claim that when he stopped reaching for his cell phone again, that's when Diane stopped charging at him! How was she about to charge him again if you had left this physical body again?"

"I came back into this physical body again when I realized that kid was trying to reach for his cell phone again."

"You came back into this physical body again when you realized that Marcus was trying to reach for his cell phone again?"

"Yes."

"Why didn't you want Marcus to retrieve his cell phone?"

"For what?! So he can call out for help to whoever was on the other end of the phone?! Wasn't happening."

"You didn't want anyone who was on the other end of the phone to know where Marcus was nor to know what was happening to him?"

"No I didn't."

"So every time Marcus tried to reach for his cell phone, you came right back inside this physical body just in the nick of time to stop him!"

"Exactly."

"Then you would leave this physical body again."

"Exactly."

"Where did you go?! Where were you even at when you realized that Marcus was trying to reach for his cell phone?"

"You don't need to know."

"I don't?"

"No."

"Why did you leave this physical body temporary in the first place?" Dr. Kahn asks.

"I can't tell you?"

"You can't?"

"No."

"Why not?"

"I just can't!"

"I see. Marcus also claim he was throwing all kinds of objects at Diane to snap her out of her state of trance and said Diane never once moved or blink while she was getting hit with those objects! He said she just stood there like a mannequin, staring at him not moving like she didn't even see or feel the objects being thrown at her! He said even when Diane got hit right smack in the face with heavy paint cans that then fell hard on her feet, she just stood there like she didn't feel any pain! Maybe that's why Diane didn't seem to feel any pain when Marcus was throwing those heavy objects at her in the hallway, hitting her real hard. She wasn't there! Was there a soul or spirit inside this physical body, by the time Marcus was throwing those heavy objects at it?"

"Not at first."

"Not at first?"

"No."

"Is that why Diane had no feelings when Marcus was throwing those objects at her in the hallway?"

"No that's not why."

"It's not?"

"No. My soul and spirit came back inside this physical body during the middle of that kid throwing those objects at it."

"What! Your soul and spirit came back inside this physical body during the middle of Marcus throwing objects at it?"

"Yes."

"So what happened when your soul and spirit came back inside this physical body during the middle of Marcus throwing objects at it? Did you feel any pain?"

"No."

"You didn't feel any pain while your soul or spirit was inside this physical body getting hit real hard with all kinds of objects Marcus was throwing at it?"

"No."

"Why not?!"

"I don't feel pain."

"You don't feel pain?" Dr. Stone asks.

"No."

"Why not?"

"I just don't."

"But Diane feels pain, because when her original soul or spirit had came back inside this physical body later on when she woke up inside her family's van, she felt the pain from those injuries and started screaming. That means she felt the pain."

"Yes she feels pain, but I don't."

"You don't feel pain at all?"

"No."

"Why not?"

"I just don't."

"Wow, then your soul or spirit is definitely not of this world! May I ask what world are you from?"

"You don't need to know."

"I don't?"

"No."

"Why not?"

"You just don't."

"I see. Marcus said after he threw those objects at Diane, he got close to the back stairwell of that third floor school hallway. He claim that when he finally made it close to the back stairwell, he notice that Diane was creeping towards him getting closer and closer to him. Then he said he saw Diane running towards him! He said when he turned and escaped into the back stairwell and ran down the stairs, he heard the third floor stairwell door bang open so hard with such a loud bang that he felt the stairwell vibrate, then he heard Diane's footsteps jumping and charging down the staircase after him! Diane claims she remembers none of that stuff! She claims she doesn't remember creeping towards Marcus on that third floor hallway then running towards him. She claim she was NEVER in that back stairwell of that school. She said she does not remember ever being there! Now if Diane does not remember creeping towards Marcus on that third floor school hallway then running towards him, and she does not remember ever being in that back stairwell of the school chasing after Marcus down the back stairwell, then who's soul or spirit WAS the one who was creeping towards Marcus on the third floor school hallway then ran towards him?! Was it your soul or spirit inside this physical body at the moment who was creeping towards Marcus then ran towards him?"

"Yes."

"What!" Dr. Stone and Dr. Kahn shout.

"It was YOU who was creeping towards Marcus then ran towards him?!" Dr. Kahn asks.

"Yes it was me," Diane D's other personality says.

"Why were you creeping towards Marcus then ran towards him?"

"Because I saw that he was getting close to the back stairwell."

"You saw Marcus getting close to the back stairwell?"

"Yes."

"That's why you ran towards him?"

"Yes."

"When Marcus ran into the back stairwell, was it your soul, spirit and personality who bang the stairwell door open real hard and then jumped and charged down the staircase after him?"

"Yes."

"So it was YOU who chased after Marcus in the back stairwell?"

"Yes it was me!"

"It was not Diane."

"No she wasn't there!"

"So that's why she doesn't remember being there."

"Exactly."

"I see."

"Why were you chasing after Marcus in the hallway then in the back stairwell?" Dr. Stone asks. "You already beated him up on the third floor school hallway. Why were you chasing after him in the back stairwell?"

"Because I wasn't done with him yet," Diane D's other personality says.

"You weren't done with him yet? What do you mean you weren't done with him yet?! You already beated him to a pulp! You kung fu kicked him and broke his ribs and practically broke all his other bones and everything else! He was bleeding all over that third floor school hallway! What more did you want to do to him that night?!"

"I wanted to kill him."

"What!" Dr. Stone and Dr. Kahn shout. "Kill him?!"

Margarita, Tomas, Mary, Barry, Tonio, Marilyn, Nicolas and Michael shockingly sit there with mouths wide open not believing what they just heard! They turn and shockingly look at each other! They turn their heads back forward and shockingly look at Diane D's other personality not believing what her other personality just said!

"You wanted to kill Marcus?!" Dr. Kahn shouts. "You wanted him dead?!"

"That's right," Diane D's other personality says.

"For God's sakes why?!"

"Because he hurted Diane!"

"Oh my God! You really wanted to kill Marcus for that?! Seriously?!"

"Yes!"

"But Diane doesn't want Marcus dead! When she and her family were at the police station and she found out from the police officer that Marcus was planning to commit suicide and would have to be on a suicide watch, she decided to try one last time to talk to him on the phone to tell him that she forgives him so he can accept her forgiveness and hopefully his nightmares of her will end so he won't feel that he has to kill himself! That's proof right there that she does not want

Marcus dead!"

"No she doesn't want him dead! But I do!"

"Really?! Oh my God, that's why you were trying to kill him in that school back stairwell?!"

"Yes!"

"Then why didn't you have already done so while you and he were all alone on that third floor school hallway?!" Dr. Stone shouts. "Marcus claim he kept screaming for help while he was trapped alone with Diane on that third floor school hallway! He says he was trapped with Diane for a while! All that time your soul or spirit was alone with him on that third floor school hallway kung fu kicking him, breaking his bones and holding him hostage, you could have killed him right then and there if you really wanted to! Why did you wait until Marcus got into that back stairwell of the school to try to kill him?!"

"Because I wanted to wait until he got far away from Diane's family to do it!"

Margarita, Tomas, Mary, Barry, Tonio, Marilyn, Nicolas and Michael continue to shockingly sit there with mouths wide open still not believing what they just heard! They turn and shockingly look at each other again! They turn their heads back forward and shockingly look back at Diane D's other personality not believing the other statement her other personality just said!

"What!" Dr. Kahn and Dr. Stone shout.

"You wanted to wait until Marcus got far away from Diane's family to kill him?!" Dr. Stone asks.

"Exactly," Diane D's other personality says.

"Why?! Why did you want to wait until Marcus got far away from Diane's family to kill him?!"

"Because I didn't want to kill him too close to her family."

"What! You didn't want to kill Marcus too close to Diane's family?!"

"No."

"Why not?!"

"So they wouldn't be involved!"

"So they wouldn't be involved?!"

"That's right!"

"Why didn't you want Diane's family involved in your heinious vicious act?!"

"Because I wanted to protect her family."

"You wanted to protect Diane's family?!"

"Yes."

"Why? Why did you want to protect her family?!"

"Because she loves her family."

"Because she loves them?"

"Yes. I didn't want her hurt by having her family involved."

"You didn't want Diane hurt by having her family involved?!"

"No."

"But don't you realize, that anything Diane becomes involved in, her family automatically becomes involved in also, because that's her family! Why did you want to kill Marcus anyway?! Don't you think you did enough damage to him?!"

"No I don't think I did enough damage to him!"

"You don't think you did?!"

"No!"

"Why not?!"

"Because I didn't get a chance to kill him!"

"But if you would have killed Marcus inside the back stairwell of that school, guess who's the one who would have got put away?! It would have been Diane! She would have got put away in jail, prison or a mental hospital if YOU would have killed Marcus! When you beat up Marcus inside that school hallway, guess who's the one who DID get put away? It was Diane! She got put away in a mental institution and was committed to the mental hospital for several months for what YOU did to Marcus! Do you at least care about that?!"

"Yes I do."

"You do?! How?! How do you care about that if you're the one who did this heinous act on that little boy and caused Diane to wind up being put away?!"

"Because while she was in the mental institution, I took her place."

"What!" Dr Kahn and Dr. Stone shout.

"You took her place?!" Dr. Stone asks. "What do you mean 'you took her place'?!"

"While she was serving time in the mental institution, I came into her physical body again," Diane D's other personality says.

"What!" Dr. Kahn and Dr. Stone shout.

"You came into this physical body while Diane was serving time in the mental institution?!" Dr. Stone shouts.

"Yes," Diane D's other personality says.

"Oh my God! How?!"

"By pulling her original soul and spirit out of this physical body!"

"What!" Dr. Kahn and Dr. Stone shout.

"By pulling her original soul and spirit out of this physical body?!" Dr. Stone shouts.

"You pulled Diane's original soul and spirit out of this physical body, while she was in the mental institution?!" Dr. Kahn shouts.

"Yes," Diane D's other personality says.

"Oh my God! Why?!"

"So I can come into her physical body again!"

"So you can come into her physical body again?"

"Yes."

"Why did you come into her physical body while she was in the mental institution?!" Dr. Stone asks.

"To serve the time for her."

"To serve the time for her?!"

"Yes."

"Why?"

"So she wouldn't have to."

"So she wouldn't have to?! You mean you come into this physical body while Diane is in the mental institution to serve time for her so she wouldn't have to serve the time herself?!"

"Exactly."

"My goodness! Are you saying, that YOU be inside this physical body while Diane is in the mental institution, and the people inside the mental institution don't even know?!"

"No they don't know."

"My goodness! Where was Diane's original soul or spirit while you were serving the time in the mental institution for her?"

"She was free as a bird, wandering the universe."

"She was free as a bird, wandering the universe again? Then whenever her soul or spirit comes back into this physical body, she claims she doesn't know why her soul or spirit was out there in the universe and doesn't know who or what put her soul or spirit out there and does not remember any actions that happened inside the mental institution, because YOU were the one who was there in that place instead of her?!"

"Exactly."

"But I don't understand, because Diane's family always stay with her while she's in the mental institution! Do you be inside this physical body while Diane's family be staying with her while she's in the mental institution?"

"No. I do not be around when her family stays there with her. Her original soul and spirit would be there."

"Her original soul and spirit would be there at the mental institution while her family is staying there with her?"

"Yes."

"I thought you said you served time for Diane while she's in the mental institution."

"I do. But only when her family steps away."

"Only when her family steps away?"

"Yes."

"Why only when her family steps away?"

"I don't normally have an encounter with her family."

"You don't?"

"No."

"Why not?"

"Because that's HER family. I leave that encounter to her."

"You do?"

"Yes I do."

"What about the times when Diane had served time in jail?" Dr. Kahn asks. "Do you be inside her physical body when she's in jail?"

"Yes I do."

"What!!" Dr. Kahn and Dr. Stone shout.

"You came into this physical body while Diane was serving time inside jail too?!" Dr. Stone shouts.

"Yes I did," Diane D's other personality says.

"My God, how?! By pulling her original soul and spirit out of this physical body while she's in jail too?!

"Exactly."

"So you can come into her physical body while she's in jail to serve the time for her there too?"

"Exactly."

"Why are you serving time for Diane while she's in jail?"

"So she wouldn't have to serve the time!"

"So she wouldn't have to serve time in jail either?!"

"Exactly."

"So you're saying, that you be inside this physical body while Diane is in jail, and the people inside the jail don't know it either?!"

"No they don't know."

"So they just assume, that you're Diane's original soul and spirit."

"Exactly."

"My goodness!"

"Where was Diane's original soul or spirit while you were serving the time in the jail?" Dr. Kahn asks.

"She was free as a bird again, wandering the universe," Diane D's other personality says.

"She was free as a bird, wandering the universe again?"

"Yes."

"What about when her family comes to visit her while she's in jail? Do you be inside this physical body while Diane's family be visiting her in jail?"

"No. I do not be around when her family comes to visit her in jail either. Her original soul and spirit would be back by then."

"Her original soul and spirit would be back by the time her family comes to visit her in jail?"

"Yes."

"Wow. So therefore, her family has never had an encounter with you inside the jail or inside the mental institution?"

"No they haven't."

"Well since you were inside this physical body while Diane was in jail, are you the one who gave those correction officers inside that jail cell a hard time when they were trying to keep Diane inside there?"

"Yes."

"It was YOU?!"

"Yes."

"Are you the one who beat up those security guards and those police officers at Diane's family's organization, which caused Diane to wind up being tossed and thrown in jail in the first place?"

"Yes."

"It was YOU?"

"Yes it was me!"

"Then it was YOU who bent that ten foot pole that was inside the jail cell, didn't you?!"

"Yes that was me."

"All of that was you?"

"Yes, all of it!"

"Why did you do that? Why did you beat up the security guards and police officers at Diane's family's organization causing Diane to be locked up for a few months?"

"Because they upsetted her! I don't like anybody upsetting Diane. If they do, then I get upset then they'll have to deal with me!"

"They'll have to deal with you?"

"That's right!"

"Were you the one inside the jail cell who looked right at a nurse who came into the jail cell the next morning to check on Diane? Because the nurse told those correction officers who were waiting outside the jail cell that morning, that when she went inside the jail cell to check on Diane, she claim that Diane had opened her eyes and was looking right at her. The nurse told those correction officers that Diane had stared at her for a while, but Diane said she never saw a nurse inside her jail cell because by the time she woke up, it was already afternoon. Are you the soul, spirit or personality who was looking right at the nurse who came into the jail cell that morning?"

"Yes it was me."

"It was YOU who looked at the nurse and was staring at her?"

"Yes."

"Where was Diane's original soul or spirit at that time?"

"Her soul and spirit was still free wandering the universe."

"It was?"

"Yes."

"Why haven't you left her physical body at that time yet? Why was your soul or spirit still inside this physical body by the time the nurse came into the cell?"

"Because I was waiting for those correction officers to come back into the cell."

"You were waiting for the correction officers to come back?"

"Yes."

"Why? Why were you waiting for them to come back into the cell?"

"Because I wasn't done with them yet."

"You weren't done with them yet?"

"What do you mean 'you weren't done with them yet'?" Dr. Stone asks.

"I wasn't done trying to attack them," Diane D's other personality says.

"You weren't done trying to attack them? What do you mean 'you weren't done trying to attack them'?"

"I didn't really get a chance to attack them the night before. They kept poking that damn pole at these ribs so I stayed in that cell overnight to wait for them to come back."

"You stayed in that cell overnight to wait for those correction officers to come back?" Dr. Kahn asks.

"Yes I did."

"So what happened? Did they ever come back? Did you ever get the chance to attack them?"

"No, because they never came back into the cell."

"I don't blame them! So what happened when the correction officers never came back into the cell? Did you continue to stay inside this physical body to wait for them?"

"No. I gave up and left this physical body that afternoon."

"You did?"

"Yes."

"So that's the only reason why you stayed inside this physical body overnight, was to wait for those correction officers to come back into the cell to put an attack on them?"

"Exactly."

"Wow! So being that the correction officers never came back into the cell, you left this physical body that afternoon, that's when Diane's original soul and spirit came back?"

"Yes."

"And by the time her original soul and spirit came back into this physical body, the nurse had already left the cell. That's why Diane never saw the nurse that morning even though the nurse said that Diane had opened her eyes and was looking right at her staring at her, because it was YOU who was still inside this physical body looking at the nurse staring at her."

"Yes it was me."

"Why were you staring at the nurse anyway?"

"To see who she was."

"To see who she was?"

"Yes."

"Why?"

"To see if it was one of those damn correction officers!"

"To see if it was one of those correction officers?"

"Yes."

"And as you're staring at the nurse, you see that she is NOT one of those correction officers that you were waiting for all night. What would have happened if it WAS one of those correction officers there inside the jail cell instead of the nurse?"

"I would have attacked them!"

"You would have attacked one of those correction officers?!"

"Yes."

"Wow. You sound like you were very determined to get them! It's a good thing they never came back into the cell!"

"I still could have gotten them, even though they never came back into the cell."

"What? Wait a minute. You just said you still could have gotten those correction officers even though they never came back into the cell?"

"Yes, if I really wanted to."

"If you really wanted to?"

"Yes."

"How? How were you going to get to them?! By kung fu kicking the cell door wide open then breaking out of the cell?!"

"No."

"Then how would you have gotten to them?!"

"I could have went and possessed one of their physical bodies if I really wanted to."

"What!" Dr. Kahn and Dr. Stone shout.

"You could have went and possessed one of those correction officer's physical body if you really wanted to?" Dr. Stone shouts. "How?"

"By leaving this physical body then approach one of their physical bodies," Diane D's other personality says. "Then I would pull their soul or spirit out of their physical body then enter their physical body and beat the hell out of the other correction officers."

"What!" Dr. Kahn and Dr. Stone shout.

"You could have done THAT?!" Dr. Kahn shouts.

"Yes I could have," Diane D's other personality says.

"My God! So what happened? You didn't do that, did you?"

"No. I decided not to do that, so I left."

"You did?"

"Yes."

"But if you would have taken over one of those correction officers' physical bodies and used their physical body to beat the hell out of the other correction officers, the other correction officers would have thought that certain correction officer suddenly went crazy!"

"Yes they would have thought that."

"They would have no idea that it would have been YOU inside his physical body."

"No they wouldn't."

"Wow. Well thank God you decided not to take over any of their physical bodies because taking over Diane's physical body is enough! Are you the one who kung fu kicked that stuck storage room door at the other hospital?"

"Yes."

"What!" Dr. Kahn and Dr. Stone shout.

"That was you too?" Dr. Stone asks.

"Yes that was me," Diane D's other personality says.

"Why did you do that? Why did you kung fu kick that stuck storage room door then went inside the storage room and did all that damage in there?"

"Because I was looking for whoever could have been hiding in there."

"You were looking for whoever could have been hiding inside that storage room?"

"That's right."

"Why were you looking for someone?"

"Because someone was spying on Diane and I didn't like it."

"Someone was spying on Diane?"

"Yes."

"Who?"

"Two hospital employees."

"Two hospital employees?"

"Yes."

"They were spying on Diane?"

"Yes."

"What were they spying on Diane doing?"

"They were eavesdropping on her while she was on the phone having a private conversation."

"They were eavesdropping on Diane while she was on the phone?"

"Yes."

"Where was she when she was on the phone?"

"She was inside one of the rooms in the clinic area with the door closed."

"Diane was inside one of the rooms in the clinic area?"

"Yes."

"Where were the two hospital employees?"

"They were outside the door eavesdropping, listening to her phone conversation."

"They were?"

"Yes."

"Did Diane know that someone was eavesdropping on her listening to her phone conversation?"

"No, not at first. She suspected it later on."

"She suspected it later on?"

"Yes."

"Did she know who the two hospital employees were who were eavesdropping on her?"

"Not at first."

"She didn't know who they were at first either?"

"No."

"Then how did she figure out who they were? The two hospital employees claimed, that Diane never saw them inside that clinic hallway that night where she heard the tray dropped. They said they were gone by the time she got to that corner of the clinic hallway. So if Diane never saw who was inside the clinic hallway, then how did she know who the two hospital employees were who was spying on her?!"

"I whispered in her head and told her."

"What!" Dr. Stone and Dr. Kahn shout.

"You whispered in her head?" Dr. Stone asks.

"Yes I did," Diane D's other personality says.

"How?"

"I can't tell you."

"You can't tell me?"

"No."

"Did she know that you whispered in her head?"

"Yes."

"She knew you whispered in her head?"

"Yes."

"How did she feel about that?"

"She was upset when she found out who was spying on her?"

"She was upset when she found out who it was?"

"Yes."

"So you know who the two hospital employees were that were spying on Diane?"

"Yes I do."

"Well who are they?"

"I can't tell you."

"You can't?"

"No."

"Why not?"

"I just can't!"

"Okay. So what did YOU do, when you found out that the two hospital emoployees were spying on Diane?"

"I decided to enter this physical body to go after them."

"What!" Dr. Stone and Dr. Kahn shout.

"You decided to entered this physical body to go after them?!" Dr. Stone asks.

"Yes," Diane D's other personality says.

"How did you enter this physical body?"

"By pulling Diane's soul and spirit out of it then entering it while she was in the stairwell."

"What? You pulled Diane's original soul and spirit out of this physical body then entered this physical body while she was in the stairwell?"

"Yes."

"Just like you pulled her soul or spirit out of this physical body and entered it while she was in the corner of the school hallway so you can go after and attack that little boy Marcus?"

"Yes."

"Just like you pulled her soul or spirit out of this physical body and entered it while she was in the jail cell so you can go after and attack those correction officers? Now you pull her soul or spirit out of this physical body and enter it while Diane was in the stairwell of the clinic area so you can go after and attack those two hospital employees?"

"Exactly."

"My God! You seem to just come along and pull Diane's original soul and spirit out of this physical body at will, then just enter into it!"

"Thats's true," Dr. Kahn says. "So what happened after you entered this physical body inside the stairwell of the clinic area?"

"I went to go after the two hospital employees," Diane D's other personality says.

"You went to go after the two hospital employees?"

"Yes."

"Where did you go?"

"I went to the lower level of the clinic area to look for them."

"You went to the lower level of the clinic area to look for them?"

"Yes."

"Then what happened when you got to the lower level of the clinic area?"

"I didn't see them anywhere."

"You didn't?"

"No."

"If you didn't see them anywhere, how did the storage room door and the storage room get damage?"

"I went in there."

"You did?"

"Yes."

"Why? Why did you go inside the storage room if you didn't see the two hospital employees anywhere?"

"I thought that the two hospital employees were hiding in there."

"You thought the two hospital employees were hiding inside the storage room?"

"Yes."

"What made you think, that they were hiding inside there?"

"Because I heard and saw the storage room door move."

"You heard and saw the storage room door moving?"

"Yes."

"So what did you do?"

"I went to the storage room door to open it."

"You did?"

"Yes."

"Then what happened?"

"I didn't get it opened at first."

"You didn't?"

"No."

"So what did you do next?"

"I backed up. Then I ran straight to the storage room door and kung fu kicked it wide open to get into the storage room to look for whoever was spying on Diane."

"You kung fu kicked the storage room door wide open?!"

"Yes I did."

"So YOU'RE the one who kung fu kicked the storage room door and damaged it and knocked it right off its hinges?"

"Yes I'm the one."

"Just to go in there to look for whoever might have been spying on Diane."

"Yes."

"My God. Then what happened when you went into the storage room?"

"I started looking for whoever could have been hiding in there."

"You did?"

"Yes."

"How did you look for them?"

"By moving and tossing all that office furniture around in there."

"You were the one who moved and tossed all that office furniture around that was inside the storage room? YOU'RE the one who damaged the storage room too?"

"Yes I'm the one."

"YOU'RE the one who turned all that heavy office furniture in there upside down?!"

"Yes that was me."

"My God. You didn't find anyone hiding inside that storage room, did you?"

"No."

"What would have happened, if you HAD found someone hiding inside that storage room?"

"I would have beat the hell out of them and kill them."

"What?!" Dr. Kahn and Dr. Stone shout.

Margarita, Tomas, Mary, Barry, Tonio, Marilyn, Nicolas and Michael shockingly sit their with mouths wide open again not believing what they just heard! They turn and shockingly look at each other again! They turn their heads back forward and shockingly look back at Diane D's other personality not believing the other statement her other personality just said!

"You would have beat the hell out of them and kill them?!" Dr. Stone shouts.

"Yes I would," Diane D's other personality says.

"Just like you had beat the hell out of Marcus and was ready to kill him in the back stairwell?!"

"Exactly."

"But why?!" Dr. Kahn asks. "Why would you had beat the hell out of someone or kill them, if you had found them hiding inside that storage room?!"

"Because that means they were the ones who were spying on Diane!"

"Not necessarily! It could have been an innocent person inside that storage room who had absolutely nothing to do with spying on Diane! It could have been another hospital employee who was hiding inside that storage room to catch up on some sleep! Would you still had beat them up or try to kill them if you had found them in there?"

"Yes I would have."

"You would?!"

"Yes!"

"Why?!"

"Because that means they would have witnessed me damaging the storage room door and the storage room, then tell everyone that it was Diane who they saw did it! And that's exactly what those two hospital employees did, told everyone that Diane damaged the storage room door and the storage room."

"Yes, and when they told everyone that Diane damaged the storage room door and the storage room, Diane got in trouble by her family. Her family had the hospital fire her! Not only that, her family wind up banning her from performing, then they sent her packing to the Dominican Republic for a while! She got punished by her family by what YOU did!"

"That's why I would have beat the hell out of or try to kill whoever I had found hiding inside that storage room, to keep them from witnessing it, to keep them from telling everyone that Diane is the one who did it!"

"So you were willing to silence the witness."

"If it means keeping Diane out of trouble, yes."

"My God! You seem to have no problem with talking about killing somebody!"

"I would kill anybody for Diane."

"You would?!"

"Yes I would."

"But I don't think Diane would kill anybody herself! Of course she loses her temper at times and would get out of control, or unless it was actually YOU who was inside her body getting out of control, but I don't think she's a killer!"

"She's not a killer!"

"Well thank God for that!"

"But I am!"

"What!" Dr. Kahn and Dr. Stone shout.

Margarita, Tomas, Mary, Barry, Tonio, Marilyn, Nicolas and Michael continue to shockingly sit their with mouths wide open not believing what they just heard! They turn and shockingly look at each other again! They turn their heads back forward and shockingly look back at Diane D's other personality not believing the statement her other personality just said!

"You are?!" Dr. Kahn asks.

"For Diane, yes," Diane D's other personality says.

"Oh my Lord," Dr. Stone shockingly says. "Have you ever killed anybody before?"

"Yes," Diane D's other personality says. "Several times."

"What!" Dr. Stone and Dr. Kahn shout. "Several times?!"

Margarita, Tomas, Mary, Barry, Tonio, Marilyn, Nicolas and Michael shockingly sit their with mouths wide open again not believing what they just heard! They turn and shockingly look at each other again! They turn their heads back forward and shockingly look back at Diane D's other personality not believing what her other personality just said!

"You have killed several times?!" Dr. Stone shouts.

"Yes I have," Diane D's other personality says.

"Oh my God, who?! Who have you killed?!"

"You don't need to know."

"Yes I do need to know! Who have you killed?! How many people and when did this happen?!"

"It happened way before your time."

"What?!" Dr. Stone and Dr. Kahn shout. They shockingly look at each other. Then they look back at Diane D's other personality.

"Way before my time?" Dr. Stone asks. "It happened way before my time?! What do you mean 'it happened way before my time'?!"

"It happened hundreds of years ago," Diane D's other personality says.

"Hundreds of years ago?!" Dr. Stone and Dr. Kahn shout. Dr. Stone and Dr. Kahn puzzled look at Diane's other personality! Then then look at each other. They look back at Diane D's other personality as Dr. Stone asks it, "How old is your soul or spirit? How long has your soul or spirit been around?!"

"My soul and spirit has been around for several hundred years," Diane D's other personality says.

"What!" Dr. Stone and Dr. Kahn shout. "Several hundred years!"

"Your soul and spirit has been around for several hundred years?!" Dr. Kahn shouts. "Oh my God! Have you ever had a physical body?"

"No," Diane D's other personality says.

"You never had a physical body?"

"No."

"So you were always a spirit?!"

"Yes."

"So how did you kill people if you never had a physical body?!"

"I approached other people's physical bodies."

"What!" Dr. Kahn and Dr. Stone shout.

"You approached other people's physical bodies?!" Dr. Kahn shouts.

"That's right," Diane D's other personality says.

"Then what happened when you approached their physical bodies?"

"I pulled their original soul and spirit out of their physical bodies. Then I entered their physical bodies and used their physical bodies to kill other people."

"What!" Dr. Stone shouts. "You pulled people's original souls and spirits out of their physical bodies, then entered their physical bodies and used their physical bodies to kill other people, just like you pulled Diane's original soul and spirit out of her physical body then entered her physical body and used her physical body to harm that little boy Marcus and other people in the past?!"

"That's right."

"So whose physical bodies have you used to kill other people with hundreds of years ago? It couldn't have been this physical body that you used because this physical body wasn't around hundreds of years ago! So whose physical bodies have you used to kill other people?!"

"A lot of people's physical bodies."

"A lot of people's physical bodies?! Like who?! Were they men or women?!"

"Mostly men."

"Mostly men?! You possessed a lot of men's physical bodies in the past and caused them to kill?!"

"Exactly."

"Where? In what part of the world?!"

"Different parts of the world."

"Different parts of the world?!"

"Yes."

"In what century?"

"In all the centuries I've been around."

"In all the centuries you've been around in?! So you have gone through different parts of the world through the centuries and entered different people's physical bodies to commit murder?!"

"That's right."

"When was the first time, your soul or spirit entered someone's physical body then used their physical body to commit murder?"

"Around several hundred years ago."

"Around several hundred years ago?! What century was that?"

"In the mid 1400's."

"In the mid 1400's?!"

"Yes."

"That was six centuries ago. What happened back then?"

"This man was meditating."

"A man was meditating? Where?"

"In Asia."

"In Asia? A man was meditating in Asia six centuries ago?"

"Yes."

"What part of Asia?"

"You don't need to know."

"I don't?"

"No."

"Why not?"

"You just don't."

"Okay. Then what happened while this man was meditating?"

"After a while, I was drawn to his physical body."

"You were drawn to his physical body?"

"Yes."

"Why?"

"Because his meditation had drawn me to him."

"His meditation drawned you to him?"

"Yes."

"Just like Diane's meditation draws you to her whenever SHE meditates!"

"Exactly."

"Then what happened once your soul and spirit was drawn to this man's physical body?"

"I pulled his original soul and spirit out of his physical body. Then I entered his physical body and killed someone."

"You pulled this man's original soul and spirit out of his physical body, then entered his physical body and killed someone?!"

"Yes."

"My God! Who was it that you killed while your soul and spirit was inside his physical body?"

"You don't need to know."

"I don't?"

"No."

"Did this man whose body you possessed ever got in trouble when you used his physical body to kill someone?"

"Yes he got in trouble."

"He got in trouble?"

"Yes."

"What happened when he got in trouble?"

"He went to jail and prison."

"He went to jail and prison?"

"Yes."

"Then what happened once he got to jail and prison? Did you take over his physical body then sat in jail or prison for him?"

"Yes I did."

"What!" Dr. Stone and Dr. Kahn shout.

"You sat in jail and prison for him too like you did for Diane?!" Dr. Stone shouts.

"Yes I did," Diane D's other personality says.

"So of course the people inside the jail or prison had no idea that another soul or spirit was inside this man's physical body."

"No they had no idea."

"My God! Then what happened after you sat in jail or prison for him?"

"I helped him escape."

"You helped this man escape?" Dr. Kahn asks.

"Yes I did."

"How did you help him escape?"

"I used his physical body to escape. Once I escaped using his physical body, I left his physical body."

"You left his physical body afterwards?"

"Yes."

"That's when his original soul and spirit returned?"

"Yes."

"Then he winds up not remembering how he escaped from jail or prison because it was really YOU who was doing the escaping."

"Exactly."

"Was he ever caught again?"

"No."

"He was never caught again?"

"No."

"So what happened to him? Did he ever live a normal life?"

"You don't need to know."

"I don't?"

"No."

"Did anybody ever knew that there was a different soul or spirit inside this man's physical body doing the killing?"

"No, no one knew until now when I just told you."

"So no one in this man's time ever knew, that his physical body was possessed by your soul or spirit."

"No, nobody knew."

"Wow."

"When was the second time your soul or spirit entered someone's physical body then used their physical body to commit murder?" Dr. Stone asks.

"Around fifty years later," Diane D's other personality says.

"Around fifty years later after the first one? So that means the second killing happened around the early 1500's?"

"Yes."

"What happened?"

"Another man was meditating."

"Another man was meditating? Where?"

"In Asia."

"In Asia again?"

"Yes."

"Then what happened?"

"I was drawn to his physical body."

"You were drawned to this man's physical body just because he was meditating too?"

"Exactly."

"Then what happened once you were drawned to this man's physical body?"

"I pulled his original soul and spirit out of his physical body, then I entered his physical body and killed someone else."

"You used that man's physical body also to commit murder?!"

"Yes."

"My God! Who was it that you killed while your soul or spirit was inside his physical body?!"

"You don't need to know."

"I don't need to know that either?"

"That's right."

"Did he ever get caught?"

"No."

"He never got caught either?" Dr. Kahn asks.

"No."

"Did he ever live a normal life after you used his physical body to commit murder?"

"You don't need to know."

"I don't?"

"No."

"Did anybody in this second man's time ever knew, that there was a different soul or spirit inside his physical body doing the killing?"

"No, no one knew."

"No? So no one in that second man's time ever knew, that this man's physical body was possessed by your soul or spirit too."

"No."

"Wow. Does your soul or spirit usually get drawned to people's physical bodies whenever they meditate?"

"Sometimes."

"Sometimes?"

"Yes."

"Why does your soul or spirit get drawned to people's physical bodies whenever they meditate?"

"It just happens?"

"Oh yeah? Just like it happens whenever Diane meditates. So people's meditations seem to open doors for you and allows your soul and spirit to approach their physical bodies and just pull their original soul or spirit out of their physical bodies then you enter their physical bodies to do harm to other people! Why did you kill someone when you entered those two men's physical bodies back in the 1400's and 1500's?"

"You don't need to know."

"I don't?"

"No."

"Wow. It sounds like Diane is not your first victim whose physical body you use to harm other people with!"

"She's not my first victim. She's my twelth."

"What?!" Dr. Kahn and Dr. Stone shout. "Your twelth?!"

"You mean you have taken the physical bodies of nine more other people in the past and used their physical bodies to harm other people with and commit murder?!" Dr. Stone shouts.

"Yes," Diane D's other personality says.

"How often have you used different people's physical bodies to commit murder?!"

"Around once every fifty years."

"Once every fifty years?! You mean ever since you committed the first murder in Asia back in the mid 1400s?!"

"Yes."

"So if you committed the first murder back in the mid 1400's, and it is now the 2000's, that means you used someone's physical body and committed murder eleven times! That means you so far killed eleven people through out the world and through out the centuries! And if you used different people's physical bodies to commit murder around once every fifty years, that means you used someone's physical body to commit murder within the past fifty years! Did you use someone's physical body to commit murder within the past fifty years?"

"Yes, I sure did."

"You did?!"

"Yes."

"Where did it happen?"

"In Europe."

"It happened in Europe this time?!"

"Yes."

"Who's physical body did you use and possess to commit murder within the past fifty years in Europe? Was it a man's physical body or a woman's physical body?"

"It was a man's physical body."

"Another man's physical body?"

"Yes."

"What man?"

"You don't need to know."

"I do need to know! And I need to know who did you kill!

"It's not for you to know!"

"It's not?!"

"No!"

"Was the person whose physical body you used to commit murder within the past fifty years ever caught?"

"No they weren't."

"They were never caught?!"

"No."

"Are they still alive? Because since this murder happened only fifty years ago, it's a possibility that person can still be alive today! Is that person whose body your soul or spirit possessed fifty years ago in Europe still alive today?"

"You don't need to know."

"I don't?"

"No."

"Why not?"

"You just don't!"

"Well maybe I should have the police come right in here and interrogate you to say who the person is or who they were, don't you think?! Because if that person is still alive, they can still be brought to justice!"

"Go right ahead, get the police! By the time the police come here and want to interrogate me, my soul and spirit will be gone away from this physical body and away from this earth. The police won't be able to catch me! But, there is only way the police will be able to catch me."

"There's only one way?"

"Yes."

"And what way is that?"

"Is if they leave this earth too."

"Is if they leave this earth too?"

"Exactly. But once they leave this world, they won't be able to come back."

"No? Why not? You don't mean because they'll be dead, do you?"

"Yes that's exactly what I mean. Now you don't want the police to have to leave this earth in order for them to try and catch me, do you?"

Dr. Stone and Dr. Kahn nervously look Diane D's other personality. Then they nervously look at each other. Dr. Stone turns back to Diane D's other personality and says, "No. I wouldn't want that to happen."

"I didn't think so. And it won't make sense for the police to get anything out of Diane either when her soul or spirit returns because she knows nothing about my past crimes. It happened way before her time as well."

"My goodness! So if your soul or spirit enter different people's physical bodies around once every fifty years and commits a murder, and your soul or spirit entered someone's physical body within the LAST fifty years and committed another murder, that means fifty years is up again! That means your soul or spirit will commit murder again within these recent years and commit another murder fifty years from now!"

"Most likely."

"My God! Have you used someone's physical body to commit murder within the past twenty or thirty years?"

"No."

"You haven't?"

"No."

"Are you planning to use someone's physical body to commit murder within the next twenty or thirty years?"

"Most likely."

"Most likely?! So who's physical body are you planning to use to commit another murder? I sure hope it won't be Diane's physical body, will it?!"

"We shall see."

"We shall see?! So since you have not used someone's physical body to commit murder within the past twenty or thirty years, that means you have never used Diane's physical body to commit murder so far."

"I was about to."

"What!" Dr. Stone and Dr. Kahn shout. "You were about to?!"

"What do you mean 'you were about to'?!" Dr. Stone shouts.

"If I would have caught up with that kid in the back stairwell of that school, that would have been my first time using this physical body to commit murder," Diane D's other personality says.

"What!" Dr. Stone and Dr. Kahn shout.

"If you would have caught up with Marcus in the back stairwell of the school, that would have been your first time using Diane's physical body to commit murder?!" Dr. Stone shouts.

"That's right," Diane D's other personality says. "If that kid hadn't escape into that back stairwell of the school, he would have been a dead kid."

"A dead kid?!" Dr. Stone and Dr. Kahn shout.

"That's right. He would have been my twelfth murder victim."

"Your twelfth murder victim?!" Dr. Stone and Dr. Kahn shout.

"Oh my Lord!" Dr. Stone shouts. "That is terrible! Don't you know that if you would had killed Marcus using this physical body, Diane would have been the one sitting in prison or in the mental institution for what YOU would have done?!"

"No she wouldn't."

"She wouldn't?"

"No."

"How not?!"

"Because I would have took her place again."

"You would have took her place in prison or in the mental institution again?!"

"Yes."

"And where would her soul or spirit be?!"

"Roaming free wandering the universe."

"Roaming free wandering the universe?! You mean you would have come into her physical body to serve time for her again and let her soul and spirit roam free wandering the universe again?!"

"Yes."

"Why?!"

"It's not her crime, it's my crime! I'll do the time!"

"You'll do the time?"

"That's right!"

"My God! You seem to have no problem with sitting in jail, prison or the mental institution for Diane!"

"No I don't. As long as it's for her, I have no problem with it."

"My God! Why do you kill people anyway?!"

"You don't need to know."

"I DO need to know! I HAVE to know! Why do you kill people in the first place, especially around once every fifty years?! And why haven't God caught up with you yet?!"

"You don't need to know!"

"Okay, calm down. Calm down. I just want to say thank God Marcus escaped into that back stairwell of that school because I think he would have definitely been your twelfth murder victim if you would have caught up with him! And thank God you didn't find anyone hiding inside that storage room at the other hospital when you kung fu kicked the door wide open because I don't think they would have made it out of there alive with the power and strength I heard your soul and spirit had that night! I think if anyone was hiding inside that storage room, they would have definitely been your twelvth murder victim instead of Marcus since he managed to escape from you in that back stairwell of the school and you weren't able to get to him! Now what I need, is for you to answer this very important question that I'm about to ask you. How do you feel about Marcus now as we speak? Do you still want to kill him?"

"Yes I do."

"What!" Dr Kahn and Dr. Stone shout.

"You still want to kill Marcus?!" Dr Kahn shouts.

"Yes," Diane D's other personality shouts.

"Even now?!"

"Yes, even now!"

"Why?! Why do you still want to kill Marcus?! You're not looking for him to be your twelvth murder victim are you?!"

"Why not?!"

"Why not?!" Dr. Stone shouts. "But if you kill Marcus, Diane is the one who's gonna be put away in a mental institution again!"

"Then I'll just take her place again!"

"But what about Marcus' family?! Don't you think if you kill Marcus, his family will be devastated?!"

"I don't care about his family!" Diane D's other personality shouts as her other personality pounds her fist against the couch causing the chains to rattle.

"You don't?!"

"No!"

"But if Marcus is dead, don't you think his family will miss him?! They will miss him terribly!"

"I don't give a damn about his family!" Diane D's other personality shouts as her other personality pounds her fist against the couch again causing the chains to rattle again!

"You don't?!"

"No!"

"My God, Marcus was right about you! You are an evil vicious soul, spirit and entity, just like he said!" Diane D's other personality suddenly holds her breath as a look of anger appear on her face. Her other personality exhales with anger as Doctor Stone says to it, "Okay, since you don't care about Marcus' family, then what about Diane's family, huh?! What about Diane?! Yeah your soul or spirit might take her place while she's serving time in jail, prison or the mental institution, but don't you think if Diane is seperated from her family while she's in jail or prison, her family will miss her terribly and she will miss them?!"

"That's all I care about is Diane."

"Good! Okay then, at least you care about SOMEBODY! So can you at least think about Diane and her family missing each other if Diane is put away in jail or prison?!"

Diane D's other personality does not respond. Dr. Stone and Dr Kahn stare at Diane D's other personality waiting for an answer. Diane D's other personality still does not respond.

"Okay then," Dr. Kahn says. "I'm going to ask you another question. What I need, is for you to answer this other very important question that I'm about to ask you, okay? When Diane went to a photo shoot one day, and the photographer there snapped a few photos of her, the photographer and his assistant saw and noticed two different images of Diane right inside the same photo. They noticed a second image of Diane standing with its back right up against the original image of her. They noticed that the second image of Diane was staring directly into the camera, while the other image of her was holding and looking at the parrot! But by the time the photographer tried to show the double image of Diane to the other people in the room including Diane's mom and Diane herself, that double image of Diane was mysteriously gone. The photographer couldn't find it anymore and didn't know what happened to it. What I need to know is, was that second image of Diane in the photograph really you? Were you the one who was in that photograph with Diane staring directly into the camera?"

"Yes," Diane D's other personality says.

"What!" Margarita, Tomas, Mary, Barry, Tonio, Marilyn, Nicolas and Michael shockingly whisper.

"That second image of Diane in the photograph was really YOU?!" Dr. Stone shouts.

"Yes," Diane D's other personality says.

"How did you show up in that photo if you don't have an appearance?!"

"I made myself up to look like Diane!"

"What!" Dr. Stone and Dr. Kahn shout.

"You made yourself up to look like Diane again, just like you do when you enter Marcus' dreams and nightmares?!" Dr. Kahn shouts.

"Yes," Diane D's other personality says.

"That's why the photographer and his assistant saw two images of Diane, because one of those images of Diane was actually YOU who made yourself look like Diane?!"

"Exactly."

"Wow! When the photographer kept trying to snap a photo of Diane, Diane's mom told us that Diane's eyes kept going off camera looking to the side when the photographer kept trying to snap her photo! What I need to know is, was it you who Diane was really looking at, when her eyes kept going off camera looking to the side?"

"Yes."

"What!" Margarita, Tomas, Mary, Barry, Tonio, Marilyn, Nicolas and Michael shockingly whisper.

"It was YOU she was looking at?!" Dr. Stone shouts.

"Yes," Diane D's other personality says.

"That's why her eyes kept going off camera, because she was actually looking at YOU?!"

"Yes."

"So that means she saw you and knew you were there?"

"Yes."

"But nobody else in that room could see you?!"

"No they couldn't."

"Just her?!"

"Yes."

"But she didn't tell anybody that you were there, did she?"

"No she didn't."

"Instead, she just kept quiet about it and told everybody that she was bothered by a fly that was flying near her face!"

"Oh no!" Margarita, Tomas, Mary, Barry, Tonio, Marilyn, Nicolas and Michael shockingly whisper.

"Is that why Diane seemed like she was getting annoyed when her eyes kept going off camera looking to the side," Dr. Kahn asks, "because she was actually annoyed by you?"

"Yes," Diane D's other personality says.

"Why was she annoyed by you?"

"She didn't want my image to appear in the picture."

"She didn't want your image to appear in the picture?!"

"No."

"Because she knew that if you were there, your image might somehow appear in the photo and she didn't want that, did she?"

"No she didn't."

"But your image appeared in the picture anyway."

"Not for long."

"Why didn't your image stay in that photo, by the time Diane's mom and everybody else in the room were looking at the camera?"

"Because Diane didn't want them to see my image in it!"

"So your image left the photo just in the nick of time, by the time Diane's mom and every one else in the room got to see it because Diane didn't want them to see it."

"No she didn't."

"My God!" Margarita, Tomas, Mary, Barry, Tonio, Marilyn, Nicolas and Michael shockingly whisper.

"Why were you around Diane at that moment anyway?!" Dr. Stone asks.

"Because she had meditated earlier," Diane D's other personality says.

"That's what drawned you to her when she was at the photo shoot, because she had meditated earlier that day?"

"Yes."

"But when Diane had meditated earlier that day, she was secretly meditating at her other grandparents' house. And she was meditating inside one of the upstairs bedrooms with the door closed, but she wasn't alone inside that room while she was meditating. Her family caught her meditating with her cousin Dana. So since you were drawned to Diane at the time because she was meditating earlier and her cousin Dana was meditating right along with her, were you drawn to Dana as well?"

"Yes."

"What!" Margarita, Tomas, Mary, Barry, Tonio, Marilyn, Nicolas and Michael shockingly whisper. "Oh no!!"

"You were drawn to ger cousin Dana too?!" Dr. Kahn shouts.

"Yes," Diane D's other personality says.

"Oh my goodness! Did Dana know that you were drawn to her, by her meditating with Diane?"

"No."

"She didn't know?!"

"No."

"Oh my God! Did anything strange or supernatural happen with Dana later on that day like it did with Diane?"

"You don't need to know."

"I don't?"

"No."

"Okay. Have you ever made yourself look like Dana, like you make yourself look like Diane?"

"Yes."

"You have?!"

"Yes."

"Where?!"

"You don't need to know."

"Does Dana know that you make yourself look like her?!"

"No."

"She doesn't know?!"

"No she doesn't."

"How many times have you made yourself look like Dana?"

"You don't need to know."

"I don't need to know that either?"

"No."

"Does Dana even know about you?"

"Not really."

"Not really?"

"No."

"Okay. Have you ever entered Dana's physical body like you enter Diane's physical body?"

"Yes."

"What!" Margarita, Tomas, Mary, Barry, Tonio, Marilyn, Nicolas and Michael shockingly whisper. "Oh nooo!!"

"You've entered Dana's physical body before?!" Dr. Stone shouts.

"Yes," Diane D's other personality says.

"How?!"

"By pulling her soul and spirit out of her physical body then enter her physical body like I do this one!"

"What!" Dr. Stone and Dr. Kahn shout.

"By pulling her soul and spirit out of her physical body then enter her physical body like you do Diane's?!" Dr. Stone shouts.

"Exactly!" Diane D's other personality shouts.

"Oh my goodness! That means you've POSSESSED BOTH Diane's and Dana's physical bodies!"

"That's correct."

"But right now, you're in Diane's physical body!"

"Yes."

"When have you entered into Dana's physical body?!"

"Only after she meditates with Diane or gets angry."

"Only after she meditates with Diane or gets angry too?!"

"Yes."

"How many times have you pulled Dana's original soul and spirit out of her physical body then enter it like you do Diane's?!"

"Whenever she meditates for gets angry."

"Whenever she meditates or gets angry just like Diane?!"

"Yes."

"Is that why Dana goes off and becomes violent and out of control at times like Diane and be in and out of mental instutions like Diane, is because it was actually you inside her physical body behaving violently?!"

"Yes."

"Oh my God!" Margarita, Tomas, Mary, Barry, Tonio, Marilyn, Nicolas and Michael shockingly whisper. "Oh nooo!!"

"Now we know why Dana gets violent and out of control sometimes and gets superhuman strength!" Barry whispers, "because she is possessed by this thing or entity, just like Diane!"

"Oh Lord!" Michael shouts.

"I see," Dr. Stone says. "Were you ever inside Dana's physical body, while she was serving time in jail, prison or the mental institution?"

"Yes," Diane D's other personality says.

"What!" Margarita, Tomas, Mary, Barry, Tonio, Marilyn, Nicolas and Michael shockingly whisper. "Oh nooo!!"

"You were inside Dana's physical body while she was serving time in jail, prison or the mental institution also, just like Diane?!" Dr. Stone asks.

"Yes," Diane D's other personality says.

"And the peope inside the jail, prison or the mental institution didn't know that it was another soul or spirit inside Dana?!"

"No they didn't."

"So they just assume that it's Dana's original soul and spirit inside her physical body, just like they assume that it's Diane's original soul and spirit inside her physical body!"

"That's correct."

"My God! Diane comes from a very large family, including two siblings, two parents, two sets of grandparents, aunts, uncles, cousins and tons of other relatives. She comes from a very close-knit family who all love each other and always do things together! What I need to know is, have you ever entered anybody else in Diane's family's physical body before?!"

"No."

"You haven't?!"

"No."

"Why not? Even though the rest of Diane's family and relatives are NOT into meditation, I'm sure they all do get angry at times because we all get angry at some point in our lives. So how come you don't enter anybody else in Diane's family's physical body? Why just Dana?"

"Because she's the only one in the family who meditates with Diane."

"Because she's the only one who meditates with Diane?"

"Exactly."

"I see! So if it wasn't for Dana meditating with Diane, you would have never pulled her original soul or spirit out of her physical body then enter into her physical body like you do Diane."

"No I wouldn't."

"So you only enter Dana's physical body because she meditates with Diane?"

"Exactly."

"And you only enter Diane's physical body because she meditates period."

"Exactly."

"My goodness!"

"Okay," Dr. Kahn says. "Now I'm going to ask you another important question that I'm about to ask you. Since you've admitted that you have used different people's physical bodies in the past to kill other people with throughout the centuries and throughout the world once every fifty years, and you have admitted that you were about to use Diane's physical body to kill that kid Marcus inside the back stairwell of that school, I need to ask you this very important question. Have you ever entered Dana's physical body and tried to use her physical body to kill someone?"

Diane D's other personality is about to answer. It suddenly pauses, then doesn't say anything. Her other personality suddenly becomes silent. Dr. Kahn and Dr. Stone puzzled stare at Diane D's other personality. Then they puzzled look at each other. They puzzled look back at Diane D's other personality.

Margarita, Tomas, Mary, Barry, Tonio, Marilyn, Nicolas and Michael shockingly look at Diane D's other personality waiting for an answer.

Dr. Kahn and Dr. Stone continue to puzzled stare at Diane D's other personality waiting for a response. Dr. Kahn then says, "Have you ever used Dana's physical body to try and kill someone or have you ever used Dana's physical body and killed someone?"

Diane D's other personality still does not respond. Her other personality remains silent.

Margarita, Tomas, Mary, Barry, Tonio, Marilyn, Nicolas and Michael shockingly stare at Diane D's other personality. They nervously look at each other as Marilyn whispers, "Oh oh. That other personality is not answering!" Marilyn, Margarita, Tomas, Mary, Barry, Tonio, Nicolas and Michael nervously look back forward.

"Well aren't you going to answer the question?" Dr. Stone asks. "You answered everything else up to this point! We're going to ask you again. Have you ever used Dana's physical body to try and kill someone or have you ever used Dana's physical body to kill anybody?!"

Diane D's other personality is about to answer. It suddenly pauses again, but does not say a word. Her other personality remains silent again.

"Oh no!" Margarita, Tomas, Mary, Barry, Tonio, Marilyn, Nicolas and Michael whisper.

"Why isn't that personality answering the question?!" Tomas whispers. Tomas, Margarita, Mary, Barry, Tonio, Marilyn, Nicolas and Michael frighteningly stare at Diane D's other personality.

"Are you still there?" Dr. Kahn asks. "Say something! We need you to answer the question! Have you ever used Dana's physical body to try and kill someone or have you ever used Dana's physical body to kill anybody?!"

Diane D's other personality still does not respond. Her other personality still remains silent.

"Oh no!" Margarita, Tomas, Mary, Barry, Tonio, Marilyn, Nicolas and Michael whisper. "That personality is still not answering the question?!" Tomas whispers.

"Oh my God!" Barry whispers.

"Maybe that personality knows something, but doesn't want to get Dana in trouble!" Marilyn whispers.

"Oh nooo!" Mary whispers. Mary, Tomas, Margarita, Barry, Tonio, Marilyn, Nicolas and Michael frighteningly stare at Diane D's other personality!

"Why aren't you answering?" Dr. Stone asks. "We need to know! Have you ever used Dana's physical body to try and kill someone or have you ever used Dana's physical body to kill?!"

"No comment," Diane D's other personality suddenly says.

"No comment?! So you're not going to answer the question?"

"No comment! Next question please!"

"Oh my Lord!" Margarita, Tomas, Mary, Barry, Tonio, Marilyn, Nicolas and Michael whisper.

"Okay," Dr. Kahn says. "Since you refuse to answer the last question, I need you to answer another very important question that I'm about to ask you, okay? When Diane and the Dianettes were performing at a park in Germany one night and Diane's body mysteriously levitated right over the stage in front of around five thousand spectators practically scaring them to death, did you have something to do with that? Did you have anything to do with this physical body levitating over the stage in Germany?"

"No," Diane D's other personality says.

"You didn't?"

"No."

"You didn't have anything to do with Diane's physical body

levitating over the stage in Germany at all?"

"No."

"Well thank God for that!"

"It was the other spirit and personality who did that."

"What!" Dr. Kahn and Dr. Stone shout. "Other spirit and personality?!"

"What other spirit and personality?!" Dr. Kahn shouts.

"You mean there's another spirit and personality around this physical body also?!" Dr. Stone shouts.

"Yes," Diane D's other personality says.

"There is?!"

"Yes."

"My God!" Dr. Kahn shouts. "Well who are they?"

"I can't tell you."

"You can't?"

"No."

"Well why not?!"

"You will have to find out for yourself."

"We will have to find out for ourselves?"

"Yes."

"Okay we will! Thanks for that information!"

"My goodness!" Dr. Stone shouts. "We are going to send you back and try to bring out and talk to the soul, spirit and personality who caused Diane's body to levitate over that stage in Germany, but before you go, I would need you to identify some people that are in this room, okay?"

"What!" Margarita, Tomas, Mary, Barry, Tonio, Marilyn, Nicolas and Michael shockingly whisper. They nervously look at each other as Marilyn whispers, "Oh no! He's going to have that other personality look at us and identify us!"

"Oh my Lord," Tonio nervously whispers. Margarita, Tomas, Mary, Barry, Tonio, Marilyn, Nicolas and Michael nervously turn back forward as they continue to sit in the middle of the room watching Dr. Stone, Dr. Kahn and Diane D's other personality.

Dr. Stone then says, "When I count to three, I want you to open your eyes." Diane D's other personality continues to lay on the couch with its eyes closed. Dr. Stone then says, "Now one ..... two ..... three! Open your eyes!" Diane D's other personality slowly opens its eyes. Her other personality suspiciously looks its eyeballs around with very puffy, swollen and sleepy eyes. Dr. Stone then says, "Hi there." Diane D's other personality looks at Dr. Stone as it continues to lay on the couch. Dr. Stone then says, "How are you feeling?" Diane D's other personality does not respond. It looks at Dr. Stone with an angry glare. "Are you feeling okay?" Dr. Stone asks. Diane D's other personality does not speak. It continues to glare at Dr. Stone.

Dr. Kahn looks at Diane D's other personality and says, "Hey." Diane D's other personality looks its eyeballs at Dr. Kahn. Dr. Kahn then says, "How are you?" Diane D's other personality glares at Dr. Kahn. Dr. Kahn then says, "How do you feel now?" Diane D's other personality does not respond. It continues to glare at Dr. Kahn. Dr. Kahn then says, "Well aren't you going to say 'hello' or anything?" Diane D's other personality still does not respond. It continues to glare at Dr. Kahn. Dr. Kahn then says, "Well, say something. Say anything." Diane D's other personality still does not respond. It continues to glare at Dr. Kahn. Dr. Kahn then says, "Wow. I see you're not a friendly one, are you?" Diane D's other personality continues to glare at Dr. Kahn.

Dr. Stone then says, "Okay." Diane D's other personality looks back at Dr. Stone as Dr. Sone says to it, "Now, I'm gonna lift the back of this couch up so you can see and identify some people that are in this room, okay?" Diane D's other personality closes its eyes again as Dr. Stone presses a button on the side. The back of the couch start to rise causing Diane D's physical body to sit up with the cuffs and chains still wrapped around her physical body.

Margarita, Tomas, Mary, Barry, Tonio, Marilyn, Nicolas and Michael nervously look at Diane D's other personality as it sits up on the couch. They nervously look at each other. They turn back forward and continue to nervously look at Diane D's other personality.

Diane D's other personality is sitting up with its eyes still closed. Dr. Stone then says to it, "Okay, open your eyes again." Diane D's other personality opens its eyes and looks forward towards the back of the room. It looks slightly to the right and suddenly sees Diane D's family sitting in the middle of the room watching it. The other personality becomes shocked! It suddenly turns the other way and tries to jump right out of the seat, but is jerked and pulled back down by the cuffs and chains causing the chains to rattle and causing Dr. Stone, Dr. Kahn and Diane D's family to frighteningly jump out their seats and stand as Dr. Stone and Dr. Kahn nervously hold their hands out to Diane D's other personality with Dr. Stone saying, "Take it easy." Diane D's other personality puzzled looks down at the cuffs, chains and shackles. Her other personality turns her head to her right and glares at Dr. Stone! Dr. Stone asks, "Is everything alright?" Diane D's other personality continues to glare at Dr. Stone.

Dr. Kahn then asks, "Is everything okay?" Diane D's other personality then turns her head to her left and glares at Dr. Kahn! Dr. Stone and Dr. Kahn nervously look at Diane D's other personality.

Margarita, Tomas, Mary, Barry, Tonio, Marilyn, Nicolas and Michael shockingly and nervously look at Diane D's other personality as they continue to frighteningly stand. Michael turns to them and nervously whispers, "Oh my God, did y'all see that?! It looked like she was getting ready to jump right off that couch and run right out of here when she saw us!"

"I know," Nicolas whispers.

Diane D's other personality looks back at Diane D's family again. Her other personality becomes shocked again! It turns the other way and tries to jump right out of the seat again, but is jerked and pulled back down by the cuffs and chains again causing the chains to rattle again and causing Dr. Stone, Dr. Kahn and Diane D's family to continue to stand there frightened as Dr. Stone and Dr. Kahn nervously hold their hands out to Diane D's other personality. Diane D's other personality puzzled looks back down at the cuffs chains and shackles. Her other personality turns her head and glares at Dr. Stone again! Dr. Stone then says, "Everything is gonna be alright." Diane D's other personality continues to glare at Dr. Stone!

Dr. Kahn then says, "Everything is gonna be okay." Diane D's other personality then turns her head back towards its left and glares at Dr. Kahn again! Dr. Kahn then says, "Just take it easy." Diane D's other personality continues to glare at Dr. Kahn! Dr. Stone and Dr. Kahn nervously look at Diane D's other personality. Diane D's other personality then turns her head back forward and looks back at Diane D's family. It starts to glare at Diane D's family.

Margarita, Tomas, Mary, Barry, Tonio, Marilyn, Nicolas and Michael nervously look at Diane D's other personality as Nicolas nervously whispers, "Oh Oh. She's giving us the evil eye!"

"She sure is," Marilyn whispers. "Maybe it IS a good thing they chained her up!"

"Marilyn!" Margarita and the rest of the family shockingly whisper.

"I'm just saying!" Marilyn and the rest of the family all turn to each other and secretly whisper among themselves as Marilyn whispers, "That other personality did admit that it had killed many people in the past! That other personality is a murderer!"

"Not only that," Tonio whispers. "That other personality also admitted that they were planning to kill that little boy Marcus right in the back stairwell of that school! That's attempted murder that other personality have caused Diane to commit!"

"It sure is," Barry whispers. "And the bad thing is, that other personality STILL wants to kill Marcus!"

"Not only that," Michael whispers. "That other personality said that they would have killed anybody they had found hiding inside that storage room, even if that person had nothing to do with spying on Diane!"

"That's true!" Margarita whispers. "That personality also admitted that it killed a person every fifty years! Not only that, it admitted that it will kill again now and will kill again fifty years from now and will probably use Diane's body to do it!"

"I know," Tomas whispers. "That personality admitted to a lot of things! That's probably why it seem shocked when it first saw us sitting here, because it didn't know that we were sitting here the whole entire time listening to everything it had said and admitted to! That's probably why it tried to break out of that seat as soon as it saw us, because it knows it was caught red handed! It realize that we had heard everything it said!"

"I know," Marilyn whispers. "Man I don't even want to be in the same room with that other personality!"

"Me neither," Michael whispers. "As a matter of fact, I don't want that personality to remain inside Diane's body any longer!"

"Neither do I," Margarita whispers. "I don't think having this hypnosis done was a good idea at all! I think Dr. Stone better hurry and send that other personality back to where ever it came from!"

"I think so too!" Tomas whispers. Tomas, Margarita, Barry, Michael, Marilyn, Tonio, Mary and Nicolas nervously look back at Diane D's other personality.

Dr. Stone and Dr. Kahn sit back down in their chairs as Diane D's other personality puzzled looks down at the cuffs and chains wrapped around her body.

Diane D's family then sit back down in the chairs. They face forward and nervously look at Diane D's other personality again.

Diane D's other personality looks up from the cuffs and chains and looks back at Diane D's family. It starts to glare at Diane D's family again.

Diane D's family nervously look back at Diane D's other personality.

Diane D's other personality continues to sit there glaring at Diane D's family.

Diane D's family nervously continue to look at Diane D's other personality.

Diane D's other personality then gives her family a cold hard stare.

Diane D's family nervously look at each other not knowing what to do.

Dr. Stone looks at Diane D's other personality and says to it, "Now, do you know who those people are over there?" as he points to Diane D's family. Diane D's other personality continues to glare at her family.

Her other personality then looks at Dr. Stone. Dr. Stone says to Diane D's other personality again, "Do you know who those people are?"

Diane D's other personality glares back at her family. It then says, "I've seen them before."

"What!" Margarita, Tomas, Mary, Barry, Tonio, Marilyn, Nicolas and Michael whisper as they shockingly look at Diane D's other personality. They then turn to each other as Barry whispers, "My God did y'all hear that?! She said she's seen us before! It's like she sees us as total strangers!"

"My God," Tomas says. They nervously look back at Diane D's personality again.

"You've seen them before?" Dr. Stone asks.

"Yes," Diane D's other personality says.

"Okay. So if you've seen those people over there before, do you know who they are?"

"Yes."

"You DO know who they are?"

"Yes."

"She just said she knows who we are!" Michael whispers. "Maybe it IS Diane's original personality!"

"Michael," Barry whispers. "Diane's original personality is not a killer like this personality is!" Barry, Michael and the rest of the family nervously continue to look at Diane D's other personality.

"Okay," Dr. Stone says. "So if you know who those people are over there, then who are they?"

"They're Diane's family," Diane D's other personality says.

"What!" Margarita, Tomas, Mary, Barry, Tonio, Marilyn, Nicolas and Michael whisper. They are shocked as they look at Diane D's other personality. They turn to each other as Nicolas shockingly whispers, "My God did y'all hear that?! She just referred to herself in the third person again!"

"That means it's not Diane!" Margarita cries. "It's still that other personality!" Margarita, Tomas, Mary, Barry, Tonio, Marilyn, Nicolas and Michael get tears in their eyes as they turn and look back at Diane D's other personality.

"Those people over there are Diane's family?" Dr. Stone asks.

"Yes," Diane D's other personality says.

"Okay. Could you identify for me each family member?"

Diane D's other personality puzzled looks at Dr. Stone. It then asks, "Identify for you each of her family members?"

"Yes."

Diane D's other personality looks back at Diane D's family. It then looks to the far right at Margarita and says, "That's Diane's grandma."

"That's Diane's grandma?"

"Yes."

"And who are the others?"

Diane D's other personality looks at Tomas and says, "That's Diane's grandpa."

"That's her grandfather?"

"Yes."

"The next person?"

Diane D's other personality looks at Mary and says, "That's Diane's mom." She then looks at Barry and says, "That's Diane's dad." She then looks at Tonio and says, "That's her uncle." She then looks at Marilyn and says, "That's her aunt." She then looks at Nicolas and says, "That's her brother." She then looks at Michael and says, "And that's her husband."

"Okay good. Now would you reckognize Diane's cousin Nancy, the one you had an encounter with in their upstairs hallway, if you saw her again?"

"Maybe."

"Maybe? Do you see Diane's cousin Nancy over there now?"

Diane D's other personality looks at her family again. It then says, "No, I don't see her cousin Nancy there."

"You don't see her cousin Nancy?"

"No."

"Okay. Thanks. Now that you identified each of Diane's family members correctly, I'm going to send you back. I'm going to put you back to sleep, okay? Now lay back down." Dr. Stone presses the button again causing the couch back to lay back down causing Diane D's other personality to lay back down. Dr. Stone then says to Diane D's other personality, "Now when I count to three, I want you to close your eyes and go back to sleep. I want you to go back to where ever you came from, okay?" Diane D's other personality continues to lay on the couch with its eyes opened glaring at Dr. Stone. Dr. Stone then says, "Now one ..... two ..... three! Go back to sleep!" Diane D's other personality's eyes closes. Dr. Stone and Dr. Kahn continue to sit near Diane D's physical body and watch her other personality as her other personality goes back to sleep. Diane D's other personality continues to lay on the couch with its eyes closed. It quickly goes back into a deep sleep. Diane D's physical body is now back into a state of hypnosis.

Margarita, Tomas, Mary, Barry, Tonio, Marilyn, Nicolas and Michael shockingly stare at Diane D's physical body. "Wow," they all say.

"Is she back to sleep already?" Marilyn asks.

"Yes Marilyn," Margarita says. "I think she is."

"That fast?"

"Well she's still under hypnosis."

"Wow." Marilyn and the rest of her family continue to stare at Diane D's physical body.

"This, is so strange," Nicolas whispers. "We see Diane talking, but hearing someone else speaking!"

"I know," Tonio says. "It's very of creepy."

"It sure is," Marilyn says. Marilyn, Tonio, Barry, Nicolas, Margarita, Tomas, Mary and Michael turn back forward and puzzled look back at Diane D's physical body.

Dr. Stone and Dr. Kahn continue to sit near Diane D's physical body as Diane D's physical body continues to lay on the couch with her eyes closed. Dr. Stone and Dr. Kahn continue to watch Diane D's physical body as she sleeps. Dr. Stone speaks to Diane D's subconscious again and says to her, "Now, is there a third soul, spirit or personality in there using this physical body also? Is there a third soul, spirit or personality in there? If there is a third soul, spirit or personality in there using this physical body also, we need you to come out and talk to us. Is there a third soul, spirit or personality in there?" Dr. Stone and Dr. Kahn stare at Diane D's physical body as her physical body continues to lay on the couch as her eyes remain closed.

Margarita, Tomas, Mary, Barry, Tonio, Marilyn, Nicolas and Michael continue to sit quietly in the middle of the room puzzled looking at Diane D's physical body.

Outside in the hospital hallway, Nancy, Charlotte, Gracy, Grandpa Mike, Mickey and the rest of Diane D's family and relatives stand near the back door of the room as Grandpa Mike says to Nancy and Charlotte, "Well since you two are afraid to be inside the room, I and someone else should be in there to take your places since the doctors said up to ten family members at a time are allowed in there."

"But how are you going to get in there Grandpa?" Mickey asks. "The door is locked."

"It is?"

"Yeah."

Grandpa Mike tries to turn the doorknob on the back door. It will not turn. It is locked. Grandpa Mike turns to the family and says, "I need to get in there. I want to find out what's going on!"

"Can you call them Dad?" Aunt Celeste asks.

"No Aunt Celeste," Nancy says. "All cell phones had to be turned off. If any of us tries to call them, the calls won't go through."

"Man I need to get in there!" Grandpa Mike shouts. "I want to find out what's happening with Diane!"

"Maybe we should knock on the door Dad," Uncle Willie says.

"We can't Willie," Gracy says. "The doctors don't want any outside disturbance heard during the hypnosis. We might as well go back down to the waiting room." Everyone worriedly stands outside the backdoor. They then turn and go down the hallway.

Back inside the hypnosis room, Dr. Stone continues to speak to Diane D's subconscious as he looks down at her physical body and asks, "Is there a third soul, spirit or personality around this physical body using this physical body also?" Dr. Stone and Dr. Kahn stare at Diane D's physical body. Diane D does not respond. Her physical body continues to lay on the couch not responding as her eyes remain closed. Dr. Stone then says, "If there is a third soul, spirit or personality inside this physical body now, we need you to come out and talk to us. We need to talk to the soul, spirit and personality that caused Diane's physical body to levitate over a stage in Germany, NOT Diane's original soul, spirit or personality now and NOT the soul, spirit or personality that her cousin Nancy encountered inside their family's home in the upstairs hallway outside the bedrooms that night, we already talked to those two souls, spirits and personalities. We need to talk to the soul, spirit or personality that caused Diane's physical body to levitate over a stage in Germany, but before we do that, we want to make sure, that this is NOT Diane's original soul, spirit or personality now and we want to make sure that this is NOT the soul, spirit or personality that her cousin Nancy encountered inside their family's home in their upstairs hallway. Now is the soul, spirit or personality that caused Diane's physical body to levitate over a stage in Germany inside this physical body now? Reveal yourself! Come out and speak to us. Is the soul, spirit or personality that caused Diane's physical body to levitate over a stage in Germany inside this physical body now?" Dr. Stone and Dr. Kahn stare at Diane D's physical body. Diane D does not respond. Her physical body continues to lay on the couch not responding as her eyes remain closed.

Margarita, Tomas, Mary, Barry, Tonio, Marilyn, Nicolas and Michael continue to sit quietly puzzled looking at Diane D's physical body.

Dr. Stone continues to look at Diane D's physical body and says, "Is there a third soul, spirit or personality there inside this physical body?" Dr. Stone and Dr. Kahn continue to stare at Diane D's physical body. Diane D's physical body continues to lay on the couch not responding as her eyes remain closed.

Margarita, Tomas, Mary, Barry, Tonio, Marilyn, Nicolas and Michael anxiously look at Diane D's physical body.

Dr. Stone then says, "If the soul, spirit or personality that caused Diane's physical body to levitate over a stage in Germany is inside this physical body now, please reveal yourself to us and talk to us. Reveal yourself to us now!" Suddenly, Diane D's physical body starts to breathe hard. Dr. Stone and Dr. Kahn anxiously look at Diane D's physical body as her chest starts to rise and eyeballs seem to roll towards the top of her head again underneath her closed eyelids.

Margarita, Tomas, Mary, Barry, Tonio, Marilyn, Nicolas and Michael anxiously look at Diane D's physical body.

Dr. Stone and Dr. Kahn anxiously look at each other, then back at Diane D's physical body. Diane D continues to breathe hard as her eyes remain closed. Suddenly her breathing slows down, her chest lowers back down. Dr. Stone then says, "Is that a soul, spirit or personality trying to come out? Is there a soul, spirit or personality in there inside this physical body now? If there is a soul, spirit or personality inside this physical body now, respond yes by waving your fingers three times when I ask again. Now is there a soul, spirit or personality inside this physical body now?" Diane D's physical body continues to lay on the couch as her eyes remain closed. Suddenly her fingers wave once, twice, then three times.

Margarita, Tomas, Mary, Barry, Tonio, Marilyn, Nicolas and Michael are anxious and nervous as Tonio turns to them and whispers, "She waved her fingers three times!" Tonio, Michael, Nicolas, Margarita, Tomas, Mary, Barry and Marilyn continue to anxiously look at Diane D's physical body.

Dr. Stone continues to speak to Diane D's subconscious as he looks down at her physical body and says, "Okay good. Now we want to talk to the soul, spirit or personality that caused Diane's physical body to levitate over a stage in Germany, NOT Diane's original soul, spirit or personality and NOT the soul, spirit or personality that Diane's cousin Nancy encountered inside their family's home. We want to talk to the soul, spirit or personality that caused Diane's physical body to levitate over a stage in Germany, but before we do that, we want to make sure that this is NOT Diane's ORIGINAL soul, spirit or personality anymore, and we want to make sure that this is NOT the soul, spirit or personality that Diane's cousin Nancy encountered inside their family's home. Now is this Diane's ORIGINAL soul, spirit or personality inside this physical body now? Is Diane's original soul, spirit or personality there inside this physical body? If Diane's original soul, spirit or personality is inside this physical body now, respond 'Yes' by waving your fingers three times when I ask. If Diane's original soul, spirit or personality is NOT the one inside this physical body now, respond 'No' by waving your fingers twice. Now is Diane's original soul, spirit or personality inside this physical body now? 'Yes' or 'no'?" Diane D's physical body continues to lay on the couch as her eyes remain closed. Suddenly her fingers wave once then twice.

"What!" Margarita, Tomas, Mary, Barry, Tonio, Marilyn, Nicolas and Michael whisper. They become shocked and more nervous as Barry turns to them and whispers, "Oh oh. She only waved her fingers twice!" Tomas, Margarita, Mary, Barry, Tonio, Marilyn, Nicolas and Michael continue to shockingly and nervously look at Diane D's physical body.

Dr. Stone then says, "Is this Diane's ORIGINAL soul, spirit or personality inside this physical body now?" Diane D's physical body continues to lay on the couch as her eyes remain closed. Suddenly her fingers wave once then twice.

"What!" Margarita, Tomas, Mary, Barry, Tonio, Marilyn, Nicolas and Michael whisper. They become shocked and more nervous as Margarita turns to them and whispers, "She only waved her fingers twice again! That means it's not her again!"
"Oh no!" the rest of the family whispers. They continue to shockingly and nervously look at Diane D's physical body.

Dr. Stone then says, "Are you saying, that this is ANOTHER soul, spirit or personality inside this physical body now?" Diane D's physical body continues to lay on the couch as her eyes remain closed. Suddenly her fingers wave once, twice, then three times.

"What!" Margarita, Tomas, Mary, Barry, Tonio, Marilyn, Nicolas and Michael whisper. They become more shocked and nervous as Marilyn turns to them and whispers, "It's the other personality again!"
"Oh oh!" Nicolas whispers. Nicolas, Marilyn, Margarita, Tomas, Mary, Barry, Tonio and Michael continue to shockingly and nervously look at Diane D's physical body.

Dr. Stone then says, "Is this STILL the soul, spirit or personality that Diane's cousin Nancy encountered inside their family's home in their upstairs hallway?" Diane D's physical body continues to lay on the couch as her eyes remain closed. Suddenly her fingers wave once then twice.

"What!" Margarita, Tomas, Mary, Barry, Tonio, Marilyn, Nicolas and Michael whisper.

Dr. Stone then says, "You're NOT the soul, spirit or personality that Diane's cousin Nancy encountered inside their family's home either?" Diane D's physical body continues to lay on the couch as her eyes remain closed. Suddenly her fingers wave once then twice.

"Oh oh!" Margarita, Tomas, Mary, Barry, Tonio, Marilyn, Nicolas and Michael whisper.

"Then who is it?!" Tonio whispers.

Dr. Stone then says, "Well since this is NOT the soul, spirit or personality that Diane's cousin Nancy encountered inside their family's home, and since this is NOT Diane's original soul, spirit or personality, are you saying, that this is a third soul, spirit or personality inside this physical body now?" Diane D's physical body continues to lay on the couch as her eyes remain closed. Suddenly her fingers wave once, twice, then three times.

"It's a third personality!" Nicolas whispers.
"Oh no!" the rest of the family whisper.

Dr. Stone then says, "Is this the soul, spirit or personality that caused Diane's physical body to levitate over a stage in Germany?" Diane D's physical body continues to lay on the couch as her eyes remain closed. Suddenly her fingers wave once, twice, then three times.

"What!" Margarita, Tomas, Mary, Barry, Tonio, Marilyn, Nicolas and Michael whisper. "Oh no!"

Dr. Stone then says, "Are you saying, that you ARE the soul, spirit or personality that caused Diane's physical body to levitate over a stage in Germany?" Diane D's physical body continues to lay on the couch as her eyes remain closed. Suddenly her fingers wave once, twice, then three times.

"Oh my God!" Margarita whispers as she, Tomas, Mary, Barry, Tonio, Marilyn, Nicolas and Michael nervously look at Diane D's physical body.

Dr. Stone continues to speak to Diane D's third personality as he says, "Okay. We want to talk to you. We need to find out some answers. We need to know what happened the night Diane and the Dianettes were performing in Germany and this physical body mysteriously levitated right over the stage. Are you able to talk about it now? Do you want to talk about it now? If you are able to talk about it now or are willing to talk about it now, respond by saying 'yes' when I ask again. Now are you able to talk about it now or are you willing to talk about it now?"

Diane D's physical body continues to lay on the couch as her eyes remain closed. Suddenly her third personality says, "Yes."

"What!" Margarita, Tomas, Mary, Barry, Tonio, Marilyn, Nicolas and Michael whisper.

"You're willing to talk about it now?" Dr. Stone asks.

"Yes," Diane D's third personality says.

"Good."

"Okay hi," Dr. Kahn says to Diane D's third personality. "I'm Doctor Kahn. I need you to answer some very important questions that I'm about to ask you, okay? Now I'm going to ask you the same questions that I asked the other soul, spirit and personality, the one Diane's cousin Nancy had an encounter with inside their family's home, okay? What I want to know is, do you have a name?"

"No," Diane D's third personality says.

"You don't have a name?"

"No."

"Okay. Do you have a gender?"

"No."

"No gender either?"

"No."

"Okay. How old is your soul or spirit? How long has your soul or spirit been around?"

"For several hundred years."

"Your soul and spirit has been around for several hundred years too?! So you're an old soul and spirit too just like the other one! My God! Have you ever had a physical body?"

"No."

"You never had a physical body either?"

"No."

"So you were always a spirit too?"

"Yes."

"Wow, I see. What world are you from?"

"You don't need to know."

"I don't?"

"No."

"Okay. Do you speak and understand a specific language?"

"Yes."

"You speak and understand a specific language?"

"Yes."

"And what language is that?"

"All languages."

"All languages? What do you mean 'all languages'?"

"I speak and understand all languages."

"You speak and understand all languages too?"

"Yes."

"Wow, just like the other soul, spirit and personality! Wow. Okay. Well since we mainly speak English, we're going to continue to comminicate to you in English, okay? Now what I want to ask you is 'have you ever used someone's physical body to kill people?"

"You don't need to know."

"I don't need to know that either?"

"No."

"Why not?"

"You just don't."

"Oh. Okay. Well, let me start by saying, that one night when Diane and the Dianettes were performing in a park in Germany, they did some amazing performances on the stage. Two of the Dianettes did a disappearing act, two other Dianettes climbed a bare wall then crawled across the ceiling and the other two Dianettes lifted heavy objects. But when it was Diane's turn to come out and she performed on stage, I heard that she did some great ballet moves, some wonderful kick-boxing moves and some fantastic martial arts moves and stunts, then she did a balancing act on her hands, then she did a hand stand on one hand on her finger tips where she was doing splits while she was upside down. She then laid on the stage floor. While she was on the stage floor, suddenly, her physical body, which is the body that your soul or spirit is in right now, mysteriously levitated in a horizontal position right over the stage. The spectators got very frightened and ran off when they saw Diane's body levitating on the stage. Then her body returned to the stage floor. When Diane stood up on the stage floor, suddenly, her physical body mysteriously levitated in a vertical position right over the stage. The spectators got very frightened again and continued to run off when they saw Diane's body levitating again. After everything was all over and done, Diane claim she has no memory of levitating over the stage. She says she doesn't remember levitating at all and doesn't believe she ever levitated! She claims she doesn't remember her balancing act on her hands either! She claims the only thing she remembers is finding herself falling and landing hard on the stage floor getting hurt. She said she didn't know or realize what was happening to herself! What we need to know is, did you have something to do with this physical body levitating over the stage in Germany that night?"

"Yes."

"What!" Margarita, Tomas, Mary, Barry, Tonio, Marilyn, Nicolas and Michael become shocked and nervous as they continue to listen to Dr. Kahn and Diane D's third personality.

"You caused this physical body to levitate over the stage?" Dr. Kahn asks.

"Yes," Diane D's third personality says.

"Wow. How did your soul or spirit wind up causing this physical body to levitate?"

"I saw this physical body laying there on the stage floor."

"You saw this physical body laying on the stage floor?"

"Yes."

"Now I'm going to ask you the same question that I asked the other soul, spirit and personality. Where were you when you saw this physical body laying on the stage floor?"

"I was hovering over it."

"You were hovering over this physical body too?"

"Yes."

"So you were an invisible soul or spirit hovering over this physical body like the other spirit was doing?"

"Yes."

"So the audience members could not see you or notice you hovering over this physical body, since you were an invisible soul or spirit there, right?"

"Yes."

"They did not know you were there."

"No."

"Okay. Why were you hovering over this physical body in the first place?"

"Because Diane had meditated."

"Diane had meditated while she was on the stage?"

"Yes."

"Is that what brought your soul or spirit to the stage, because Diane meditated?"

"Yes."

"So Diane herself brought you there on the stage just by meditating?"

"Yes."

"Wow, just like she brought the other soul, spirit or personality into her family's home by meditating. Did Diane know that she brought you there on the stage by her meditating?"

"No."

"She didn't know that she brought you there?"

"No."

"I see. Does Diane ALWAYS attract you around her every time she meditates?"

"Sometimes."

"Sometimes?"

"Yes."

"Does she KNOW that she attracts you around her every time she meditates?"

"Sometimes."

"She knows sometimes?"

"Yes."

"Wow. So how did you make this physical body levitate over the stage?"

"I came to this physical body and pulled her original soul and spirit out of it while she was meditating."

"What!" Dr. Kahn and Dr. Stone shout.

"You pulled Diane's original soul and spirit out of this physical body while she was on the stage meditating?" Dr. Stone asks.

"Yes," Diane D's third personality says.

"Then what happened after you pulled Diane's original soul and spirit out of this physical body?"

"I lifted this physical body off the stage floor."

"What!" Dr. Kahn and Dr. Stone shout.

"You lift this physical body off the stage?" Kahn asks.

"Yes," Diane D's third personality says.

"That's how Diane levitated over the stage?"

"Yes."

"And the people in the audience didn't know that you were lifting this physical body off the stage floor?"

"No."

"Wow. Now when you first saw Diane's physical body meditating on the stage floor, walk us through from the time you first approached her physical body to the time you left her physical body."

DIANE D'S THIRD PERSONALITY'S FLASHBACK:

It is around 12:30 at night in Germany in a large park. There is a large oval shape stage with around five thousand spectators half way around it. The stage is dark and dimly lit. Diane D's physical body is on the stage floor with her legs in a split position with her face, chest, arms and both of her hands down to the floor as she meditates. The third soul, spirit or personality hovers over Diane D's physical body looking at her physical body watching it. The third soul, spirit or personality hovers over Diane D's physical body for a while. It slowly moves closer to Diane D's physical body. The third soul, spirit or personality then speeds towards Diane D's physical body! Diane D's physical body continues to remain motionless on the stage floor. "Diane D!" voices from the crowd shout. Diane D does not respond. She continues to remain motionless. She appears to be sound asleep. "Diane D!" voices from the crowd shout again.

Diane D's physical body still remains motionless with her face, chest and arms still down to the stage floor with her legs still in a split position. As the music changes and starts to pump again, suddenly, Diane D's torso and hips slowly rise a few inches off the stage floor as her face, arms, both of her hands, legs and feet remain on the stage floor. The audience starts to cheer. Diane D's legs and feet suddenly rise a few inches off the stage floor also as they remain in a split position. The audience continues to cheer. As Diane D's torso and hips raise higher, her legs and feet raise higher and slowly start to come closer to each other. Diane D's torso, hips, legs and feet are still rising as her legs and feet come a little more close to each other with her face, arms and both of her hands remaining on the stage floor. Her lower body is now one foot off the stage floor with her legs and feet still spread apart as her face, arms and both of her hands remain on the stage floor! Diane D raises her entire lower body in a slight diagonal position. She then holds her body stiff as she balances her entire weight on her head, arms and hands.

Diane D's head and arms suddenly rise a few inches off the stage floor causing her torso, hips, legs and feet to rise even more higher with her legs and feet still spread apart as her hands remain on the stage floor. Diane D's arms start to straighten and stand as her head and arms suddenly rise higher causing her torso, hips, legs and feet to raise even more higher. Diane D's arms are straightening more and standing more as her head, torso, hips, legs and feet are all raising two feet off the floor with her hands remaining on the floor! Diane D's arms are now standing completely straight as her entire body is now balancing two feet off the stage floor in a complete horizontal position! She is balancing her entire weight on her arms and hands with her legs and feet still spread apart.

As Diane D's body remain in a horizontal position, suddenly her hips go all the way up in the air putting her upper body vertical in an upside-down position as her hands remain on the stage floor. Suddenly her legs and feet go all the way up in the air putting her legs and feet vertical in an upside-down position as her hands remain on the stage floor. Diane D's entire body is now raised in a complete vertical position! She is completely upside down as she balances her entire weight on her hands doing a complete hand stand!

Diane D then spins and twirls her entire body around on her hands as her legs and feet start to spread apart again doing different split positions right in the air! She suddenly removes her right hand off the stage floor. She is now doing a hand stand on one hand!

Diane D is balancing her entire weight on one hand as she starts to spin and twirl the rest of her body around! Her legs move about and sway around in the air in different split positions as she continues to hold her balance and entire body weight on one hand.

Diane D's left palm suddenly raises off the stage floor, leaving just her left fingertips touching the stage floor!

Diane D's left fingertips turn making her entire body turn while her legs continue to move about and sway around in the air in different split positions as she continues to balance her entire weight on her left finger tips! Diane D's left palm lowers again. Her left palm slowly raises again as her left fingertips turn again, making her entire body turn again as her legs continue to move about and sway around in the air in different split positions as she continues to hold her balance on her left finger tips. The two cameramen riding on the cart circle Diane D and point the camera at her. Diane D's left palm lowers back to the stage floor again. Her right hand comes back down to the stage floor as she does the hand stand back on both hands. Her legs and feet slowly come back down. Her torso and hips slowly come back down as her legs remain a split position. She suddenly turns around making herself lay face up on her back with her eyes closed and her head back appearing to be unconscious as her right leg and foot remain all the way up to her head in a split position. Diane D's right leg suddenly comes down near her left leg having both legs on the stage floor near each other. Diane D's legs and arms suddenly spread out on the floor far apart from each other. Suddenly Diane D raises her arms and hands off the stage floor with her hands balled up into fists as she tries to lift her body up. Her entire body seems to rise an inch off the floor then spins around in a horizontal position to a different part of the stage appearing to be sort of weightless as her eyes remain closed and her head back!

Diane D's body then stops spinning and seems to land back down on the stage floor as she spreads her arms out on the floor. Diane D raises her arms and fists off the stage floor again as she tries to lift her body up again. Her entire body seems to rise an inch off the floor again then spins around in a horizontal position again to another part of the stage appearing to be weightless again!

Diane D's body stops spinning again and seems to land back down on the stage floor as she spreads her arms out on the floor again. She raises her arms and fists off the stage floor again as she tries to lift her body up again. Her entire body seems to rise an inch off the floor again then spins around in a horizontal position again back to the center of the stage appearing to be weightless again!

Diane D's body stops spinning again and lands back down on the stage floor as she spreads her arms out on the stage floor again. As Diane D's arms remain spread out on the stage floor with her eyes closed and her head back, suddenly, her entire body seems to rise an inch off the floor again. It then rises another inch! It then rises a few more inches!

Diane D's body continues to rise higher as she starts to do an eerie levitation performance! The crowd starts to scream in fear as Diane D's body levitates one foot off the stage floor! Her body continues to rise higher! The crowd continues to scream in fear as Diane D's body levitates two feet off the stage floor! Her body continues to rise higher! The crowd continues to scream in fear as Diane D's body levitates three feet off the stage floor! Her body continues to rise higher! The crowd continues to scream as Diane D's body levitates four feet off the stage floor! The cameramen and security guards look on shocked as one of them shouts, "Oh my God she's levitating!"

"Oh shit!" one of the cameramen says.

"How the hell she do that?!" the second security guard shouts. The cameramen and security guards shockingly and frighteningly look at Diane D's body as it levitates in mid air! The cameramen and security guards look up in the air above Diane D and are shocked to see no means of support! They look down underneath Diane D and are shocked to see no means of support underneath her either.

"There's nothing holding her!" the first security guard shouts. "I don't see any evidence of anything physical that could be making her body levitate in mid-air!"

"You sure it's not the wind?!" the second security guard shouts.

"No it's not the wind! Nobody else is floating!"

The two cameramen on the cart continue to point the camera right at Diane D! Diane D's body start to spin around in mid air as her head remains back with her eyes closed and her arms, hands and feet wave around as if deliberately spinning her body around in mid air. One of the security guard shouts, "Oh my God! She's spinning around in mid air! What are we gonna do?!"

"I don't know!" a second security guard shouts. "I've never seen or experience anything like this before!"

"Me neither!" the cameraman shouts.

"Maybe we should go near her to protect her just in case she falls and gets hurt!" the first security guard shouts.

"I don't want to go near that! I'm afraid!"

"But we have to! We can't just leave her to float in mid air alone!" The security guards and cameramen nervously look at each other. They then look back at Diane D's body and rush towards her body!

Diane D's body continues to spin! Her feet almost hits the security guards and cameramen causing them to duck and quickly get out of her way! The security guards and cameramen bend back up and shockingly look at Diane D's body. "My God she almost kicked us!" the third security guard shouts.

"I know!" the first security guard shouts. "We gotto be very careful with her! I hear her kicks really hurt!"

"I heard that too!" the second security guard shouts.

"So what should we do?!" the fourth security guard shouts.

"We got to circle her to catch her whichever direction she goes in just in case she falls!" the first security guard shouts.

The men nervously turn to each other. They frighteningly look back at Diane D's body. They circle her body as it continues to float and spin! "Oh my God!" the cameraman shouts.

"This is unbelievable!" the first security guard shouts. Diane D appears to remain unconscious as her body slowly stops spinning with her head still back and eyes closed as the crowd continues to scream! Diane D's body stops spinning as her arms and hands hang from her torso. Her head and upper body slowly goes downward towards the stage floor leaving her legs and feet higher in the air. "Oh my God!" the first security guard shouts.

The fourth cameraman runs to the other side of Diane D's body! The third security guards nervously turns to him and shouts, "What are you doing?!"

"I want to get this shot!" the fourth cameraman shouts. "This is a once in a lifetime thing!" The cameraman goes down to the floor underneath Diane D's body. He points and shoots the camera right up at her back as her upper body slowly comes back down to the stage floor with her legs and feet still higher in the air! Diane D's upper body slowly lands back down on the stage floor then her lower body lands.

She lays right near the fourth cameraman as her eyes remain closed. The fourth camera man continues to point and shoot the camera at Diane D's body. He then points and shoots the camera right at Diane D's face. Diane D still appears to be unconscious not knowing what's going on. The rest of the cameramen and security guards bend to the floor to Diane D. They look at Diane D's face as one of them asks, "Is she alright?"

"I don't know," the second guard says. "She looks unconscious!"

The men continue to puzzled look down at Diane D. Suddenly, Diane D's left leg bends all the way up bringing her left knee right up to her chest. The cameramen and security guards frighteningly back away a little! They puzzled look at Diane D. They then bend back to her and nervously look at her face. Suddenly, her lower left leg kicks all the way up kicking one of the security guards right in the face! "Aaaaaahh!" the security guard screams and holds his face in pain as Diane D's left foot continues to kick all the way up near her head, having her legs going into a split position again as she lays on her back. The men frighteningly back away from Diane D as the security guards shouts, "My God! She kicked me!" as he continues to hold his face.

"Yeah I know!" the other security guard shouts. "That's why I said we got to be careful!" Diane D continues to lay on the stage floor in a split position with her eyes closed and head back still appearing to be unconscious as her body suddenly turns over face down in the split position. The men shockingly look at Diane D and frighteningly back away from her as the crowd continues to scream in fear. Diane D's hips suddenly raise with her feet and hands remaining on the stage floor. Her legs and feet start to stand. The cameramen and security guards frighteningly back further away from Diane D! They puzzled stare at Diane D as her eyes remain closed. Her body seems to be moving completely on its own without her doing it or being aware of it! Diane D's head and upper body then come up, having her body stand up right! The cameramen and security guards frighteningly back further away from Diane D!

Diane D turns toward the center of the audience. Her eyes are now half open with most of her eyeballs hidden behind her half closed eyelids. She appears to be in a state of trance as she looks way up towards the back of the audience, giving the back of the audience a stone cold blank look! She throws her left arm and fist up in the air! She suddenly brings her right knee up. Different music starts to play. Diane D stands on her left leg and holds her right leg in the air with her right arm and hand around it. She suddenly looks up in the air as she holds her head back. She kicks her right leg out and starts to levitate again in a vertical position as her body rises four feet in the air!

Diane D's body starts to spin in mid air with her head forward and eyes closed again. Her head then falls backward towards the side, her arms and legs hang from her body as her body continues to spin! She appears to be hanged and spinned by an invisible rope and noose as the crowd continues to scream in fear!

The audience turn around running away out of the field! They are pushing and shoving each other as they desperately try to get away! There is panicking and a stampede among the crowd as several people hold their chests, then fall to the grass!

As Mary, Margarita, Barry, Tomas and the rest of Diane D's family almost reach the stage, Diane D's body suddenly falls! She quickly waves her arms, hands, legs and feet out and kicks another security guard in the face as she falls! "Aaaaaahh!" the security guard screams and holds his face in pain as Diane D's body drops and lands hard on the stage floor!

Diane D's family reach the stage! They see Diane D on the stage floor and shout, "Diane!" They rush right on the large stage and run towards Diane D!

Diane D suddenly lays up on the stage floor as her eyes remain shut. She shakes her head. She then opens her eyes and awakens out of her trance. Her eyes appear as if she has just woken up from a long sleep as she looks around in a daze not seeming to know where she is and not seeming to know what is happening to her. She then grabs her backside and holds herself in pain.

"Diane!" her family shockingly shouts as they continue to rush to her!

Diane D painfully and worriedly looks at her family and the rest of her relatives as they rush to her.

Diane D's family approach her! They bend down on the stage floor to her and shout, "Diane! Diane!" They then grab Diane D. They tightly hold her as they shout to her, "Diane!"

"Estas bien?!" Mary shouts. "Que ha pasado?!"

"Diane!" Margarita shouts. "Hable a nosotros! Diga algo!"

"Diane are you okay?!" Barry shouts. Diane D puzzled looks at her family! "What in the world happened to you?!" Barry shouts. Diane D's eyes are half closed with her head back. Barry then wraps his arm entirely around Diane D. Diane D has her head laid back against Barry's arm as her family worriedly looks at her and continue to hold her.

The security guards, the cameramen and other witnesses approach Diane D! Other people rush to Diane D.

Several ambulances arrive in the field. They tend to several people that are on the ground.

The security guards, Diane D's family and people on the stage continue to surround Diane D as three male paramedics rush to them with a stretcher. "Okay everyone let us through!" the paramedics shout. The people look at the paramedics and start to clear out of the way.

The paramedics in the field have several people laying in stretchers. They lift the stretchers and place them into the ambulances.

The paramedics on the stage lift the first security guard who got kicked in the face by Diane D onto a stretcher as they hold a bloody cloth over his face. They quickly walk the stretcher with the security guard away as they continue to hold the bloody cloth over his face. The other three male paramedics have Diane D laying and strapped tightly in a stretcher as they rush her and the stretcher off the stage! Diane D's family, the security officers and cameramen rush and follow off after Diane D's stretcher! Other paramedics lift the second security guard who got kicked in the face by Diane D onto a stretcher as they hold a bloody cloth over his face. They quickly walk the security guard and the stretcher away as they continue to hold the bloody cloth over his face.

BACK TO THE PRESENT:

"So a lot of people and spectators got hurt during all that chaos?" Dr. Kahn asks.
"Yes," Diane D's third personality says.
"Where was Diane's original soul or spirit, while the levitation part was all happening? Where was her original soul or spirit, while you were lifting her physical body up in the air?"
"Wandering the universe."
"Her original soul and spirit was wandering the universe, again?"
"Yes."
"Who or what put her soul and spirit out there? Was it you?"
"Yes."
"It was YOU?"
"Yes."
"Why?"
"Because she was meditating."
"Because she was meditating?"
"Yes."
"So you just come along and pull her original soul and spirit right out of this physical body, then put her soul or spirit out there in space wandering the universe, just for meditating?"
"Exactly."
"You know you and the other soul and spirit who had an encounter with her cousin Nancy seem to have no problem with coming right along and just pulling Diane's original soul or spirit right out of this physical body and placing her soul or spirit out into the universe whenever you want!"
"It's not whenever we want! Only when she meditates or gets

206

angry."

"Only when she meditates or gets angry?"

"Exactly."

"So by her meditating or getting angry, she draws you and the other spirit to her, and in return, you and the other spirit pull her original soul or spirit out of her physical body and place her soul or spirit out into the universe for the time being and then you enter into her physical body and use it, right?"

"That's right."

"Wow. Did Diane know that you caused her physical body to levitate over the stage?"

"No."

"She didn't know that you caused this physical body to levitate?"

"No."

"My God! What about when Diane stood back up and then levitated in a verticle position? Were you the one who lifted this physical body up in the verticle position?"

"Yes."

"It was YOU who did that too?"

"Yes."

"Wow. I see."

"Why was Diane's physical body suddenly dropped to the stage floor while her physical body was levitating in the verticle position?" Dr. Stone asks.

"It was an accident," Diane D's third personality says.

"An accident?"

"Yes."

"What do you mean 'an accident'?"

"We didn't mean to drop her."

"We? What do you mean 'we'?"

"Who's we?" Dr. Kahn puzzled asks.

"Me and the other spirit," Diane D's third personality says.

"What!" Dr. Stone and Dr. Kahn shout.

"You and the other spirit?!" Dr. Kahn shouts.

"What other spirit?!" Dr. Stone shouts. "You mean the same spirit who we talked to earlier a little while ago, the one that had an encounter with Diane's cousin Nancy inside their family's home, and the same spirit who beat up that little boy Marcus in the school hallway who keeps entering his dreams and nightmares, and the same spirit who kung fu kicked that stuck storage room door at the hospital and the same spirit who tried to attack those correction officers inside the jail cell?! That spirit? That spirit said they had nothing to do with Diane's physical body levitating. You mean that spirit?"

"No, not that one," Diane D's third personality says. "Another one."

"What!" Dr. Stone and Dr. Kahn shout. "Another one?!"

"You mean there's a third spirit around this physical body too besides you and the other one who had an encounter with her cousin

Nancy?" Dr. Kahn asks.

"Yes," Diane D's third personality says.

"Oh my God! Who's the third spirit?!"

"I can't tell you."

"You can't?!"

"No."

"Why not?!"

"I just can't!"

"My God! And this third spirit is also behind this physical body being levitated over the stage?!"

"Yes."

"My Goodness!"

"How many spirits come around Diane whenever she meditates or gets angry?!" Dr. Stone shouts.

"Several of us," Diane D's third personality says.

"Several of you?!" Dr. Stone and Dr. Kahn shout.

"How many altogether?!" Dr. Stone asks.

"You don't need to know how many altogether!" Diane D's third personality shouts. "It's several of us, that's all you need to know!"

"Oh my God! And you all come around whenever Diane meditates or gets angry?!"

"Yes we do."

"All the time?"

"Most of the time."

"Why?!"

"Because we look out for her, that's why!"

"You look out for her?"

"Yes we do."

"Then why was her physical body all of a sudden dropped to the stage floor as soon as her family got close to the stage?! Because Diane's family claimed to have never seen her levitate! They said by the time they got to the stage, the only thing they saw, was Diane dropping and falling to the stage floor. They thought that she fell from one of her gymnastic flips. Since they thought she fell from one of her gymnastics flips, that means you and the other spirits that were involved in her levitation dropped her physical body just in the nick of time! Why was her physical body suddenly dropped to the stage as soon as her family got there?"

"Because we didn't want her family to witness her being in the air, when we realized they were coming to the stage."

"What?" Dr. Stone and Dr. Kahn say.

"You didn't want Diane's family to witness her levitating?" Dr. Kahn say.

"No we didn't," Diane D's third personality says.

"That's why her physical body was suddenly dropped to the stage floor as soon as her family got there?"

"Yes."

"Why didn't you want Diane's family to see her levitating?"

"Because we wanted to protect her family."

"You wanted to protect Diane's family?" Dr. Stone asks.

"Yes."

"From what?!"

"From seeing her in the air!"

"Why did you want to protect Diane's family from seeing her in the air?"

"So they wouldn't be involved."

"So they wouldn't be involved?"

"That's right."

"Why didn't you want Diane's family involved?"

"Because she loves her family! We didn't want Diane hurt by having her family involved."

"You didn't?"

"No."

"That's exactly what the other spirit who had an encounter with her cousin Nancy said, that they didn't want to kill Marcus too close to where Diane's family was because they didn't want Diane hurt by having her family involved. It's good that you and the other spirits don't want Diane hurt by having her family involved, but you all have to understand and realize, that anything that happens to Diane, her family automatically becomes involved in it, because that's her family!"

"That's why we didn't want her family to see her in the air!"

"So you and the other spirit just dropped her physical body to the stage floor just in the nick of time to keep her family from witnessing her being in the air?!"

"We didn't mean to drop her! It was a spur of the moment thing when we realize her family was coming towards the stage."

"So if Diane's family had never came out of that trailer and never came to the stage, her physical body would have continued to levitate over the stage?"

"No. We would have brought it back down eventually. By her family coming to the stage, it just made us bring her physical body down sooner."

"But dropping her physical body caused her physical body to land hard on the stage floor causing Diane to get hurt! Don't you think you hurted Diane by doing that?!"

"We didn't mean for her to get hurt! It was an accident!"

"An accident?"

"That's right."

"Well maybe the accident wouldn't have happened in the first place, if you and the other spirits had left this physical body grounded to the stage floor."

"The last thing we want to do, is hurt Diane or anybody in her family."

"You don't want to hurt Diane or anybody in her family?"

"No."

"But you don't mind hurting or attacking other people, do you?"

"Only if they hurt or upset Diane, we don't mind hurting or attacking them."

"Even if it's a child?"

"Even if it's a child, we don't mind hurting them."

"But Diane said she would never hurt a child."

"She won't. But we will."

"Really?"

"Yes."

"My GoOdness! That's terrible! And by Diane getting angry, she draws you and the other spirits to her and then you all just pull her soul or spirit out of her physical body again and just throw and toss her soul or spirit out into the universe for the time being and then enter her physical body to take care of and attack people with it, right?"

"Exactly."

"Why do you want to use this physical body and attack people with it whenever they get Diane angry?"

"Because we don't like anybody messing with Diane, that's why!"

"You don't?"

"No! We don't like anyone getting her upset or angry! We look out for her! We protect her!"

"You protect her?"

"Yes we do! We got her back."

"You got her back too?"

"Of course we do!"

"I see. Is there any reason why you and the other spirits are so protective of Diane?"

"We just are."

"Why?! Is she your leader or something?"

"Sort of."

"Sort of?!" Dr. Stone Dr. and Kahn shouts.

"What do you mean 'sort of'?" Dr. Stone asks.

"We're her soldiers," Diane D's third personality says.

"Soldiers?!"

"That's right!"

"Does Diane know that you and the rest of her soldiers be causing all this chaos?"

"Sometimes she knows."

"She knows?"

"Yes."

"What does she do or what does she think about that?"

"She doesn't really approve of it."

"She doesn't?"

"No."

"Has she ever said anything to you and the other spirits about it?" Dr. Kahn asks.

"Yes she has."

"She has?! Well what has she said to you all?"

"She told us to cool it."

"What?" Dr. Kahn and Dr. Stone say.

"Diane told you all to cool it?" Dr. Stone asks.

"Yes," Diane D's third personality says.

"Well obviously y'all haven't listen to her if you all are still causing a lot of havoc!"

"We cool it sometimes."

"Sometimes?"

"Yes we do."

"Why cool it only sometimes and not cool it all the time?"

"Because we look out for Diane and have her back!"

"Even though she tells you all to cool it, you're not going to listen to her?"

"It's not that we're not going to listen to her. It's that we're going to always have her back."

"You are?"

"Yes."

"I see. Okay thanks. Thanks for that information. Now we are going to send you back to where you came from, but before you go, I would need you and the other spirits to do Diane a favor. I need you and the other spirits to leave Diane alone from now on."

"Leave Diane alone? What do you mean 'leave her alone'?"

"Let me put it this way. I want you and the other spirits not to bother Diane ever again. I want you all to leave her soul, her spirit and her physical body alone from now on and not to go anywhere near her soul or spirit nor enter her physical body anymore whether she's meditating or not! And I want you all to leave her soul, her spirit and her physical body alone and not to go anywhere near her soul or spirit nor enter her physical body anymore whether she gets angry or not! I want you all not to send or put her soul or spirit out into space wandering the universe anymore and I want that other soul, spirit and personality, that murderous one who has been killing people through out the centuries once every fifty years, that same one who had an encounter with her cousin Nancy inside their family's home, that same one who beat up that kid Marcus inside the school hallway and that same one who claimed to have even entered Dana's physical body not to come into Diane's family's home anymore and I want that same one not to bother Marcus anymore. I want that spirit to stay away from Marcus and not enter into his dreams nor come into his nightmares anymore! And I want that same one to leave Dana's soul, spirit and her physical body alone from now on and not to go anywhere near her soul or spirit nor enter her physical body anymore whether she's meditating or not or whether she gets angry or not! I want you and all the other souls, spirits and personalities to stay away from Diane, her family including her cousin Dana and that kid Marcus, you got that?!"

"How dare you tell us to stay away from Diane. We only come to her or around her and Dana whenever they meditate or get angry."

"Well I guess we have to make sure, that Diane and Dana never meditate or get angry anymore in order to keep you souls, spirits and personalities away from them! We are going to have to keep a close eye on Diane to see and make sure that she does not meditate nor gets angry anymore. We are going to have her on some type of counseling, medication and prescription drugs and we're going to have her sent back to anger management. That way she can control her temper to make sure she doesn't get angry much anymore. That way you and the other souls, spirits and personalities get to leave HER alone and leave her PHYSICAL BODY alone as well and not cause anymore havoc!"

"So you're planning to take Diane away from us?!"

"Yes that's exactly what I'm planning to do. I'm planning to separate all you souls, spirits and personalities away from her for good!"

"Oh yeah?!"

"Yes!"

"How dare you plan to take Diane away from us. How dare you try to separate us from her! Just for planning to do that, I am going to fire you up!" Diane D's third personality suddenly tries to get up off the couch, but is jerked and pulled back down by the chains that are wrapped around her physical body as her physical eyes remain swollen shut.

"Fire me up? What are you talking about?"

"I am going to wring your neck for trying to take Diane away from us!" Diane D's third personality tries to get up off the couch again but is jerked and pulled back down by the chains again. Diane D's third personality suddenly tries to break loose from the chains!

"Oh my God what is she doing!" Michael whispers.

"I think she's trying to break loose from the chains!" Barry whispers as he, Margarita, Tomas, Mary, Tonio, Marilyn, Nicolas and Michael shockingly look at Diane D's third personality.

"What are you doing?!" Dr. Stone nervously shouts to Diane D's third personality.

"Getting out of these damn things so I can wring your fuckin neck!" Diane D's third personality shouts as it continues to try to break loose from the chains. "After I wring your neck, I'm gonna go after that damn kid and wring HIS neck too!"

"Go after that kid and wring his neck too? What kid? You mean Marcus?!"

"Yes HIM!"

"Oh no! Not you too! How would you even find Marcus?! You don't know where he is!"

"I DO know where he is, and when I catch up to him, I'm going to kill him!"

"What!" Dr. Stone and Dr. Kahn shout as they jump out of their seats. "Kill him?!"

"Oh no!" Dr. Stone shouts. "That's what that murderous soul, spirit and personality who chased Marcus down the back stairwell of the school wanted to do, kill him! And it STILL wants to kill him! Now you want to kill him too!"

"That's right!" Diane D's third personality shouts.

"Oh no!"

"Oh no!" Margarita shouts as she, Tomas, Barry, Mary, Tonio, Marilyn, Nicolas and Michael quickly get up and rush from their seats! They rush towards the rope that's still surrounding Diane D's third personality, Dr. Stone and Dr. Kahn.

Chapter 14

The Beast Within Goes Berserk!

Diane D's third personality continues to try to break loose from the chains as her physical eyes remain swollen and shut. Dr. Stone then shouts to Diane D's third personality, "You're not going anywhere! So you might as well forget about trying to break loose from the chains coming after me or going after that kid Marcus, because I'm gonna send you back to where you came from! I'm gonna put you back to sleep! Now when I count to three, I want you to go back to sleep and go back to where you came from and stay there! Now one ..... two ..... three! Go back to sleep!" Diane D's third personality does not go back to sleep. Her third personality continues to try and break loose from the chains! Everyone becomes shocked and stunned as Diane D's third personality does not go back to sleep! Her third personality tries to raise her shoulders and upper arms from off the chains! Her third personality then squeezes her upper arms and torso very tight. Her third personality suddenly gets superhuman strenth and pulls the chains wrapped around Diane D's upper arms upwards causing the metal bars beneath it to bend upwards! Diane D's third personality then breaks the chains wrapped around her upper arms loose from the metal bars beneath the couch making loud metal crash noises! Dr. Stone, Dr. Kahn and Diane D's family become shocked and horrified screaming in horror as they quickly step back! Both chains wrapped around Diane D's upper arms are broken making Diane D's upper arms free from the couch as the broken chains hang from around her upper arms! Dr. Stone again shouts to Diane D's third personality, "Go back to sleep I say! One ..... two ..... three! Go back to sleep!" Diane D's third personality still does not go back to sleep. Her third personality continues to try breaking loose from the other chains! Dr. Stone turns to Dr. Kahn and shouts, "Get the security!" Dr. Kahn presses a button on the side.

Diane D's third personality suddenly gets superhuman strength again! It pulls the chain attached to Diane D's right handcuff, the chain strapped around her right shoulder, the chain wrapped around her right leg and the chain attached to her right shackle upward causing the metal bars beneath them to bend upwards! Diane D's third personality then breaks the chain attached to her right handcuff, the chain strapped around her right shoulder, the chain wrapped around her right leg and the chain attached to her right shackle loose from the metal bars beneath the couch making loud metal crash noises again! Dr. Stone, Dr. Kahn and Diane D's family scream in horror again! Dr. Stone again shouts to Diane D's third personality, "Go back to sleep I say! One ..... two ..... three! Go back to sleep!" Diane D's third personality still refuses to go back to sleep! The long chain attached to Diane D's right handcuff, the chain strapped around her right shoulder, the chain wrapped around her right leg and the chain attached to her right shackle are all broken making Diane D's right side of the body free from the couch as the broken chains hang from her right wrist, right shoulder, right leg and right shackle! Her third personality continues to try breaking loose from the other chains on her left side as her third personality spreads her legs and feet further apart breaking the chain between the shackles making loud metal crash noises again! Dr. Stone, Dr. Kahn and Diane D's family continue to scream in horror!

Diane D's third personality pulls the chain wrapped around Diane D's left leg and the chain attached to Diane D's left shackle upward causing the metal bar beneath it to bend upwards! Diane D's third personality then breaks the chain wrapped around Diane D's left leg and the chain attached to her left shackle loose from the metal bar beneath the couch making loud metal crash noises again as Dr. Stone, Dr. Kahn and Diane D's family continue to scream in horror! The long chain wrapped around Diane D's left leg and the chain attached to her left shackle are broken making Diane D's left leg free from the couch causing both of her legs to be free from the couch as the broken chains hang from both of her legs and both of her shackles! Everyone in the room is shocked and horrified continuing to scream in horror as Diane D's third personality suddenly throws her lower body and legs high up in the air with her left shoulder and left handcuff still chained to the couch! Dr. Stone again shouts to Diane D's third personality, "Go back to sleep I say! One ..... two ..... three! Go back to sleep!" Diane D's third personality still refuses to go back to sleep! Her third personality starts to swing her legs and feet high up in the air again causing the long broken chains hanging from the shackles to swirl high in the air like a whip hitting Dr. Stone and Dr. Kahn right in their heads! "Aaaaahhhh," scream Dr. Stone and Dr. Kahn as they are about to fall and painfully hold their heads! Diane D's third personality continues to try breaking loose from the other chains taking its superhuman strength and pulls the chain wrapped around her left shoulder upwards causing the metal bar beneath it to bend upwards! Diane D's third personality then breaks the chain wrapped around Diane D's left shoulder loose from the metal bar beneath the couch making loud metal crash noises again! The chain wrapped around her left shoulder is broken making Diane D's left shoulder free from the couch causing both of her shoulders to be free from the couch as the broken chains hang from both of her shoulders! All of Diane D's limbs are now free from the couch except for the long chain attached to her left handcuff which is still attached to the metal bar beneath the couch!

As Diane D's third personality tries to break loose from the remaining chain that's still attached to her left handcuff, Dr. Stone and Dr. Kahn quickly turn and start to run for the front door, but Diane D's third personality takes its superhuman strength, lifts the couch right up off the floor and throws the couch right at Dr. Stone and Dr. Kahn as the couch pulls the remaining chain and Diane D's body along with it! The couch lands hard on the floor as Diane D's third personality throws her entire body horizontally in the air and kung fu kicks Dr. Kahn right in the back! Dr. Kahn's body is thrown forward as Diane D's third personality quickly twists her legs around in the air and fung fu kicks Dr. Kahn right in the forehead with her other feet throwing his body backwards! "Aaaaahh!" Dr. Kahn screams as he falls backwards and lands on the floor with his forehead bleeding! Dr. Stone becomes shocked and horrified as Dr. Kahn shouts to him, "Aaaahhh! Get the security! And the priest!"

Dr. Stone turns and runs towards the front door again, but Diane D's third personality takes its superhuman strength, lifts the couch right up off the floor again and throws the couch right at Dr. Stone as the couch pulls the remaining chain and Diane D's body along with it again! The couch lands hard on the floor as Diane D's third personality throws her entire body horizontally in the air again and kung fu kicks Dr. Stone right in the back! Dr. Stone's body is thrown forward as Diane D's third personality quickly twists her legs around in the air again and fung fu kicks Dr. Stone right in the forehead with her other feet throwing his body backwards also! "Aaaaahh!" Dr. Stone screams as he falls backwards and lands on the floor with his forehead bleeding also!

Diane D's third personality still tries to break loose from the remaining chain that's still attached to her left handcuff! Her third personality pulls the remaining chain upward causing the metal bar beneath it to bend upwards! Diane D's third personality then breaks the chain attached to her left handcuff loose from the metal bar beneath the couch making loud metal crash noises again as her family screams in horror! The chain attached to her left handcuff is broken making Diane D's left handcuff free from the couch making her entire body free from the couch as the broken chain hang from her left handcuff! Diane D's third personality quickly bends and lifts the psychiatrist couch right up off the floor again as the long broken pieces of the chains still attached to her body hang from her body! Her third personality then takes its superhuman strength and holds the couch high up in the air! Her third personality then spins her entire body around as the long broken pieces of the chains attached to her body hang and swirl around with her body whipping her right in the face and torso!

A couple of security guards and the priest burst into the front door! As the security guards and the priest head straight towards Diane D's third personality, her third personality takes its superhuman strength and throws the couch twenty feet right across the room at the security guards and the priest slamming the couch right into their heads bashing their heads in knocking them down! The security guards, the priest and the couch land hard on the floor! Diane D's third personality runs right to the couch with the long broken pieces of the chains still attached to her body and shackles! Her third personality uses Diane D's gymnastic skills then jumps and throws Diane D's hands on top of the couch lifting her entire body upside down in the air doing a hand stand! Her third personality then uses Diane D's martial arts skills and swings Diane D's legs and feet high up in the air causing the long broken chains attached to the shackles to swirl high in the air like a whip again! Diane D's third personality then becomes a contortionist, bends her entire body backward in a circle and whips the security guards and the priest right in their heads with the chains that are attached to the shackles! "Aaaaahhhh," the security guards and the priest scream holding their heads as their heads start to bleed!

Diane D's third personality then throws her entire body to the side of the couch landing on her feet! Her third personality bends and lifts the psychiatrist couch right up off the floor again, holds it high up in the air again and quickly spins her entire body around again as the long broken pieces of the chains attached to her body hang and swirl around with her body again whipping her right in the face and torso again!

A few more security guards burst into the back door, but Diane D's third personality quickly throws the couch thirty feet right across the room at the security guards slamming the couch right into their heads bashing their heads in knocking them down also! The security guards and the couch land hard on the floor! Diane D's third personality runs to the couch again with the long broken pieces of the chains still attached to her body! Her third personality uses Diane D's gymnastic skills again then jumps and throws Diane D's hands on top of the couch lifting her entire body upside down doing a hand stand again! Her third personality uses Diane D's martial arts skills again and swings Diane D's legs and feet high up in the air again causing the long broken chains attached to the shackles to swirl high in the air like a whip again! Diane D's third personality becomes a contortionist again as she bends her entire body backward in a circle and whips the security guards right in their heads with the chains attached to the shackles! "Aaaaahhhh," the security guards scream holding their heads as their heads start to bleed also!

Diane D's third personality then throws her entire body back straight up in the air again then throws her body to the side of the couch and lands on her feet! Her third personality bends and lifts the psychiatrist couch right up off the floor again, holds it high up in the air again and quickly spins her entire body around again as the long broken pieces of the chains attached to her body hang and swirl around with her body again whipping her right in the face and torso again! Margarita, Tomas, Barry, Mary, Tonio, Marilyn, Nicolas and Michael anxiously try to approach Diane D's third personality as they shout to it, "Diane!"

Four police officers burst into the front door with tasers drawn, but Diane D's third personality throws the couch thirty feet right across the room at the police officers slamming the couch right into their heads bashing their heads in knocking them down! The police officers and the couch land hard on the floor! Two of the police officers are knocked out cold with their heads and the other officers' heads bleeding! Margarita, Tomas, Barry, Mary, Tonio, Marilyn, Nicolas and Michael scream in horror! They turn and anxiously try to approach Diane D's third personality again, but Diane D's third personality runs to the couch again as Margarita, Tomas, Barry and Mary shout, "Diane!" Diane D's third personality uses Diane D's gymnastic skills again then jumps and throws Diane D's hands on top of the couch again lifting her entire body upside down doing a hand stand again! Her third personality swings Diane D's legs and feet high up in the air again causing the long broken chains attached to the shackles to swirl high in the air like a whip again and whips the broken chains attached to the shackles down hard on the other police officers' arms, hands and fingers whipping the tasers right out of their hands! "Aaaaahhhh," the other police officers scream painfully holding their arms, hands and fingers as their arms, hands and fingers start to bleed! Margarita, Tomas, Barry, Mary and Michael turn and rush to Doctor Stone.

Doctor Stone is knocked out on the floor with his head bleeding! Margarita, Tomas, Barry, Nicolas and Michael bend down to him and jerk him up off the floor as Margarita shouts to him, "Doctor Stone, wake up! Come on wake up!" Dr. Stone wakes up. He is woozy as Margarita, Tomas, Barry, Nicolas and Michael try to stand him up as Margarita shouts to him, "Doctor Stone can't you put her back to sleep?!"

"That's right Doctor Stone!" Michael shouts. "You have to put her back to sleep?!"

"I tried to put her back to sleep!" Dr. Stone shouts in a daze. "It didn't work!"

"Well you have to try again!" Tomas shouts. "She's hurting people!"

"Come on Doctor Stone!" Barry shouts. "Let's go! You started this, now fix it!" Barry, Tomas, Margarita, Nicolas and Michael jerk Dr. Stone and pull him towards Diane D's third personality!

Barry, Margarita, Tomas, Nicolas and Michael pull Dr. Stone near Diane D's third personality as Barry shouts to him, "Go ahead Doctor! Put her back to sleep!"

Dr. Stone is still in a daze. He then shouts to Diane D's third personality, "One ..... two ..... three! Go back to sleep!" Diane D's third personality still does not go back to sleep! It continues to cause havoc!

The injured police officers laying on the floor painfully try to reach for their tasers, but Diane D's third personality quickly jumps and throws her hands right on top of the couch again lifting her entire body upside down doing a hand stand again! Her third personality swings Diane D's legs and feet high up in the air again causing the broken chains attached to the shackles to swirl high in the air again and whips the chains down hard on the police officers' arms, hands and fingers whipping the tasers right out of their hands again! "Aaaaahhhh," the police officers scream again painfully holding their arms, hands and fingers as their arms, hands and fingers start to bleed more! "Aaaaahhhh!" one of the officers laying on the floor shouts. "I think my arm and fingers are broken! Aaaaahhh!" Margarita, Tomas, Barry, Mary, Tonio, Marilyn, Nicolas and Michael shockingly look at the officer as Diane D's third personality throws her entire body back straight up in the air again then throws her body to the side of the couch and lands on her feet! Margarita, Tomas, Barry, Mary, Tonio, Marilyn, Nicolas and Michael turn and try to approach Diane D's third personality again as Diane D's third personality lifts the psychiatrist couch right up off the floor again, holds it high up in the air again and quickly spins her entire body around again as the long broken pieces of the chains attached to her body hang and swirl around with her body again hitting her in the face and torso again! They shout to it, "Diane stop it!"

Out in the hallway, Gracy, Grandpa Mike, Mickey, Nancy, Charlotte and the rest of Diane D's family and relatives rush down the hallway back towards the hypnosis room! They suddenly hear a loud BANG against the wall coming from inside the hypnosis room! They stop and become startled as they feel the vibration! They then see four police officers running up the hallway with guns drawn! Diane D's family and relatives rush towards the police officers as Grandpa Mike shouts to them, "What the hell is going on!"

"Stay back sir!" one of the officers rushes to him and shouts as the other three police officers charge towards the hypnosis room front door!

Back inside the hypnosis room, the three police officers burst into the front door with the guns drawn, but Margarita, Tomas, Barry, Mary, Tonio, Marilyn, Nicolas and Michael rush right in front of the police officers and shout to them, "You better not try to shoot her!"

"That's right!" Barry shouts. "Or else you got to come through us!"

Barry and the rest of his family use their bodies as human shields shielding Diane D's third personality from the police officers' guns.

"We're not trying to shoot her sir!" one of the police officers shouts. "We just want to subdue her!" Margarita, Tomas, Barry, Mary, Tonio, Marilyn, Nicolas and Michael suddenly duck as the couch speeds right over their heads towards the police officers slamming right into the police officers' heads bashing their heads in knocking them down! The police officers and the couch land hard on the floor! One of the police officers is knocked out cold with his head and the other officers' heads bleeding as Diane D's third personality runs to the couch again! Her third personality jumps and throws her hands on top of the couch again lifting her entire body upside down doing a hand stand again! Her third personality swings Diane D's legs and feet high up in the air again and whips the broken chains attached to the shackles down hard on the police officers' arms, hands and fingers whipping the guns right out of their hands! "Aaaahh!" the officers scream painfully holding their arms, hands and fingers as their arms, hands and fingers start to bleed!

Diane D's third personality then throws her entire body back straight up in the air again then throws her body to the side of the couch and lands on her feet again! Her third personality bends and lifts the psychiatrist couch right up off the floor again, holds it high up in the air again and quickly spins her body around again as the long broken pieces of the chains attached to her body hang and swirl around with her body again hitting her right in the face and torso again! Suddenly, her third personality throws the couch thirty feet right across the room towards the back door!

As four more police officers are about to burst into the back door with more guns drawn, the couch slams right into their heads bashing their heads in knocking them down! The police officers and the couch land hard on the floor! Two more police officers are knocked out cold with their heads and the other officers' heads bleeding as Diane D's third personality runs to the couch again! Her third personality then jumps and throws her hands on top of the couch again lifting her entire body upside down doing a hand stand again and whips the long chains attached to the shackles down hard on the police officers' arms, hands and fingers whipping the guns right out of their hands causing one of the guns to go off! "Aaaaahhhh," the police officers scream as a bullet hits one them! The officer then screams, "Aaaaah! I've been shot!"

"Aaaahh!" other officers scream painfully holding their arms, hands and fingers as their arms, hands and fingers start to bleed!

Diane D's third personality then throws her entire body back straight up in the air again then throws her body to the side of the couch and lands on her feet again! Her third personality bends and lifts the psychiatrist couch right up off the floor again and holds it high up in the air again! Her third personality quickly spins her entire body around again as the long broken pieces of the chains attached to her body hang and swirl around with her body again hitting her in the face and torso again! Margarita, Tomas, Barry and Mary try to approach Diane D's third personality again and shout to it, "Diane please stop!" Diane D's third personality ignores her family as her third personality continues to spin her entire body around with the long chains still swirling around with her body still hitting her in the face and torso! Margarita, Tomas and Barry turn and rush back over to Doctor Stone again!

Out in the hallway, Gracy, Grandpa Mike, Mickey, Nancy, Charlotte and the rest of Diane D's family and relatives try to rush towards the hypnosis room again but two officers rush right in front of them blocking their way as the first officer shouts to them, "You all can't go in there!"

"Why not?!" Grandpa Mike shouts. "My family is in there! That's my granddaughter in there!"

"Who Diane D?!"

"Yes, her!"

"Well your granddaughter Diane D is going berserk inside that room because she just caused an officer to get shot!"

"She what?!" the rest of the family and relatives shout.

"Yes! I'm trying to keep you guys out of harm's way!"

"Oh no!" Gracy, Grandpa Mike and the rest of the family are shocked as they frighteningly look at the officer. They suddenly hear another loud BANG against a wall coming from inside the hypnosis room! They become startled again as they feel the vibration again!

Back inside the hypnosis room, some of the injured police officers laying on the floor painfully try to reach for their guns, but Diane D's third personality quickly jumps and throws her hands on top of the couch again lifting her entire body upside down doing a hand stand again and whips the chains down hard on the police officers' arms, hands and fingers whipping the guns right out of their hands again causing another gun to go off! "Aaaaahhhh," the police officers scream as a bullet hits another officer! The officer screams, "Aaaaah! I've been shot too! Aaaaaahh!"

Out in the hallway, Gracy, Grandpa Mike, Mickey, Nancy, Charlotte and the rest of Diane D's family and relatives nervously look at each other as Aunt Celeste shouts, "I think that was a gun shot! I heard it! Then I heard someone screaming!"

"I heard it too!" Mickey shouts. "Our family is in there! They might get shot too! I'm gonna go in there!"

"Me too!" Grandpa Mike shouts.

"Me too!" Uncle Willie shouts. They suddenly hear another loud BANG against a wall coming from inside the hypnosis room again! They become startled again as they feel the vibration again! Diane D's family is frightened by the constant loud banging!

"Oh my God!" Mickey shouts. "I see two people's heads laying on the floor near the back door!"

"Oh my God!" Aunt Celeste shouts. "I see it too! It looks like their heads are bleeding!"

"I think their heads ARE bleeding Aunt Celeste! That looks like a pool of blood near their heads!"

"Oh my goodness! They didn't get shot in the heads did they?!"

"I hope not Aunt Celeste! I sure hope not!"

"And look!" Charlotte shouts as she points towards the front door. "I see someone's legs and feet laying near the front door!"

"I see it too!"

"Oh my God!" Gracy shouts. "Are these people dead?!"

"I hope not Grandma!" Mickey and the rest of the family suddenly hear another loud BANG against a wall coming from inside the hypnosis room again! They become startled again as they feel the vibration again! They suddenly see a police swat team with six members running up the hallway with shotguns drawn! Nancy and Charlotte are crying and scared as Nancy screams, "What's happening Grandpa Mike! What's happening?!"

"I don't know Nancy!" Grandpa Mike shouts. He then turns to the swat team members and shouts to them, "Wait a minute!"

"Just stay back sir!" the first police officer shouts to him again.

"But I gotta go in there!"

"You can't go in there! Another officer was shot!"

"What!" the family shouts. "Another officer was shot?!"

"Yes! Do you all want to be next?! That's why I need you folks to stay back for your safety!"

"But we have other family members inside that room you know!" Uncle Willie shouts. "There're eight of them in there! What about their safety?!"

"Well that's what the swat team is here for, to get your other family members out of that room safely!" the officer shouts as the police swat team charge towards the hypnosis room front door!

Back inside the hypnosis room, Diane D's third personality quickly throws the couch right across the room at the front door! As the swat team members are about to burst into the front door with the shotguns, the couch slams right into their heads bashing their heads in knocking them down! The swat team members and the couch land hard on the floor! Two of the swat team members are knocked out cold with their heads and the other swat team members' heads bleeding! Diane D's third personality quickly runs right to the couch again! Her third personality bends and lifts the psychiatrist couch right up off the floor again, holds it high up in the air again, swirls her body around with the long broken pieces of the chains swirling around with her body and throws the couch right across the room at the back door!

As four more swat team members are about to burst into the back door with shotguns, the couch slams right into their heads bashing their heads in knocking them down! The swat team members and the couch land hard on the floor! Another swat team member is knocked out cold with his head and the other swat team members' heads bleeding! Diane D's third personality runs to the couch again! Her third personality then jumps and throws her hands on top of the couch again lifting her entire body upside down again and whips the broken chains attached to the shackles down hard on the swat team members' arms, hands and fingers whipping the shotguns right out of their hands! "Aaaaahhhh!" the injured swat team members scream painfully holding their arms, hands and fingers as their arms, hands and fingers start to bleed!

Diane D's third personality then throws her entire body straight back up in the air again then throws her body to the side of the couch and lands on her feet again! Her third personality bends and lifts the psychiatrist couch right up off the floor again, holds it high up in the air and quickly spins her entire body around again as the long broken pieces of the chains attached to her body hang and swirl around with her body again hitting her in the face and torso again!

Margarita, Tomas, Barry and Michael jerk Dr. Stone who is still bleeding and woozy and pull him towards Diane D's third personality again as Tomas shouts to him, "Come on Doctor Stone, put her back to sleep! Put her back to sleep now!"

Dr. Stone then shouts to Diane D's third personality, "One ..... two ..... three! Go back to sleep!" Diane D's third personality still does not go back to sleep. Her third personality continues to spin her body around holding the couch high up in the air as the long broken pieces of the chains attached to her body hang and swirl around with her body hitting her right in the face and torso again! Dr. Stone again shouts, "One ..... two ..... three! Go back to sleep!" Diane D's third personality stops spinning and is about to throw the couch right across the room at the injured bleeding unconscious police officers and the injured bleeding unconscious swat team members again as they lay helpless on the floor, but Dr. Stone rushes right in front of her third personality and shouts to it, "One ..... two ..... three, go back to sleep! One ..... two ..... three, go BACK to where you came from!" Diane D's head suddenly falls backward! Dr. Stone quickly steps back as the rest of Diane D's physical body falls backward still holding the couch high up in the air! "Aaaaahhh Diaaane!" her family screams and shouts as her physical body and the couch crash to the floor! Diane D's physical body lands face up on the floor with the long broken pieces of the chains still attached to her body, limbs and shackles! Her physical body lays motionless on the floor with her eyes still puffy and swollen shut as her family shouts, "Diaaane!" Her family is about to rush right to her physical body but Dr. Stone shouts to them all, "Wait now everybody, just hold on! Stop right where you are!" Diane D's family stop right in their tracks! They turn their heads around towards Dr. Stone as he shouts to them, "Don't anybody approach her yet! She's still under hypnosis! That other personality might still be there!" Diane D's family shockingly stare at Dr. Stone. Dr. Stone then shouts, "We might not be out of the woods yet! That other personality might come out and strike again!" Diane D's family nervously stare at Dr. Stone. They slowly and nervously turn their heads back forward towards Diane D's physical body. They nervously stare at her physical body as her physical body lays motionless on the floor with the long broken pieces of the chains still attached to her body, limbs and shackles. Dr. Stone then shouts, "I think it's best to keep back from her until I get her ORIGINAL soul, spirit or personality to come back! So what I need, is for you all to back away from her!" Diane D's family slowly and nervously back away from Diane D's physical body as they stare at it.

Five more police officers burst into the front door with guns drawn! More security guards, security officers, hospital staff and paramedics burst into the front door! They and the police officers look around the room. They are all shocked to see all the bloodshed that has just happened in there! They see blood all over the room! They see injured security guards, an injured priest, injured police officers and injured swat team members lying on the floor bleeding everywhere! They then see Dr. Kahn on the floor injured and bleeding also! They also see five police officers and two swat team members knocked out cold. They see furniture knocked down everywhere. They see two video cameras knocked down.

Gracy, Grandpa Mike, Mickey, Aunt Celeste and the rest of Diane D's family and relatives suddenly burst into the room. They are shocked to see all the bloodshed! They see a lot of authority figures on the floor injured, bleeding and knocked out! They see furniture knocked down everywhere! The other police officers, the security guards, hospital staff and paramedics see Diane D's physical body laying across the room motionless on the floor with the long broken pieces of the chains still attached to her body, limbs and shackles. They are about to head towards Diane D's physical body but Dr. Stone shouts to them, "Wait! Stop right where you are!" The other police officers, the security guards, hospital staff and paramedics stops right in their tracks! They turn their heads around towards Dr. Stone as he shouts to them, "Don't anybody move! I'm not sure if it's safe for anybody to get close to her! She's still under hypnosis! That other personality might still be there!" The other police officers, the security guards, hospital staff and paramedics shockingly stare at Dr. Stone. Dr. Stone then shouts, "We might not be out of the woods yet! If you approach her and that other personality comes out and strikes again, you are at your own risk!" The other police officers, the security guards, hospital staff and paramedics nervously stare at Dr. Stone. They slowly and nervously turn their heads back forward towards Diane D's physical body. They nervously stare at her physical body as her physical body continues to lay motionless on the floor. Dr. Stone then shouts, "I think it's best to step back from her until I get her original soul, spirit or personality to come back! So what I need is for everyone to back away from her now!" The other police officers, the security guards, hospital staff and paramedics slowly and nervously back away from Diane D's physical body. The other police officers, the security guards, hospital staff and paramedics back up towards Dr. Stone.

Margarita, Tomas, Barry, Mary, Tonio, Marilyn, Nicolas, Michael, Gracy, Grandpa Mike, Mickey, the rest of Diane D's family and relatives turn and rush to Dr. Stone as Mary anxiously asks him, "When are you gonna try to wake her up Doctor Stone?! When are you gonna try to bring her back?!"

"I have to make sure it's safe for any of us to get close to her Miss Mary!" Dr. Stone shouts. "Look at all the chaos that she did!" Everyone shockingly looks around the room at the bloodshed! They look at the injured security guards, the injured priest, injured police officers, injured swat team members and an injured Dr. Kahn laying on the floor bleeding as some hospital staff and paramedics tend to them. They also look at the knocked down furniture laying across the room. Dr. Stone looks back at Diane D's family and shouts, "It looks like a war zone happened in here! See what I mean? Now you see why we felt the need to cuff and chain her up?! Her other personality went crazy and literally broke th0se chains loose from the couch!" Dr. Stone points towards the broken chains on the floor still attached to Diane D's physical body and shouts, "That is proof right there and you saw the proof happening with your very own eyes! Her other personality broke the chains loose from the couch to attack me and Dr. Kahn threatening to wring my neck, then was planning to go after that kid Marcus to kill him, claiming to know where he is! You heard it with your own ears! Obviously that other personality is not done with Marcus! I'm afraid that poor kid is going to have a lot on his plate!" Diane D's family worriedly look at Dr. Stone. He then tells them, "Just don't get close to her yet. I have to check on her slowly. Once I get her original soul, spirit or personality back, we still have to make sure that it's her ORIGINAL soul, spirit or personality and NOT the other souls, spirits or personalities."

"And how are you going to do that Doctor Stone?" Barry asks. "Have her identify us again?"

"Yes I'm gonna have to."

"Just hurry Doctor," Margarita pleads.

"Okay," Dr. Stone says. "But I cannot do that in this room. There are too many people in this room. I need a more private room to snap her out of hypnosis."

"A more private room?"

"Yes, with no more than ten family members again to witness."

"Okay," Tomas says. "What room Doctor?"

"I will have to get her transferred to the room next door where it's more private and safe to snap her out of hypnosis."

"How are you going to get her in there Doctor Stone?" Michael asks.

"I would have the security remove the cuffs, chains and shackles from off her physical body then have the paramedics place her physical body on the stretcher, then bring her physical body and the stretcher into the other room. And once we get her physical body into the other room, we have to make sure that the doors in the other room be locked just in case her other personality is still there and tries to break out of that room to harm more people!" Dr. Stone looks towards a couple of male security officers and says to them, "I need you guys to remove the cuffs, chains and shackles from off her." Two male security officers approach Dr. Stone as he says to them, "Come so you can remove the cuffs, chains and shackles from off her." Dr. Stone turns to Diane D's family and says, "Wait right here." Dr. Stone and the two male security officers turn and head towards Diane D's physical body.

Dr. Stone and the two male security officers anxiously approach Diane D's physical body as her physical body continues to lay motionless on the floor with the long broken chains still attached to her physical body with her eyes still swollen shut. The security officers shockingly stare at the broken psychiatrist couch, the bent metal bars underneath it and the broken chain pieces still on it. They shockingly look at Diane D. They then bend down to the floor and get on their knees to Diane D's physical body and check on her.

Everyone else in the room anxiously look on as Margarita shouts to Dr. Stone, "Is she okay Doctor?"

"I don't know yet," Dr. Stone says.

"She's still alive is she?" Michael asks.

"Yes she's still alive."

Dr. Stone turns to the security officers and says, "Remove the cuffs, chains and shackles off her now." The security officers start to unlock the cuffs, chains and shackles from off Diane D's physical body.

Back across the room, one of the male paramedics tending to the injured police officers turns to a male security guard next to him and whispers, "My God what the hell happened in here? Did all these people get shot?! It looks like a massacre happened in here! What happened?!"

"I think Diane D went berserk and attacked the doctors, then the security guards and a priest when they bursted in here!" the security guard whispers.

"What! She did?!"

"Yeah. Then she went berserk on the police officers and a swat team when they bursted in here and attacked them as well!"

"What! Diane D went berserk and attacked security guards and police officers again, and this time, doctors and a priest too?"

"Yeah and caused two officers to get shot?"

"What! Two officers got shot?!"

"Yeah! Then she attacked the swat team when they bursted in here!"

"A swat team too?! Oh no!"

"Yeah! I mean she is something else!"

"My God! What did Diane D attack all these people with, a gun? Because it looks like a tiny war zone happened in here!"

"It sure does, but she didn't attack any of these people with a gun, she had no gun on her! She attacked them with that psychiatrist couch."

"What! She attacked them with that psychiatrist couch? What do you mean 'she attacked them with that psychiatrist couch'?!"

"She picked it up right off the floor and started throwing it across the room at them!"

"What! Wait a minute. Are you telling me, that Diane D picked that psychiatrist couch right up off the floor and threw that couch across the room at the security guards, the priest, police officers, the swat team and that doctor laying over there?"

"Yeah!"

"My God, how the hell she do that?! How was she able to lift that psychiatrist couch and then throw it across the room?! That psychiatrist couch is pretty heavy you know!"

"Yeah it is heavy, but it didn't stop her from lifting it up, holding it high up in the air then throw it across the room like a piece of rag!"

"She threw the couch across the room?!"

"She sure did! I caught the tail end of all of this!"

"You did?!"

"Yeah!"

"My goodness!" The paramedic guy and the security guard shockingly look around the room at dozens of injured authority figures on the floor bleeding. They then look towards Diane D's physical body laying several yards away on the floor as the security officers continue to unhook the cuffs, chains and shackles from her physical body. "Why does she have broken chains hooked and attached around her?"

"Because the doctors had her in chains!"

"What! The doctors had Diane D in chains? What do you mean 'they had her in chains'?"

"They had her body and limbs wrapped in chains and chained her body to the couch!"

"What! They had Diane D's body and limbs wrapped in chains and chained her body to the couch?"

"Yeah!"

"For what?!"

"They were afraid that when they hypnotize her and bring her other personality out, her other personality might wind up going

227

berserk and that's exactly what happened, her other personality went berserk and out of control on everybody!"

"What! Her other personality came out?!"

"Yeah!"

"And went berserk?!"

"Yeah, and this is the result!"

"Oh my lord! I heard about that other personality of hers. That other personality of hers don't play!"

"It sure doesn't. When her other personality came out, it broke the chains loose from the couch freeing herself from the couch and chains!"

"What! Her other personality broke the chains loose from the couch?!"

"Hell yeah! It was like she became a modern day Houdini when she freed herself from being wrapped in chains!"

"My God. How was she able to break the chains loose from the couch?!"

"Somehow her other personality wind up having superhuman strength and turned into the Incredible Hulk!"

"Her other personality had superhuman strength and turned into the Incredible Hulk?"

"Yeah."

"My God! I heard about her other personality's superhuman strength!"

"That's why she was able to lift that couch right up off the floor and throw it across the room because of her other personality's superhuman strength! Then her other personality used the doctors' own chains and couch as weapons against them, the security guards, the priest, the police officers and the swat team!"

"Her other personality used those chains and the couch as weapons against all these people?!"

"Yeah!"

"My God! Thank goodness I wasn't in here when it all happened, because I know I would be laying on this floor right along with the rest of these people!" The paramedic guy and the security guard shockingly look around the room at dozens of injured authority figures on the floor bleeding. They then look back towards Diane D's physical body as the security officers continue to remove the cuffs, chains and shackles from off her physical body.

The security officers finish removing the cuffs, chains and shackles from off Diane D's physical body. Dr. Stone then asks, "Are all the cuffs, chains and shackles removed from her?"

"Yes Doctor, all of them," one of the security officers says.

"Okay." Two more male paramedics burst into the room with a stretcher. Dr. Stone looks towards them and shouts, "Bring the stretcher here!" The two paramdics rush the stretcher towards Diane D's physical body. They bring the strectcher to Diane D's physical body. Dr. Stone tells them, "Okay let's lift her and put her on the stretcher then bring her and the stretcher into the next room." The two paramedics bend down to Diane D's physical body. They and the security officers grab Diane D's physical body. They lift her physical body up and gently place her physical body face up on top of the stretcher. They then place a sheet over her lower body. Dr. Stone turns to Diane D's family and says, "I need only up to ten family members to come over here. Everyone else stay back."

Margarita, Tomas, Barry, Mary, Tonio, Marilyn, Nicolas, Michael, Gracy and Grandpa Mike anxiously head towards Diane D's physical body as everyone else stays back.

Margarita, Tomas, Barry, Mary, Tonio, Marilyn, Nicolas, Michael, Gracy and Grandpa Mike anxiously approach Diane D's physical body and shout, "Diane!" They are about to grab her, but Dr. Stone shouts to them, "Wait! Hold on now everybody, don't any family member touch her!" Margarita, Tomas, Barry, Mary, Tonio, Marilyn, Nicolas, Michael, Gracy and Grandpa Mike stop and look at Dr. Stone as he says to them, "She's still under hynosis! If you touch her and call out to her, you will interfere with the hypnosis and it will be harder for me to bring her ORIGINAL soul, spirit and personality back! Do you want her original soul and spirit to come back or not?!" Margarita, Tomas, Barry, Mary, Tonio, Marilyn, Nicolas, Michael, Gracy and Grandpa Mike look at Dr. Stone as he says to them, "What I need, is for all of you to back up from her a little, give her some room and remain quiet while we try to get her into the next room." Margarita, Tomas, Barry, Mary, Tonio, Marilyn, Nicolas, Michael, Gracy and Grandpa Mike look back at Diane D's physical body. They back up a little. Dr. Stone then says to the paramedics, "Let's get her into the other room." The paramedics and the security officers roll the stretcher away with Diane D laying on it as her family members follow them. The paramedics roll the stretcher and Diane D out the back door. Dr. Stone and Diane D's family follow out the back door behind the paramedics and the security officers as the broken and bent out of shape psychiatrist couch, cuffs, chains and shackles remain on the floor.

Fifteen minutes later inside the next room, Dr. Stone sits in a chair next to the stretcher on the right side of Diane D's head again as he is slightly leaned towards her physical body again with a bandage wrapped around his bleeding head. Another doctor, Dr. Harvey, a white male around his mid fifties who's taking injured Dr. Kahn's place, sits in a chair next to the stretcher on the left side of Diane D's head as he is slightly leaned towards her physical body. Dr. Stone speaks to Diane D's subconscious again as he looks down at her physical body and asks, "Is there a soul, spirit or personality there inside this physical body?" Dr. Stone and Dr. Harvey stare at Diane D's physical body. Diane D does not respond. Her physical body continues to lay face up on the stretcher not responding as her eyes remain swollen and shut.

Margarita, Tomas, Barry, Mary, Tonio, Marilyn, Nicolas, Michael, Gracy and Grandpa Mike are sitting across the room in the middle of the second room anxiously watching Dr. Stone, Dr. Harvey and Diane D's physical body.

Dr. Stone and Dr. Harvey continue to look down at Diane as Dr. Stone asks, "Is there a soul, spirit or personality inside this physical body now? We need Diane's ORIGINAL soul, spirit and personality to return. Is Diane's original soul, spirit or personality in there now? Reveal yourself. Come out to us. Is Diane's original soul, spirit or personality in there now?" Dr. Stone and Dr. Harvey continue to stare at Diane D's physical body as her physical body continues to lay face up on the stretcher not responding.

Margarita, Tomas, Barry, Mary, Tonio, Marilyn, Nicolas, Michael, Gracy and Grandpa Mike continue to anxiously and nervously look at Diane D's physical body.

Dr. Stone and Dr. Harvey continue to look down at Diane D's physical body as Dr. Stone speaks to Diane D's subconscious again and asks, "Is there a soul, spirit or personality in there?" Dr. Stone and Dr. Harvey stare at Diane D's physical body as her physical body continues to lay on the stretcher not responding.

Margarita, Tomas, Barry, Mary, Tonio, Marilyn, Nicolas, Michael, Gracy and Grandpa Mike continue to sit quietly in the middle of the room puzzled looking at Diane D's physical body.

Outside in the hallway, Nancy, Charlotte, Mickey and the rest of Diane D's family and relatives stand around worried and nervously as Nancy says, "My God, I sure hope they're able to bring Diane's original personality back."
"Me too, Charlotte says. "This whole thing is just scary!"
"It is," Aunt Celeste says as everyone worriedly stands around.

Back inside the room, Dr. Stone and Dr. Harvey continue to look down at Diane D's physical body as Dr. Stone speaks to Diane D's subconscious again and asks, "Is there a soul, spirit or personality in there?" Dr. Stone and Dr. Harvey continue to stare at Diane D's physical body. Diane D still does not respond. Her physical body continues to lay on the couch not responding as her eyes remain swollen and shut. Dr. Stone then says, "If there is a soul, spirit or personality inside this physical body now, we need to know. We need

Diane's original soul, spirit and personality to come back, NOT the soul, spirit or personality that her cousin Nancy encountered inside their family's home inside their upstairs hallway, NOT the same one who beat up that kid Marcus inside that school hallway and was planning to kill him, NOT the same one who kung fu kicked the stuck storage room door at another hospital, NOT the same one who terrorized those correction officers inside the jail cell trying to attack them and NOT the one who caused Diane's physical body to levitate over the stage in Germany. I want Diane's original soul, spirit or personality to come back, I want her original soul, spirit and personality to return, but before we do that, I want to make sure, that the soul, spirit or personality that her cousin Nancy encountered inside their family's home inside their upstairs hallway does NOT return! I want to make sure, that SAME soul, spirit or personality who beat up that kid Marcus inside that school hallway and was planning to kill him does NOT return! I want to make sure, that SAME soul, spirit or personality who kung fu kicked the stuck storage room door at the hospital does NOT return! I want to make sure, that SAME soul, spirit or personality who terrorized those correction officers inside the jail cell trying to attack them does NOT return, and I want to make sure, that the soul, spirit or personality who caused Diane's physical body to levitate over the stage in Germany does NOT return either! Now is there a soul, spirit or personality there inside this physical body?" Dr. Kahn and Dr. Harvey continue to stare at Diane D's physical body as her physical body continues to lay on the couch not responding.

Margarita, Tomas, Barry, Mary, Tonio, Marilyn, Nicolas, Michael, Gracy and Grandpa Mike anxiously look at Diane D's physical body.

Dr. Stone then says, "Is Diane's original soul, spirit or personality inside this physical body now? Reveal yourself. Come out. We need you to return. Your family wants you to return. They want you back Diane, they are here waiting for you to return. Come back to your family Diane, come back now." Dr. Stone and Dr. Harvey stare at Diane D's physical body. Diane D still does not respond. Her physical body continues to lay on the couch not responding.

Margarita, Tomas, Barry, Mary, Tonio, Marilyn, Nicolas, Michael, Gracy and Grandpa Mike continue to sit quietly anxiously looking at Diane D as they pray silently for her original soul, spirit and personality to return.

Dr. Stone continues to look at Diane D's physical body and says, "Is Diane's original soul, spirit or personality inside this physical body now? If Diane's original soul, spirit or personality is inside this physical body now, please reveal yourself to us and come out. We need you to return to your family. Return back to your family now!"

Suddenly, Diane D's physical body starts to breathe hard. Dr. Stone and Dr. Harvey anxiously look at Diane D's physical body as her chest starts to rise and eyeballs seem to roll towards the top of her head again underneath her closed eyelids.

Margarita, Tomas, Barry, Mary, Tonio, Marilyn, Nicolas, Michael, Gracy and Grandpa Mike become excited and anxiously look at Diane D's physical body.

Dr. Stone and Dr. Harvey anxiously look at each other, then back at Diane D's physical body. Diane D's physical body continues to breathe hard as her eyes remain swollen and shut. Her physical body suddenly jerks as her legs kick up in the air as Dr. Stone and Dr. Harvey practically jump out of their seats. Diane D's physical body suddenly becomes motionless again. "What was that?" Dr. Harvey says. "She's not moving again. Why isn't she moving?"

"I don't know," Dr. Stone says. "I sure hope that wasn't the wrong soul, spirit or personslity trying to come back."

"Oh God." Dr. Harvey and Dr. Stone continue to look at Diane D's physical body.

Dr. Stone then speaks back to Diane D's subconscious and says, "Was that a soul, spirit or personality trying to come out? Was it Diane's original soul, spirit or personality? Is Diane's original soul spirit or personality there? Please come out and return to your family Diane. Return to your family now." Suddenly, Diane D's physical body starts to breathe hard again. Dr. Stone and Dr. Harvey anxiously look at Diane D's physical body again as her chest starts to rise and eyeballs seem to roll towards the top of her head again underneath her closed eyelids.

Margarita, Tomas, Barry, Mary, Tonio, Marilyn, Nicolas, Michael, Gracy and Grandpa Mike anxiously look at Diane D's physical body.

Dr. Stone and Dr. Harvey anxiously look at each other, then back at Diane D's physical body. Diane D's physical body continues to breathe hard as her eyes remain swollen and shut. Suddenly her breathing slows down, her chest lowers back down. Dr. Stone then says, "Is that a soul, spirit or personality trying to come out? Is there a soul, spirit or personality in there inside this physical body now? If there is a soul, spirit or personality inside this physical body now, respond 'yes' by waving your fingers three times when I ask again. Now is there a soul, spirit or personality inside this physical body now?" Diane D's physical body continues to lay on the couch as her eyes remain swollen shut. Suddenly her fingers wave once, twice, then three times.

Margarita, Tomas, Barry, Mary, Tonio, Marilyn, Nicolas, Michael, Gracy and Grandpa Mike become more excited and nervous as Michael turns to them and whispers, "She waved her fingers three times!" Margarita, Tomas, Barry, Mary, Tonio, Marilyn, Nicolas, Michael, Gracy and Grandpa Mike continue to anxiously look at Diane D.

Dr. Stone continues to speak to Diane D's subconscious as he looks down at her physical body and says, "Good. Now we want Diane's ORIGINAL soul, spirit or personality to come out, NOT the soul, spirit or personality that her cousin Nancy encountered inside their family's home inside their upstairs hallway, NOT the same soul, spirit or personality who beat up that kid Marcus inside that school hallway, NOT the same soul, spirit or personality who kung fu kicked that stuck storage room door at another hospital, NOT the same soul, spirit or personality who terrorized those correction officers inside the jail cell and NOT the souls, spirits or personalities who caused this physical body to levitate over the stage in Germany. We want Diane's original soul, spirit or personality to be back, but we want to make sure that this is NOT the soul, spirit or personality that Diane's cousin Nancy encountered inside their family's home, we want to make sure that this is NOT the same soul, spirit or personality who beat up that kid Marcus inside that school hallway, we want to make sure that this is NOT the same soul, spirit or personality who kung fu kicked the stuck storage room door, we want to make sure that this is NOT the same soul, spirit or personality who terrorized those correction officers inside the jail cell and we want to make sure that this is NOT the souls, spirits or personalities who caused this physical body to levitate over the stage in Germany. Now is this the soul, spirit or personality that Diane's cousin Nancy encountered inside their family's home? Is the soul, spirit or personality Diane's cousin Nancy had an encounter with and the same one who beat up that kid Marcus, inside this physical body now? If that soul, spirit or personality IS inside this physical body now, respond 'Yes' by waving your fingers three times when I ask. If that soul, spirit or personality is NOT the one inside this physical body now, respond 'No' by waving your fingers, twice. Now is the soul, spirit or personality Diane's cousin Nancy had an encounter with inside this physical body now? 'Yes' or 'no'?" Diane D's physical body continues to lay on the stretcher as her eyes remain closed. Suddenly her fingers wave once then twice.

"What!" Margarita, Tomas, Barry, Mary, Tonio, Marilyn, Nicolas, Michael, Gracy and Grandpa Mike whisper. They become excited and more nervous as Margarita turns to them and whispers, "She only waved her fingers twice! That means it's NOT the personality Nancy had the encounter with!"
"That's a good sign!" Tomas whispers.
"Come on Doctor Stone you can do it," Barry whispers. "Bring Diane's original personality back!" Barry, Tomas, Margarita, Mary, Tonio, Marilyn, Nicolas, Michael, Gracy and Grandpa Mike continue to

anxiously and nervously look at Dr. Stone and Diane D's physical body.

Dr. Stone then says to Diane D's subconscious, "Is this the soul, spirit or personality Diane's cousin Nancy encountered inside their family's home and the same one who beat up that kid Marcus, yes or no?" Diane D continues to lay on the couch as her eyes remain swollen and shut. Suddenly her fingers wave once then twice again.

"Oh good!" Margarita, Tomas, Barry, Mary, Tonio, Marilyn, Nicolas, Michael, Gracy and Grandpa Mike whisper.
They become more excited and nervous as Mary turns to them and whispers, "She only waved her fingers twice again!" The family continues to nervously look at Diane D's physical body.

Dr. Stone then says to Diane D's subconscious, "Are you saying, that this is another soul, spirit or personality inside this physical body now?" Diane D continues to lay on the couch as her eyes remain closed. Suddenly her fingers wave once, twice, then three times.

Margarita, Tomas, Barry, Mary, Tonio, Marilyn, Nicolas, Michael, Gracy and Grandpa Mike become more anxious and nervous as Marilyn turns to them and whispers, "They're saying it's another soul, spirit or personality! We're not out of the woods yet! It's probably that third personality again, the one that attacked the security guards, the police officers and the swat team members in the other room!"
"We sure hope not!" Mary whispers.

Dr. Stone then says to Diane D's subconscious, "Now is this the soul, spirit or personality who caused Diane's physical body to levitate over the stage in Germany, the same soul, spirit or personality who just attacked me, Dr. Kahn, the security guards, the priest, the police officers and swat team members in the other room? Is that soul, spirit or personality inside this physical body now? If that soul, spirit or personality IS inside this physical body now, respond 'Yes' by waving your fingers three times when I ask. If that soul, spirit or personality is NOT the one inside this physical body now, respond 'No' by waving your fingers, twice. Now is the soul, spirit or personality that caused Diane's physical body to levitate over the stage in Germany and the same soul, spirit or personality who went on the attack inside the other room, inside this physical body now? 'Yes' or 'no'?" Diane D's physical body continues to lay on the stretcher as her eyes remain closed. Suddenly her fingers wave once then twice.

"What!" Margarita, Tomas, Barry, Mary, Tonio, Marilyn, Nicolas, Michael, Gracy and Grandpa Mike shout. They become more excited and nervous as Marilyn turns to them and whispers, "It's not the third personality either, the one that went on the attack in the other room!"

"Oh let's keep our fingers crossed that this IS Diane's original personality!" Margarita whispers.

Dr. Stone then says to Diane D's subconscious, "Are you saying, that this is a different soul, spirit or personality inside this physical body now?" Diane D continues to lay on the couch as her eyes remain closed. Suddenly her fingers wave once, twice, then three times.

Margarita, Tomas, Barry, Mary, Tonio, Marilyn, Nicolas, Michael, Gracy and Grandpa Mike become more shocked and nervous as Marilyn turns to them and whispers, "It's a different personality! I think she's back!"

"Hopefully it's Diane's original one Marilyn," Barry says. "Let's not get our hopes up too high just yet!" Barry, Marilyn, Mary, Margarita, Tomas, Tonio, Nicolas, Michael, Gracy and Grandpa Mike nervously look at Diane D's physical body as they cross their fingers.

Dr. Stone then says to Diane D's subconscious, "Well if it's not the soul, spirit or personality that caused Diane's physical body to levitate over the stage in Germany which is the same soul, spirit or personality that went on the attack in the other room, and if it's not the same soul, spirit or personality who had the encounter with her cousin Nancy which is the same soul, spirit or personality that beat up that kid Marcus and kung fu kicked the stuck storage room door and terrorized the correction officers inside the jail cell, then is this Diane's ORIGINAL soul, spirit or personality inside this physical body now?" Diane D continues to lay on the couch as her eyes remain closed. Suddenly her fingers wave once, twice, then three times.

"Yesssss!" Margarita, Tomas, Barry, Mary, Tonio, Marilyn, Nicolas, Michael, Gracy and Grandpa Mike excitingly jump and shout. "It's her!"

Dr. Stone turns to Diane D's family and shouts, "I need silence please!" Dr. Stone turns back to Diane D's subconscious and says, "Are you saying, that this is Diane's ORIGINAL soul, spirit or personality back inside this physical body?" Diane D continues to lay on the couch as her eyes remain closed. Suddenly her fingers wave once, twice, then three times.

"She's back!" Margarita whispers as she, Tomas, Barry, Mary, Tonio, Marilyn, Nicolas, Michael, Gracy and Grandpa Mike jump and scream.

"Okay," Dr. Stone says to Diane D's subconscious. "I am going to wake you back up. But before I do that, I need to talk to you. I still need to make sure, that you are Diane's ORIGINAL personality, that this IS Diane's original personality, okay? Now are you able to talk now? Do you want to talk now? If you are able to talk now or are willing to talk now, respond by saying 'yes' when I ask again. Now are you able to talk now or are you willing to talk now?"

Diane D's physical body continues to lay on the couch as her eyes remain closed. Her orginal personality suddenly says, "Yes."

"Yes!" Margarita, Tomas, Mary, Barry, Tonio, Marilyn, Nicolas and Michael whisper.

"You're willing to talk?" Dr. Stone asks.
"Yes," Diane D's original personality says.
"Good. Now I need you to answer some simple questions, okay? What I need to know is, do you have a name."
"Yes."
"You have a name?"
"Yes."
"So what is your name then?"
"Diane."
"Your name is Diane?"
"Yes."

"Yes!" Margarita, Tomas, Mary, Barry, Tonio, Marilyn, Nicolas and Michael excitingly whisper. "It's her!"

"Good!" Dr. Stone says. "Do you speak and understand a specific language?"
"Yes," Diane D's original personality says.
"And what specific language is that? What specific language do you speak and understand?"
"English."
"You speak and understand English."
"Yes."
"Is there another language you specifically speak and understand?"
"Spanish."
"You can speak and understand Spanish."
"Yes."
"Good. Is there another language that you can speak and understand?"
"French."
"French? You can speak and understand French."
"Yes."
"All French or some French?"
"Some French."
"You can speak and understand only some French?"
"Yes."
"Okay. Is there any other language in this world that you can

speak and understand?"

"No."

"There isn't?"

"No."

"Think. Think very hard. Can you speak and understand any other language on this planet?"

"No."

"You cannot speak or understand any other language at all?"

"No."

"So you can mainly speak and understand English, Spanish and some French?"

"Yes."

"Yes!" Margarita, Tomas, Mary, Barry, Tonio, Marilyn, Nicolas and Michael whisper. They shockingly look at each other and whisper, "It's her! She's back!" They shockingly look back at Diane D.

"Okay," Dr. Stone says to Diane D's subconscious. "I am going to wake you back up now. When I count to three, I want you to wake up and open your eyes, okay? One ..... two ..... three! Open your eyes!" Diane D's original soul, spirit and personality opens her eyes.

"She's back!" Margarita, Tomas, Barry, Mary, Tonio, Marilyn, Nicolas, Michael, Gracy and Grandpa Mike whisper with excitment.

Diane D suspiciously looks her eyes around. She then looks at Dr. Stone as she continues to lay on the couch.

"She's back!" Margarita, Tomas, Barry, Mary, Tonio, Marilyn, Nicolas, Michael, Gracy and Grandpa Mike whisper again as they continue to stand with excitement.

Dr. Stone then says to Diane D, "Hi there. How are you feeling?" Diane D puzzled looks at Dr. Stone.

Dr. Harvey then says to Diane D, "Hi there. I'm Doctor Harvey." Diane D puzzled looks at Dr. Harvey.

Diane D suddenly jerks and starts screaming in pain, "Aaaaahhhh!"

"Diaaaane!" Margarita, Tomas, Barry, Mary, Tonio, Marilyn, Nicolas, Michael, Gracy and Grandpa Mike shout as they get out of their seats and rush towards Diane D!

Margarita, Tomas, Barry, Mary, Tonio, Marilyn, Nicolas, Michael, Gracy and Grandpa Mike approach Diane D and shout, "Diane!" They grab Diane D and start holding and hugging on to her very tight as she continues to scream in pain!

"Aaaaahhh!" Diane D screams.

"Oh Diane!" Her family looks at her and shout. "You're back!" Margarita, Tomas, Barry, Mary, Tonio, Marilyn, Nicolas, Michael, Gracy and Grandpa Mike continue to hold and hug on Diane D very tight.

"Aaaaaahh!" Diane D screams again.

"Wait!" Dr. Stone shouts as Diane D's family stop and look at him. "You have to be careful! I know you're happy to have her back, but she's in pain!"

"She's in pain?!" Diane D's family excitingly asks.

"Yes! She's in pain from when she broke loose from the chains!"

"Well if she feels pain, that means it's her original personality!" Magarita happily shouts as she and the rest of the family turn back to Diane D and continue to hold and hug her.

"Aaaahh!" Diane D screams again.

"She's in pain everybody!" Dr. Stone angrily shouts as Diane D's family stop and look back at him. "And by you all grabbing, hugging and holding her real tight, you're making her pain worst!"

"We know Dr. Stone!" Mary happily shouts. "Since she's in pain right now, that's a good sign that it IS her original personality back, NOT the other personalities who DON'T feel pain!"

"That's right Doctor Stone!" Tomas happily shouts. "Even though she's in pain, we're just happy to have her back!"

"Yes thank you so much for bringing her back Doctor Stone!" Barry happily shouts as he, Margarita and Mary excitingly turn back to Diane D and continue to hug and hold her tightly.

"Aaaaahhh!" Diane D screams again! Tomas, Tonio, Marilyn, Nicolas, Michael, Gracy and Grandpa Mike also continue to happily hold and hug Diane D very tightly, not thinking about the pain they are causing her. They're just happy to have her original personality back as Dr. Stone and Dr. Harvey stand there looking on happy to have Diane D's original personality back also.

Dr. Harvey turns to Dr. Stone and says, "Hey, I think you better hurry and get some medical attention for your injury too."

"Okay," Dr. Stone says.

"I'll let the paremedics in." Dr. Harvey turns and rushes to the door. He unlocks and opens the door. Paramedics rush into the room with a wheel chair. A couple of paramedics head towards Dr. Stone with the wheel chair as a few paramedics head towards Diane D.

One of the paramedics with Dr. Stone says to him, "Here Doctor. Sit in this wheel chair."

Dr. Stone sits in the wheel chair. He turns to the paremedics that are with Diane D and tells them, "She needs to be admitted. She's in a lot of pain right now from when she broke loose from the chains. She might have bruises all over herself. Tell the doctors that she's going to have to be sedated."

"Okay," the paramedics says.

Dr. Harvey approaches Diane D's family as Michael asks him,

"She's being admitted?"

"Well yes, "Dr. Harvey says. "She's not well." Dr. Harvey turns to the paramedics and says, "Bring her upstairs." The paramedics take Diane D and the stretcher and bring her and the stretcher towards the front door as her family follows.

Diane D's family then approach Dr. Stone as Barry asks, "So what's supposed to happen with her now Doctor Stone?"

"She's being admitted in the hospital for a while," Doctor Stone says. "The other doctors are gonna give her X-rays from the injuries she sustained when she broke loose from the chains to see if she has any broken bones."

"Oh yeah?" Margarita asks. "Then what's suppose to happen next?"

"We're going to have her commited again."

"Commited again?!" Diane D's family shouts.

"Yes!"

"Why?!" Barry shouts.

"Didn't you see all the chaos that she caused while she was under hypnosis, breaking the chains loose from the couch then having all those security guards, the priest, police officers and a swat team be hurt and injured when she tossed the couch across the room at them slamming the couch right into their heads bashing them in the heads knocking them down then chain whips them while they're down causing two guns to go off and causing two police officers to be shot! Look what she did to me and Doctor Kahn, she kung fu kicked us in the head and back and hit us with the chains! This is what we were afraid of!"

"But Diane didn't realize what she was doing Doctor Stone!" Mary shouts.

"I know, that's why we felt we had to chain her up! But obviously, it didn't work!"

"That's why we did not want that other personality to come out to the surface in the first place Doctor Stone when you and Doctor Kahn were planning to hypnotize her!" Margarita shouts, "but you and Dr. Kahn wanted to hypnotize her anyway!"

"Yeah look where it got us! Now we're both are going to have to be laying up here in this hospital ourselves!"

"But why do you still have to have her committed Doctor Stone?!" Tomas shouts.

"Didn't you hear what she said while she was under hypnosis?! She threatened to go after that kid Marcus to kill him! She literally breaks the chains loose from the couch to go do so! Those chains didn't stop her from attacking me, Doctor Kahn, the priest, the security guards, police officers and a swat team then trying to go after that kid Marcus! You all keep saying that it's Marcus' own subconscious that's causing his nightmares about Diane coming after him, but even though Diane herself says she's not angry with Marcus anymore and not thinking about him, obviously her subconscious is still angry with him!"

"So that means my sister has to be sent away again Doctor Stone?" Nicolas asks.

"Well we can't send the other souls, spirits or personalities away. They have no physical bodies! Unfortunately, they used Diane's!"

"Oh no!" Diane's family shouts.

"How long will she be committed Doctor?!" Michael asks.

"I don't know," Dr. Stone says. "It depends on her evaluation."

"Oh no!" Diane's family shouts again.

"I'm sorry folks."

One of the paramedics turns to Diane D's family and says, "We have to take him for medical treatment." The paramedics turn Dr. Stone's wheel chair and take him towards the door.

Dr. Stone turns towards Diane D's family and says, "I'll get back to you. Doctor Harvey will take my place while I'm out for my injury. He will take care of everything." The paramedics head Dr. Stone and the wheel chair towards the front door as Diane D's family sadly look on.

"Wait a minute Doctor Stone!" Barry suddenly shouts as he rushes to Dr. Stone. Mary, Margarita and Tomas rush after Barry.

The paramedic stop the wheel chair as he and Dr. Stone turn towards Barry. Barry, Mary, Margarita and Tomas approach Dr. Stone as Barry says, "Dr. Stone? What are we going to do about Dana? Since that other soul, spirit or personality kept quiet about whether they ever used her physical body to kill anybody, should we ask Dana herself has she ever killed anybody?"

"No!" Dr. Stone shouts. "Absolutely not! If you ask Dana has she ever killed anybody, she's not going to admit to it! She's not going to incriminate herself! Not only that, if that other soul, spirit or personality ever did use Dana's physical body to kill, most likely, Dana is not going to remember it!"

"She's not?" Margarita asks.

"No! Just like Diane doesn't remember her violent actions whenever that other soul, spirit or personality take over her physical body to do harm! Because if you ask Dana has she ever killed anybody before, she's not going to know what the heck you're talking about! Then she's gonna want to know why would you ask her something like that! So if that other soul, spirit or personality ever did use Dana's physical body to kill someone, Dana is not going to remember it! You're never going to get a true answer from her! We might have to investigate Dana's past in another way. Since you all are part of her family, have you ever know of her ever killing somebody?"

"No," Margarita, Barry, Mary and Tomas say.

"Not that any of us know of," Barry says. "If that other soul, spirit or personality ever did use Dana's physical body to kill someone, that other soul, spirit or personality is not going to do it in front of any of us or near any of us! It will most likely do it far away from us so we won't be involved, just like it was planning to kill Marcus far away from us in the back stairwell of the school so we won't be involved."

240

"Yeah that's true. Obviously, this other soul, spirit and personality doesn't realize that anything Diane or Dana become involved in, your whole family will be dragged into it." Margarita, Barry, Mary and Tomas sadly look at Dr. Stone. Dr. Stone then says, "Well, I have to get going." The paramedic turns Dr. Stone's wheel chair. Dr. Stone turns back towards Diane D's family and says, "I'll talk to you later." The paramedic heads Dr. Stone and the wheel chair out the front door as Diane D's family sadly look on.

Margarita, Barry, Mary and Tomas then turn to each other as Margarita says, "Not only do we have to worry about Diane with this other soul, spirit and personality, but we have to worry about Dana now too!"

"I know Mom," Barry says. "The only thing we can do, is be there for both Diane and Dana." They all start to get tears in their eyes. Barry then says, "Come on. We got to get to Diane." Barry, Mary, Margarita and Tomas turn to the rest of the family in the room as Barry shouts to them, "Come on everybody! We're going to Diane!" The rest of the family hurry towards Barry, Mary, Margarita and Tomas.

That same evening, Margarita, Tomas, Mary, Barry, Tonio, Marilyn, Nicolas and Michael are all laying on cots downstairs in the emergency room with their eyes closed as Dr. Harvey and other doctors surround them. They are all traumatized by what they have heard and witnessed with Diane D's other personalities earlier. Dr. Harvey approaches Margarita laying on a cot with her eyes closed and face sort of sweaty. He says to her, "Are you okay Miss Margarita? Miss Margarita?" Margarita tries to respond, but is not able to as her eyes remain closed. Dr. Harvey then turns from Margarita as he sadly looks at her. He starts to head towards Mary.

Dr. Harvey approaches Mary laying on another cot with her eyes closed also and her face sort of sweaty. He says to her, "Miss Mary. Are you okay?" Mary tries to respond, but is not able to either as her eyes remain closed. Dr. Harvey then turns from Mary and sadly looks at her. He starts to head towards Barry.

Dr. Harvey approaches Barry as Barry lays on another cot with his eyes closed and face slightly sweaty. He says to him, "Mr. Barry? Mr. Barry can you hear me?" Barry tries to respond also, but is not able to either as his eyes remain closed. Dr. Harvey then turns from Barry and sadly looks at him. He starts to head towards Tomas.

Dr. Harvey approaches Tomas laying on another cot with his eyes closed and face a little sweaty. He says to him, "Mr. Tomas? Mr. Tomas?" Tomas tries to respond also, but is not able to either as his eyes remain closed. Dr. Harvey then turns from Tomas and sadly looks at him. He starts to head towards Michael.

Dr. Harvey approaches Michael laying on another cot with his eyes closed and face slightly sweaty also. He says to him, "Mr. Michael? Mr. Michael." Michael does not respond. His eyes remain closed. Dr.

Harvey then turns from Michael and sadly looks at him. He starts to head towards Marilyn.

Dr. Harvey approaches Marilyn laying on another cot with her eyes closed and face a little sweaty. He says to her, "Miss Marilyn can you hear me? Miss Marilyn." Marilyn tries to respond also, but is not able to either as her eyes remain closed. Dr. Harvey then turns from Marilyn and sadly looks at her. He starts to head towards Nicolas.

Dr. Harvey approaches Nicolas laying on another cot with his eyes closed and face sweaty. He says to him, "Mr. Nicolas can you hear me? Are you able to speak Mr. Nicolas? Mr. Nicolas?" Nicolas does respond. His eyes remain closed. Dr. Harvey then turns from Nicolas and sadly looks at him. He starts to head towards Tonio.

Dr. Harvey approaches Tonio laying on another cot with his eyes closed and face sweaty. He says to him, "Mr. Tonio? Wake up Mr. Tonio." Tonio does not respond either as his eyes remain closed. Dr. Harvey then turns from Tonio and sadly looks at him. He starts to head to one of the other doctors.

Dr. Harvey approaches one of the other doctors and says, "They're all out of it."

"I see," a male white doctor around his mid forties says as he and Dr. Harvey look at Margarita and the rest of the family.

"If they don't come out of being shocked and traumatized by the end of tonight, I'm afraid I'm going to have them all admitted."

"I know." The other doctor and Dr. Harvey continue to look at Margarita and the rest of the family.

"Well, I'm gonna head back upstairs to the hypnosis room now. I'll be back to check on them."

"Okay Doctor Harvey."

Dr. Harvey takes one last look at Diane D's family. He then turns and heads down the hallway.

Several minutes later, Dr. Harvey is back upstairs inside the hypnosis room. He, other hospital staff members, hospital authorities, Officer Henley, other police officers, news reporters and photographers are all shockingly looking around at all the damage and bloodshed that has happened in there. There are objects and some furniture knocked down all across the room. There are papers all over the floor and video cameras knocked down. Everybody then turns and looks at the damaged and broken bent out of shape psychiatrist couch which is still on the floor with broken chains, broken cuffs and broken shackles on the floor around it. They see the metal bars beneath the couch all broken and bent out of shape. The see broken pieces of the chains still attached to it. They see long broken pieces of other chains laying across the floor. The photographers approach the broken couch and broken chains laying on the floor. They snap pictures of the broken couch and broken chains. One of the reporters turns to Dr. Harvey and says, "Wow Diane D did all of this?!"

"I'm afraid she did," Dr. Harvey says.

"My God! How is her family taking all of this? Are they all still downstairs in the emergency room, traumatized by what they all saw and witnessed?"

"Yes they still are. They still can't believe what they saw and witnessed! They still can't believe all the stuff they heard Diane D's other personalities saying!"

"They heard everything Diane D's other personalities said?!"

"Yes everything, from the beginning to the end. And they witnessed her other personality's superhuman strength when her other personality went berserk on the doctors, the security guards, a priest, the police officers and a swat team!"

"What! They witnessed all that?!"

"They sure did! I think they're so traumatized that some of them or all of them might have to be admitted if they don't come to!"

"What? You're not saying that they might have to be in the hospital themselves?"

"I'm afraid so if they don't get over being traumatized."

"So that means Diane D caused all those authority figures AND her own family as well to be admitted into the hospital!"

"Well not her, it's her other personality. I'm afraid her other personality might have caused her own family to be admitted, if they don't pull through."

"Did they get physically hurt also when all the authority figures got hurt?"

"They almost did get hurt when the couch flew right over their heads!"

"What! Diane D's other personality threw the couch right over her own family's heads?"

"Yeah but her other personality was aiming the couch at the police officers when her other personality was throwing the couch across the room at them! If Diane D's family hadn't duck their heads in time, the couch would have slammed right into their heads instead."

"Oh my God! No wonder why they're all traumatized right now! I can imagine what they must be going through right now! I feel bad for them!"

"Yeah, me too."

"But I don't get it. They saw and witnessed everything that happened with Diane D earlier, but yet they never saw or witnessed what happened with Diane D when her body supposedly levitated over a stage in Germany?"

"No they never saw or witnessed that from what I heard. But I'm sure that if they HAD witnessed Diane D levitating over that stage in Germany, I'm sure they would have been traumatized by that as well."

"But this time, they witnessed everything right before their eyes?"

"Yes that's why they're all traumatized. I'm afraid they might need some counseling themselves after all of this."

"Wow." The reporter and Dr. Harvey turn and continue to look at the damaged hypnosis room.

Chapter 15

Injured Police Officers' Families Threaten To Sue

That same night inside another hospital room, many injured police officers are laying in hospital beds surrounded by their families.

Dr. Harvey, news reporters and photographers are all standing outside in the hallway.

The police officers' families step out of the room and enter the hallway. Mrs. Jenkins, one of the injured officer's wife, a white female around her early 40's with dark hair approaches Dr. Harvey and shouts to him, "You know this is so unbelievable! We want to press charges against Diane D!"

"That's right!" Mrs. Peterson, the wife of another police officer, a white female around her early forties with brunette hair shouts. "Diane D is a dangerous person! Look what she did to my husband and the other police officers! They said she threw a psychiatrist couch across the room at them, a priest, security guards and a swat team when they were about to burst into the doorway of the hypnosis room! They said she knocked them all down with that couch! Some of the police officers and swat team members got knocked out cold! Then she chain whipped all of them with the chains that were attached to her shackles! My husband and another cop wind up getting shot when she chain whipped the guns right out of their hands causing one of the guns to go off! Now my husband and all these other officers are laying here in the hospital, including two doctors, security guards, a priest and a swat team! I mean all these authority figures and their guns couldn't stop Diane D?!"

"That's right! When some of the police officers came to, they said that couch came flying at them so fast that they didn't even know what hit them!"

"They didn't?" Dr. Harvey asks.

"No, not at first! They found out later on that it was a psychiatrist couch! They said they never had time to even get in the door when that couch came flying at them at sixty, seventy or eighty miles and hour! A lot of these officers have serious head injuries! A few of their heads got split opened! Some them even have brain hemorrhage!"

"Oh no!" the rest of the officers' families shout.

"Those two doctors, Doctor Stone and Doctor Kahn, brought that monster right out of Diane D! They turned Diane D into a vicious monster! And once they turned her into a vicious monster, they couldn't even control their monster while their monster was going mad turning loose on the security guards, a priest, police officers and a swat team!"

"I'm sorry Mrs. Jenkins," Dr. Harvey says, "but you have to understand, Diane didn't know what she was doing! She was under hypnosis! She's not aware of what she did! She's not aware of any of this!"

"She isn't?"

"No!"

"Why not?! Is she still under hypnosis?!"

"No, she's not under hypnosis anymore, she's sedated."

"Sedated?!"

"Yes."

"Why?!"

"Because of the pain she was in from herself breaking loose from the chains! She's got bruises all over her arms, her shoulders, her wrists, her legs and her ankles! She's still not aware of what's going on right now! She doesn't even know that she's the cause of your husband, the other police officers, the security guards, the priest and a swat team being in the hospital!"

"Wow," Mrs. Peterson says. "All these people are in the hospital! And this is all because Doctor Stone and Doctor Kahn put Diane D under hypnosis and brought that monster or demon personality out of her?!"

"I'm afraid that's what happened."

"Alright! We're going to sue those two doctors then!"

"Sue them?! What do you mean you're going to sue them?!"

"They're the ones who brought that monster or demon personality out of Diane D which caused her to wind up attacking my husband, the other officers, the security guards, the priest and a swat team with that couch and those chains! The other police officers and security guards who were laying on the floor injured said that Diane D had superhuman strength when she threw and tossed that phychiatrist couch right across the room at the other officers and security guards! They said they've never seen anything like that before! They said they saw that couch came speeding at them and other officers so fast that it felt like they got hit and knocked down by a flying speeding car! They said then Diane D threw her hands right on top the couch, did a hand stand and chain whipped them all with the chains that were attached to her shackles causing two guns to go off! Those other police officers and my husband are hurt real bad! Dr. Stone made Diane D into a vicious monster! He's just like Doctor Frankenstein!"

"Doctor Frankenstein?!"

"Yes! Or should I call him Doctor FrankenStone?!"

"Doctor FrankenStone?! Now you didn't have to go there Mrs. Peterson."

"It's easy for you to say that Doctor Harvey! It's not your loved ones laying in the hospital hurt! My husband might die from that gunshot wound and having his head split opened!"

Dr. Harvey sadly looks at Mrs. Peterson.

Chapter 16

People Read Headlines Of Diane D's Other Personality

The following day, a white grandmother with very dark hair around her mid fifties and her daughter around her mid thirties are sitting inside a coffee shop with cups of coffee and cheesecake on their table. The daughter has a stroller right next to her with her female toddler in it as she gives her female toddler a bottle of milk. The grandmother is reading a newspaper with a headline that reads: DOCTORS HYPNOTIZE DIANE D AND BRING OUT HER OTHER PERSONALITY AFTER IT WAS DISCOVERED THAT HER COUSIN NANCY HAD AN ENCOUNTER WITH IT INSIDE THEIR FAMILY'S HOME: "Hey!" the grandmother suddenly says. "This article says that two doctors hypnotized Diane D and brought out her other personality after her cousin Nancy encountered it inside their family's home!"

"What!" the daughter says. "Doctors hypnotized Diane D and brought out her other personality when her cousin Nancy encountered it inside their house?!"

"Yes, that's what it says!"

"Oh my God!" The daughter takes a quick glance at the article and says, "Isn't her cousin Nancy one of the Dianettes who backs up and sings with her?"

"Yes she sure is."

"And they live in the same house with their grandparents right?"

"Yeah they do, up in the northern part of Westchester."

"Wow. Does it mean that their family's house is haunted?"

"Nooo, I don't think it's their house that's haunted. I think it's Diane D herself that's haunted!"

"You really think so Mom?"

"Of course I do! I've heard about her other personality that be going on the attack attacking people and she winds up not remembering it! I think she had a split personality when she beat up that little boy inside that school hallway that night because she claims

248

she does not remember beating him up!"

"I know! Ain't that weird?"

"It sure is! Some people believe she's possessed!"

"I heard! What do you think Mom? You think it's a possibilty that Diane D could be possessed?"

"I believe so!"

"You do?!"

"Of course I do! I think she's possessed by these vicious souls, spirits or other personalities that be taking over her! I believe that these vicious souls, spirits or other personalities aren't after her family's house, I believe they're after Diane D herself because I hear she keeps meditating! And I believe whenever she meditates, she be inviting these other personalities or entities to take over herself and she doesn't even be aware of it! And that incident usually happens inside her family's house! When she went into a state of trance and beat up that little boy inside that school hallway, that didn't happen inside their family's home, that happened right inside a school hallway, but that doesn't mean that the school hallway or the school itself is haunted, does it?"

"No, of course not."

"And when those two hospital employees who worked the night shift at a hospital saw another personality take over Diane D when they saw her literally kung fu kick a stuck storage room door wide open and broke it right off its hinges, that happened inside a hospital clinic area, but that doesn't mean that the hospital clinic area or the hospital itself is haunted, does it?"

"No."

"So I don't think it matters where Diane D be at! Those other personalities or entities will take over her no matter where she is! So it's not the places that are haunted, it's Diane D herself that's haunted!"

"If that's the case, then how come that little boy had refused to attend that school anymore if it's not the school itself that's haunted?"

"Because of the memories of what happened to him inside that school? If he even looks at or sees that school, it will remind him of what he went through with Diane D. It will remind him of that terrible incident when Diane D beat him up in there! It will remind him of seeing Diane D being possessed and in a state of trance in there! He doesn't want to be reminded of what he went through with Diane D inside that school and I don't blame him! Not only that. Those two hospital employees who witnessed Diane D kung fu kick that stuck storage room door wide open inside a hospital clinic area one night had to be transferred to work at another hospital themselves! They couldn't take the memories of what they saw and witnessed Diane D do either!"

"My God! You know Mom, I would be afraid to live in a house with someone like Diane D, someone who seems possessed then gets into these weird state of trances then gets out of control and attacks people and winds up not rememdering them!"

"Me too!"

"I'm glad we don't have anybody like that in our family because who knows when that other personality might all of a sudden come out if we had someone like that in our family. If we had someone like that in our family and their other personality just come out like that, I would run right out of the house and not look back because that is scaaary!"

"It certainly is." The grandmother and her daughter continue to look at the newspaper.

At another location, two white men and a white woman in the street who are around their late thirties and early forties are reading a newspaper with a different headline that reads: **SEVERAL POLICE OFFICERS KNOCKED OUT COLD! DOCTORS HYPNOTIZE DIANE D AND BRING OUT HER OTHER PERSONALITY WHICH THEN GOES BERSERK AND ATTACK THE DOCTORS, A PRIEST AND AUTHORITY FIGURES CAUSING TWO COPS TO GET SHOT!**: "Oh my God!" one of the men says. "This article says doctors hypnotized Diane D and brought out her other personality!"

"Yeah I saw it on the news!" the second man says. "Her other personality caused two cops to get shot too!"

"Two cops got shot?!" the woman asks.

"Yeah!"

"That is crazy!"

"It is!" the first man says. "It says that Diane D's own family was right inside the hypnosis room when she got hypnotized and they heard and witnessed everything her other personality said and did! It says that they got traumatized by that incident!"

"They got traumatized?!"

"Yeah. It says so right here!"

"Man that is fucked up!" the second man says.

"It sure is! I really feel for what Diane D's family is going through, having to deal with something like this."

"I know." The men and woman continue to read the newspaper article.

That same day, a black man around his early forties at an office job is reading a newspaper with a different headline that reads: **DIANE D WRAPPED IN CHAINS AND SHACKLES! DOCTORS BRING OUT DIANE D'S OTHER PERSONALITY WHICH MANAGES TO BREAK LOOSE FROM THE CHAINS AND SHACKLES! HER OTHER PERSONALITY THEN GOES BERSERK AND ATTACK THE DOCTORS, A PRIEST AND AUTHORITY FIGURES! TWO COPS SHOT IN THE PROCESS!**: "Oh my God!" the man shouts. "This article says that two doctors had Diane D hypnotized at a hospital, then had her body wrapped in chains and brought out her other personality!"

"What!" other office workers shout as they rush to the man.

The office workers approach the man as one of the women shouts, "Two doctors had Diane D hypnotized at a hospital, then had her body wrapped in chains and brought out her other personality! Diane D was wrapped in chains?!"

"Yeah!" the man says.

"Then two doctors brought out her other personality?!"

"Yeah! Then it says right here that her other personality broke loose from the chains and attacked the doctors with the chains!"

"What!" the other workers shout.

"She broke loose from the chains?!" a male co-worker shouts.

"Yeah!" the first man says.

"Then attacked the doctors with the chains?!"

"Yeah and with the psychiatrist couch she was chained too!"

"What!" the other workers shout. "With the psychiatrist couch she was chained to?!"

"You mean Diane D was chained to a couch?" the male co-worker asks.

"According to this article she was!" the first man says. "And it says that when the security guards and a priest burst into the room, her other personality went on the attack and threw the psychiatrist couch right across the room at their heads smashing the couch right into their heads knocking them down!"

"What! She threw a psychiatrist couch across the room?!"

"That's what it says!"

"Then she smashed the couch right into their heads and knocked the security guards and the priest down with the couch?!"

"Yeah! It says that the couch came speeding at their heads at sixty, seventy or eighty miles an hour!"

"Sixty, seventy or eighty miles an hour?!" the other workers shout.

"Yeah!"

"My God that's as fast as a car!" the male co-worker says.

"Yeah! That's how fast Diane D's other personality threw that couch!"

"My God! What was a priest doing there in the first place?"

"I don't know! Maybe they had the priest there for a reason! And it says that when police officers and a swat team were about to burst into the doorway of the hypnosis room, Diane D's other personality threw the psychiatrist couch right across the room at their heads smashing the couch right into their heads bashing their heads in knocking them down too!"

"What!" a second male co-worker shouts. "She threw the psychiatrist couch across the room again, smashing the couch into the police officers and a swat team knocking them down with the couch too?!"

"Yeah!"

"Ain't that psychiatrist couch heavy?"

"Of course it's heavy! It says that the couch was so heavy that some of the police officers got knocked out cold when the couch came speeding at them knocking them down!"

"They got knocked out cold?!" the other workers shout.

"Yeah! Their guns fell right out of their hands when they got knocked out!"

"Their guns fell out of their hands?!" a second woman asks.

"Yeah! Some of their heads got split open!"

"Oh gosh!" the other workers shout.

"And when the other injured officers on the floor tried to reach for their guns, that's when Diane D's other personality threw her body upside down on top of the couch and did a hand stand and chain whips the security guards' and police officers' hands with the long chains that were strapped to her shackles!"

"She did a hand stand while chains were strapped to her shackles?!" the male co-worker asks.

"Yeah, then she used those chains as whips and swung those chains then chain whips the guns right out of the police officers' hands!"

"She did what?!"

"Yeah! It caused two of the guns to go off! Two cops got shot?!"

"What!" the other workers shout. "Two cops got shot?!"

"Yeah!"

"That's crazy!" the second woman shouts. "Did they survive?!"

"They're both still alive right now, but one of them is in critical condition!"

"One of them is in critical condition?!"

"Yeah! He got shot in the chest!"

"Oh no!" the other workers shout.

"Didn't her cousin Dana caused a female officer to get shot in the back a couple of years ago?" a second male co-worker asks.

"Yep, she sure did!" the first man says. "Now that female officer is paralyzed and can never walk again. That female officer became disabled and now Diane D herself caused two officers to get shot!"

"Oh God!" the other workers shout.

"It says that Diane D's own family was right inside the room when this shit was going down!"

"What!"

"Diane D's family was inside the room?!" the first male co-worker shouts. "You mean they witnessed all of that?!"

"Yeah!" the first man shouts.

"Oh my lord, they could have gotten shot too when the guns went off! My God! How did Diane D even manage to break those chains loose from the couch?! How was she even able to lift that couch and toss it across a room?!"

"Her other personality probably did that!" the first woman shouts.

"Other personality my foot!" the first man shouts. "That was no other personality!"

"It wasn't?!"

"No, split personalities don't do that!"

"No? So what was it then?!"

"It was a goddamn demon, that's what it was! Anybody that is able to break out of chains like that or lift a heavy couch high up in the air and throw it across a room at sixty, seventy or eighty miles and hour which is faster than most cars, has to be the work of a demon! I mean no one is that powerful to break loose from chains that are wrapped around them and a couch or lift a heavy object high up in the air and toss it right across a room at a killer speed! That is not normal! That is definitely the work of a demon!"

"So what are you trying to say?" the second male co-worker says. "Are you saying that a demon took over Diane D?"

"Yes that's exactly what I'm saying! That woman doesn't have a split personality, she is possessed! And she is possessed by a demon! That's probably why those doctors had a priest inside that room in the first place because they were scared! They wanted to get prepared to excorsize that demon out of Diane D!"

"Yeah you're right," the first woman says, "because that's the same thing that kid Marcus said about her when she beat him up inside that school hallway a few years ago! He said he felt the presence of a demon inside Diane D!"

"Well now we all know, that kid Marcus was right! Diane D is possessed! And she probably got possessed by doing that meditation stuff she does! I think that woman be inviting these demons into her with that meditation jazz and she might not even be aware of it!"

"But I don't understand! A lot of people meditate! But they don't become possessed or anything!"

"They don't become possessed! But for some reason, Diane D seems to be the only one who becomes possessed whenever she meditates!"

"Maybe it could be something about her meditation that seems to make her become possessed," the second male co-worker says. "Maybe she's doing something special in her meditation."

"Like what, worshipping the devil?! Either way, the sad thing is, is that her family had to witness all of that stuff and deal with it! It says right here that eight family members of hers are traumatized by what they had all heard and witnessed and had to be admitted into the hospital emergency room themselves!"

"Eight family members of hers are traumatized?" the first male co-worker asks.

"Yes, eight family members, including her grandparents!"

"What!" everyone shouts. "Her grandparents?!"

"Her grandparents were in the room when all that stuff happened?!" the first male co-worker shouts. "You mean they witnessed that stuff too?!"

"Yeah they witnessed it!" the first man shouts, "including Diane D's own parents!"

"Oh no!"

"And her husband and older brother!"

"What!" everyone shouts. "Her husband and older brother?!"

"Yeah! I'm sure they're all traumatized by that whole thing! I would be traumatized too if I realize that I'm in the same room with a demon or realize that I'm living in the same house with one!"

"Living in the same house with a demon!" the first woman says. "Oooohhh that is scary!"

"It is!" Everyone looks back at the newspaper article.

That same day, Vanessa and Jessica are inside the livingroom in their apartment. The doorbell suddenly rings. "I'll go get it," Vanessa says. Vanessa turns and heads towards the front door.

Vanessa approaches the front door. She looks through the peephole. She then opens the door and sees Officer Henley at the door. She then says, "Officer Henley, how are you?"

"How am I?" Officer Henley says. "The question is, 'how are you'."

"Okay I guess."

"Good. Did you see today's paper?"

"No not yet. Come on in." Vanessa opens the door wider and lets Officer Henley in.

Officer Henley enters the apartment. He sees Jessica, Marcus and Richard standing in the living room. He enters the living room and says, "Hey guys. I'm sorry to barge in on you."

"No that's okay Officer Henley," Jessica says. "What's up?"

"I came to show you today's paper just in case you haven't read it or gotten it yet."

"Oh yeah? What happened?"

"Read this." Officer Henley hands the newspaper to Jessica.

Jessica, Vanessa, Marcus and Richard read the newspaper with a headline that reads: **DIANE D TURNS INTO A MODERN DAY HOUDINI AS SHE BREAKS LOOSE FROM CHAINS:** "Diane D turns into a modern day Houdini?" Jessica says. "What's this about?" Jessica opens the newspaper. She, Vanessa, Marcus and Richard read the article. "What!" Jessica shouts. "This article says that doctors hypnotized Diane D and brought out her other personality!"

"What!" Marcus, Vanessa and Richard shout.

"Doctors hypnotized Diane D and brought her other personality out?!" Marcus shouts.

"Yeah!" Jessica shouts.

"Oh my goodness!" Vanessa shouts.

"It then says that Diane D's other personality threatened the doctors!"

"What!" Marcus, Vanessa and Richard shout.

"Her other personality threatened the doctors?!" Richard shouts.

"Yes!" Jessica shouts. "It says her other personality threatened that it was going to wring the doctor's neck!"

"What!" Marcus, Vanessa and Richard shout. "Wring the doctor's neck?!"

"Her other personality threatened to wring the doctor's neck?!" Vanessa shouts.

"Yeah!" Jessica shouts. "Then it says her other personality went berserk and broke loose from the chains she was strapped in and attacked the doctors!"

"What!" Marcus, Vanessa and Richard shout. "Broke loose from the chains she was strapped in?!"

They all shockingly look at Officer Henley as Vanessa shouts, "Diane D was wrapped in chains?!"

"Yes," Officer Henley says.

"Then her other personality threatened to wring the doctor's neck?!"

"It sure did."

"Then her other personality literally breaks loose from the chains and attacks the doctors?!"

"I'm afraid so."

"It then says that security guards and a priest bursted into the room!" Jessica shouts. "When security guards and the priest bursted into the room, Diane D's other personality threw a psychiatrist couch right across the room at them knocking them down!"

"What!" Vanessa, Richard and Marcus shout.

Vanessa turns to Officer Henley and shouts, "Diane D's other personality threw a psychiatrist couch across the room at security guards and a priest knocking them down?!"

"Yes," Officer Henley says. "I'm afraid her other personality did."

"How was her other personality even able to lift a couch and throw it across the room?!"

"I have no idea Mrs. Whitley."

"It then says the police bursted into the doorway with tasers drawn!" Jessica shouts.

"Tasers?!" Vanessa, Richard and Marcus shout.

"Yeah! And when they bursted into the doorway with the tasers, Diane D's other personality threw the psychiatrist couch right across the room at them, knocking them down also!"

"What!" Vanessa, Richard and Marcus shout.

Vanessa turns to Officer Henley and shouts, "Diane D's other personality threw the psychiatrist couch across the room, at police officers too, knocking them down also?!"

"Yes!" Officer Henley says. "I'm afraid her other personality did that too."

"It says some of some of the police officers got knocked out cold!" Jessica shouts.

"What!" Vanessa, Richard and Marcus shout. "Knocked out cold?!"

Vanessa turns to Officer Henley and shouts, "Some of the police officers got knocked out cold?!"

"Yes!" Officer Henley says.

"Oh my God!"

"Then it says that some of their heads got split opened!" Jessica shouts.

"What!" Vanessa, Richard and Marcus shout. "Some of their heads got split opened?!"

Vanessa turns to Officer Henley and shouts, "Some of the police officers' heads got split opened?!"

"Yes Mrs. Whitley!" Officer Henley says.

"Oh my God!"

"Then it says that Diane D's other personality did a hand stand right over the couch and chain whips the injured police officers' hands with the long chains that were still strapped to her shackles and wind up knocking the tasers right out of their hands!" Jessica shouts.

"What!" Vanessa, Richard and Marcus shout.

"She knocked the tasers out of their hands?!" Richard shouts. "With the chains?!"

"Yeah!" Jessica shouts. "Some of their arms and fingers got broken!"

"What!" Vanessa, Richard and Marcus shout.

"Their arms and fingers got broken?!" Marcus shouts.

"That's what it says!" Jessica shouts. "Then more police officers were about to bursted into the doorway, this time with guns drawn!"

"With guns drawn?!" Vanessa, Richard and Marcus shout.

"Oh my goodness!" Vanessa shouts.

"And when the police were about to burst into the doorway with the guns, Diane D's other personality threw the psychiatrist couch right across the room at them too, knocking them down also!" Jessica shouts.

"What!" Vanessa, Richard and Marcus shout.

"She threw the psychiatrist couch at them too?!" Richard shouts.

"Yeah!" Jessica shouts. "Some of them got knocked out cold too!"

"Oh no!" Vanessa, Richard and Marcus shout.

"And their heads got split opened too!"

"Oh no!"

"Then it says that Diane D's other personality did a hand stand right over the couch and chain whips the injured police officers' hands with the long chains that were still strapped to her shackles and wind up knocking the guns right out of their hands!"

"What!" Vanessa, Richard and Marcus shout.

"She knocked the guns out of their hands?!" Richard shouts. "With the chains too?!"

"Yeah!" Jessica shouts. "One of the guns go off and strikes an officer!"

"What!" Vanessa, Richard and Marcus shout.

Vanessa looks at Officer Henley and shouts, "A police officer got shot?!"

"I'm afraid so Mrs. Whitley," Officer Henley says.

"Oh no!" Vanessa, Richard and Marcus shout.

"When the police officers tried to reach for their guns, that's when Diane D's other personality did a hand stand over the couch again and chain whips the injured police officers' hands again causing another gun to go off striking another officer!" Jessica shouts.

"What!" Vanessa, Richard and Marcus shout.

Vanessa looks at Officer Henley again and shouts, "Another officer got shot?!"

"I'm afraid so," Officer Henley says.

"Oh no!" Vanessa, Richard and Marcus shout.

"Then it says that a swat team was about to burst into the doorway with shotguns!" Jessica shouts.

"Shotguns?!" Vanessa, Richard and Marcus shout.

"Oh my goodness!" Vanessa shouts.

"And when the swat team was about to burst into the doorway with the shotguns, Diane D's other personality threw the psychiatrist couch right across the room at them too, knocking them down also!" Jessica shouts.

"Oh my lord!"

"It says some of them got knocked out cold too!"

"What!" Vanessa, Richard and Marcus shout.

Vanessa looks at Officer Henley again and shouts, "My goodness! How many people did Diane D's other personality knock out cold?!"

"A whole lot of people Mrs. Whitley," Officer Henley says. "A whole lot."

"Oh no!" Vanessa, Richard and Marcus shout.

"It says that some of the injured police officers claim before they knew it, a large object came speeding and smashing right into their heads knocking a few of them out cold!" Jessica shouts. "When a few of them came to, they said it felt just like they got hit and ran over by a car! It says that Diane D's family was right inside the room during her hypnosis and witnessed everything!"

"They did?!" Vanessa shouts.

"Yeah! It says that her family was so traumatized by witnessing this whole thing that they all wound up passed out in the emergency room!"

"Really?! She wound up causing her own family to be hospitalized?! My goodness! Diane D is a dangerous woman! She needs to be locked up in a cage!"

"She sure do!"

Vanessa turns to Officer Henley and asks, "How are the police officers' conditions Officer Henley?! Did they survive?!"

"They're still alive for now Mrs. Whitley," Officer Henley says. "The doctors don't think some of them will make it."

"What!" Vanessa, Richard and Marcus shout. "Oh no!"

Jessica continues to read the article. She suddenly shouts, "Oh no!

Oh noooo!"

Vanessa puzzled looks at Jessica and says, "Oh no?! What do you mean 'Oh no' Jessica?! What happened?!"

"It says that when Diane D's other personality threatened the doctors, a few of her family members told the police, that her other personality made threats against Marcus!"

"What!" Vanessa and Richard shout. "Threats against Marcus!" They all frighteningly look at Marcus, then at Officer Henley.

"Her other personality made threats against me?!" Marcus shouts. "What do they mean her other personality made threats against me?!"

"Well Marcus," Officer Henley says. "I'm sorry to tell you this, but it was discovered that Diane D has more than one other personality!"

"What!" Marcus, Jessica, Vanessa and Richard shout. "More than one other personality?!"

"Diane D has more than one other personality?!" Vanessa shouts. "What do you mean?!"

"Well," Officer Henley says. "It was discovered, that the doctors brought out two other personalities besides Diane D's original personality."

"What!" Vanessa, Marcus, Jessica and Richard shout. "Doctors brought out two other personalities?!"

"Besides Diane D's original personality?!" Vanessa shouts. "You mean she has three different personalities altogether?!"

"Yes, according to a few of her family members," Officer Henley says. "Her family members said that both of Diane D's other personalities made threats against Marcus!"

"What!" Marcus, Jessica, Vanessa and Richard shout. "Both of her other personalities?!"

"Both of her other personalities made threats against me?!" Marcus shouts. "Oh no! Well what did her other personalities say about me?!"

"Her other personalities threatened to come after you Marcus!" Officer Henley says.

"What!" Jessica, Vanessa and Richard shout. "Threatened to come after him?!"

"Both of her other personalities threatened to come after Marcus?!" Jessica shouts.

"I'm afraid so," Officer Henley says.

"Oh no!"

"How are Diane D's other personalities going to come after Marcus anyway?!" Vanessa shouts. "Her other personalities don't know where Marcus is right now and her other personalities do not even know where Marcus lives! Not even Diane D's original personality know where Marcus is right now nor knows where he lives!"

"I'm Sorry Mrs. Whitley," Officer Henley says. "But one of her other personalities did tell the doctors that they already know where Marcus is!"

"What!" Jessica, Vanessa Marcus, and Richard shout.

"One of her other personalities told the doctors that they already know where Marcus is?!" Vanessa shouts.

"According to Diane D's family it did," Officer Henley says.

"Oh no!" Jessica, Vanessa Marcus, and Richard shout.

"What made Diane D's family tell the police about the threats her other personalities made about Marcus?!" Vanessa shouts.

"They claim they're concerned about Marcus safety!" Officer Henley shouts.

"They're concerned about his safety?!"

"Of course they are! Plus they claim they don't want Diane D's ORIGINAL personality to be blamed for anything her OTHER personalities do, just in case any of her other personalities do succeed in coming after Marcus."

"What!" Jessica and Vanessa shout.

"Just in case any of her other personalities succeed in coming after him?!" Vanessa shouts. "Well what did her ORIGINAL personality say?! Did her ORIGINAL personality make threats against Marcus?!"

"No, according to Diane D's family," Officer Henley says. "They said her original personality didn't make any threats against Marcus at all."

"It didn't?"

"No."

"Well how was her original personality behaving?!" Jessica shouts. "Was her ORIGINAL personality aggressive like her other personalities?!"

"No. According to Diane D's family, they said her original personality wasn't aggressive at all and was as cool as a cucumber, it's her other two personalities that have to be watched out for!"

"Her other two personalities that have to be watched out for?!"

"Yes!"

"Oh noooo!" Marcus shouts. "If Diane D's other personalities already know where I'm at, that means her other personalities are stalking me! It means they're the ones who are coming into my dreams and nightmares! See?! I told you all that Diane D was never really over that hoax letter Richard and I sent to her and her family! Yeah she claim that she has forgiven me, not thinking about me and that she has moved on with her life, but her subconscious is still upset at me! Her subconscious has not forgiven me!"

"Oh my God Officer Henley!" Vanessa shouts. "What's going to happen, now that Diane D's own subconscious has admitted that she's going to come after Marcus and knows where he is?!"

"She will have to be committed again," Officer Henley says.

"Committed again?!"

"Of course, to keep Marcus safe!"

"Even if she is committed again, that's not going to stop Marcus' nightmares about her coming after him trying to kill him, because he was still having nightmares about Diane D coming after him even while she was committed before! What are we gonna do?!"

"I don't know what you're gonna do Mrs. Whitley, but I know one thing you should do."

"Oh yeah? And what's that?!"

"Have Marcus accepted Diane D's forgiveness as soon as possible, that's what you should do! Sometimes when everything else fails, you have no choice but to go for your last option. Have Marcus accepted Diane D's forgiveness once and for all because his nightmares, I honestly cannot help him with it. Listen I have to go now. But if you have any problems at all, please do not hesitate to call me, alright? Take care." Officer Henley turns around and heads towards the front door as Vanessa worriedly follows behind him.

Vanessa opens the front door for Officer Henley. Officer Henley looks at Vanessa and says, "Take care. Call me right away if anything happens." Vanessa worriedly looks at Officer Henley. Officer Henley then turns and goes out the front door.

Vanessa worriedly watches Officer Henley. She then steps back and closes the front door. She turns around, leans on the front door, looks at Marcus and cries, "Oh Marcus!"

"See Grandma?" Marcus says. "There is only one way to escape Diane D's torment."

"No Marcus! I don't want to hear you talk like that, do you understand?!"

"But Grandma...!"

"Do you understand?!"

"But Grandma...!"

"Do you understand Marcus?!"

"Yes Grandma."

"Good. Now, the first thing we're going to do, is take you up to that hospital and face Diane D and tell her that you accept her forgiveness so that you can end this torment once and for all!"

"No! You can't make me do that!"

"Marcus this might be the only way!" Jessica cries and shouts. "Please try to accept Diane D's forgiveness or you're going to keep having nightmares about her and her other personalities might come after you!"

"No! I can't face her! I caaaan't!" Marcus turns and runs away down the hallway towards his bedroom.

Richard looks at Jessica and cries, "Mom, what are we gonna do?! We can't let Diane D's other personalities come after Marcus!"

"We're not going to let her other personalities come after Marcus Richard," Jessica says. "You know why? Because I'm going to try to get a gun license and own a gun!"

"What!" Richard and Vanessa shout. "Get a gun license and own a gun?!"

"That's right! Now Diane D's original personality might be as cool

260

as a cucumber, but I'm not going to let her other personalities come after my child and I just sit back and do nothing! I'm going to protect my child! I don't like guns but I will get one and use it if I have to, to protect my children!"

"Jessica!" Vanessa shouts. "The police and a swat team were not able to stop Diane D's other personality from attacking them, even though they were armed with guns! Her other personality still managed to take them down with that couch knocking them out cold and split their heads open while they had guns on them! What makes you think YOUR gun will stop her other personality's powerful wrath?!"

"I don't know Mom! I just don't want to take any chances! If her other personality can beat up and attack Marcus once before inside that school hallway and have no conscious about it, her other personality can always do it again!" Jessica then cries, "All I know, is that I have to protect my child from that dangerous monster!" Jessica turns and runs down the hallway towards Marcus' bedroom as Vanessa and Richard stand there crying, worriedly looking on.

A man is sitting on the bus reading a newspaper article with a headline that reads: BLOODSHED INSIDE THE HYPNOSIS ROOM AS DIANE D'S FAMILY FRIGHTENINGLY WITNESS HER OTHER PERSONALITY'S VIOLENT OUT OF CONTROL BEHAVIOR AFTER SHE BECAME HYPNOTIZED BY DOCTORS!:

A woman is sitting in a hair salon reading a newspaper article with a headline that reads: TWO DOCTORS HURT AND TWO COPS SHOT AS OTHER AUTHORITY FIGURES GET KNOCKED OUT COLD BY THE WRATH OF DIANE D'S OTHER PERSONALITY!:

Inside the hospital lobby, Grandpa Mike, Grandma Gracy, the rest of Diane D's family and relatives and the police officers' families are standing around Dr. Harvey as Grandpa Mike shows Dr. Harvey a newspaper article with a headline that reads: DOCTOR FRANKENSTONE! INJURED POLICE OFFICERS AND THEIR FAMILY MEMBERS ACCUSE DOCTOR STONE OF BRINGING THE MONSTER OUT OF DIANE D, CLAIMING THAT DOCTOR STONE COULD NOT CONTROL HIS MONSTER AS HIS MONSTER WAS GOING MAD AND TURNING LOOSE ON AUTHORITY FIGURES!: "You know I don't appreciate this!" Grandpa Mike shouts. "These people are calling Diane a monster! I don't appreciate anybody calling my grandchild a monster!" Grandpa Mike turns to Mrs. Peterson and shouts, "I mean who the hell do you people think you are?!"

"Well that's how your grandchild was behaving Mr. Brown!" Mrs. Peterson shouts. "She is a monster! She went out of control again!"

"You still don't have to call our granddaughter a monster!" Gracy shouts.

"And your granddaughter did not have to do what she did! I mean what do you call a person or thing that turns loose and starts attacking people, especially when the person or thing gets superhuman strength and starts breaking loose from chains that they're wrapped in and starts lifting extremely heavy objects in the air! What do you call a person or thing that keeps spinning their entire body around while they're holding the extremely heavy object high up in the air and then toss the heavy object right across a room like a piece of rag?! That is not normal behavior!"

"You still shouldn't be calling my granddaughter a monster Mrs. Peterson!" Gracy shouts.

"Yeah that's easy for you to say Mrs. Brown! It's not your loved ones laying here in the hospital shot! My husband might die because of your granddaughter!" Mrs. Peterson cries. The rest of Diane D's family sadly look at Mrs. Peterson. They then take the newspaper and look at the headlines. Underneath the headlines, they see a sketch, drawing and painting of Diane D's forearms, wrists and hands bound together with cuffs and chains with her arms and hands way up in the air ready to pull and break the cuffs and chains apart! Nancy takes the newspaper and holds it looking at it. She and Charlotte frighteningly stare at the sketch, drawing and painting of Diane D's forearms, wrists and hands bound together with cuffs and chains with her arms and hands way up in the air.

That same afternoon, Margarita, Tomas, Mary, Barry, Tonio, Marilyn, Nicolas and Michael are standing outside of the hospital emergency room in the hallway. They are released from the hospital emergency room after spending over eighteen hours in there! They are still traumatized as other family members, Dr. Harvey, hospital staff members, news reporters and photographers surround them clapping and cheering for them! Dr. Harvey approaches Margarita, Tomas, Mary, Barry, Tonio, Marilyn, Nicolas and Michael and tells them, "We're just all glad to see that you all are okay."

"Yes," one of the other doctors says. "We were really worried about you guys."

"Thanks everybody," Margarita sadly says.

"Where are you all heading to now?" Dr. Harvey asks.

"We're gonna go upstairs to see and check on Diane," Barry says.

"Is she okay Doctor Harvey?" Michael asks.

"Yes, she's still sedated," Dr. Harvey says.

"She is?"

"Yes. Some of your other family members are with her."

"Oh. Okay."

"Come on. I'll take you all up to her." Dr. Harvey turns and helps Michael, Margarita, Tomas, Mary, Barry, Tonio, Marilyn and Nicolas leading them away as everyone continues to clap and cheer for them.

Chapter 17

Diane D Lays Unconscious Inside Hospital Room

Thirty minutes later, Margarita, Tomas, Mary, Barry, Tonio, Marilyn, Nicolas, Michael, Dr. Harvey and other family and relatives are inside Diane D's hospital room. They surround Diane D worriedly looking at her as she lays face up in the hospital bed unconscious hooked to monitors with her face slightly bruised with eyes still puffy and swollen shut with casts and bandages wrapped around her upper arms, shoulders and wrists with a blanket over her lower body. There is a long chain attached to one of her ankles and the other end of the chain attached to the metal bars of the bed.

Later on that same evening, Barry, Tomas, Gracy, Grandpa Mike, Nicolas, Mickey, Nancy, Charlotte and Michael stand around Diane D's hospital bed sadly staring at her as Mary and Margarita stand at the head of Diane D's hospital bed patting Diane D's forehead, eyes and neck with damp cloths as Diane D still lays unconscious hooked to monitors with eyes swollen shut and face slightly bruised. "When will she wake back up Grandma?" Mickey whispers.

"As soon as the sedation wears off," Margarita whispers as she and Mary continue to pat Diane D's head, face and neck with the damp cloths.

"My God did she really do that?" Nancy whispers, "broke the chains loose from the couch?"

"Yes," Barry whispers, "that's why she's bandaged up. She wound up hurting herself when she did that."

"Yes she did," Margarita whispers. "And most likely, she's not going to remember doing that."

"My God," Nancy whispers.

"Did she really say that she was going to go after that kid Marcus and kill him?" Charlotte whispers.

"Yes she did say that Charlotte," Barry whispers. "And most likely, she's not going to remember saying that either."

"Wow."

"Did she really lift that psychiatrist couch and throw it across the room?" Aunt Celeste whispers.

"Yep," Tonio whispers. "She sure did."

"Wow! How many times did she do that?!"

"I can't even count! It was a whole lot of times!"

"I know it was a whole lot of times because we kept hearing that couch being thrown and banged against the wall while we were outside in the hallway! We kept feeling the vibration! It really shook us up!"

"I bet it did! It shook us up too."

"Isn't that psychiatrist couch heavy?"

"Yeah it's heavy, but it wasn't heavy for her other personality to lift up and throw across the room banging it hard against the wall hitting the doctors and authority figures with."

"Why was her other personality throwing and banging the couch against the wall?!" Nancy whispers.

"I don't know. I guess it got so angry when the doctor told it to stay away from Diane."

"My God," Charlotte whispers. "It's a good thing Nancy and I left the room before they brought that other personality out of her because I wouldn't want to hear what her other personality was saying nor witness any of that stuff her other personality did!"

"Me neither," Nancy says.

"Well you did miss a lot girls," Tonio says.

"You missed a whole lot," Marilyn says. "And it's a good thing you did miss a lot or you would be traumatized too."

"See?" Nancy whispers. "I told you! When Charlotte and I started to leave that hypnosis room, I asked were any of you coming with me and her, but you all chose to stay!"

"Well some of us had to stay in the room with Diane Nancy!" Margarita whispers. "If we all had left the room, there would be no family members in the room with Diane! She would have been in there all alone with no family members in there for her! And we would have never heard with our own ears all those things her other personality or personalities were saying and admitting to!"

"Wow. I'm traumatized just hearing about all of this! Maybe I shouldn't have said anything about my encounter with her other personality."

"No?" Barry whispers. "Why not?"

"Because look what happened! All these people got hurt! The doctors got hurt, the priest got hurt, security guards, police officers, a swat team, even Diane herself got hurt!"

"We almost got hurt too Nancy," Marilyn whispers. "That psychiatrist couch practically skinned our heads when it flew right over our heads towards the police officers! If we didn't duck down in time, that couch would have smashed right into our heads instead of those police officers' heads."

"Wow," Charlotte says. "How were you all able to duck down just in the nick of time to keep from getting hit with the couch when the police officers didn't duck down in time and wind up getting hit with that couch? Did you all knew the couch was coming?"

"Well our instincts automatically had us duck down real quick when we felt something about to fly right at our heads Charlotte," Barry says.

"Your instincts?"

"Yeah."

"Well what about the police officers' instincts? Didn't they have instincts too?"

"I guess their instincts wasn't fast enough for some reason."

"See?!" Nancy shouts. "See what I mean?! If I never said anything, you wouldn't have almost got hurt! You all almost got hurt and got traumatized and I feel like it's my fault for saying something!"

"No Nancy!" Margarita says. "If you see something, say something! You saw that something wasn't right with Diane and you spoke up about it! That's what you should do."

"Yeah you did the right thing Nancy," Tomas says. They all sadly look back at Diane D as she remains unconscious.

The next morning, a man and a woman in the street who are around their late forties are reading a newspaper with a different headline that reads: **THE SUDDEN SILENCE: DIANE D'S FAMILY BECOME SHOCKED WHEN HER OTHER PERSONALITY ALL OF A SUDDEN BECOMES SILENT WHEN DOCTORS ASKED HER OTHER PERSONALITY A SPECIFIC QUESTION ABOUT HER COUSIN DANA**: "Wow," the woman says. "This article says when the doctors spoke to Diane D's other personality and asked it questions about her cousin Dana, it answered all the questions except for one! When the doctors asked Diane D's other personality, this specific question about her cousin Dana, her family became shocked when her other personality all of a sudden became silent and didn't answer the specific question about her cousin Dana!"

"Oh yeah?" the man says. "What specific question did the doctors ask Diane D's other personality about her cousin Dana?"

"It doesn't say. The doctors and Diane D's family think that the other personality might know something about her cousin Dana but is somehow hiding it to protect Dana."

"Hiding it to protect Dana?"

"Yeah!"

"That's what they think?"

"Yeah, that's what I think too!"

"Well maybe that other personality could be hiding something, so it probably plead the Fith Amendment, 'the right to remain silent' and that's exactly what that other personality sound like it did. Remained silent during a specific question."

"Wow. Now everybody in town is wondering, 'what could Diane D's other personality be hiding about her cousin Dana that it doesn't want anybody else to know about'!"

"Wow. That is a mystery."

"It is." The man and woman continue to look at the article.

Later on that day, Margarita, Tomas and Dr. Harvey are inside Dr. Kahn's hospital room standing by his bedside as Dr. Kahn lays in a hospital bed unconscious hooked to tubes and monitors with bandages wrapped around his head and neck. "How is he Doctor Harvey?" Margarita asks.

"I don't know," Dr. Harvey says. "He suffered a brain hemorrhage."

"A brain hemmorage!" Margarita and Tomas shout.

"Oh God!" Margarita shouts. "I'm so sorry this all happened!"

"Is there anything we can do for him Doctor Harvey?" Tomas asks.

"The only thing we can do for him Mister Tomas, is pray," Dr. Harvey says.

"Oh God," Margarita says as she cries on Tomas' shoulders as Tomas sadly tries to comfort her.

Around an hour later, Margarita, Tomas and Dr. Harvey are inside Dr. Stone's hospital room as Dr. Stone lays awake in a hospital bed with a bandage wrapped around his head. "How are you feeling Doctor Stone?" Margarita sadly asks.

"Not good at all," Doctor Stone says. "I guess you all are right. Maybe it wasn't a good idea to bring that other personality out of Diane, look where it's got us! I'm laying here in the hospital, Doctor Kahn is laying here in the hospital, the security guards are laying here in the hospital so is a priest, police officers and a swat team?! We're all laying in here! This is exactly what Doctor Kahn and I were afraid of, laying here in this very same hospital. As you can see, our worst fears came true. Then I hear the police officers' families want to sue me and Doctor Kahn!"

"Wow Doctor Stone," Tomas says. "We're so sorry this happened. We all now see, that this wasn't a good idea."

"It wasn't! We only wanted to hypnotize Diane because of the encounter your other granddaughter Nancy had with her other personality! We were trying to see, if this same personality had anything to do with beating up Marcus inside the school and entering his dreams and nightmares! We found out, that it did! We only wanted to help Diane with her split personality situation and at the same time help Marcus end his nightmares of her! We wanted to help both of them, but it didn't work out."

"So sorry Doctor Stone," Margarita says.

"How's Doctor Kahn doing?"

"He's still sedated," Dr. Harvey says.

"He is?"

"Yes. He was hurt real bad."

"Oh God." Dr. Stone then looks at Margarita and Tomas and says, "How about you guys, how do you feel? I heard you were all traumatized by what happened."

"Yes Doctor Stone," Margarita says. "We're still traumatized by what happened."

"That's right Doctor Stone," Tomas says. "We were so traumatized that we almost had to be admitted into the hospital ourselves! We're still not quite over what happened yesterday, seeing Diane talking, but hearing someone else speaking! It was very creepy for us."

"It was! Then hearing her other personality admitting to all these other things in Diane's past like beating up Marcus, kung fu kicking the stuck storage room door wide open at the other hospital, attacking the correction officers inside the jail cell, waiting in Diane's physical body all night long for those correction officers to come back to the cell, then looking at the nurse who came into the cell to check on her, then hearing her other personality admitting to things that happened way before Diane herself was even born, like killing people through out the centuries once every fifty years, then seeing her third personality go off like that attacking you doctors, having superhuman strength by breaking the chains loose from the couch, then lifting that heavy couch, spinning it in the air then tossing it across the room at the authority figures knocking some of them out cold then chain whips them with the chains while she's upside down doing hand stands and winds up causing two officers to be shot! That is still so unbelievable!"

"It is! What happened yesterday was all too much for us to take Doctor Stone! When that couch came speeding and slamming into those security guards', police officers' and the swat team members' heads, I was so scared that they were going to be decapitated or something!"

"Yeah me too!"

"I don't think it's anything my family and I will ever get over! We were not prepared for that! Especially seeing something like that happening in front of our eyes and happening within our own family! We were not prepared for that at all!"

"I know," Dr. Stone says. "Sorry we all had to witness that. See? This is exactly what Doctor Kahn and I were afraid of, knowing Diane's other personality's violent history, that's why we wanted to chain her physical body up! But obviously we all saw, that the chains did not stop her other personality's powerful wrath!"

"It certainly didn't."

"How is Diane by the way? How is she doing? Have you seen her again since you were released from the emergency room?"

"Yes we were all in her hospital room a little while ago," Margarita says.

"You were? Well how is she?"

"She's still sedated Doctor Stone," Tomas says.

"She is?"

"Yes."

"So she still has no idea what went on."

"No she has no idea."

"She does not know that authority figures are laying in the very same hospital she's in because of the injuries she inflicted on them?"

"No Doctor Stone she does not know," Margarita says. "And I'm afraid she's not going to know for a while because they might have her sedated for a while."

"Oh yeah? Wow. I see."

"Well we're going to let you get some rest Doctor Stone," Dr. Harvey says.

"Okay Doctor Harvey."

"Get better."

"Okay."

"By Doctor Stone," Margarita says.

"By Miss Margarita."

Margarita, Tomas and Dr. Harvey turn and leave Dr. Stone's bedside as they sadly stare at him.

Injured police officers lay in another hospital room in hospital beds with bandages wrapped around all their heads and necks.

In the next room, Margarita, Tomas and Dr. Harvey stand beside one of the injured officers who was shot in the chest. The officer is unconscious as he lays hooked to tubes and monitors with a bandage wrapped around his head and a brace wrapped around his neck. Margarita sadly places her hand on the injured officer's shoulder and cries to him, "I'm so sorry for this. I'm sorry this all happened." Margarita takes her hand off the injured officer's shoulder as she and Tomas tearfully look at him.

Dr. Harvey turns to them and says, "We better leave now." Dr. Harvey, Margarita and Tomas then turn and leave the injured officer's bedside as they sadly stare at him.

Dr. Harvey, Margarita and Tomas step out into the hospital hallway. Margarita and Tomas turn to Dr. Harvey as Margarita says, "So they're not sure if he's going to make it?"

"No, they're not sure Miss Margarita," Dr. Harvey says. "His neck is also broken."

"What!" Margarita and Tomas shout.

"His neck is broken?!" Tomas shouts.

"I'm afraid so," Dr. Harvey says. "Even if he does survive from what happened, he could still wind up being paralyzed."

"Paralyzed!" Margarita and Tomas shout.

"Yes! He's not the only one with a broken neck. A few other officers' necks got broken too."

"A few other officers?!" Margarita shouts.

"I'm afraid so. If they survive, they might wind up being paralyzed too."

"Oh nooo!"

"A couple of other officers are in comas."

"Comas?!" Margarita and Tomas shouts.

"Yeah. Other officers and swat team members got their heads split opened."

"Heads split opened?!"

"Oh yeah. Didn't you notice that all the officers, swat team members and security officers we just went to visit all had bandages wrapped around their heads? Every single person that got hurt by that couch have bandages wrapped around their heads and necks! Even Doctor Stone and Doctor Kahn have bandages wrapped around their heads!"

"This is so hard to believe!" Tomas shouts.

"Well believe it Mister Tomas. It's possible for several people to have broken necks, heads split open and in comas if a heavy object comes speeding at them then slamming right into them at sixty, seventy or eighty miles an hour! That other personality of Diane's did a lot of serious damage to these people! Her other personality became a one person army! I just hope and pray this officer and all the other people pull through." Margarita and Tomas sadly look at Dr. Harvey as Dr. Harvey sadly looks back at him. Dr. Harvey then says, "Come on, let's go." Dr. Harvey, Margarita and Tomas turn and sadly walk down the hallway.

Chapter 18

Margarita Puts Her Foot Down!

Hours later, Diane D's family and relatives are all standing in the hospital hallway still traumatized by the ordeal they have all went through two days ago as they surround an angry Margarita who is pacing back and forth shouting, "Okay listen up everyone!" Margarita stops pacing and shouts, "We cannot let what happened with Diane the other day ever happen again! We have to make sure that she does not meditate again attracting these vicious souls, spirits or personalities to her or this will happen again! We can't be going through this! And to make sure that Diane does not ever meditate again, she is going to have to be watched over like a hawk!"

"Watched over like a hawk?" Nicolas asks.

"Yes!"

"What do you mean Grandma?" Michael asks.

"I mean every move she makes have to be watched so she won't have to sneak behind our backs to meditate again! We can't have these souls, spirits or personalities coming into her physical body and cause all this havoc again! Especially that other soul, spirit and personality saying that they were gonna use her physical body to try and kill that kid Marcus in the back stairwell of that school and saying that they might use her physical body to kill in the future?! I don't want that killer soul, spirit or personality to come around Diane ever again! Look what that second other personality did! It caused a lot of chaos! It caused the doctors, the security guards, a priest, a lot of police officers and a swat team to get hurt! Some of them got knocked out cold by that other personality throwing that heavy couch across the room at them! Some of their heads got split opened!"

"Oh no!" the family and relatives shout.

"Some of their necks got broken!"

"Necks got broken?! Oh no!"

"A couple of officers got shot and other officers are in comas!"

"Oh no!"

"We're not even sure if a couple or few of the officers, the security guards or swat team members are going to make it! If any of these people die, the courts are definitely going to have Diane committed again and for a long time! That's why Diane has to be watched at all times! She has to be watched every move she makes because I do not trust her! She went behind our backs and still meditated after we told her not to! If she can go behind our backs and sneak to meditate before, she can always do it again! If or whenever Diane comes back home, I want her to be watched even when she goes to the bathroom!"

"What!" the rest of the family shout.

"You want Diane to be watched while she's in the bathroom Mom?!" Barry shouts.

"Exactly!" Margarita shouts. "From now on whenever Diane has to use the bathroom, one of us has to be in the bathroom with her!"

"What!" the rest of the family shouts.

"One of us has to be in the bathroom with her?!" Marilyn asks.

"You got it!" Margarita shouts.

"But Mom, wouldn't that be invading Diane's privacy?"

"Of course it's going to invade Diane's privacy Marilyn! Diane brought this on herself and on us! She should have thought about all of that before she decided to sneak off behind our backs to meditate! She costed herself to lose her own privacy! That's why one of us is going to have to be in the bathroom with her, one of us females."

"One of us females?" Charlotte asks.

"That's right!"

"But Grandma!" Nancy shouts. "What if that other soul, spirit or personality comes out of Diane while one of us is in the bathroom with her?! I don't want to be in the bathroom with that other soul, spirit or personality, especially now that I know that other soul, spirit or personality is a killer and would probably kill again! I don't want to meet that other soul, spirit or personality again! I don't want to be in the same room with it! I don't want to be under the same roof with it either! I don't want to go through that same experience I went through with that other soul, spirit or personality again! It really creeped me out!"

"That other soul, spirit or personality won't come out of Diane as long as you keep and eye on her to make sure she doesn't meditate Nancy!"

"I'm still not feeling this Grandma! From now on, every time I look at Diane I have to wonder, is it HER or is it that other soul, spirit or personality!"

"Nancy, if Diane's face is NOT pale, then it's HER! If her face IS pale, then it's not her! It's that other soul, spirit or personality!"

"Oh gosh!"

"If that other soul, spirit or personality happens to emerge out of Diane, I want you to come get me right away! I have a thing or two I would like to say to that other soul, spirit or personality!"

"What!" the family shouts.

"You do?" Nancy asks.

"Yes!" Margarita shouts.

"What are you going to say to it Mom?" Barry asks.

"I'm gonna tell that soul, spirit or personality to stay the hell away from Diane and to leave Diane alone, that's what I'm gonna say to it!"

"Mom, Doctor Stone already told that other soul, spirit or personality to leave Diane alone and to stay away from her! It didn't work! Look what that other soul, spirit or personality did to him, Dr. Kahn, security guards, the priest, police officers and a swat team! All those people couldn't stop that other soul, spirit or personality's rage and fury even though they had tasers, guns and shotguns drawn!"

"That's why I have to straighten that other soul, spirit or personality out Barry! I can't let that other soul, spirit or personality keep coming around Diane taking over her physical body doing whatever it wants with it! If Doctor Stone's method of telling that other soul, spirit or personality to stay away from Diane didn't work, maybe I can try it!"

"What!" the family shouts. "You?!"

"Yes me!"

"How are you going to do that Grandma?" Nicolas asks.

"I don't know. I have to figure something out."

"But Grandma, if you tell that other soul, spirit or personality off, you'll be telling Diane off!"

"No I won't be telling Diane off Nicolas, because most likely, Diane will not remember it! I have to tell that other soul, spirit or personality off if that other soul, spirit or personality comes into Diane's physical body again for Diane's sake and our sake! So therefore us females will have to keep an eye on Diane whenever she's in the bathroom to make sure she does not meditate!"

"Do I have to Grandma?" Nancy asks.

"Yes you do Nancy. Yes you do. But you don't have to worry about it now. While Diane is in the hospital, I'll keep an eye on her while she's in the bathroom, then if or whenever she comes home, I am going to let her have it for meditating behind our backs! And not only do I want Diane watched, I want Dana watched as well!"

"Dana?!" the family shout.

"Yes Dana! I became very worried and concerned about her ever since during the hypnosis, when that other soul, spirit or personality refused to answer the doctors' question about whether it ever used Dana's physical body to try and kill someone or ever used her physical body to kill!"

"But Mom," Tonio says. "That other soul, spirit or personality never said that it DID use Dana's physical body to try and kill someone or used her physical body to kill! It never said it did! It just never answered the question!"

"I know it never answered the question Tonio, that's what scared me, the sudden silence! Why did that other soul, spirit or personality all of a sudden become silent when it was asked has it ever used Dana's physical body to try and kill someone or has it ever used Dana's physical body to kill?! Now we all have to wonder whether or not this other soul, spirit or personality ever used Dana's physical body to try and kill or ever used her physical body to kill! That's why I want Dana watched too, to make sure she doesn't meditate either!"

"But Aunt Margarita," Uncle Willie says, "you don't really have to worry about Dana meditating at all, unless she's with Diane!"

"What? Unless she's with Diane? What do you mean 'unless she's with Diane'?"

"We've never seen Dana meditating unless she's with Diane!"

"You haven't?"

"No! If Diane is not around, believe me, Dana will not be meditating! We've never seen Dana meditating alone, only when she's with Diane!"

"What? So you're saying that Dana only meditates because Diane probably be infuencing her to meditate?!"

"Yes that's exactly what I'm saying! If it wasn't for Diane, none of us will ever find Dana meditating at all!"

"No?"

"No."

"Wow. Well that's good! But I still worry the fact, that instead of Dana stopping Diane from meditating, she might just go right along with Diane and join her again! If Dana can join Diane and meditate with her before, she can always do it again! I don't want Diane to keep infuencing Dana into meditating! I mean it's bad enough that she keeps meditating and have these supernatural occurences follow her, but now she got Dana dragged into it! We saw what happened inside the hypnosis room with that sudden silence that other personality had when the doctors asked that certain question about Dana! All of a sudden that other personality had nothing to say! It just kept remaining silent!" Everybody frighteningly stares at Margarita. "Come on everybody! Let's go check on Diane." Margarita turns away as everyone else worriedly follows her.

Chapter 19

Two Officers And A Swat Team Member Pass Away

The next day, Mrs. Jenkins, her family, the family of another police officer and the family of a swat team member are crying their eyes out. Mrs. Jenkins cries on Dr. Harvey's shoulders and shouts, "He's gone, he's gone! My husband is gone! He just died! The other officer died late last night and the swat team member died this morning!" Mrs. Jenkins continues to cry her eyes out.

"I'm so sorry Mrs. Jenkins," Dr. Harvey says with tears in his eyes. "I really am."

Mrs. Jenkins lifts her head up and looks at Dr. Harvey and shouts, "That Diane D is a murderer! She's not only a murderer, she's a cop killer! Does she know what she did?! Does she realize what she did to our families?!"

"I'm afraid that Diane is still unaware of what went on Mrs. Jenkins. She's still unconscious. She's been sedated since she was brought out of hypnosis."

"Since she was brought out of hypnosis?!"

"Yes."

"Why did those other doctors have to hypnotize her?! Why did they have to bring out that monster personality of hers?! That monster personality of hers destroyed all of our families! Why didn't those other doctors just leave that monster personality of hers wherever it came from?! That monster personality of her ruined our lives! Thanks to that other personality of hers, I'm now a widow!" Mrs. Jenkins continues to cry her eyes out on Dr. Harvey's shoulder.

The next day, people on the train are reading a newspaper article with a headline that reads: TWO OFFICERS AND A SWAT TEAM MEMBER WHO WERE VICTIM'S OF DIANE D'S OTHER PERSONALITY'S WRATH PASS AWAY:

Three days later, there is a funeral for the two police officers at the funeral hall. Mrs. Jenkins is crying at the casket with the widow of the other police officer. There are thousands of other officers and civilians gathered at the funeral.

Margarita, Tomas, Barry, Mary and Michael are at the entrance of the funeral. A white female around her late 40's who is one of the police officers' relative approach Margarita and Tomas and says, "Aren't you guys going to come in?"

"We would love to come in Miss," Margarita says. "But I'm sure we're the last people those officers' families want to see."

"At least you can go show them your support."

"We do want to show our support Miss," Tomas says, "that's why we're here. But at the same time, we don't want to impose because we're not sure we'll be wanted here because of what Diane did."

"I understand. Thanks for showing up anyway."

"You're welcome."

The woman sadly turns and walks away as Margarita, Tomas, Barry, Mary and Michael continue to stand at the entrance of the funeral hall.

The next morning, there is a funeral for the swat team member at a church. The swat team member's family and friends are all crying at the casket. There are thousands of police officers and civilians gathered at the funeral.

Later on that day, a Hispanic man and a plus-size black woman working inside a school office who are around their late forties are reading a newspaper article with a headline that reads: **TWO POLICE OFFICERS LAYED TO REST AS THEIR FAMILIES AND COMMUNITIES GATHER AT FUNERAL**: "Hey" the man says. "Here's the article of those slain officers' funerals, the funerals we saw on TV yesterday."

"Wow," the woman says.

"And one of the swat team members had a funeral this morning."

"Wow. That is so sad."

"It is."

"You know I don't understand, how in the world, was Diane D able to take down all those authority figures like that without using any guns!"

"She used another weapon! She used a psychiatrist couch as a weapon and threw that psychiatrist couch right across the room at those police officers, security guards and swat team members slamming that couch right into their heads!"

"I know! Man that is messed up! But even though all those authority figures were equipped with guns and shotguns, they couldn't stop her?"

"No, because one of the survivors who witnessed what went on inside that hypnosis room said, that when he and the other officers were about to burst into the doorway, that psychiatrist couch was already flying at them!"

"What! What do you mean 'that psychiatrist couch was already flying at them'? You mean to tell me, that when those police officers and the swat team were about to burst into the doorway, that psychiatrist couch was already airborne?"

"Yeah! That officer said that when he and the other officers drew their guns and were about to burst into the doorway, the next thing they know, is that something in the air had flew and slammed right into their heads knocking them down that they didn't even have time to see the object or move out of the way in time! That officer said that he and the other officers didn't even know what hit them!"

"They didn't?"

"No! Those officers who had their funeral yesterday were still knocked out cold when they died!"

"You mean they were in a coma?"

"Yeah! They never came to! In other words, they died not knowing what hit them!"

"Oh my God, that is so sad!"

"It is!"

"But I don't understand. If Diane D threw that couch across the room at the doorway before those police officers and the swat team members even entered the doorway, how did she knew they were coming? Why did she throw the couch towards that direction in the first place if she didn't see those authority figures there yet?!"

"I don't know. Maybe she heard their footsteps coming because witnesses said that her eyes seemed closed that whole entire time she was going berserk inside that hypnosis room!"

"Her eyes seemed closed?"

"Yeah! They said her eyes looked like they were swollen shut."

"Swollen shut?!"

"Yeah! They said they didn't know how Diane D was even able to see what she was doing with her eyes swollen shut."

"Maybe her eyes appeared swollen shut. She probably was able to see only a little bit.

"Well that little bit of sight she had didn't seem to stop her from doing all that damage and causing all that chaos in that room! She did a hell of a lot of damage and caused a lot of chaos for somebody that can only see a little bit."

"Yeah that's true. I wonder how she feels that she killed people, especially police officers and a swat team member?"

"I don't think she knows about it yet!"

"She doesn't know about it yet? What do you mean she doesn't know about it yet?"

"I heard she's still unconscious at the hospital."

"She's still unconscious? She hasn't come to yet either?"

"No.   I heard she's been sedated since that incident when the doctors brought her out of hypnosis! So far right now, she has no idea what went on. She has no idea what she's done."

"Oh Lord." The woman and the man continue to look at the article.

Chapter 20

Marcus' Last Nightmare!

Marcus is laying in his bed tossing and turning. He is having another nightmare!

NIGHTMARE:

Marcus finds himself right back in the same area in the dark dim isolated school hallway where it all started. He is frightened, scared, bleeding and injured as he steps backwards towards the end of the hallway looking back towards the end of the hallway as he continues to cry and slowly back away with his body bent forward in pain. He is getting closer to the end of the hallway where the large window and exit sign are. The eerie sounds of the crickets coming from outside the window become louder as Marcus gets closer to the end of the hallway. He quickly turns his head back forward and looks back at Diane D who is standing way down the hallway staring at him giving him a cold stare as she ignores her cell while it is ringing inside her pants pocket. Marcus gets further away from Diane D. He suddenly hears Diane D's cell phone stop ringing. He stops right in his tracks and anxiously looks towards Diane D's cell phone again. He frighteningly looks at Diane D again as he slowly starts to back away from her again. Suddenly, he hears his cell phone ringing again which is still laying on the floor in the distance not too far from Diane D. Marcus stops right in his tracks again. He anxiously looks at his cell phone! He frighteningly looks at Diane D again!

Diane D continues to stand there in the dark in a trance like state giving Marcus a firm hard stare as her face remains pale, bruised, bleeding and half dead with her eyes very puffy, practically swollen shut and half dead.

Marcus frighteningly runs and rolls down the stairwell screaming! He looks up and hears heavy footsteps jumping and charging down the top flight of stairs after him! He screams even more with his body still bent forward in pain!

Marcus reaches the first floor landing as he continues to cry and scream! He quickly runs towards the first floor stairwell doors as his body remains bent forward shouting, "Aaaaaahh! Help me! Somebody help me please! Aaaaaahh!"

Suddenly Diane D jumps and charges down the flight of stairs with a long cord or wire in her hands and runs right towards Marcus! She catches up to Marcus and violently grabs him by the neck! "Aaaaahh!" Marcus screams as Diane D jerks him then throws the cord or wire right over his head! She then wraps the cord or wire right around Marcus' neck! "Aaaaahh!" Marcus screams as Diane D makes the wire into a noose around his neck! Diane D tightens the noose as Marcus chokes and struggles to break free from the cord or wire! Diane D then takes the other end of the cord or wire then drags the other end of the cord or wire the other way towards the back of the stairwell as the other end of the cord or wire chokes, pulls and drags Marcus by the neck! Marcus struggles to breathe and tries to free himself from the cord or wire! "Aaaahh someone please help me!" Marcus coughs and screams as he is being choked by the wired noose! "Help meee! Someone help me please!" Marcus coughs and screams as he is being dragged away!

Diane D drags Marcus behind the stairwell! She then goes right through the wall behind the stairwell and drags Marcus right through the wall dragging him into a dark universe that's behind the wall. "Aaaahh!" Marcus screams as he goes into the dark universe. "Aaaaaahh!........"

PRESENT:

"Aaaaaahhh!" Marcus wakes up screaming from his nightmare again! Jessica, Vanessa and Richard rush right into his room again!

They rush right to him and shout, "Marcus!" They bend to him and grab him! They sit on his bed and hold tightly onto him as Vanessa shouts, "Marcus Marcus Marcus! It's okay! It's us!"

"Aaaahhh, help me, help me!" Marcus screams as he sits up on his bed. "She's still after me! She keeps coming after me in the back stairwell of the school! This time in the dream, she actually caught up with me!"

"What!" Vanessa, Jessica and Richard shout.

"Diane D caught up with you this time?!" Vanessa shouts. "Because in all your other dreams and nightmares, she's never caught up with you! You were always able to escape her!"

"But this time, I didn't escape her Grandma!" Marcus shouts. "This time, she actually caught up to me!"

"Oh Lord!"

"What did Diane D do when she caught up with you Marcus?!" Jessica asks.

"She grabbed me!" Marcus shouts.

"She grabbed you?!"

"Yes!"

"Then what happened?"

"She wrapped a cord or wire around my neck!"

"She what!" Jessica, Vanessa and Richard shout.

"She wrapped a cord or wire around your neck?!" Jessica shouts.

"Yes!" Marcus shouts.

"My God! Then what happened?"

"She started to drag me!"

"She dragged you?!"

"Yes!"

"To where?!"

"I don't know! All I know, is that she was dragging me to a dark place behind the stairwell!"

"To a dark place behind the stairwell?" Vanessa shouts.

"Yeah! Sort of like a dark universe."

"A dark universe?!"

"Yes!"

"How did her face look like?"

"Almost like a dead person!"

"What!" Vanessa, Jessica and Richard shout. "Like a dead person?!"

"What do you mean almost like a dead person Marcus?!" Vanessa shouts. "A dead person's face normally have no color! Their face is usually pale! Was her face pale? Is that what you're trying to say?"

"Yes Grandma!" Marcus shouts. "Her face was pale!"

"It was?! My God! So altogether, Diane D caught up to you, grabbed you, wrapped a cord or wire around your neck, then dragged you to a dark place behind the stairwell?"

"Exactly!"

"Oh my God Marcus!" Jessica shouts. "Since you said Diane D has never caught up to you before in any of your other dreams and nightmares, but caught up to you in your nightmare this time, I hope it's not a sign!"

"A sign?"

"Yeah! I hope it doesn't mean that her other personality or personalities are going to REALLY come after you!"

"Oh no! You think it could really be a sign Mom?!"

"It's a possibility! One of her other personalities already killed two police officers!"

"Oh no!" Marcus and Richard shout.

"Two police officers already died, so did a swat team member!"

"A swat team member too?!" Marcus shouts. "Oh no! That's three people Diane D's other personality killed so far!"

"That's right that's three people! We don't know how many more of those injured authority figures might pass away! Remember Officer Henley told us that one of Diane D's other personalities did tell the doctors that it already knows where you are!"

"Oh no!"

"But don't worry Marcus. There's only one way to handle this situation."

"One way?"

"Yes."

"And what way is that Mom?!"

"Get my gun and SHOOT the monster!"

"What! You would really do that Mom?!"

"Of course I would do that Marcus! You're my child! What kind of mother would I be, if I didn't try to protect my children?!"

"Marcus why don't you just accept Diane D's foregiveness," Vanessa says. "Maybe this will all end!"

"No I'm not going to accept her forgiveness Grandma!" Marcus shouts.

"Why not?!"

"Because I don't want to face her!"

"So you would rather face her in your dreams and nightmares for the rest of your life?!"

"I don't know! I don't know what I'm going to do!"

"I know what you can do Marcus. Try to accept Diane D's foregiveness once and for all because we cannot keep going through this! This has been going on for the past three years! I have had lots of sleepless nights because this! This can't keep going on! Think about accepting Diane D's forgiveness, for my sake, okay?"

"That's right Marcus," Jessica says. "Accept Diane D's forgiveness, because I don't want her other personality or personalities to make anymore threats against you then act on those threats! Do you want what happened to you inside that school hallway three years ago to happen again?! I don't want to have to use my gun, but I will use it if that monster decides to step foot anywhere towards this direction!"

Marcus nervously looks at his family. He then says, "Okay."

"Okay?!" Jessica and Vanessa shout.

"Okay what Marcus?!" Vanessa asks.

"I will accept Diane D's foregiveness," Marcus says.

"What!" Jessica and Vanessa shout. "Really Marcus?!"

"Yeah."

"Oh that is so good to hear!" Jessica shouts.

"I'm so glad to hear that Marcus!" Vanessa shouts. "I'm sure this will all finally end if you would just accept Diane D's forgiveness."

"That's right Marcus. Now that we got that out of the bag, do you want to come sleep in my room since this nightmare has gotten worse?"

"No that's okay Mom," Marcus nervously says. "I think I'll be okay."

"Oh yeah? Are you sure?"

"Yeah I'm sure. I'll be okay."

"Now that's what I want to hear! Are you planning to go back to sleep?"

"No, I think I'll stay up. It's almost daylight."

"Okay Marcus. We're going to head back to sleep. See you at breakfast."

"Okay Mom. Bye."

"Bye baby." Jessica, Vanessa and Richard stand back up. They lean to Marcus and give him a loving kiss. They turn and head towards the doorway. They take one last look at Marcus and leave the room.

Marcus looks towards the doorway. He then whispers to himself, "No you won't see me at breakfast because what you all just gave me, was a goodbye kiss! I won't be here anymore." He then looks up in the air and says, "Okay Diane D's other personality! You want me so bad? Well you got me because here I come!" Marcus gets out of the bed. He turns to his bed and grabs the sheets. He starts to pull all the sheets off his bed. He balls up all the sheets. He holds the sheets and quietly heads for the doorway. He goes out the bedroom into the hallway with the sheets.

Marcus quietly walks through the hallway holding the balled up sheets and heads towards the bathroom as he looks around. He quietly goes into the bathroom. He then shuts the door behind himself.

Later on that morning, Jessica is surrounded by Officer Henley and other police officers as she cries her eyes out shouting, "See? Marcus was right! There IS a monster inside Diane D! I always knew that woman was possessed by something when Marcus first told me what he went through with her on that third floor school hallway that night! I always knew! I don't know why you officers didn't just arrest her when Marcus first told you about the nightmares he's been having about her!"

"Miss Whitley, Diane D hasn't been around Marcus since that night he had an encounter with her on that third floor school hallway a few years ago!" Officer Henley says. "She has nothing to do with Marcus' death, she was nowhere around when his death happened. She was in the hospital when this horrible incident happened and she still is in the hospital. She hasn't been released yet." Jessica continues to cry her eyes out. Officer Henley then asks, "How is your mom doing?"

"My mom is traumatized! Marcus was her life! She's so traumatized that she had to be taken to the hospital!"

"She was taken to the hospital?"

"Yes!"

"I'm sorry to hear about that Miss Whitley. How is Richard doing?"

"He's traumatized too! He had to be taken to the hospital also! He literally passed out when he realized what happened to his brother!"

"Oh no."

Jessica continues to cry her eyes out as Officer Henley and the other police officers sadly continue to surround her.

The next day, Candis is inside her apartment with Jonathan her ex-Jamaican boyfriend/fiance who is also Diane D's former lover. Candis and Jonathan are looking at a newspaper article with a headline that reads: **MARCUS, THE LITTLE BOY CLAIMED TO HAVE BEEN BEAT UP BY DIANE D INSIDE A SCHOOL HALLWAY THREE YEARS AGO TAKES HIS OWN LIFE!**: "Wow!" Candis shouts. "See Jonathan?! I told you that there's something about Diane D that gives me the creeps, I told you that! You see what she put that poor little boy through?! His nightmares of her caused him to take his own life!"

"Oh my God!" Jonathan says. "Does it say how he killed himself?"

"Yeah. It says he had hung himself with bedsheets inside his family's bathroom!"

"Oh no!"

"I know! It's sad! It's sad that the only way this kid felt to escape his torment of Diane D was to take his own life! My God! I almost had nightmares about Diane D myself, when I found out that she sped her car all the way from her family's organization t0 come several miles away to beat me up in the parking lot behind this building?! And the creepy thing is, I didn't even know she knew about me, but she knew all about me! She knew exactly where to find me when she sped her car all the way over here to attack me in the parking lot! And you need to stay away from her too Johnathan! If you get her upset, that other soul, spirit, personality or personalities of hers might come after you too then you'll wind up going through what that poor little boy went through, having nightmares about Diane D!"

"Candis I haven't been around Diane D in a few years! The only time I see her, is when she's on stage when I come to see her family's shows, that's it!"

"Does she know about that kid Marcus taking his own life because of her?! Does she know about it?!"

"I don't know Candis. As far as I know, Diane D is still in the hospital sedated because of her injuries. Once she's released from that hospital, I think they're going to have her transferred right back to the mental institution again."

"Really?"

"Yeah."

"Good! This time, I hope she stays in the mental institution and never comes out! When is this little boy's funeral? I would like to go there and give his family some moral support. I want to show my condolences."

"You do?"

"Yeah."

"Well I don't know when his funeral is Candis."

"That's okay, I'll try to find out." Candis continues to read the article as Jonathan sadly looks at the article.

Four days later, Marcus has a funeral. He is inside a closed casket as Officer Henley, other police officers, Candis, Jonathan, Marcus' old school teachers, his new school teachers, his old classmates, his new classmates and thousands of other people attend his funeral. Jessica is at the side crying her eyes out as Officer Henley and other people try to comfort her. Candis approaches Officer Henley. She says to him, "Um excuse me Officer?" Officer Henley turns to Candis as she says to him, "I'm just curious to know, where is her mom and her older son?"

"They are both traumatized by all of this," Officer Henley says. "They couldn't be here."

"No?"

"No. They're in the hospital."

"What! They're in the hospital?!"

"Yes they are."

"Oh my God. Sorry this all happened. Did that kid Marcus' nightmares of Diane D cause him to take his own life?"

"I'm afraid it did."

"Oh my! That poor kid! The doctors couldn't help him?"

"They tried to, but didn't succeed."

"Wow. Well I hope the kid is finally resting in peace."

"I think he is. After the ordeal he went through for three years, I think he deserves some peace now."

"Yeah me too. Thank you Officer."

"You're welcome." Officer Henley and Candis sadly look at Jessica. Candis and Jonathan then turn and walk away.

Candis and Jonathan approach Marcus' casket and sadly look at it. Candis then turns around and looks at the crowd. She then says, "Oh my God."

Jonathan puzzled looks at Candis and asks, "What's wrong?"

"I see Diane D's family!"

"What! You see her family?"

"Yeah."

"Where?"

"At the entrance!"

"Oh my God." Jonathan turns and looks at the entrance. He sees Margarita, Tomas, Barry, Michael and Mickey at the entrance. He becomes nervous and whispers, "I don't think I want Diane D's family to see me here."

"No? Why not?"

"Because they hate me Candis! They might not have gotten over the affair Diane D had with me years ago, especially her husband! I don't want to run into him. He might want to punch me out! I don't want to run into the rest of her family either! I better ease out of here before they see me. You should ease out of here before they see you too Candis."

"What's wrong with them seeing me? I'm not the one guilty of anything, Diane D is! She's the one who cheated on her husband with you! As long as she's not here, I shouldn't have to leave. She's not here is she? Because she is one person I do not care to run into."

"I don't think Diane D is here Candis. I think she might still be in the hospital. Even though she might not be here and still be in the hospital, you did had an issue with her at the police station years ago while her family was there. Your image will always reflect on that! Do you want to run into her family again and have them be reminded of that incident?"

"No. I guess not."

"Okay then. I think we should leave out the side door."

"Okay. Let's go." Candis and Jonathan take one last look at Diane D's family then head towards the side and leave the area.

Margarita, Tomas, Barry, Michael and Mickey stand at the entrance looking at the crowd. They see Jessica near the front crying her eyes out. Mickey turns to Margarita and Tomas and sadly says, "Grandma, Grandpa, you think we should go over to Marcus' mom and give her our condolences?"

"We would love to Mickey," Margarita says. "But I think we would be the last people on earth Marcus' mom would rather see. After all, it WAS Diane her child kept having nightmares about, causing him to take his own life, and Diane is our family member."

"That's true."

"I don't see Marcus' grandmother or his brother here," Michael says.

"I heard they got traumatized by this," Barry says.

"They got traumatized too?" Mickey asks.

"Yeah Mickey. It seems like we all are getting traumatized these days." Barry, Margarita, Tomas, Michael and Mickey stand at the entrance looking at the crowd.

"Come on everybody," Margarita then says. "Let's get back to the hospital because I have to get ready to stay with Diane again tonight."

"Okay Margarita," Tomas says as he, Margarita, Barry, Michael and Mickey take one last look towards Marcus' coffin, then turn and leave the area.

Chapter 21

Margarita's Encounter With The Other Personality

That same evening, Diane D's family including the Dianettes are standing around her hospital bed looking at her with Diane D being in a deep sleep laying face up still hooked to monitors with both her shoulders, both arms and both wrists completely in casts and bandages. Diane D has a long chain still attached to one of her shackles and the other end of the chain attached to the metal bars of the bed as Mary and Margarita stand at the head of her hospital bed patting her forehead, eyes and neck with damp cloths again. "Are you going to spend the night with her again Grandma?" Michael asks.

"Yes," Margarita says. "I'm gonna spend the night with her every night this week," Margarita says as she and Mary fix Diane D's clothes and blanket.

It is late at night around 2:00 in the morning. Diane D's hospital room is dimly lit. Margarita and Dr. Kern are in Diane D's hospital room standing over Diane D's hospital bed looking down at Diane D with Diane D still in a deep sleep hooked to monitors with both her shoulders, both arms and both wrists still in casts and bandages as she lays face up in the bed. Margarita then says, "How long is she going to be bed ridden Doctor?"

"For a while Miss Margarita," Dr. Kern says. Dr. Kern then turns to Margarita and says, "She really got injured bad when her other personality broke the chains loose from the couch."

"My God."

"She just needs plenty of rest."

"Okay Doctor." Margarita and Dr. Kern continue to look at Diane D. They then turn and walk away from Diane D's bedside as they stare at her. They turn their heads forward and walk towards the doorway.

Dr. Kern and Margarita step out of Diane D's hospital room into the hallway. Dr. Kern turns to Margarita and says, "I'll check back on her in the morning. You get some rest."

"Sure Doctor Kern. I will."

"See you in the morning."

"Okay."

Dr. Kern turns and walks away as Margarita leans on the wall watching him go down the hallway. Margarita then looks around the hospital hallway. She then gets up off the wall and turns back towards Diane D's hospital room. She then heads back into the room.

Margarita is back inside the hospital room closing the door behind herself. She leans on the door holding her head up with her eyes closed. She then holds her head back straight and opens her eyes. She looks towards Diane D's hospital bed. She becomes shocked to see Diane D's hospital bed empty! She does not see Diane D in the bed! She becomes hysterical and shouts, "Diane!" She hurries to Diane D's empty hospital bed!

Margarita approaches Diane D's hospital bed and shouts, "Diane! Where are you?!" She hysterically looks around the hospital room and shouts, "Diane!" She then looks towards the bathroom. She sees the long chain that's hooked to Diane D's shackle and the wires hooked to the monitors are leading to the bathroom. Margarita looks at the bathroom and sees that the door is closed. She starts to head to the bathroom and shouts, "Diane! Qué estás haciendo en el baño?! Pensé que estás postrado en cama!"

Margarita approaches the bathroom door. She then opens it. She stands in the doorway and looks into the dimly lit bathroom which has only a small night light on. She becomes shocked to see Diane D just standing there facing the mirror with her back towards her not saying a word with both her shoulders, both arms and both wrists still in casts and bandages with wires from the monitors still hooked to her and the long chain still hooked to her shackle. Margarita then says, "Diane? Estas bien?" Diane D continues to face the mirror with her back towards Margarita not saying a word. Margarita then shouts, "Diane, estoy hablando con usted!" Diane D slowly turns around towards Margarita. Her face has that eerie pale unearthly half dead appearance to it again and her eyes are very puffy, swollen and appear to be half dead as she firmly looks at Margarita. Margarita becomes shocked and stunned seeing Diane D's strange facial appearance. She then becomes frightened and shouts, "Oh nooo! It's YOU! That other personality!" Margarita becomes hysterical again as she frighteningly backs up and shouts, "Oh my God! Where's Diane?!" She then cries, "What have you done with her?!" Diane D's other personality continues to stare at Margarita giving Margarita a cold stare with half dead eyes. Margarita then shouts, "Don't tell me you pulled her soul and spirit out of her body and placed it out in space wandering the universe again!"

"Yes I have," Diane D's other personality firmly says.

"What! Why?! Bring her back! Bring her back now!"

"I will bring her back."

"What are you doing here?! Why are you here?!"

"I'm here because of you."

"Because of me?"

"Yes."

"What do you mean 'because of me'?!"

"You want to talk to me, don't you?"

"I want to talk to you? What do you mean?!"

"I know what you said to your family the other day. You told your family that you would like to have a word with me, didn't you?"

"Yes! Yes I did tell them that! How do you know?!"

"I just know."

Margarita shockingly and frighteningly stares at Diane D's other personality. She then shouts, "Oh my God! Which soul, spirit and personality are you?! The one who had an encounter with my other granddaughter Nancy, and the one who kept entering Marcus' dreams and nightmares, who also claim to have entered Dana's physical body before, or the other one who admitted that they cause Diane to levitate in Germany then attacked the doctors, security guards, the priest, police officers and a swat team?! Which one are you?!"

"The one who encountered your other granddaughter."

"Nancy?! YOU'RE the one who Nancy had an encounter with inside my home?!"

"Yes."

"Oh my God! And you're the one who kept entering Marcus dreams and nightmares?!"

"Yes I'm the one."

"Oh my goodness! And you're the one, who claim to have entered Dana's physical body before too?!"

"Yes it's me."

"Oh my God!"

"Well, I'm here. Here's your chance to talk to me. What do you want to say to me?"

"What do I want to say to you?!"

"Yes."

"What I want to say to you is, I want you to leave Diane alone, that's what I want to say to you! I don't want your soul, spirit or personality coming around Diane again, taking over her physical body anymore causing a lot of havoc! She's in this hospital injured because of what that other soul, spirit and personality did to her physical body! I don't want you or that other soul, spirit or personality putting Diane's soul or spirit through this anymore! I don't want you or that other soul, spirit or personality putting her physical body through this anymore! As a matter of fact, her physical body shouldn't even be out of the bed! She's bed ridden! But then you come along and just snatch her soul and spirit right out her physical body while she's sedated! Then you just enter her physical body and bring her physical body right out of the bed when it shouldn't even be out of the bed! I don't want you or that other soul, spirit or personality putting her physical body through this anymore and I don't want you or that other soul, spirit or personality putting us her family through this anymore! We've had enough of all of this!" Diane D's other personality continues to give Margarita a cold stare with the eerie pale face and puffy swollen, half dead eyes as Margarita shouts, "We're all still traumatized and going through nervous break downs because of all of this and seeing security guards, police officers and all those other people being hurt and injured because of YOU and that OTHER soul, spirit or personality! What I want you to do right now, is put my grandchild's physical body right back in that bed where it should be! And once you put her physical body back in the bed, I want you to go away and stay away! And leave my grandchild's soul, spirit and body alone from now on, you got that?!"

Diane D's other personality continues to give Margarita a cold stare. Her other personality then says, "Okay. I will leave Diane alone from now on."

"You will?"

"Yes. I'm only doing this for you because you're her family."

"Because I'm her family?"

"Yes."

"Why because I'm her family?!"

"Because she loves her family. She doesn't want her family hurt or upset. If her family gets hurt or upset, then she'll be hurt and upset and I don't want her hurt and upset. That's why I'm willing to leave her soul, spirit and body alone, for her family's sake and for her sake. But let me tell you something. I will always have Diane's back no matter what."

Margarita continues to frighteningly stare at Diane D's other personality. She then asks, "Why?"

"Because I look out for her."

"Why?! Why do you look out for her?!"

"We just do."

"We? Who's we?! You and that other soul, spirit and personality who attacked those security guards, the priest, police officers and the swat team?!"

"Yes."

"But I don't understand! You and that other soul, spirit or personality say that you're protective of Diane and look out for her and don't want anybody hurting her! But the only ones who are really hurting Diane, is YOU and that OTHER soul, spirit or personality, causing her physical body to be injured, causing her to have bruises all over her physical body, and she would have no idea in the world where the bruises be coming from! If you don't want anybody hurting Diane, then you shouldn't be hurting her either!"

"Don't worry. We won't cause anymore havoc, unless we really have to."

"Unless you really have to?!"

"Yes."

Margarita continues to frighteningly stare at Diane D's other personality. She then asks, "What about if Diane meditates again?"

"What about it?"

"Will you and that other soul, spirit or personality still come around her if she meditates again?!"

"Her meditation draws us to her. That we have no control over."

"You have no control over it?"

"No."

"I see. What about that kid Marcus?"

"What about him?"

"He killed himself! Do you know about that?"

"Yes I do."

"You do?!"

"Yes."

"Well is he resting in peace? Do you know where his soul or spirit is?!"

"Yes I do."

"You do?!"

"Yes."

"Well where is he?!"

"You don't need to know."

"Why not?"

"You just don't."

Margarita frighteningly stares at Diane D's other personality.

Diane D's other personality then says, "Now if you would excuse me, I will replace Diane's physical body back on the bed and let her soul and spirit return to you."

"You will?!"

"Yes."

"Oh thank you!" Margarita anxiously shouts. "Thank you!" Margarita puzzled stares at Diane D's other personality again. Then she nervously says, "Before you go, I just need to ask you. That killing you told the doctors that you be doing once every fifty years through out the centuries, is that fifty years up?"

"Yes it is."

"It is?!"

"Yes."

"Are you planning to commit murder again?"

"You don't need to know."

"I don't?!"

"No."

"Well if you do plan to commit murder again, you're not planning to use Diane's physical body to do any of your killings are you?! Because I won't let you! That other soul, spirit and personality already used her physical body to kill two police officers and a swat team member!"

"You have nothing to worry about. I won't use this physical body to do any killings."

"You won't?"

"No."

"But when the doctors asked you who's physical body are you planning to use to commit another murder, and asked you will it be Diane's physical body, you told them 'we shall see'! Were you really planning to use my grandchild's physical body to commit another murder?!"

"It was a possibility," Diane D's other personality says as Margarita gasps. Diane D's other personality then says, "But I changed my decision. I won't do that to Diane. I won't put her or her family through that."

"You won't?!"

"No."

"Oh thank you!" Margarita sighs and says. "Thank you so much! So if you do kill somebody again, whose physical body will you use to do it? I sure hope you don't plan to use Dana's physical body! Because I won't let you use her physical body either!"

"Don't worry. It won't be anybody you know."

"It won't?"

"No."

"Not even Dana?!"

"No. I won't do that to her either."

"Thank God!" Margarita sighs. "What about the future murder victim? Who will the future murder victim be? Will it be someone I know?"

"No, the murder victim won't be anyone you know either."

"They won't?"

"No. It won't even happen in this part of the world."

"It won't?"

"No."

"So where will it happen then?!"

"Far far away from here."

"Far far away from here?! Where?!"

"You don't need to know."

"But why do you kill people anyway?!"

"I just do."

"Why?! And why do you do it once every fifty years?! Is it something you have to do?! Is it some type of ritual?!"

"You don't need to know."

Margarita frighteningly stares at Diane D's other personality again. She then says, "Oh. Well I'm glad you don't plan on using Diane's physical body or Dana's physical body." Margarita frighteningly stares at Diane D's other personality again. She then says, "By the way, I need to ask you something. When the doctors asked you 'have you ever used Dana's physical body to kill anybody', you suddenly became silent and never answered that question. Why is that?" Diane D's other personality gives Margarita a cold stare. Margarita then says, "Since you remained silent and never answered that question, I'm going to ask you that very same question myself and I hope you answer me. Have you ever entered Dana's physical body, and used her physical body to kill someone?" Diane D's other personality does not answer the question. Her other personality continues to give Margarita a cold stare. Margarita then says, "Well? I'm waiting for an answer. Have you ever used Dana's physical body to kill someone?" Diane D's other personality continues to remain silent as her other personality continues to give Margarita a cold stare. Margarita then shouts, "Answer the question! Have you ever used Dana's physical body to commit murder?!"

"I was about to."

Margarita gasps! She then says, "Oh nooo!! You were about to?! What do you mean you were about to?! What happened?!"

"I was about to kill this person one night."

Margarita gasps! She then says, "You were about to kill this person one night?!"

"Yes."

"Using Dana's physical body?!"

"Yes."

"Oh my God! Who?! Who were you about to kill?!"

"Some young woman you don't know."

"A young woman I don't know?! When?!"

"Several years ago."

"Several years ago?! Where?!"

"In this part of the world."

"In this part of the world?!"

"Yes."

"Where exactly?!"

"In the stairwell."

"What! In the stairwell again?! Where, inside a school?!"

"No."

"Not inside a school?! Then where?!"

"Inside an apartment building."

"Inside an apartment building stairwell?!"

"Yes."

"Oh my God! What apartment building stairwell?!"

"You don't need to know."

"Oh my God! Why were you about to kill this young woman?!"

"You don't need to know."

"I don't?"

"No."

"How were you about to kill her?!

292

"By taking a hammer and bashing her in the head."

Margarita gasps! She then says, "By taking a hammer and bashing the young woman in the head?!"

"That's right."

"Oh my God! That is so cruel!"

"Don't worry. I didn't get to kill her because she had escaped and ran off in the stairwell before I got the chance to catch her."

"She escaped and ran off in the stairwell?!"

"Yes."

"Oh my God! That woman must have ran off because she probably saw you or should I say saw Dana coming after her with a hammer! Did the woman see Dana's physical body coming after her with a hammer?"

"Yes."

"She did?!"

"Yes, that's why she ran off."

"Oh my God! Just like when Marcus ran off and escaped from Diane or should I say escaped from YOU in the back stairwell of that school! So if that young woman hadn't escaped from you and you would have caught up to her, you would have tried to kill her with the hammer?!"

"Exactly. I would have bashed her right in the skull."

"You would have bashed her in the skull, using Dana's physical body?!"

"Exactly."

"Oh nooo! So you were about to make Dana into a vicious murderer, just like you were about to make Diane into a vicious murderer when you had her physical body go after Marcus! Oh my God! Does Dana remember going after this young woman with a hammer when you used her physical body go after that woman?"

"No she doesn't."

"She doesn't remember?!"

"No, how can she remember? Her soul and spirit wasn't there."

"It wasn't?"

"No."

"Then where was it?"

"Wandering the universe."

"Wandering the universe too?! Who put her soul or spirit out there?!"

"I did."

"You did! So you snatched Dana's soul and spirit right out of her physical body, threw her soul and spirit out there in space wandering the universe for the time being just like you do Diane, then entered her physical body and used her physical body to do an attempted murder by going after that young woman in the stairwell with a hammer?!"

"Exactly."

"And while Dana's soul and spirit was out there in space wandering the universe, she had no idea in this world, that her own physical body down here on earth was about to be used in an attempted murder?!"

"No she had no idea."

"Oh my God! Just like Diane had no idea that her own physical body was about to be used in an attempted murder! Oh my Goodness! So when Dana's original soul and spirit returned into her physical body, she had no memory of what went on with her physical body?!"

"No she had no memory of what went on."

"Oh my God! What drawned you to Dana's physical body that night anyway?"

"She was meditating with Diane earlier that evening."

"She was meditating with Diane earlier that evening? That's what made you drawned to her?!"

"Yes."

"Is that the only reason why you were drawned to Dana in the first place, because she was meditating with Diane earlier that evening?"

"Yes that's the only reason."

"Oh my God." Margarita frighteningly stares at Diane D's other personality.

"Now if you would excuse me, I will replace Diane's physical body back on the bed now and let her soul and spirit return to you."

"Oh. Okay, thank you! Thank you!" Margarita puzzled stares at Diane D's other personality.

Diane D's other personality continues to give Margarita a cold stare, waiting for Margarita to move out of the way.

Margarita then says, "I'll step out of your way." Margarita nervously backs up and steps out of the bathroom doorway.

Margarita hurries away from the bathroom doorway towards the hospital room door.

Diane D's other personality steps out the bathroom with the monitor wires still hooked to her and the long chain still hooked to her shackle dragging the long chain. Her other personality then stops and gives Margarita a cold stare again.

Margarita leans on the hospital room door frighteningly looking at Diane D's other personality.

Diane D's other personality then turns away from Margarita and heads to the hospital bed. Her other personality approaches the hospital bed. Her other personality then turns her head and gives Margarita another cold stare.

Margarita continues to lean on the hospital room door frighteningly looking at Diane D's other personality.

Diane D's other personality then turns back forward and sits on the hospital bed. Her other personality then lays down on the hospital bed. Her other personality then places the sheet and blanket over itself. It then looks back at Margarita.

Margarita frighteningly continues to watch Diane D's other

personality.

Diane D's other personality then lays down on its back with its face up towards the ceiling. Her other personality then closes its eyes and goes to sleep.

Margarita frighteningly watches Diane D's other personality going to sleep. She stands there leaning against the door for a while. She then sees Diane D's other personality going into a deep sleep. She stands there leaning on the door for several seconds and starts to cry. She sees Diane D's other personality completely still, not moving. She then says, "Diane?" Margarita frighteningly leans off the door looking at Diane D's physical body. She then stands there and stares at Diane D's physical body. Then she slowly and nervously heads towards Diane D's physical body and says, "Diane? Are you back?" Margarity approaches Diane D's physical body as it lays on the hospital bed appearing to be in a deep sleep. Margarita looks at Diane D's physical face. She sees that Diane D's physical face is not pale anymore. She sees that the color has come back to Diane D's face. She sees Diane D's physical face back to normal! She becomes anxious and excited and shouts, "Diane!" Margarita grabs Diane D's physical body by the shoulders and starts to gently shake Diane D's physical body shouting, "Diane! Wake up baby! It's me! Wake up!" Margarita continues to gently shake Diane D by the shoulders and shouts, "Diane wake up baby! Wake up!" Margarita then shakes Diane D real hard desperately trying to bring Diane D's original soul and spirit back as she shouts, "Diane despierte! Voy a seguir molestando hasta que vuelvas, ahora se despierte! Despierte a Diane! Por favor despiértese!" Margarita starts to shake Diane D more harder! Suddenly Diane D starts moaning and groaning in pain. Margarita becomes excited and shouts, "Diane es que USTED?! Es usted vuelta?!" Margarita continues to roughly shake Diane D by the shoulders! Suddenly Diane D starts to moan and groan louder. "Diane!" Margarita excitingly shouts. "Oh mi Dios Diane, estás de vuelta?!"

Diane D gets a look of pain on her face and shouts, "Aahh!"

"Diane!" Margarita shouts. "Usted está gritando de dolor! Se siente el dolor?! Déjame saber si usted siente dolor! Se siente el dolor?!" Margarita continues to roughly shake Diane D's physical body by the shoulders and shouts, "Puedes sentir esto?!" She roughly shakes D's physical body by the shoulders again and shouts, "Puedes sentir eso?!"

"Aaah!" Diane D screams in pain again! She opens her eyes a little. She looks at Margarita and shouts, "Grandma! What are you doing?!"

"Oh Diane!" Margarita excitingly shouts and smiles as she looks at Diane D. "Usted está de vuelta!" Margarita lifts Diane D's physical body up a little and grabs her physical body holding Diane D very tightly giving Diane D a huge big hug.

"Grandma!" Diane D screams in pain again. "You're hurting me!"

"I'm hurting you?!"

"Yeah!"

"That means you feel pain! If you feel pain, that means it's YOU!! You're back!" Margarita cries and shouts. "My baby is back, my baby is back!" Margarita starts to cry real hard. She then turns her face to Diane D and starts kissing all over Diane D's head and face real hard. "You're back baby, you're back!" Margarita continues to cry real hard. She then holds, hugs and kisses on Diane D very tightly. She starts to gently rock Diane D as she leans her head against Diane D's head. She continues to cry. She then says, "It's okay baby, it's okay." Margarita turns her face towards Diane D and gives Diane D another kiss on the head. She then looks up in the air with tears in her eyes. She then whispers to the other soul, spirit and personality, "Thank you. Thank you for bringing her back." Margarita continues to stare in the air. She then looks back at Diane D and continues to hold, hug and kiss on Diane D very tight. She continues to gently rock Diane's physical body as she continues to cry.

The next morning, Margarita's family and relatives, doctors and hospital staff are standing in the hospital hallway anxiously and frighteningly surrounding Margarita. They just heard the news of Margarita having her own encounter with Diane D's other personality! "Oh my God Mom!" Barry shouts. "Are you alright?! First it was Nancy having an encounter with that other personality, now you! Who's going to be next?!"

"Are you alright Grandma?!" Michael hysterically asks. "Did Diane ... I mean did that other personality act like it wanted to hurt you or harm you?!"

"No, it didn't," Margarita nervously says with tears in her eyes.

"It didn't?"

"No."

"Thank goodness!"

"Are you okay Miss Margarita?" one of the doctors asks.

"No I'm not okay!" Margarita shouts. "I'm worried and upset about what's happening to my grandchild!"

"Oh Miss Margarita? It'll be okay! Don't cry! It's going to be okay! How's Diane D doing now?"

"She's still suffering in a lot of pain from that ordeal when she broke loose from the chains."

"You mean when her other personality broke the chains loose from the couch?"

"Yes. Her aunts and her other grandma are in the room with her trying to massage her aches and pains."

"Her aunts and her other grandmother?"

"Yes." Everyone tries to comfort Margarita.

Inside Diane D's hospital room, Diane D is laying chest down on her hospital bed unconscious with monitor wires still hooked to her with her arms all the way up to her head with both her upper arms, both her lower arms, both her wrists and both her hands still wrapped entirely in casts and bandages as she lays her head on top of her hands with her head facing her right with her eyes still swollen shut. There is a pillow beneath her head as her hair is in one long thick braid. Her muscular shoulders and muscular back are completely bare with the sheet and blanket covering her hips on down. There are bandages wrapped around the sides of her torso where it is slightly bruised as Aunt Jean stands near Diane D's left shoulder massaging her left shoulder and Aunt Celeste massages Diane D's bare back rubbing some mineral oil on her back. Aunt Laura stands to the side holding the mineral oil as Gracy fixes Diane D's sheet and blanket.

Dana and her sisters, Missy, Landa, Londa and Linda, suddenly enter the hospital room holding gifts, huge teddy bears and food as Missy says, "Hi everybody."

"Hey you all," Gracy and Aunt Jean say.

"We brought more gifts for Diane," Londa says.

"And we got her some soup too," Dana says.

"I don't think Diane is still able to eat right now Dana," Gracy says. "She was still in a lot of pain."

"That's why we brought soup for her so she can eat it whenever she feels better."

"I think that soup is gonna sit around a long time Dana. Diane is still unconscious."

"She is?"

"Yeah. They sedated her again."

"They did? Why?"

"Because of the pain she was in. So she's not going to able to eat that soup for a while. It's gonna get spoiled. So you girls might as well eat it."

"Okay Grandma." Dana, Missy, Landa, Londa and Linda put the food on the side. They then walk towards Diane D's hospital bed.

Dana and her sisters approach Diane D's hospital bed and look down at her. They sadly stare at Diane D as she continues to lay there on her chest unconscious with her face to the side. Missy turns to Gracy and asks, "How she doing Grandma?"

"She was still in a lot of pain Missy," Gracy says. "That's why they sedated her again."

"She's sedated again?"

"Yes."

"Oh." Missy, Dana, Landa, Londa and Linda continue to look at Diane D. They then look at the slight bruises on the side of her back underneath the bandages as Missy asks, "Why does she have slight bruises on her side? Where did those bruises come from?"

"It came from when she spun her body around holding the couch high up in the air while she still had the chains attached to her body.

When the chains were swirling an spinning right along with her body, the chains wind up whipping her on the sides."

"It did?"

"Yes, but she still kept spinning her body around while the chains were whipping her. That's how she got the bruises on her sides. The bruises came from the chains."

"She didn't feel the chains whipping her?"

"I guess not. It didn't stop her from spinning her body around because she still kept spinning her body around while she was holding the couch high up in the air."

"She didn't realize what was happening with herself?

"No she didn't realize it at all."

"Wow, that is so sad."

"It is."

Landa then looks at Gracy, Aunt Celeste, Aunt Jean and Aunt Laura and says, "Did any of you see the hypnosis room yet since that incident?"

"No we haven't Landa," Aunt Celeste whispers.

"How come?"

"I don't know if we are able to see it."

"Why not? I want to see it."

"You want to see it?" Aunt Laura whispers.

"Sure. I heard it got real damaged in there. I heard there was blood everywhere."

"It was," Aunt Celeste whispers. "That's why you can't see it. I don't think they're going to allow anybody in that room."

"Why not?"

"Because it's a crime scene, that's why."

"What!" Missy, Landa, Londa and Linda whisper. "A crime scene?!"

"Yes."

"How is it a crime scene Aunt Celeste?" Missy whispers.

"Don't you know?! Three people died from that incident! Two police officers and a swat team member! They lost their life from what happened inside that hypnosis room, other authority figures got seriously injured! Who knows if more of them might pass away later on from that incident!" Missy, Landa, Londa and Linda shockingly look at Aunt Celeste with their mouths open. They then turn their heads towards the head of the bed and look at Diane D. They shockingly stare at her again. Then they turn their heads towards the foot of the bed and look at her feet. They see the long chain that's attached to her shackle. They see the other end of the chain attached to the metal bar of her hospital bed.

Linda turns to Gracy and whispers, "Does Diane know that anybody died from what she did?"

"No she still doesn't know anything yet Linda," Gracy whispers.

"She doesn't?"

"No! She's been sedated and unconscious back and forth since the doctors brought her out of hypnosis."

"What!" Londa whispers. "You mean to tell us, that she killed three people, and don't even know it?!"

"Well it wasn't her that did it Londa. It was her other personality who killed those people."

"Her other personality?"

"Yes!"

"Oh gosh. Wow, that is messed up."

"It is."

"Has she eaten yet Grandma?" Missy asks.

"Well, they're feeding her through the IV needle right there Missy, that's how she's eating."

"Oh, I see."

"Where's your mom and dad?"

"They're on their way up."

"Okay." Gracy walks to the head of the bed near Diane D's right shoulder as Aunt Jean remains at Diane D's left shoulder massaging her left shoulder. Gracy looks at Diane D's head and says to Aunt Jean, "I think we should remove her arm and hand from underneath her head before her arm and hand lose circulation."

"Okay Mom," Aunt Jean says. Aunt Celeste approaches near Aunt Jean and reaches her hands underneath Diane D's head. She and Gracy gently lift Diane D's head a little as Aunt Jean gently removes Diane D's left arm and hand from underneath Diane D's head and Gracy removes Diane D's right arm and hand from underneath Diane D's head. Aunt Celeste and Gracy gently place Diane D's head back down on the pillow. Aunt Jean gently places Diane D's left elbow on the side of the pillow as Gracy places places Diane D's right elbow on the opposite side of the pillow. Diane D's head faces her left side now as she continues to lay unconscious with her shoulders and back still bare and hands folded above her head. They all sadly look at Diane D again as Aunt Jean continue to rub her left shoulder.

Aunt Jean finish rubbing Diane D's left shoulder. She Aunt Celeste and Gracy then take the sheet and blanket and bring the sheet and blanket all the way up to Diane D's shoulders covering her whole body as she continues to lay unconscious. They sadly look at Diane D again as Gracy gives Diane D a loving kiss on the head.

Chapter 22

Another Officer Passes Away

The next day, Mrs. Peterson, her family and in-laws are inside a hospital room crying their eyes out as Mrs. Peterson shouts, "Why did this have to happen?! Why why whyyy?!" Mrs. Peterson continues to cry her eyes out.

The officer's mother and father approach Mrs. Peterson as his mother shouts, "My son is gone, my son is gone! How can this happen?!" The officer's mother and Mrs. Peterson start to cry on each other's shoulders.

Dr. Harvey approaches Mrs. Peterson and the officer's mother and says, "Mrs. Petersons. I'm so sorry for both of your loss."

"Sorry my foot Doctor Harvey!" Mrs. Peterson shouts as she looks at Dr. Harvey. "Diane D is a murderer! She killed my husband! She's a cop killer! She needs to be arrested and charged!"

"That's right Doctor Harvey!" the officer's father shouts. "When are they going to arrest Diane D! So far, her other personality just claimed its fourth victim here, my son! When are they going to arrest her Doctor Harvey?!"

"Diane is still in the hospital Mr. Peterson!" Dr. Harvey says. "They sort of do have her under arrest because she's laying in the hospital with a chain hooked to one of her shackles!"

"A chain hooked to one of her shackles?!"

"Yes!"

"Oh what's that gonna do?! Huh?! If her other personality was capable of breaking loose from chains before, then her other personality can do it again and break loose from that chain that's attached to her shackle!"

"Well thank God her other personality is not there anymore Mr. Peterson, because Diane's original personality came back! If her other personality was still there, she would have been broke loose from that chain attached to her shackle!"

"Then her other personality would escape right out of the hospital and cause more chaos, then more police officers and a swat team would have to come after that other personality of hers with guns, then more deaths would occur! Wow! I cannot believe how vicious her other personality is! Throwing a couch across the room at authority figures slamming the couch right into their heads bashing them right in their heads knocking them out cold, causing some of their heads to split wide open, causing my son and another officer to get shot then die later on! That is so cruel Doctor Harvey! It really is! This is exactly why I never wanted my son to become a police officer, because we got crazy people like that other personality of Diane D's roaming the streets when they should be locked up! Diane D needs to be locked up for good Doctor Harvey, that way her other personality can't use her physical body to harm more people!"

"That's right Doctor Harvey!" Mrs. Peterson shouts. "Thanks to Diane D's other personality, both Mrs. Jenkins and I are now widows!"

"I'm sorry Mrs. Peterson," Dr. Harvey says. "I really am."

"Oh what do you know?!" Mr. Peterson shouts as he frustratedly turns and walks away from Dr. Harvey. Dr. Harvey sadly looks at Mr. Peterson. Then sadly looks at Mrs. Peterson and her mother in-law as they continue to cry on each other's shoulders.

The next day, three High School teachers, two black women and a black male who are around their mid forties, are inside the school office. As one of the female teachers is pouring some coffee from a coffee pot inside a coffee cup, the male teacher is reading a newspaper article with a headline that reads: **ANOTHER POLICE OFFICER WHO WAS A VICTIM OF DIANE D'S OTHER PERSONALITY'S WRATH PASSES AWAY**: "Wow" the man says. "Another one bites the dust."

The two female teachers look at the man as one of them says, "Another one bites the dust? What are you talking about?"

"I'm talking about this article here! It says that another police officer who got injured by Diane D's other personality died yesterday!"

"What! Another officer died?"

"Yeah! The one who got shot in the chest!"

"The one who got shot in the chest!" the second woman shouts.

"Yeah!"

"My God!" The women walk to the male teacher to look at the article. "You know this is the fourth person that has died from Diane D's other personality injuring them! That means that Diane D has killed four people so far!"

"Man that sucks!"

"It does! I really feel bad for her family! They have a murderer on their hands!"

"Her family claim it's not her doing that, that her other personality did it!"

"It's the same thing as far as I'm concerned! Of course her family is going to defend her actions! But it was still her body doing that stuff wasn't it?!"

"Well, yeah!"

"Do you think the authorities are going to just lock up Diane D's other personality without locking Diane D up herself?! If the authorities lock up her other personality, then I'm sorry, Diane D just have to go get locked up right along with it! So as far as I'm concerned, she killed those people!"

"I heard she's not even aware of it! I heard she's still sedated at the hospital!"

"You mean so far she has no idea in this world that she has killed people?!" the first woman says.

"No she has no idea at all!"

"Oh my God! That's horrible! First of all, it's horrible to kill people, second of all, it's horrible to kill people and not even be aware that you did it!"

"Yeah that's true."

"You know last year I was thinking about having Diane D come to this school to perform for the students here!"

"You were?"

"Yeah! But after hearing about all this her other personality did, going berserk attacking the doctors and killing authority figures, I change my mind! I can't have her come here performing for the students, then all of a sudden that other personality of hers comes out and goes after the students! The students will run right out of the school and there will be a horrible stampede here!"

"It sure would be!" the second woman says. "Many people have died from stampedes you know! Then that would be another death that Diane D's other personality caused!"

"It sure would be! Her other personality already caused that kid Marcus to take his own life by appearing in his nightmares practically every night! We can't have another kid dying because of her other personality!"

"We sure can't! We can't have that monster personality of hers come here! We have to protect the students!"

"And ourselves too!" The people continue to look at the article as the women drink their coffee.

Three days later, there is a funeral for the police officer at a church. Mrs. Peterson, her mother in-law, her father in-law and the rest of their family are crying their eyes out at the casket. There are thousands of other officers and civilians gathered at the funeral.

Chapter 23

Dr. Stone Goes To Court

A month later, Dr. Stone sits in the front of the courtroom wearing the bandage around his head. He is sitting with two lawyers. One of his lawyers Carl Roberts, a male white around his late forties with dark hair, stands up and says, "I would like to call my client to the stand." Dr. Stone stands and walks to the front of the courtroom towards the stand.

Dr. Stone approaches the stand. He then turns and faces Carl Roberts.

Carl Roberts tells Dr. Stone, "Raise your right hand please." Dr. Stone raises his right hand as Carl Roberts says to him, "State your full name please."

"Jake Maurice Stone," Dr. Stone says.

"Okay Doctor Stone, do you swear to tell the truth, the whole truth and nothing but the truth so help me God?"

"Yes."

"Sit down please."

Dr. Stone sits down in the stand.

"Okay Doctor Stone, do you have a patient who suffers from mental illness?"

"Yes I do," Dr. Stone says.

"Who is the patient? What is your patient's name?"

"The patient's name is Diane Deniece Brown."

"Diane Deniece Brown?"

"Yes."

"And what other name is Diane Deniece Brown known by?"

"She is known by her stage name which is 'Diane D'."

"She is known by her stage name 'Diane D' whose family owns and runs a charity and entertainment organization in which she performs for, right?"

"That's correct."

"Okay Doctor Stone. And what is Diane D's mental illness?"

"She suffers from Split Personality Disorder."

"Split Personality Disorder?"

"Yes."

"What usually happens during her Split Personality Disorder?"

"She would have outbursts, get out of control and later on would not remember her outbursts and out of control behavior."

"She would have outburst and be out of control and not remember it?"

"That's correct."

"What happened during her most recent outburst and out of control behavior?"

"Doctor Kahn and I had hypnotized her and brought her other personality out to the surface. We spoke with her other personality and her other personality spoke back with us answering our questions."

"Her other personality spoke back with you answering your questions?"

"Yes it did. Later on, I told Diane's other personality to stay away from Diane and not to come around Diane anymore."

"You did?"

"Yes."

"Then what happened after that?"

"That's when her other personality got angry and wanted to come after me."

"Her other personality got angry and wanted to come after you, after you told it to stay away from Diane?"

"Yes."

"Then what happened after that?"

"Her other personality broke the chains loose from the psychiatrist couch Diane's physical body was chained to."

"I heard!"

"That's when her other personality attacked me and Doctor Kahn."

"And how did her other personality attack you and Doctor Kahn? What did her other personality do?"

"Her other personality gave me and Doctor Kahn kung fu kicks to each of our backs and heads."

"Her other personality gave you and Doctor Kahn kung fu kicks to the back and head?"

"Yes."

"Is that where the bandage on your head came from, when Diane D's other personality attacked you?"

"Yes."

"Is Diane D aware of what she did to you and Doctor Kahn?"

"No she's not aware of it at all."

"She isn't? Why not?"

"Because it was her OTHER personality who did the attack, not her ORIGINAL personality."

"So her original personality is not going to know or be aware of what her other personality do or did?"

"No."

"So what happened after her other personality kung fu kicked you and Dr. Kahn?"

"Her other personality threw the psychiatrist couch right across the room at the security guards, a priest, police officers and swat team members when they bursted into the hypnosis room doorway."

"Wow. Why did you and Doctor Kahn hypnotize Diane D in the first place?"

"Because we needed to talk to her other personality."

"Why did you need to talk to her other personality?"

"Because her cousin Nancy had an encounter with her other personality inside their family's home one night, and that kid Marcus who claimed that Diane beat him up inside the school hallway three years ago claim to constantly have nightmares about her still coming after him. We needed to find out if the personality her cousin Nancy encountered inside their family's home is the same personality who was entering Marcus dreams and nightmares."

"You wanted to find that out?"

"Yes."

"And what did you find out?"

"We found out, that the soul, spirit and personality that her cousin Nancy encountered inside their family's home IS the same soul, spirit and personality who entered Marcus' dreams and nightmares."

"You found out that it's the same soul, spirit and personality?"

"Yes."

"Where is Diane D at now?"

"She's still in the hospital."

"She's still in the hospital?"

"Yes."

"What is her condition right now?"

"Unconscious and bed ridden with bruises on her body."

"She's unconscious and bed ridden with bruises on her body?"

"Yes."

"Why is she unconscious and bed ridden with bruises on her body?"

"She got injured when her other personality broke the chains she was wrapped in loose from the couch. That's why she's sedated and unconscious, so she can get some rest and heel from her injuries. That's why she's incompetent to stand trial."

"I see. Do you have proof that your patient Diane D did not know what she was doing inside that hypnosis room when she attacked you and Doctor Kahn then threw the psychiatrist couch across the room at the security guards, the priest, police officers and swat team members?"

"Yes I have proof. The recording of the hypnosis was captured on video."

"It was?"

"Yes."

"Do you have the video with you?"

"No, Diane's family have the video. I would need them to give me permission to show the video to the courts if it could help Diane's case."

"Okay." The court procedure continues to go on.

Chapter 24

Teresa And Joseph Visit Diane D In Hospital

Two days later, Margarita is in the hospital lobby talking to Marilyn. She says to Marilyn, "Voy a conseguir algo de café. ¿Quieres un café?"

"No that's okay Mom," Marilyn says. "Voy a ir volver arriba a Diane."

"Okay. Voy a estar ahí arriba." Margarita turns and starts to head towards the cafeteria as Marilyn turns the other way and heads towards the elevators.

Margarita heads towards the cafeteria. She looks towards the front door and sees Teresa who's a friend of both Diane D and Dana who is a beautiful black woman with a deep dark skinned comlexion with shoulder length hair and her boyfriend Joseph, a black man with a dark complexion, coming inside the hospital lobby. She stops, smiles and says, "Hi Teresa! Hey Joseph!"

"Hi Miss Margarita!" Teresa and Joseph say as they approach Margarita. Teresa then says, "How are you Miss Margarita?"

"I'm okay. And yourself?"

"We're fine. How's Diane doing? I would like to know if it's okay if we see her."

"Yes, but not too long Teresa. Diane needs plenty of rest."

"I understand."

"How is she doing?" Joseph asks.

"She's sedated right now," Margarita says.

"She's still sedated?"

"I'm afraid so."

"Are you planning to spend the night with her again Miss Margarita?" Teresa asks.

"Of course I am."

"You are? Aren't you afraid or nervous that other personality might suddenly appear in Diane again?!"

"I know Teresa, but Diane is my grandchild. My family and I are going to be here for her no matter what. It's something my family and I just have to deal with."

"Oh wow. I'm sorry you all are going through this."

"Thanks Teresa. You can see Diane real quick. Just don't approach her or try to wake her up."

"Okay Miss Margarita, as long as you're there in the room with us."

"As long as I'm there in the room?"

"Well yeah. We're kind of afraid to be there in the room with Diane by ourselves after everything we heard happened with her."

"I understand Teresa. But of course I'm gonna be there in the room with you, plus some of my family members are up there in the room with Diane now."

"They are?"

"Yeah. Marilyn just went up there."

"She did?"

"Yeah. Come on. I'll let you two to see Diane real quick."

"Okay."

Margarita turns and heads towards the elevators as Teresa and Joseph nervously follow her.

Margarita is walking in the upstairs hospital hallway as Teresa and Joseph continue to nervously follow behind her. Margarita heads towards Diane D's hospital room as Mickey suddenly comes out of Diane D's hospital room. Mickey sees Teresa and Joseph and says, "Hi Teresa! Hi Joseph!"

"Hi Mickey!" Teresa and Joseph say.

"How are you?" Joseph asks.

"Good, and yourself?" Mickey asks.

"Okay."

"Diane está todavía dormido Mickey?" Margarita asks.

"Sí, ella aún está dormido Grandma," Mickey says. "Estaré de vuelta."

"Okay baby." Margarita approaches Diane D's hospital room door as Mickey walks away. She goes into the hospital room.

Margarita is inside the hospital room. She turns to Teresa and Joseph and says, "Come on in." Teresa and Joseph slowly and nervously enter the hospital room. They see a whole bunch of gifts and flowers everywhere. They see Nicolas and Marilyn adjusting the flat screen TV. They then see Diane D sound asleep still sedated, sleeping face up with her arms folded up and still in casts and bandages with her hands behind and beneath her head. They see Diane D dressed in a dark green opened pajama top with long sleeves over the cast and bandages wearing a light green bustier inside it with the bed spread on top of her chest. The long chain attached to her shackle is still attached to the metal bar of the bed. There is a little Spanish boy around 2-

years old sleeping right on top of Diane D laying his head right on top of her chest as Diane D continues to sleep. A little Spanish girl around the same age jumps right on top of the bed. She approaches Diane D. The little boy looks at the little girl and screams to her, "Noooo! Ir lejos!" He tries to hit the little girl.

"Noooo!" the little girl screams as she tries to hit the little boy. They begin to sort of fight over Diane D.

"Hey!" Nicolas shouts as he approaches them. "Bajarse de la cama y salir de la habitación!" He grabs both kids and picks them up off the bed with one kid in each arm. He then carries them towards the doorway pass Teresa and Joseph as Teresa and Joseph smile at the kids. Nicolas then takes the kids out into the hallway. Teresa and Joseph turn to Margarita as Joseph asks, "Who are those kids?"

"Oh those are my sister Marlena's great-grandchildren from the Dominican Republic," Margarita says.

"Your sister Marlena's great-grandchildren?"

"Yes. Their whole family came up here from the Dominican Republic when they heard about what happened to Diane."

"They did?"

"Yes."

"Oh that's nice. Where is your sister Marlena at now?"

"She and the rest of them went downstairs to the gift shop to buy some gifts for Diane. They'll be back up shortly."

"Oh okay."

Teresa then looks at Diane D. She turns to Margarita and whispers, "So does she remember anything that happened during her hypnosis ordeal with the doctors?"

"We don't really know yet Teresa," Margarita whispers. "Diane hasn't talked yet."

"She hasn't?"

"No. She's been unconscious and sedated the whole entire time since after that ordeal."

"She has?"

"Yes."

"What about the time you had a conversation with her other personality in the bathroom when you found her body not in the bed?"

"Well since that wasn't Diane's original personality, I cannot include that."

"I see."

Margarita goes to the side of the bed. She grabs a damp cloth that is folded on the night stand beneath the lamp. She starts to gently wipe Diane D's face, forehead and hair with the cloth.

"How is she Miss Margarita?"

"She's doing okay so far."

"That's good." Teresa and Joseph sadly stare at Diane D. They then look at the chain that's attached to her shackle and the metal bar of the bed.

309

Margarita finishes wiping Diane D's face with the cloth. She gently places the cloth back on the night stand. She takes another look at Diane D as she starts to head back towards Teresa and Joseph.

Margarita approaches Teresa and Joseph and says, "Okay Teresa?"

"Okay," Teresa says. "Thanks for letting us see her."

"You're welcome. I'll walk you two downstairs."

"Okay." Teresa and Joseph turn towards the doorway as they sadly look back at Diane D. They then look forward and head out the hospital room door as Margarita follows behind them.

Chapter 25

Another Swat Team Member Passes Away

Family members of another swat team member are standing at his bedside. The swat team member, a middle aged white male, is on his death bed as he looks at his wife with half opened eyes. His wife, a middle aged white female, is leaning towards him as she whispers to him, "You said you had a horrible dream?"

"Yes," the swat team member says with his dying breath.

"What happened in your dream?"

"I saw her."

"You saw her? You saw who? Who did you see in your dream?"

"I saw Diane D in my dream."

"What! You saw Diane D in your dream?"

"Yeah."

"Oh no! What the hell was she doing in your dream?"

"She was saying something to me."

"She what? She said something to you?"

"Yeah."

"What did she say to you?"

"She said she was going to get me."

"What! She said she was going to get you?!"

"Yes. She said she was going to get me like she got the other four."

"What! She said she was going to get you like she got the other four? What other four? The other four who?"

"The other four who already passed away."

"The other four who already passed away?"

"Yes. She told me, I was going to be next."

"She said you were going to be next?! Oh no! Don't tell me that Diane D came into your dream and told you that you're going to pass away like the three police officers and the other swat team member?!"

"I think that's what she was telling me."

"Oh nooo!"

"Someone needs to stop her."

"Someone needs to stop her?!"

"Yes."

"From what?! From entering your dreams and nightmares?!"

"Yes."

"How?! Diane D doesn't have the power to enter people's dreams or nightmares!"

"Yes she does, I saw her! She said she was going to get me! Someone needs to stop her, before it's too late!" The swat team member closes his eyes as his head turns to the side. He passes away.

His wife looks at him then shouts, "Oh no! Oh nooooo! Don't leave honey! Come back! Come back! Oh no! Oh nooo!!" The swat team member's wife cries her eyes out screaming as hospital staff members and the rest of her family rush to her!

An hour later, the swat team member's body is still in the hospital bed covered with a sheet over his head. His wife cries out and shouts, "My husband is gone!" as her family members cry their eyes out trying to comfort her.

The next day, two black males around their late thirties and one white male around his late thirties also are at a bar chit-chatting as one of the black males looks at a newspaper article with a headline that reads: **ANOTHER SWAT TEAM MEMBER PASSES AWAY**: "Hey!" the black male says. "I can't believe it!"

"You can't believe what?" the second black male says.

"Another swat team member passed away yesterday!"

"Another swat team member passed away? What swat team member?"

"You know! The swat team members who Diane D's other personality attacked at the hospital with the psychiatrist couch when she threw the psychiatrist couch right across the room and slammed the couch right into their heads?! One of them passed away yesterday!"

"One of them passed away yesterday?! You're kidding! Seriously?!"

"Yeah it's true!" the white male says. "I saw it on the news this morning!

"What! You mean another person died from Diane D's other personality's wrath!"

"Yeah!" the first black male says. "It says so right here!"

"Oh my God! Let me see it." The first black male hands the second black male the newspaper article. The second black male looks at and reads the article. He then says, "My God, I can't believe it! She killed another person!"

"I can't believe it either!" the white male says. "You know this is the fifth person that has died from Diane D's other personality's attack! So far, her other personality killed five people altogether!"

"Five people?!"

"Yeah!"

"Goddamn!"

"And they were all cops and swat team members!"

"All cops and swat team members?!"

"Yeah!"

"Man, that is fucked up! If her other personality killed all those people and she's still unconscious at the hospital, that means she's a murderer and don't even know it!"

"It's true!"

"Man I would never want to come across her other personality."

"Me neither. How does her husband handle being married to someone like that? How does he even sleep with someone like that whose other personality might come out and strike at any time?!"

"I know!" the first black male says. "Imagine him sleeping with her making love to her, then all of a sudden, her other personality comes out and says 'I'm not Diane', not only that, her other personality might try to kill him and then when her original personality comes back, her original personality won't even remember it! I mean if her other personality can kill once before or five times before, I'm sure her other personality can always do it again! Remember, her other personality injured over twenty people that day! Who knows if any of those other police officers, any of those other swat team members or any of those security guards might pass away later on! Then Diane D's other personality will have another death on its hands!"

"I know! If I was her husband, I would go find the nearest divorce attorney and say 'Look, I can't continue to be married to this dangerous person anymore, I'm afraid for my life! I want a divorce right away!'"

"I don't blame you! I would do the same thing too!" The three men continue to look at the article.

Three days later, there is a funeral for the swat team member at the funeral hall. There are thousands of other swat team members, police officers and civilians gathered at the funeral.

Chapter 26

Diane D Is Finally Awake

A few days later, Tomas, Barry and Dr. Stone are standing and talking in the hospital hallway with Dr. Stone still wearing the bandage around his head as he says, "So how is everything?"

"Everything is okay for now," Tomas says. "How is everything with you?"

"Could be better. Could be better."

"Yeah," Barry says. "It's so terrible what happened to the police officers and swat team members, huh?!"

"I know."

"It's terrible what happened to Marcus too."

"I know. I tried to help him. But you can only help a person so much. How's Diane doing by the way? Is she awake?"

"Yeah she's awake now Doctor Stone."

"She is? Finally?"

"Yeah."

"Is she talking?"

"Yeah she's talking."

"She's talking too?"

"Yeah. She's still sort of woozy, but she's talking."

"Oh that's good! Does she know what happened to Marcus?"

"No we didn't want to tell her yet Doctor Stone," Tomas says. "We figure it's not a good time right now to tell her about it."

"I understand. What about all those authority figures that got hurt with some of them passing away? Does she know about that?"

"No, we didn't want to tell her about that part yet either."

"No?"

"Uh uh. We'll bring you to her now."

"Okay." Dr. Stone, Tomas and Barry turn and walk down the hallway.

Inside Diane D's hospital room, Diane D is laying in the hospital bed woozy as her family and relatives surround her. She is awake with her eyes half closed as her family talks with her. "So how do you feel Diane?" Mary asks. "Are you still in pain honey?"

"Yeah Mom," Diane D painfully says as her family continues to surround her sadly smiling at her.

Dr. Stone, Tomas and Barry walk into the room. Dr. Stone then says, "Hello everbody!"

Diane D's family turn and look at Dr. Stone and says, "Hi Doctor Stone."

"Hello."

Dr. Stone approaches Diane D. He looks at her and says, "Diane! I see that you're finally awake! How are you?!" Diane D puzzled looks at Dr. Stone as Dr. Stone says to her, "How do you feel?"

"I'm okay," Diane D says.

"You are?"

"Yeah." Diane D puzzled looks at the bandage wrapped around Dr. Stone's head and says, "My God, what happened to you?"

"What happened to me?"

"Yeah. You got a bandage wrapped around your head. What happened?"

"Uum. I got hurt Diane."

"You got hurt?"

"Yes, I did."

"Oh my God, how?" Dr. Stone and Diane D's family suspiciously look at each other. Diane D looks at her family and Dr. Stone. She becomes suspicious. She then says, "Oh oh."

Dr. Stone and Diane D's family puzzled look at Diane D as Margarita says, "Oh oh? Oh oh what Diane?"

"I hope it wasn't something I did."

"Something you did?"

"Yeah."

"Why would you think that Diane?" Dr. Stone asks.

"I don't know. The last time I saw you, you and Doctor Kahn were starting to hypnotize me. The next thing I know, is that I woke up here in the hospital feeling pain all over my body. And when that happens, I usually hear that I went off on people attacking them and I don't be remembering it. I'm wondering if the same thing happened again this time, because you and Doctor Kahn were the last people I saw before I was hypnotized. Now I see a bandage wrapped around your head? I hope I didn't do anything wrong Doctor Stone. Did I do that Doctor Stone? Were you hurt or injured by me?"

"Well, not by YOU Diane."

"Not by me?"

"No."

"Then by who?"

"I can't talk about it right now Diane."

"You can't?"

"No."

"Why not? Because it was by me, wasn't it?"

"No it wasn't by you?"

"Then by who?"

"Is it alright if we talk about it later? It's not the time to talk about it right now."

"Oh. Okay then. I'll change the subject. So how did my hypnosis procedure go Doctor? My family won't tell me about it."

"They won't?"

"No. They refuse to tell me what happened. So why don't you tell me what happened Doctor Stone? What happened during my hypnosis procedure? What happened between the time I was first about to be hypnotized to the time I woke up again?"

"A lot of things happened Diane."

"A lot of things?"

"Yes."

"Like what?"

"We can't talk about it now."

"You can't talk about that either?"

"No."

"Didn't you record it on video?"

"We started to record it on video, but I'm not sure of how much footage of your hypnosis was captured on video."

"You're not sure?"

"No. We would have to check on it and talk about it later after you get better, okay? I just came in here to check on you to make sure you're okay. Are you okay?"

"I feel okay Doctor."

"You do? Are you still in pain?"

"Yes I still am."

"Well I'm going to speak to Doctor Kern and see if we can get you some pain medication for the time being, then we're going to get you some physical therapy when you feel better, okay?"

"Okay."

"Good. Well I have to get your prescription and medication ready, okay?"

"Okay."

"I'll see you later." Dr. Stone looks at Diane D's family and says, "Bye everybody."

"Bye Doctor Stone," Diane D's family says.

Dr. Stone turns and heads towards the doorway as Margarita and Tomas turn and follow him. Margarita and Tomas walk with Dr. Stone out to the hallway.

Margarita, Tomas and Dr. Stone step out into the hospital hallway. They stop as Margarita and Tomas turn to Dr. Stone. Margarita says to him, "So when do you think we should tell her about what happened Doctor Stone? When do you think we should show her the video of her hypnosis?"

"No time soon of course," Dr. Stone says. "I don't even know if we got the end of all that chaos on video! The video cameras were knocked down and practically destroyed with everything else inside the hypnosis room. I need the video as evidence to show my lawyers and the judge to let them know that Diane is truly not well and didn't know what she was saying when she said all that stuff about Marcus while under hypnosis, and didn't know what she was doing when she attacked me, Doctor Kahn, the priest and all the authority figures while she was still under hypnosis. They need to see the video as soon as possible."

"We understand Doctor Stone," Tomas says. "We'll give you a copy of the video."

"Thanks."

"Do you think that other personality or other personalities will ever come back Doctor Stone?"

"Anything is possible. You heard it yourself. The other souls, spirits and personalities did say, that Diane's meditations draw them to her. So in order for the other souls, spirits or personalities not to come back, Diane has to restrain herself from meditating. I know meditation is good for a lot of people, but for some reason, it's not good for her."

"And why is that Doctor Stone?" Margarita asks. "Why is meditation good for other people, but not good for Diane when she loves meditating?"

"I have no idea why it's not good for her Miss Margarita. I have no idea. We all are just going to have to keep a close eye on her."

"Are you still planning to have her committed back into the mental institution Doctor Stone?"

"Yes, of course, I have to! Her other personality took the lives of three police officers and two swat team members when it slammed the couch right into their heads at full force! That's five people that her other personality has killed so far! More police officers, security guards and swat team members might pass away, we don't know! That's why the judge have to see the video of Diane's hypnosis to see that Diane wasn't herself and didn't know what she was doing when she did all that stuff. If the judge sees that, then she will be committed back into the mental hospital and not prison."

"But remember Doctor Stone," Tomas says. "If Diane gets sent back to jail, prison or the mental institution, that other personality did say, that it will pull her original soul and spirit out of her physical body again and take her place again while she's serving time in the jail, prison or the mental institution. The people inside the jail, prison or the mental institution won't even know that it's the other soul, spirit or personality sitting right amongst them. They'll just assume that it's Diane."

Doctor Stone frighteningly and worriedly looks at Tomas and Margarita as Tomas and Margarita frighteningly and worriedly look at him. He does not know what to say. He then says, "Well, I have to get going. I'll be back to check on Diane tomorrow."

"Thank you Doctor Stone," Margarita says.

"You're welcome. Take care."

"Okay," Margarita and Tomas says.

Doctor Stone turns and heads down the hallway as Margarita and Tomas sadly stare at him.

The next day inside Diane D's hospital room, the Dianettes are surrounding Diane D sitting on her hospital bed as Diane D sits up on the hospital bed with her legs wide apart beneath the sheets and blanket. She appears all dazed out and in pain with her eyes less puffy and less swollen. She is dressed in a navy bustier without the bandages showing her bare arms, bare shoulders, bare waist and muscular physique. There are slight bruises around her shoulders, upper arms, waist and wrists as the Dianettes hold her arms, shoulders and waist looking at and touching her bruises. Lonna then asks, "Are you sure you don't remember how you got these bruises Diane?"

"No I don't have a clue," Diane D frustratedly says with tears in her eyes.

"Auuh don't cry Diane. It's gonna be okay."

"Yeah Diane," Bernice says. "We're here to try and make you feel better."

"Thanks," Diane D smiles and says as the Dianettes start to rub mineral ice on her bruises.

Two weeks later, Diane D is sitting up in her hospital bed dressed in pajamas as her family and relatives surround her again. "How are you feeling baby?" Mary asks. "Are you okay?"

"So far Mom," Diane D says.

"Good."

"Diane," Barry says. "Dr. Stone wants us to bring you downstairs to the hypnosis room."

"He does?" Diane D asks.

"Yeah."

"How come? He's not planning to put me under hypnosis again is he?"

"No. He just wants to ask you a few questions."

"A few questions? In the hypnosis room?"

"Yeah, so come on. We're gonna bring you down to the hypnosis room real quick. Are you able to walk or do you need a wheel chair?"

"I can walk. I'm still limping, but I can walk."

"Good. Let's get you going." Barry and Mary start to help Diane D out of the bed.

Fifteen minutes later, Mary, Barry and two security guards are walking Diane D downstairs in the hallway that leads to the hypnosis room as Diane D limps down the hallway.

Mary, Barry, Diane D and two security guards approach the hypnosis room door which is closed. "Let's go in Diane," Mary says. "Doctor Stone is waiting." Mary opens the hypnosis room door. She goes inside the hypnosis room as Diane D, Barry and the two security guards follow in after her.

Mary, Barry, Diane D and the two security guards look around the hypnosis room. Diane D suddenly becomes shock and sees all the damage inside the hypnosis room! She sees blood everywhere and shouts, "Oh my God! What the hell happened in here?!" Diane D continues to look around at the damaged hypnosis room.

Dr. Stone approaches Diane D and says, "Hi Diane."

Diane D turns and looks at Dr. Stone and says, "Hey Doctor Stone. What happened in here?! Did a tornado happen in here?! I see blood everywhere! It looks like several people got hurt and injured! It looks like a massacre happened! What happened?!" Diane D then sees the damaged bent out of shape psychiatrist couch. She approaches the psychiatrist couch and says, "Hey! This looks like the couch I was on when you and Doctor Kahn were about to hypnotize me Doctor Stone! Where is the couch you had me hypnotized on?"

"You're looking at it Diane."

Diane D looks at Dr. Stone and says, "What?"

"It's the same couch."

"It's the same couch you started hypnotizing me on?"

"Yes it is."

"No, it can't be the same couch you had put me on, because the couch you had put me on did not look like this."

"Yes you're right Diane. The couch I had put you on did not look like this, at first. But it looks like this now."

"Oh yeah? Why? Why does it look like this Doctor Stone? What happened to it?!" Diane D then looks at the long broken chains laying on the floor next to the psychiatrist couch and asks, "What are those chains doing on the floor Doctor Stone? Why are they there? Why are they broken? Why are they near the couch and why are some pieces of the chains attached to the couch?" Diane D puzzled looks at the couch. Then she puzzled looks at Dr. Stone. She then says, "Oh oh."

"Oh oh what Diane?"

"You said that this is the exact same couch I was on, right?"

"Yes."

"Doctor Stone, you didn't have me chained up and chained to the couch while I was under hypnosis, did you?"

"What makes you think that Diane?"

"Because I had pain and bruises all over my body when I woke up! I'm wondering what the hell happened, wondering why I feel pain all over my body. The pain and bruises all over my body came from somewhere. The pain and bruises didn't come from these chains, did they?"

"I need you to tell me that Diane."

Diane D looks back down at the chains on the floor. Then she puzzled looks at the bruises on her wrists. She starts to compare the bruises on her wrists to the chains on the floor. She then looks up at the walls and says, "Oh my God! What happened to the walls?!"

"Something was banged against the walls Diane."

"Something was banged against the walls? Something like what?"

"Don't you remember?"

"Remember what? Oh Oh. You're not saying that I had something to do with that, are you?"

"Diane, do you remember anything that happened inside this room during your hypnosis?"

"No, I don't remember anything at all! But that's the same question I was asked when I was brought to that damaged storage room at the other hospital! I looked around in it and was asked do I remember anything that happened in there and the same thing is happening now, with me being brought inside this damaged hypnosis room!"

"Well that's why we bring you into these damaged rooms Diane, to see if you can remember anything. When Doctor Kahn and I were about to hypnotize you, what do you remember after that?"

"Well one thing I remember, is that you and Doctor Kahn were at the beginning stage of hypnotizing me. I don't know what happened during the middle or the end. The next thing I know, is that I'm waking up inside a different room feeling pain all over myself. Then my family starts holding and hugging me real tight, making my pain feel worse. I tried to get my family off of me to stop them from hugging me so tight because of the pain, but it was hard for me to tell them the pain I was in. All I can do was scream."

"So you remember that part which was after you woke back up from the hypnosis."

"Right."

"Do you remember anything else that happened after Doctor Kahn and I started hypnotizing you besides waking back up feeling pain all over your body? Do you remember anything at all during the hypnosis?"

"Yes. As a matter of fact, there is one thing I do remember during my hypnosis."

"Oh yeah?!"

"Yeah."

"And what's that?"

"You had me sit up and identify my family."

"You remember that part Diane?" Mary asks.

Diane D looks at Mary and says, "Yeah Mom, I do."

"Do you remember identifying us with Nancy and Charlotte in the room or without them in the room?" Barry asks.

Diane D puzzledly looks at Barry and asks, "What do you mean 'do I remember identifying you all with Nancy and Charlotte in the room or without them in the room' Dad? You mean I identified you all twice?"

"Yes Diane, you did. Do you remember seeing Nancy and Charlotte in the room when you identified us?"

"Yes I remember seeing them sitting with you all when I identified all of you."

"You do?"

"Yes. I don't remember identifying you without them there."

"You don't?"

"No. Why would I need to identify you twice anyway?"

"We had to make sure it was your original personality Diane," Dr. Stone says.

Diane D looks at Dr. Stone and says, "What? You had to make sure it was my original personality? What do you mean?"

"We had to know whether or not it was YOU, or another personality that was identifying your family."

"What? You had to know whether or not it was me or another personality that was identifying my family? Oh oh. You're not talking about this other personality that my cousin Nancy claimed to have an encounter with inside my family's home that night, are you?"

"Yes, that's exactly what I'm talking about Diane."

"Well I have no idea what my cousin Nancy is talking about Doctor Stone, because I don't remember saying those crazy things she said I said to her that night."

"You still don't remember it?"

"No. Sorry I don't."

"Do you think your cousin Nancy would make up a story about the strange things you said to her that night?"

"No I don't think Nancy would make up that story Doctor Stone. I mean I don't think she would lie about something like that. I'm just saying that I don't remember it. Now if I did say those crazy things she said I said to her that night, maybe I could have been just sleepwalking."

"Sleepwalking?"

"Yes, and she just happen to catch me in the middle of it. After all, I did fall out in my family's livingroom that night when I went downstairs to the bar to make the drinks. I probably fell asleep automatically then sleepwalked and came up the stairs, that's when she probably ran into me. My family have told me that I've sleepwalked before and I usually don't remember that either."

"You don't?"

"No, I'm afraid I don't."

"But Nancy said your facial appearance looked different when she ran into you in the hallway that night."

"That's because I was probably still asleep. Doesn't everybody's face look different while they're still asleep or just waking up? I'm no different from anybody else Doctor Stone. I think my cousin Nancy's theory was just blown out of proportion."

"You think so Diane?"

"Yes I do." Diane D starts to look around the room again as Mary, Barry and Dr. Stone sadly look at her. Mary and Barry then approach Diane D as she continues to look at the damaged hypnosis room.

In the next room, Margarita, Tomas, Gracy, Grandpa Mike, detectives and some police officers are behind a one-way glass secretly watching Diane D as Diane D, Mary, Barry and Dr. Stone look around at the damaged hypnosis room again. One of the detectives whispers to Margarita, Tomas, Gracy and Grandpa Mike and says, "Wow. She really doesn't remember what happened in that room."

"No she doesn't officer," Margarita says.

"Wow." The detective, Margarita, Tomas and the police officers continue to watch behind the one-way glass secretly watching Diane D.

A week later, Margarita, Tomas, Mary, Barry and Michael are standing in the courtroom as Dr. Stone says to them, "Well, the good news, is that Diane will be released from the hospital and released into your custody and her other grandparents' custody for a while, but the bad news, is that she is going to have to be on house arrest."

"Yeah we know Doctor Stone," Margarita happily says.

"She will have to have an ankle monitor strapped to her ankle while she's on house arrest."

"Yeah we know," Barry happily says. "At least she'll be home with us. Then what happens after that?"

"Then after that, she has to be committed back into the mental hospital."

"For how long Doctor Stone?" Mary asks.

"I don't know. Her other personality committed a horrible crime which unfortunately she has to pay for."

"We understand Doctor Stone," Margarita sadly says.

"I'm sorry."

"It's okay Doctor Stone. We're just happy that she's coming home."

"That's good."

Across the courtroom, police officers' families and swat team members' families are upset. Mrs. Peterson turns to Dr. Stone's lawyers, Diane D's lawyers, the judge and Grandpa Mike and shouts, "Diane D kills several authority figures, and all she gets is house arrest while she's in the temporary custody of her family?! Then after that, she gets committed back to the state hospital?! That isn't right! I think she should get prison for life?!"

"We're very sorry Mrs. Peterson!" Grandpa Mike shouts. "But we have to lose our loved one too! Diane is going to be sent away to the state hospital after she leaves our custody!"

"At least she's still alive Mister Brown! My husband passed away! He will never come home again, thanks to your granddaughter!"

"I'm sorry Mrs. Peterson! I'm sorry for both of our losses!" Grandpa Mike turns and walks away.

"Your loss my foot! Damn you!" Mrs. Peterson shouts towards Grandpa Mike as a white male court officer grabs her arm and pulls her back. Margarita approaches Mrs. Peterson and tries to comfort her as Mrs. Peterson pulls away from her and shouts, "Don't touch me! Your granddaughter is a murderer! She took the life of my husband! She's a cop killer! She made me a widower and now my kids will never see their father again!" Mrs. Peterson jerks her arm away from the court officer! She turns and runs towards the exit doors in the back of the courtroom! She then runs out the courtroom out into the hallway as the court officer runs towards the exit doors and leaves the courtroom after her. Margarita, Tomas, Mary, Barry, Michael and Dr. Stone sadly look towards the exit doors.

Barry turns to Dr. Stone and says, "Doctor Stone, I just want to know. All these people that got hurt by Diane's other personality, do you think that there will be any personal retaliation against her, or us?"

"With the reputation Diane's other personality has, I'm not really sure if anybody really wants to challenge her other personality," Dr. Stone says. "Even the authority figures with their guns and their shotguns couldn't stop her other personality's powerful wrath! Her other personality wind up throwing the couch right across the room at them at full force smashing the couch right into them knocking them and their shotguns down before they could even step into the room! It's like her other personality already knew they were coming! When her other personality was spinning that couch around in the air, it was like her other personality was getting ready and prepared to throw the couch across the room and slam it right into those authority figures before her other personality even saw them! I think people might be afraid Diane's other personality might enter into their dreams and nightmares like it did to Marcus for the past three years. You see where he's at now. He was driven to suicide! Not only that, the widow of the last swat team member who passed away told authorities, that her husband told her that Diane had came into his dream, saying that she was coming to get him just before he passed away. Now look where he's at. You think all these other people want to go through that?"

"We heard about the last swat team member's dream Doctor Stone," Margarita says. "But the last swat team member and his wife don't think it was actually Diane in his dream do they? Because Diane already said that she does not have the power to enter anybody's dreams or nightmares, but that other soul, spirit or personality admit that it DOES have the power to enter people's dreams and nightmares! So it was actually the other soul, spirit or personality who that swat team member saw in his dream, not Diane!"

"Yeah you know that and I know that, but he didn't know that! Whatever he saw in his dream looked like Diane! If it looked like Diane, as far as he was concerned, it WAS Diane, to him! Marcus also saw what looked like Diane in his dreams and nightmares, so as far as he was concerned, it WAS Diane!"

"Wow," Barry says. "I'm sorry what happened to that swat team member."

"So am I," Tomas says. "What about Doctor Kahn? What's going to happen to him now?"

"He might have to close his practice due to his injuries," Dr. Stone says.

"What!" Margarita, Tomas, Mary, Barry and Michael shout. "Close his practice?!"

"Oh no!" Margarita shouts.

"We're so sorry about that Doctor Stone," Michael tearfully says. "I mean Doctor Kahn was really helpful during Diane's hypnosis. You and he were both great at communicating with her other personalities."

"That's right Doctor Stone," Margarita says. "You were wonderful at bringing Diane's original personality back. I don't know what we would have done without you."

"Yeah that's true Doctor Stone," Tomas says. "That's why we would really hate to see Dr. Kahn go. We would hate to see any of you go. Sorry that the both of you got hurt."

"Thanks," Dr. Stone says as he sadly looks at them all and they sadly look at him. He then says, "But anyway, Diane can start packing up Thursday morning."

"Thank you so much Doctor Stone," Mary says.

"You're welcome. Come on, let's go." Dr. Stone, Mary, Tomas, Margarita, Barry and Michael turn and walk towards the courtroom exit.

Outside the courtroom down the end of the hallway, Mrs. Peterson is crying her eyes out as the male court officer tries to comfort her. The court officer then says to her, "I'm so sorry Mrs. Peterson. I'm so sorry for your loss."

Mrs. Peterson turns to the court officer and cries, "Why didn't they just send Diane D to prison?! She has a history of being out of control and harming people!"

"Well her grandfather Mike came to her rescue and hired good lawyers for her. Not only that, her doctor has backed it up and states that Diane D did not know what she was doing when she went out of control inside that hypnosis room. Her doctor showed the video of Diane D's hypnosis to the judge to prove that she's not well, that's why she's going to be committed to the state hospital, for people who are not well."

"Well people who are not well should not be out in the streets! They should be locked up in cages! My husband did not sign up for this! He signed up to protect and to serve, not sign up to have his head smashed into by a flying psychiatrist couch that sped into him at over sixty miles an hour knocking him and the other officers down, then gets shot while he's laying on the floor injured and winds up dying because of it! He did not sign up for this! He did not sign up for this at all!"

"I'm so sorry Mrs. Peterson."

Mrs. Peterson continues to cry her eyes out as the court officer tries to comfort her.

Chapter 27

Diane D Is Released Into Her Family's Custody

The following week, Teresa is inside her apartment sitting on the sofa as she dials a number on her smartphone. She puts the phone to her ear and listens. She then says, "Hi Miss Margarita!"

"Hi Teresa!" Margarita says from the other end. "How are you today?"

"Pretty good! I heard that Diane was released from the hospital and is staying back at your place!"

"She is!"

"Oh that's good! I hear she's on house arrest. Is that true?"

"I'm afraid so Teresa."

"Oh I see. Well I just wanted to check on her and see how she's doing?"

"Diane is doing pretty good Teresa."

"She is?"

"So far."

"That's good. What is she doing now? Is she awake?"

"She was awake. She just went back to sleep not too long ago."

"She's sleeping right now?"

"Yes."

"Where is she sleeping, in her room?"

"No, she's sleeping in my bed."

"What! She's in your bed Miss Margarita?!"

"Yes."

"How come?"

"Diane is not allowed to be alone Teresa. I have to keep my eye on her. She has to be monitored, I don't trust her. She might secretly meditate again and the next thing we all know, is all that havoc might occur again. My family and I don't need that. We already been through enough."

"I understand. So does she remember anything that happened

during her hypnosis?"

"Well the only thing she remembers during her hypnosis, is when the doctors had her identify us. She doesn't remember anything else before or after that."

"She doesn't?"

"No."

"She doesn't remember attacking the doctors or anything?"

"No. She doesn't remember attacking the doctors, she doesn't remember attacking the security guards, she doesn't remember attacking the priest, she doesn't remember attacking the police officers, she doesn't remember attacking the swat members nor she remembers what she said to me inside that bathroom in her hospital room that night."

"What! You told her about that part?"

"I certainly did."

"Oh my God! What did she say to that?"

"She said she doesn't remember any of that."

"She doesn't? She doesn't remember any of that at all?"

"I'm afraid she doesn't Teresa. She said how would she get out of the hospital bed and go into the bathroom if she was suppose to had been bedridden."

"But you did find her in the bathroom that night."

"Yes I did. She just doesn't remember."

"Wooow that is something. Has she even seen the video of herself attacking the doctors, the security guards, the priest, the police officers and the swat team members yet?"

"No she hasn't. She hasn't been well. She has been bed ridden and was still in a lot of pain at the hospital, so we didn't want to make her feel any worse by letting her see that video of herself behaving like that."

"Yeah that's true. So what have you all done with Diane since she's been home?"

"Well we were all in my room late last night on the bed with Diane surrounding her while we were all watching a late night movie."

"Y'all were on the bed with Diane surrounding her while y'all were watching TV?"

"Yes. We were eating popcorn too while we were watching the movie."

"Y'all were?"

"Yes."

"Wow. How many of you all were on the bed together watching the late night movie with Diane?"

"Around fifteen of us, including Dana and her sisters."

"Oh Dana was there last night too?"

"Yeah. She had made Diane some soup yesterday afternoon."

"She did?"

"Yeah."

"Wow. Is Dana still there?"

"Well she stepped out for a minute to pick up some things for Diane, but she'll be back."

"Wow. It sounds like your family had a lot of fun with Diane last night. You all deserve to have a good time with her and have some peace after what you all been through with her condition. Wow Diane is really lucky to have all her family by her side. Not everyone has that."

"I know Teresa."

"Well, okay. Tell Diane I said hi and I hope she feels better."

"Thanks Teresa. I'll tell her you called."

"Thanks Miss Margarita. You take care."

"You too Teresa. Bye now."

"Bye." Teresa hangs up the smartphone.

The next day, Margarita is inside her kitchen as her cell phone rings. She picks up her phone and looks at it. She puts the phone to her ear and says, "Hey Teresa."

"Hi Miss Margarita," Teresa says from her apartment. "How is everything?"

"So far so good."

"That's good. How's Diane doing?"

"Not too good Teresa."

"No? Why? What happened?"

"Yesterday we decided to tell her about what happened with that kid Marcus."

"What! You told her about Marcus?!"

"We sure did Teresa. We felt the time was right to tell her about what happened to him."

"Oh no! How did she take it?"

"She is real devastated by it Teresa!"

"She is?"

"Of course she is! Even though she knew that Marcus was afraid of her and terrified of her, she would not want him to kill himself! She's sad about what happened to him! She would like to give condolences to Marcus' family, but she thinks she's the last person on earth that Marcus' family would want to see!"

"Oh Lord!"

"We also told her about what happened inside the hypnosis room during her hypnosis."

"Oh no! What did you tell her?!"

"We told her everything about what she said during her hypnosis!"

"You did!"

"Yes! We also told her everything about her physical body being wrapped in chains and chained to the psychiatrist couch!"

"What! You told her that?!"

328

"Yes! We also told her about herself breaking loose from the chains breaking the chains loose from the psychiatrist couch, that's where the bruises on her body came from!"

"You told her that too?!"

"Yes! We also told her about herself attacking the doctors then lifting up the psychiatrist couch, spinning it around in the air then throwing it across the room at the security guards, the priest, the police officers and a swat team!"

"You told her all of that too?!"

"Yes!"

"What did she say to that?!"

"She didn't believe us Teresa!"

"She didn't?!"

"No!"

"What about the video recording of her hypnosis?! Did you all show her that?!"

"Her doctor don't think it's the time to show her the video of her hypnosis yet."

"No?"

"No."

"My goodness! What is Diane doing now?"

"She's laying down on the bed very upset about what happened to Marcus."

"She is?"

"Yes."

"Oh my goodness! Is there anything I can do for Diane Miss Margarita?"

"No Teresa. She's just going to have to way it out right now."

"I'm so sorry about this."

"Yes we all are. Well I have to go now Teresa."

"Okay Miss Margarita. Tell Diane I said hi and I'll try to see her soon."

"Okay Teresa. Take care now."

"You too Miss Margarita. Bye."

"Bye Teresa." Margarita hangs up her cell phone. Barry walks into the kitchen with a coffee cup in his hand. Margarita turns to him and says, "Where's Diane? Is she still laying down in the bed?"

"Not anymore Mom," Barry says. "She got up."

"She did? What is she doing now?"

"She's about to get in the shower."

"She's about to get in the shower?! Is anybody going to watch her?! I don't want Diane alone in there! I don't want her to go behind our backs and start meditating while she's in the shower!"

"I know. Marilyn is getting ready to go in there and watch her."

"Marilyn stepped out for a minute, she's not here! Someone else would have to be in the bathroom to watch Diane!"

"Well Dana is still sleeping. I can wake her up and tell her to go in

329

the bathroom to watch Diane."

"Dana?!"

"Yeah."

"That's a bad move Barry! I mean Dana is no better than Diane! If you put Dana in the bathroom to watch Diane and Diane decides to meditate right there in the shower, Dana probably won't even stop her! She'll probably just meditate right there along with Diane! Since she has meditated right along with Diane before, she needs to be watched at all times herself to make sure she doesn't go along and starts meditating with Diane again! Where's Nancy?"

"Nancy is upstairs in her room."

"Well tell Nancy I said to get herself inside that bathroom with Diane to watch Diane while Diane is taking a shower! Tell her to keep her eyes on Diane and not to take her eyes off Diane at all!"

"Okay Mom." Barry turns and heads out the kitchen doorway.

Twenty minutes later, Nancy is standing in the bathroom near the shower curtain which is practically halfway opened with her arms folded. She is holding a large towel around her arms and a gold garment underneath the towel. She is looking behind the halfway opened shower curtain at Diane D while Diane D is behind the shower curtain taking a shower. Nancy then says to Diane D, "Is it you this time Diane?"

"Yeah it's me Nancy," Diane D's voice calmly says.

"Are you sure it's you?"

"Yes I'm sure Nancy. It's me."

"Okay good." Nancy continues to look behind the shower curtain at Diane D. She suddenly gets a shocked and surprised look on her face and shouts, "Diane! Your eyes are puffy, just like the night I had that encounter with your other personality! Is it YOU this time?!"

"Nancy, my eyes always get puffy whenever I take a shower and water hits my face, you know that."

"Oh that's right," Nancy smiles and says. She gives a sigh of relief and says, "What a relief! Because I was about to run right out of here!"

"Run out of here?"

"Yeah!"

"Why?"

"Because I don't want to go through what I went through with you that night Diane, seeing that strange appearance on your face, seeing your strange behavior and hearing you say stuff like 'you're not Diane' that 'Diane is not here right now that she will be back'! It was scary to hear you talk like that!"

"You don't need to worry Nancy. It's me."

"Are you sure?!"

"Yes I'm sure."

"Okay, prove that it is really YOU. What did we do last night?"

"What did we do last night?"

"Yeah."

"We were playing cards last night."

"Okay. What did we do the night before?"

"We were watching a movie in Grandma and Grandpa's room late the other night."

"So you remember that."

"Yeah I remember that."

"Good, I just want to make sure it's you."

"It's me Nancy."

"Good. But really, are you sure it's YOU this time Diane?"

"Yeah Nancy!"

"Okay, okay." The shower water goes off. Nancy then asks, "Are you finished?"

"Yeah I'm done."

"Okay." Nancy continues to look behind the halfway opened shower curtain at Diane D. She then asks, "How are the bruises on your arms, legs and shoulders doing? Do they still hurt?"

"Yeah I'm still hurting from them."

"You're still hurting from them?"

"Yeah."

"That means you're feeling pain?"

"Yes I'm feeling pain Nancy."

"So it is YOU! As long as you feel pain, I know it's YOU Diane."

"Yes Nancy I'm feeling pain from whatever happened."

"From whatever happened? You still don't remember what happened during your hypnosis Diane?"

"No I don't remember what happened Nancy. All I know, is that I have bruises all over myself and I'm still hurting from them."

"Wow, sorry that you're going through this. You need help with anything?"

"No that's okay Nancy. I got it. I just have to take it real slow."

"Oh. Okay." Nancy continues to look behind the shower curtain at Diane D. She then looks up in the air thinking. Loud clanking noises suddenly comes from behind the shower curtain. Nancy looks back at Diane D and asks, "Is everything okay?"

"Yeah," Diane D's voice says. "I just want to clean off these scrub brushes."

"Oh, okay," Nancy says. Diane D starts making loud sounds cleaning the scrub brushes as Nancy continues to watch her behind the curtain. Nancy then says, "Oh by the way Diane, Miranda and Bernice designed and made an outfit for you."

"They did?"

"Yeah. They said they want me to put the outfit on you whenever I get the chance. See? Here's the outfit, look." Nancy pulls the gold garment from underneath the towel. She holds a gold shirt and gold pants outfit up to show Diane D. Nancy smiles behind the shower curtain at Diane D. She puzzled looks at Diane D and says, "What, you don't like it?"

"It's okay."

"Come on Diane. I can tell you wasn't too enthusiast with this outfit because you just looked at it, then looked away from it and didn't say anything. You just went about your business." Nancy starts to laugh and say, "I could tell you don't like this outfit, do you Diane?"

"It's okay Nancy."

"Are you sure?"

"Yeah I'm sure."

"Okaaay." Nancy places the gold outfit back underneath the towel as she continues to watch Diane D.

Diane D continues to make loud sounds cleaning the scrub brushes as Nancy continues to watch her. She then says, "You can hand me the towel Nancy."

"Okay, here." Nancy hands the towel to Diane D. She continues to look behind the shower watching Diane D drying up. She then says, "So Diane, how do you feel about that kid Marcus taking his own life?"

"How do I feel about it?"

"Yeah."

"I feel bad for him Nancy."

"You do?"

"Of course I do."

"Why?"

"What do you mean 'why'? Why shouldn't I feel bad for him? I think it was his own demons that got the best of him."

"You think it was his own demons that got the best of him?"

"Yeah. I think his own demons caused him to be afraid of me even though I wasn't thinking about him."

"You think so?"

"Yeah I think so. If he would have only accepted my forgiveness, I think his own subconscious would have saved him from the torture of his own mind."

"You think it was his own mind torturing him?"

"Well what else could it be Nancy? No one else was around that kid harming him. I wasn't around him. I wasn't anywhere near him when he killed himself, I was in the hospital, you all saw me there. The last time I was anywhere near that kid was three years ago inside the school hallway that night when I started backing away from him then saw him from down the corner of the hallway. That was the last time I saw him or was near him. I think his own mind caused him to take his own life."

"Wow." Nancy continues to look behind the shower watching Diane D drying up.

Five minutes later, Diane D is slightly limping down the upstairs hallway outside the bedrooms dressed in a dark green robe drying her damp hair with a towel as Nancy follows behind her. Diane D turns and heads towards her bedroom as Nancy continues to follow her and says, "Grandma will be up here to rub some mineral oil on your back."

"Okay," Diane D says as she heads into her bedroom. Nancy follows Diane D into the bedroom as she closes the door behind herself.

A few days later, Nicolas, Mickey, Nancy, Charlotte and Michael are standing in the kitchen as Margarita stands in front of them and says, "Diane is gonna stay at Grandma Gracy and Grandpa Mike's house for a while. I'm gonna send her there Sunday."

"You are?" Nicolas asks.

"Yes. Not only am I going to send her there, I'm sending you all there also."

"You're sending us there too?" Nancy asks.

"Yes."

"How come Grandma?" Charlotte asks.

"To help keep an eye on Diane, to make sure that she does not secretly meditate again. Not only do I need you all to help keep an eye on Diane, I need you all to help keep an eye on Dana as well."

"Dana too?" Mickey asks.

"Yes, to make sure she does not go along with Diane and meditate with her, just in case Diane tries to sneak off and influence Dana to try to meditate with her again. I don't want Dana to get influenced by Diane anymore if Diane tries to meditate again. So I need you all to help keep a close eye on Dana too! I don't want her and Diane alone together, a third person has to be in the same room with them at all times, okay?"

"Okay Grandma," Nicolas says. "We'll try our best."

"Okay good. Now your Grandpa Tomas and two probation officers are going to drive Diane to Queens this coming Sunday, and I want the rest of you all to be packed by Sunday also because you all are going to be riding in the van with them."

"Okay Grandma," Nicolas, Mickey, Nancy, Charlotte and Michael say.

A week later one afternoon, Margarita is inside her office at the organization sitting behind her desk. She is neatly pulling and ripping some papers apart. There is a knock at the door. Margarita looks towards the door and says, "Come in!"

The door opens. Alex walks into the office and says, "Hey Margarita."

"Hey Alex."

"What's going on? I thought you'd be away for a while taking care of Diane."

"I was, but Diane went to her other grandparents' house in Queens."

"Who Gracy and Mike?"

"Yeah, she went there a few days ago. She's staying over their place for a while."

"She is? So they're going to be taking care of her?"

"Yes, she's in their custody also. I sent Nicolas, Mickey, Michael, Nancy and Charlotte over there with her."

"You did? They're all staying at Gracy and Mike's house too?"

"Yes."

"Why did you send them all there with Diane?"

"Oh so they can all help keep an eye on Diane and Dana."

"Dana too?"

"Yeah. The more eyes that are kept on Diane and Dana, the better."

"Isn't Diane still on probation or house arrest?"

"Yes she's still on probation and house arrest. That's why she's in my family's custody. She'll be back and forth between my home and Gracy and Mike's home until she goes back into the mental hospital. While she's staying at Gracy and Mike's place, that'll give me some time to catch up on some work here."

"Oh I see. Is she still wearing that ankle monitor while she's at Gracy and Mike's house?"

"Of course she is. It doesn't matter whose house she's staying at, she's still gonna have that ankle monitor strapped around her ankle."

"I see. You need help with anything?"

"Sure. I need you to take these papers to my other office."

"Sure." Alex takes the papers off the desk. He then turns and walks towards the doorway.

Later that night in Queens, NY, Diane D, Nancy and Charlotte are in one of the upstairs bedrooms inside Gracy and Grandpa Mike's house sitting on the beds chit-chatting. Charlotte then says to Diane D, "You're still not able to walk well Diane?"

"No not yet Charlotte," Diane D says.

"How did your therapy go today?" Nancy asks.

"Pretty good. I'm slowly getting my strength back."

"Oh that's good. Besides, you left your crutches downstairs. I brought them upstairs for you. I left it in Grandma Gracy and Grandpa Mike's room. I'll go get it." Nancy is about to get off the bed.

"No stay there Nancy. I'll go get the crutches. I need the exercise anyway to help with my therapy. I'll be back."

"You said that last time Diane. You never came back."

"I'll be back Nancy. Where am I gonna go? I can't get too far anyway, not with this ankle monitor strapped around my ankle."

"Okay Diane. Make sure you come back."

"Okay Nancy." Diane D gets up off the bed. She turns and slightly limps towards the doorway. She then walks out the doorway and leaves the room.

Around thirty minutes later, Nancy and Charlotte are still inside the bedroom chit-chatting. Charlotte looks towards the bedroom door. She then says, "Oh oh, Diane is taking a while to come back in here. Why is she taking a while to come back with the crutches?" Charlotte and Nancy frighteningly look at each other.

"Oh no, not again!" Nancy shouts. "I hope she didn't pass out like she did before, then came back a totally different person!"

"Well this is why Grandma says that Diane has to be watched at all times! We got to go to Grandma Gracy and Grandpa Mike's room to check on Diane to make sure she's okay!"

"No, Charlotte, I'm scared! After what I went through encountering that other personality of hers, I'm afraid I might run into it again! It was scary to hear Diane or whatever talk like that! That was a bad experience for me and I hope I never go through that again!"

"Well we just can't sit here and not know what's going on with Diane, knowing her history!"

"I know. Hey. Why don't we just call out to her and hope she answers."

"Yeah you're right. Let's do it."

"Okay."

"Ready? One two three."

"Diane!" Charlotte and Nancy shout. They do not hear a response.

"Why isn't she answering?" Charlotte nervously asks. "I'm sure she could hear us from Grandma Gracy and Grandpa Mike's room!"

"I'm sure she can too," Nancy says. "Let's try it again. One two three."

"Diane!" Charlotte and Nancy shout again. They still do not hear a response.

"She's still not answering!" Charlotte nervously shouts.

"I know!" Nancy nervously shouts.

"She didn't secretly meditate earlier did she?"

"She couldn't have meditated earlier because she was never left alone! Somebody in the family would have saw her doing it!"

"But what if Dana saw Diane meditating but didn't stop her, but instead meditated right along with Diane like she's done before?!"

"Dana was never alone with Diane Charlotte! Somebody was always with her and Diane when they were together!" Charlotte and Nancy worriedly look at each other. Nancy then says, "I think we better go to Grandma Gracy and Grandpa Mike's room together to check and see if Diane is in there. If she's not there in the room and Grandma Gracy and Grandpa Mike are not there, let's call out and scream to Grandma Gracy and Grandpa Mike so they can get Diane."

"Okay." Charlotte and Nancy get off the beds. They approach each other and nervously hold on to each other then turn towards the doorway. They nervously walk towards the doorway. They then leave

335

the room.

Charlotte and Nancy step into the well lit upstairs hallway. They look around the hallway and see no sign of Diane D. They start to walk towards the master bedroom.

Charlotte and Nancy approach the master bedroom doorway. They look into the master bedroom and do not see anyone in there. "Nobody is in here," Nancy says. She turns to Charlotte and says, "I'm scared to go downstairs and run into that other personality! Let's call out to Grandma Gracy and Grandpa Mike so they can get Diane."

"Wait a minute," Charlotte says. She looks towards Dana's bedroom and says, "I think Dana is in her room. Maybe Diane is in the room with her!"

"Oh no! That means they're both alone in there!"

"Maybe not! Let's go check to see if Diane is in Dana's room with her. If she's not there, then let's see if Dana can go get her."

"But we will have to go with Dana to keep her from being alone with Diane!"

"Okay then we'll just have to go with her!" Charlotte and Nancy turn and start to head down the hallway towards Dana's bedroom.

Charlotte and Nancy approach Dana's bedroom doorway. They look in the room and see Dana in there stacking some empty boxes on top of a shelf. They do not see anyone else in the room with her. "Dana!" Charlotte and Nancy call out to her. Dana turns her head towards Charlotte and Nancy as she continues to stack some boxes.

"What's up Dana?" Charlotte says.

"What's up?" Dana says. She puzzled looks at Charlotte and Nancy and says, "What's wrong with y'all? Are you two alright?"

"Yeah," Nancy says. "We were just worried about where did Diane go? She never came back in the other room."

"She was supposed to come back in there?"

"Yeah."

"Well she went downstairs."

"She did?"

"Yeah. I told her that I was going to make her some chicken soup so she went downstairs to the kitchen to wait for me."

"Oh she's downstairs in the kitchen?"

"Yeah."

"Are you going down there now?"

"In a few minutes. Why, what's wrong?"

"Diane was supposed to go in Grandma Gracy and Grandpa Mike's room to get her crutches and come back into the room with us. She never came back. We went and checked Grandma Gracy and Grandpa Mike's room, she's not in there either so we got worried."

"You got worried?"

"Yeah."

"You don't have to worry, she's downstairs in the kitchen." Dana continues to stack the boxes.

"Is anybody down in the kitchen with her, or is she alone down there?"

"I think she's alone down there."

"What!" Charlotte and Nancy shout. "Alone down there?!"

"Are you able to go down there now to check on her Dana?" Charlotte asks. "Nancy and I just want to put our mind at ease and make sure she's okay."

"Put your mind at ease?" Dana asks.

"Yeah."

"Well if you want to put your mind at ease, just go down to the kitchen and check on her, simple as that."

"Well can you go down to the kitchen and check on her for us Dana? We're kind of afraid to go down there."

Dana stops stacking the boxes as she turns to Charlotte and says, "You're afraid to go down to the kitchen?"

"Well yeah."

"Why?"

"Because Diane could be secretly meditating while she's down in the kitchen waiting for you!"

"So what. What's wrong with her meditating?"

"What's wrong with her meditating?!" Charlotte and Nancy shout.

"Dana don't you know that strange things usually occur whenever Diane meditates?!" Nancy shouts.

"Yeah," Dana says. "But those strange things have nothing to do with her meditating."

"What!" Nancy and Charlotte shouts.

"It doesn't?" Charlotte asks."

"No," Dana says.

"So what do you think it is then?"

"I think they're coincidences."

"Coincidences!" Charlotte and Nancy shout.

"You think when Diane gets into these state of trances during her meditation, it's a coincidence?" Charlotte asks.

"Yeah," Dana says.

"Wow. Well could you go downstairs to check on her? We don't want to run into that other personality of hers just in case it emerges out of her again."

"That other personality? Is that what's bothering y'all?"

"Yeah, aren't you afraid?"

"Afraid of what?"

"The other personality."

"No."

"You're not!" Charlotte and Nancy shockingly shout.

"No."

"Why not?!" Charlotte shouts.

"Because there's no such thing."

"What!" Charlotte and Nancy shout. "There's no such thing?!"

"You don't believe in split personalities Dana?" Nancy worriedly asks.

"No," Dana says.

"You don't believe that another personality caused Diane to attack the doctors, a priest, security guards, police officers and a swat team?!"

"No."

"Then what do you believe happened then?"

"I believe Diane attacked them and got so angry that she forgot she did it."

"What!" Nancy and Charlotte shout.

"You believe her original personality attacked those people and she simply forgot?" Charlotte asks.

"Yeah because she was so angry that she blocked it out," Dana says. "That could happen to anybody."

"It could?! Something like that?!"

"Yeah."

"A person cannot forget something like that Dana."

"Yes they could, if they get mad enough and wind up blocking it out. That's what I believe happened to Diane."

"So you don't believe it was another personality?" Nancy asks.

"No."

"What about when Diane broke loose from those chains she was wrapped in breaking it loose from the couch she was chained to? Then lifting that heavy couch and throwing it across the room?! You don't think it was another personality?"

"No I don't. Like I said, coincidences, coincidences."

"So you don't believe in split personalities at all?"

"No I don't believe in that."

"Wow, neither does Diane! She doesn't believe in split personalities either and yet SHE'S the one who's actually suffering from it! Oh my goodness." Nancy and Charlotte worriedly look at each other. Then they worriedly look at Dana. Nancy then says, "Well could you just go downstairs to check on Diane anyway?"

"Hold on. I'm coming." Dana pushes the boxes way in the back of the upper shelf. She turns towards Charlotte and Nancy and starts to head towards them.

Dana approaches Charlotte and Nancy and says, "Let's go." She then goes past Charlotte and Nancy and heads out the doorway as Nancy and Charlotte turn and follow her.

Dana is walking in the upstairs hallway towards the stairs. Nancy and Charlotte rush to Dana and hold on to her arms and shoulders as they hide their faces behind her back and shoulders. Dana stops and says to them, "What's the matter?"

"We're scared," Charlotte says.

"Scared? Scared of what?"

"That other personality!"

"I told you, there's no such thing."

"Listen Dana," Nancy says. "I saw and met that other personality face to face, and I do not want to see or meet that other personality again. We have to get to Diane before she decides to secretly meditate while no one is watching her."

Dana continues to go forward as Charlotta and Nancy continue to hold on to her.

A minute later, Dana is having difficulty walking down the stairs with Charlotte and Nancy walking behind her holding tightly and nervously on to her arms and shoulders continuing to hide their faces behind her back and shoulders.

Dana comes down the bottom of the stairs with Nancy and Charlotte still holding on to her hiding their faces behind her back and shoulders. She, Nancy and Charlotte walk to the living room then enter the living room.

Dana, Nancy and Charlotte are in the living room as Nancy and Charlotte peek their faces from behind Dana and look around. They see Nicolas sleeping on the sofa. They then turn and head to the kitchen.

Dana, Nancy and Charlotte enter the kitchen. Dana then calls out, "Diane!" Nancy and Charlotte peek their faces from behind Dana's shoulders and look around. They do not see Diane D anywhere.

"Where is she?" Charlotte worriedly asks.

"Maybe she's in the basement," Dana says.

"Basement?!" Charlotte and Nancy worriedly shout.

"Oh no!" Charlotte shouts. "She's probably down there right now meditating! Can you go down the basement and check Dana? I'm scared to go down there."

"Yeah me too," Nancy says.

"Okay," Dana says. "I'll go down there."

"Okay good. But you can't go down there alone Dana. We're not allowed to have you and Diane alone just in case she tries to get you to meditate with her."

"Is that what you're worried about?"

"Yeah. That's what we're all worried about Dana."

"Okay. If it makes you feel better, I won't meditate with Diane."

"You won't?"

"No."

"Are you sure?"

"I'm sure."

"Promise you won't meditate with Diane, even if she tries to get you to meditate with her."

"I promise I won't meditate with her, even if she tries to get me to do it."

"Are you sure Dana?"

"I'm sure."

"Good." Nancy and Charlotte let go of Dana's arms and shoulders.

Dana turns to them and says, "Don't worry girls. I'll be back."

"Okay Dana."

Dana turns and starts to head to the basement steps. She approaches the basement steps then goes down the dark basement steps. Charlotte and Nancy nervously watch Dana go down the basement steps.

Fifteen minutes later, Charlotte and Nancy are in the kitchen sitting down at the table chit-chatting as Charlotte says to Nancy, "So you think Dana is in denial?"

"Of course she's in denial Charlotte," Nancy says. "After all, she does meditate right along with Diane."

"Well maybe that's why she sees nothing wrong with it. You think she was saying all those things are coincidences to throw off our suspicion?"

"Of course she wants to throw off our suspicion because she has been caught being in a state of trance right along with Diane and I don't think she be aware of herself being in a state of trance either."

"She doesn't?"

"No. When Grandma Gracy, Uncle Willie and Nicolas told Dana that they saw her in a state of trance right along with Diane, Dana didn't seem to remember it."

"She didn't?"

"No. She had no idea what Grandma Gracy, Uncle Willie and Nicolas were talking about."

"Wow."

"That's why Grandma wants her to be watched as well."

"Is Grandma still planning to make arrangements for Dana to get counseling?"

"Oh yeeaahh. She and Grandpa were on the phone talking with Grandma Gracy and Grandpa Mike this afternoon."

"They were?"

"Yeah. They were all talking about making arrangements for Dana to have counseling."

"Oh boy!" Charlotte looks towards the kitchen doorway. She then whispers, "Oh oh, now Dana is taking a while to come back up here!" Charlotte and Nancy frighteningly look at each other. They then look towards the kitchen doorway.

"Oh no!" Nancy whispers. "Not her too! This is why Grandma says that Dana needs to be watched at all times while she's with Diane! Now we have to call out to her and hope she answers!"

"Okay! Ready? One two three."

"Dana!" Charlotte and Nancy shout. They do not hear a response.

"She's not answering either!" Charlotte nervously shouts. "And I'm sure she could hear us from the basement!"

"Let's try it again," Nancy says.

"Okay. One two three."

"Dana!" Charlotte and Nancy shout again. They still do not hear a response.

"She's still not answering!" Charlotte nervously shouts.

"I know!" Nancy nervously shouts. "First Diane disappears right inside this house, now Dana does! I mean what the hell is going on?!"

"I don't know! Diane can't get too far with that ankle monitor on her foot!"

"I know!"

"You think when Dana went downstairs, she probably caught Diane secretly meditating or caught her in a state of trance and is trying to snap her out of the trance before we and the rest of the family get suspicious and find out about it?"

"It's a possibility Charlotte. Maybe that's why she's taking a while to come back up the stairs, unless, Diane succeeded in influencing Dana to meditate right along with her again and Dana just went along with it and meditated with Diane anyway because she sees nothing wrong with it."

"But Dana made a promise that she wouldn't meditate with Diane! I hope she didn't lie to me about it just to keep me quiet."

"I hope not either. If Dana doesn't hurry and show up with Diane, then we have to go in the living room to wake Nicolas up to go get them." Nancy and Charlotte suddenly hear a couple of footsteps and voices coming up the basement steps. They nervously look at each other. "I think I hear their footsteps coming," Nancy whispers.

"I hear it too. I think Dana found Diane." Charlotte and Nancy hear the voices coming towards the kitchen. They look towards the kitchen entryway and see Dana entering the kitchen.

"Dana!" Charlotte and Nancy shout.

"Diane's coming," Dana says as she enters the kitchen. She turns to Nancy and Charlotte and says, "Are you two okay now?"

"Yeah we're fine Dana," Charlotte smiles and says.

"Are you sure?"

"Yeah we're sure Dana," Nancy smiles and says. "We're fine. Thanks."

"Okay." Dana turns and heads towards the stove.

Charlotte and Nancy look towards the kitchen entryway again and see Diane D who appears to be normal entering the kitchen. They become excited and shout, "Diane!"

"Hey girls!" Diane D says as she limps into the kitchen.

"My goodness Diane!" Nancy says. "Where have you been?!"

"I'm sorry it took so long for me to come back upstairs to the room, but I was down in the basement talking with Michael, Mickey and Uncle Willie."

"What?" Nancy and Charlotte say.

"Michael, Mickey and Uncle Willie?" Charlotte says. "They're down in the basement?"

"Yeah," Diane D says.

"Oh, we didn't know they were down there."

"Yeah they are."

"Wow," Nancy says. "You seem normal Diane."

"I seem normal? What do you mean 'I seem normal'?"

"You still seem like yourself."

"I still seem like myself?"

"Yeah."

"Well why wouldn't I be myself?"

"Oh never mind. I'm just happy that you're okay."

"I feel okay Nancy."

Nancy and Charlotte laugh and both give a sigh of relief. Nancy then says to Diane D, "You haven't secretly meditated lately have you?"

"No I haven't secretly meditated lately because you know why? First of all, Grandma and Grandpa forbid me from meditating anymore and second, even if I want to secretly meditate, I can't, not with the way Grandma have everyone in the family watching my every move."

Nancy and Charlotte laugh again. Michael, Mickey and Uncle Willie suddenly enter the kitchen as Michael says, "Good evening Nancy and Charlotte."

"Hey Michael, Mickey, Uncle Willie," Charlotte and Nancy say.

"Hey girls," Uncle Willie says. "Why didn't you two come down the stairs with Dana?"

"Yeah," Mickey says. "We were watching the game."

"Y'all were?" Charlotte asks.

"Yeah." Mickey looks towards Dana and says, "I decided to have some Gumbo soup too Dana."

"Yeah me too," Uncle Willie says.

"Okay," Dana says as she puts a large pot on the stove. Uncle Willie, Mickey and Michael start to sit at the table and chit chat with Diane D, Nancy and Charlotte. Dana turns to Nancy and Charlotte and asks, "You two want some Gumbo soup?"

"Gumbo soup?" Charlotte says. "I thought you were gonna make chicken soup."

"I was but I changed my mind because Diane decided she wants Gumbo soup instead of chicken soup."

"Oh. Okay. I guess I'll have some Gumbo soup too."

"Me too," Nancy says.

Nicolas suddenly enters the kitchen awoken from his sleep in the living room as he stretches his arms. "Hey Nicolas," everyone says.

"What's going on?" Nicolas asks.

"I'm getting ready to make Gumbo for everybody," Dana says. "You want some?"

"Gumbo soup sounds good. Yeah I'll have some Dana, thanks."

"Are there any crackers in the house?" Nancy asks.

"Yeah," Dana says. "It's in the cabinet."

"Okay, I'll get it." Nancy gets up from the chair. She turns to Diane D and says, "You want some crackers Diane?"

"Sure," Diane D says. "Why not." Diane D and Nancy chit-chat as they turn and walk towards the cabinet with Diane D still slightly limping.

Three days later, Gracy and Nicolas are in the kitchen preparing breakfast as Grandpa Mike, Aunt Celeste, Aunt Laura, Aunt Jean, Uncle Willie and Mickey sit at the large kitchen table. Nicolas turns to Grandpa Mike and says, "You ready for your coffee Grandpa?"

"Yes I'm ready Nicolas," Grandpa Mike says as he sits at the end of the table. "Are the girls coming down for breakfast?"

"Yeah. Missy, Landa and Londa are all still upstairs trying on some new make-up. They want to try the new make-up on Dana."

"Oh yeah?" Aunt Celeste says. "Dana doesn't wear make-up."

"The girls know that. That's why they want to try the new make-up on her to see how it looks on her."

"I see." Suddenly the doorbell rings.

"I'll get it," Nicolas says. He turns and heads towards the livingroom.

Nicolas goes through the livingroom to the front door. He approaches the front door and looks through the peephole. He opens the front door and sees Teresa standing outside of it. "Hey Teresa," he says.

"Hey Nicolas," Teresa says. "How are you?"

"I'm okay and yourself?"

"Pretty good. I just want to know if it's alright if I visit Diane?"

"I'm not sure if Diane is allowed anybody to visit her while she's on house arrest Teresa."

"Oh."

"But let me ask my grandparents. Hold on." Nicolas closes the front door. He turns and heads back towards the kitchen.

Nicolas enters the kitchen and says, "Grandma Grandpa, Teresa is at the door. She wants to know if she can visit Diane."

"Diane is on house arrest Nicolas," Grandpa Mike says. "She's not allowed any visitors. If they're not family, they cannot come in here and visit her."

"Well Teresa might not be family," Gracy says, "but she has been a friend of Diane's and Dana's for a long time. I guess it won't hurt if she sees Diane real quick."

"Okay. She can visit Diane real quick, but she cannot stay too long."

"Okay Grandpa," Nicolas says.

"Before you let her in, go upstairs and let Diane know that she's out there and see if it's okay with her for Teresa to come in and visit her."

"Okay Grandpa." Nicolas turns and heads back out the kitchen.

Three minutes later, Nicolas comes back into the kitchen. He says, "Diane says okay. She says Teresa can visit her real quick."

"Are you sure it's alright with her Nicolas?" Grandpa Mike asks.

"Yeah she says it's alright only for a few minutes because she says she's not really up to any visitors anyway, but Teresa can come up real quick."

"Okay, let her in, but she cannot stay too long."

"Okay Grandpa." Nicolas turns and heads back towards the front door.

Nicolas opens the front door and says, "Come in Teresa." Nicolas lets Teresa in. Teresa nervously enters the house as Nicolas says to her, "You can visit Diane real quick, but not for long because she's still under house arrest."

"Does she still have that ankle monitor wrapped around her ankle?" Teresa asks.

"Yes she still does."

"Wow."

"Now whatever you do, don't mention or ask Diane anything about what happened inside that hypnosis room because all she's going to do is deny it and says she did not do it, then she's not gonna want to talk about it."

"Okay I won't mention anything to her about it or ask her anything about it."

"Thanks."

"So I'll ask you. Since you were one of the family members who was there inside that hypnosis room and witnessed everything from beginning to end, did Diane really do all that stuff that happened inside the hypnosis room? Did she really break the chains she was wrapped in loose from the couch then threw that couch right across the room?"

"Well Teresa, all I can say is, that it WAS her body that did do all that stuff."

"It was her body?"

"Yeah. Now her mind is another story. Her mind was not there."

"Wow."

"From what my family and I heard, it was not Diane who was speaking when she threatened the doctors. Yeah we see Diane talking and see her physical mouth moving, but it's like we heard someone else saying all those things."

"Wow! I can imagine how creepy that was!"

"It was very creepy Teresa. My family and I are still haunted by it."

"I bet you are!"

"Let's take you up to Diane."

"Okay. Is Dana here?"

"Yeah Dana is here. She and her sisters are upstairs. I think Linda is still laying on the bed. Come on." Nicolas turns and leads Teresa towards the stairs.

Nicolas is walking in the upstairs hallway as Teresa follows behind him. Nicolas heads towards one of the bedroom doorways.

Nicolas goes into the doorway and sees Linda in the room laying in one of the beds reading. He then says, "Hey Linda." Linda turns to Nicolas as he says to her, "Where's Diane?"

"Oh she just went to the bathroom to get some dental floss," Linda says.

"She did?"

"Yeah. She's coming back."

"Okay. Is it okay for Teresa to wait for Diane in here with you?"

"Yeah she can come in here."

"Thanks Linda." Nicolas turns to Teresa and says, "You can wait for Diane in here with Linda. I'll tell her you're in here."

"Okay Nicolas," Teresa says. Teresa goes into the room as Nicolas turns and walks away.

Teresa sees Linda and says, "What's up Linda? How's it going?"

"Okay I guess," Linda says.

"Good. Are you tired?"

"No. Just resting. Have a seat."

"Thanks." Teresa sits down on the other bed. She then asks, "So where's Dana?"

"Dana just went into my grandparents' room with my other sisters."

"She did?"

"Yeah."

"She knows I'm here?"

"I think she does."

"Oh. Okay. Where's Michael?"

"He went to the pharmacy to pick up Diane's medication."

"He did?"

"Yeah. He'll be back soon."

"Okay." Teresa turns around and suddenly sees a serious looking Diane D standing in the doorway wearing a white bustier and black leggings baring her muscular physique with her long black hair down and bangs around her forehead wearing an ankle monitor around her left ankle and holding a dental floss. "Diane!" Teresa nervously says. "What's up Diane?"

"What's up Teresa?" Diane D says as she comes into the room with the dental floss.

"How you doing?"

"I'm okay Teresa," Diane D says as she approaches the foot of the bed.

"So how is everything? Is everything okay?"

"Everything's okay Teresa," Diane D says as she sits down at the foot of the bed. She still has slight bruises on her body.

"Good. I just came to see how you doing."

"I'm doing okay," Diane D says as she grabs a chair and places the chair in front of herself.

"You are?"

"Yeah," Diane D says as she puts a mirror on the chair.

"Good. How are your bruises doing? I see you still have them. Are they getting better?"

Diane D takes a quick look at her arm and says, "It's healing."

"It is?"

"Yeah," Diane D says as she takes the dental floss case and pulls some floss out of the case.

"Good. How's your Grandma Margarita?"

"She's good," Diane D says as she takes the floss.

"She is?"

"Yeah."

"Where is she? Is she here?"

"No, she's still up in Westchester."

"She is?"

"Yeah. Let me just use this dental floss real quick Teresa, and I'll get back to you."

"Oh. Okay."

Diane D bends a little towards the mirror and looks into the mirror. She opens her mouth, takes both hands and gently starts using the floss on her teeth as Teresa watches her. Teresa sadly looks at Diane D. She then looks at the ankle monitor wrapped around Diane D's left ankle as Diane D continues to use the dental floss. Teresa then turns and looks at Linda and sees Linda sitting up on the bed looking at and using her smartphone. She turns and looks back at Diane D as Diane D continues to bend down to the mirror using the dental floss.

Two weeks later, Diane D is back at Margarita and Tomas' mansion in Northern Westchester, NY. She is sitting in the living room with Michael, Mary, Barry, Tomas, Tonio, Marilyn and Nicolas as she and Michael sit on the couch together with Michael holding and hugging onto her as she leans against him. They are all facing a large flat screen TV which is blank. Margarita then enters the living room. She walks to the flat screen TV. She then goes in front of the flat screen TV and stands in front of everybody facing everybody. She then shouts, "Okay listen up everybody!" Everyone faces and looks at Margarita as she shouts, "We are about to watch the video of Diane's hypnosis! We are getting ready to show her the video of her hypnosis! Are we all ready to show her?"

"I don't know Grandma," Michael says. "I don't know if I want to even see that video. It's like living through that horror all over again!"

"Yeah it's true Mom," Marilyn says. "I don't know if I want to see that video either. I get chills just thinking about what we all witnessed and what we all went through in there!"

"Me too Mom," Tonio says.

"I understand how you all feel," Margarita says, "but it is important for Diane to see the video of her hypnosis since she didn't believe us when we first told her about her behavior during her hypnosis!" Margarita then looks at Diane D and says, "Diane. You still do not believe what we said happened during your hypnosis?"

"No Grandma," Diane D says. "I still don't believe it because I do not behave the way you all said I did during my hypnosis!"

"So you still have your doubts?"

"Yes Grandma, I do."

"Are you ready to watch the video?"

"Not really Grandma."

Margarita looks back at the rest of the family and says, "Is anybody ready to watch the video of Diane's hypnosis?"

"Wait a minute Margarita," Tomas says. "Where're Nancy and Charlotte? They're not in here yet."

"Nancy and Charlotte do not want to be in the room."

"They don't?"

"No."

"How come?"

"They're afraid to see the video."

"They're afraid to see it?"

"Yeah."

"Well I guess we can't blame them."

"I'm afraid to see the video myself Grandma," Nicolas says. "But I'll watch the first part of the video when the doctors were speaking to Diane, but I'm not sure if I can take seeing the other parts with the chains being busted and broken and the metal bars of the couch being bent out of shape then the doctors, the priest and the authority figures getting hurt and slammed in the heads by that couch!"

"Well the part of the doctors, the priest and the authority figures getting hurt might not have been caught on video because the cameras were knocked down," Margarita says. "You can probably still hear the audio part of it I'm not sure, because this will be my first time watching the video myself. I'll tell you all what. I'll have the entire video running. If anybody can't take watching the video anymore, you can get up and leave the room up to the part you cannot take looking at it anymore, including you Diane, okay?"

"Okay Grandma," Diane D says.

"Okay." Margarita turns to everybody and says, "I'm about to turn the video on. Here goes." Margarita turns to the TV and plays the video. The video of Diane D's hypnosis starts to play on the TV screen as Margarita goes and sits next to Tomas.

SCENE IN VIDEO:

Dr. Stone and Dr. Kahn are sitting near Diane D's head leaning towards her head. Dr. Stone speaks to Diane D's subconscious again and says to her, "Is there a soul, spirit or personality there inside this physical body?" Dr. Stone and Dr. Kahn stare at Diane D. Diane D does not respond. Her physical body continues to lay on the psychiatrist couch not responding as her eyes remain closed.

BACK IN MARGARITA AND TOMAS' LIVING ROOM:

Diane D, Michael, Margarita, Tomas, Mary, Barry, Tonio, Marilyn and Nicolas nervously watch the video. Michael, Margarita, Tomas, Mary, Barry, Tonio, Marilyn and Nicolas then turn and look at Diane D trying to see her reaction. They see Diane D staring at the video of herself in disbelief. Michael, Margarita, Tomas, Mary, Barry, Tonio, Marilyn and Nicolas turn and look back at the video.

SCENE IN VIDEO:

Dr. Stone continues to speak to Diane D's subconscious again as he looks down at her and says, "Is there a soul, spirit or personality inside this physical body now? If there is a soul, spirit or personality inside this physical body now, we need you to come out and talk to us. We need to talk to Diane's original soul, spirit and personality first. Is Diane's original soul, spirit or personality in there now? Reveal yourself. Come out and speak to us. Is Diane's original soul, spirit or personality in there now?" Dr. Stone and Dr. Kahn continue to stare at Diane D. Diane D's physical body continues to lay on the couch not responding as her eyes remain closed.

BACK IN MARGARITA AND TOMAS' LIVING ROOM:

Diane D, Michael, Margarita, Tomas, Mary, Barry, Tonio, Marilyn and Nicolas continue to watch the video. Michael, Margarita, Tomas, Mary, Barry, Tonio, Marilyn and Nicolas turn and look back at Diane D trying to see her reaction again. They see Diane D still staring at the video of herself in disbelief. Michael, Margarita, Tomas, Mary, Barry,

Tonio, Marilyn and Nicolas turn and look back at the video.

The next day, Margarita, Tomas, Mary, Barry and Michael are standing with Dr. Stone inside his office as Dr. Stone says to them, "Diane saw the video of her hypnosis yesterday, and she still doesn't believe it's herself in the video?"

"No Doctor Stone!" Margarita shouts. "She doesn't!"

"Did she see the entire video?"

"Yes we showed her the entire video from the beginning, until the end when we only heard the audio when the cameras were knocked down!"

"And she still doesn't believe it's herself?"

"No, she thinks it's somebody else!"

"Somebody else?!"

"Yes!"

"Well who does she think the person in the video is?"

"She thinks it's someone who looks like her Doctor Stone," Michael says.

"Someone who looks like her?"

"Yes because she claims she does not behave that way!"

"It's true, she DOESN'T behave that way! It's those other souls, spirits and personalities who were behaving that way through HER body! Did she see the part of the other personalities talking through her physical body on the video?"

"Yes Doctor Stone," Barry says, "but she also thinks that she could have been talking in her sleep when she saw herself in the video saying all that stuff."

"Talking in her sleep? She thinks she was probably talking in her sleep when she saw herself in the video saying those things?"

"Exactly."

"What about all that chaos in the background when the cameras fell? Did she hear and listen to that part?"

"Yes she did."

"Well what does she think about that part?"

"She doesn't think she did all that stuff she heard in the background!"

"She doesn't believe she did that either?"

"No! She said if she did do that stuff she heard in the background, maybe she could have been sleepwalking when she heard all the chaos happening in the audio part of the video."

"Sleepwalking? She thinks it's a possibility of herself sleepwalking when she heard all the chaos happening in the audio part?"

"Exactly."

"So all in all, she believes that she was sleeptalking and sleepwalking when she saw and heard herself in the video. Well what does she think about the authority figures who she heard were getting hurt in the audio part?"

"She says she feels real bad for them Doctor Stone, but she claims it's not her doing that stuff."

"She claims it's not her doing that?"

"Yes!"

"You did tell her that she's right? That it's not her doing that stuff, but another personality doing that?"

"We tried to tell Diane that it was another personality doing that stuff Doctor Stone!" Tomas shouts, "but she claims she doesn't believe in split personalities!"

"She still doesn't believe in split personlities? She still don't believe SHE has a split personality disorder?!"

"No! She just claim she didn't do it!"

"Well that's the same thing she said about beating up Marcus inside that school hallway years ago. She claim she didn't do it when Marcus claim, she did do it! That's the same thing she said about kung fu kicking that stuck storage room door at the other hospital wide open. She claim she didn't do it when two hospital eye witnesses said, she did do it! Well she's half right, she didn't do it. It's the other personalities who did do it! Well I guess all we can do for Diane, is to have her committed back into the state hospital again."

"Doctor Stone," Mary says. "Are you having my child committed back into the state hospital again because of what my family just told you?"

"No, it's not because of what your family just told me Miss Mary. Diane was still going to be committed back into the state hospital regardless of what your family just said. She's being committed back into the state hospital because of what happened during her hypnosis when she attacked those authority figures who later died! What your family just told me will only help keep your child out of prison and instead be committed back into the mental institution."

"Well Diane would not be committed back into the mental institution if we had followed our guts and not let her be hypnotized in the first place Doctor Stone!"

"That's right," Margarita cries. "We should have never let her be hypnotized! If Diane was never hypnotized, her other personality would not have come out to the surface and commit those violent acts, and she would not be committed back into the state hospital! She would still be home with us, her family! I'm sorry we even allowed her to be hypnotized because she wouldn't be sent away!"

"I'm sorry Miss Margarita."

"Sorry my foot Doctor Stone!" Mary angrily shouts. "I'm telling you right now, that hypnosis will be the last time my child ever gets hypnotized no matter what! I don't care if anybody else happen to have an encounter with her other personality in the future, or if anybody else out there claims to have nightmares about her claiming that she's entering into their dreams and nightmares, that's it! I will not have my baby going through this anymore, then being committed back into the state hospital because my child will not be hypnotized ever again!"

"Heyyy wait a minute now Miss Mary! You can't blame your child's other personality coming out to the surface all on her being hypnotized! Her other personality came out to the surface before in the past WITHOUT her being hypnotized! All she has to do, is get real angry or meditate and there it goes, her other personality would come out to the surface! Did someone hypnotized her the night she beat the crap out of Marcus inside that school hallway breaking all his bones and everything?! I don't think so! I don't think Marcus was qualified to hypnotize her! Did someone hypnotized her the night she kung fu kicked that stuck storage room door wide opened damaging that storage room by turning everything in there upside down?! I don't think so! I don't think those two hospital eye witnesses who saw her go into that storage room were qualified to hypnotize her! Did someone hypnotized her the night she tried to attack those correction officers inside the jail cell?! I don't think so!"

"Alright Doctor Stone!" Margarita shouts. "We get it! We know Diane doesn't have to be hypnotized in order for her other personality to come out to the surface and get out of control."

"I'm sorry the way this all turned out. I really am! But when you all came to me for help, because Nancy had an encounter with Diane's other personality, I had to get into Diane's brain to find out what's going on! And the only way I can get deep into her subconscious, was to hypnotize her. We found out a whole lot of answers during her hypnosis. We found out that the other soul, spirit or personality WAS the one Nancy had an encounter with that night, when Diane claims she does not remember it. We found out that the other soul, spirit or personality WAS the one who beat up Marcus inside that third floor school hallway that night, when Diane claims she does not remember it. We found out that the other soul, spirit or personality WAS the one who kung fu kicked that stuck storage room door wide open at the other hospital, when Diane claims she does not remember it. We found out that the other soul, spirit or personality WAS the one inside that jail cell trying to attack the correction officers and looking at the nurse who came into the cell the next morning, when Diane claims she does not remember it. We found out that her third personality, WAS the one who caused Diane's physical body to levitate over the stage in Germany, when Diane claims she does not remember levitating. We found out a whole lot of other things during Diane's hypnosis. Even though we succeeded in finding out a lot of answers during Diane's hypnosis, I'm sorry that all that chaos happened at the end, because once I told her third personality to stay away from Diane and not to come around Diane anymore, that was it! Her third personality decided to come after me like a bull! It threatened me, it broke the chains loose from the couch freeing itself from the couch then came after me and Doctor Kahn and kung fu kicked us and knocked us out for it, then attacked all the authority figures with that couch and winds up killing some of them! So many people got hurt that fateful day, I can't even count it! You're right, maybe we should have never hypnotized Diane. If she was never hypnotized, her third personality would not have come out to the surface and commit those violent acts causing me, Doctor Kahn, security guards, a priest, police officers and a swat team to get hurt and killed! Some of those police officers and swat team members would still be alive and Doctor Kahn would not be closing his practice! You're right, we should have never hypnotized Diane."

"So sorry all of that happened Doctor Stone," Michael says.

"Yeah thanks." Dr. Stone then says, "Well, shall we get the paper work started?" Doctor Stone turns towards his desk and goes around it as Michael, Mary, Margarita, Tomas and Barry sadly look at him.

Chapter 28

The Priest Passes Away

The priest has just passed away. His body is in the hospital bed covered with a sheet over his head. His family members and several other priests are standing at his hospital bedside crying their eyes out. One of the other priests, who is his brother, cries out, "He's gone, he's gone!" He then looks up in the air and shouts, "God! Why did you have to take my brother?! I was hoping you let him pull through this! Why did you have to take him?! Why couldn't he just stay here on earth much much longer?!" The priest's brother continues to cry his eyes out as everyone else cry their eyes out trying to comfort him.

The next day, a group of people are sitting at a bowling alley table. A white female around her mid forties is looking at a newspaper article with a headline that reads: **DIANE D'S OTHER PERSONALITY HAS CLAIMED ITS SIXTH VICTIM AS THE PRIEST PASSES AWAY**: "Oh no!" the white woman shouts. "Another person who got injured by Diane D's other personality just passed away!"

"What!" the rest of the group shouts.

"Another person who got injured by Diane D's other personality died?!" a white male around his early fifties shouts.

"Yeah!"

"Who?!"

"This time, it was the priest who passed away!"

"What!" everyone else shouts. "The priest?!"

"Yeah!"

"You got to be kidding!" a young white male shouts. "The priest this time?!"

"Yeah!"

"Oh my God!" a heavy-set black woman shouts. "Let me see!" Everyone leans on the table to look at the article. "Did it say when the priest died?"

"Yeah, it says he died last night!"

"Last night?! Oh good Lord!"

"Wow!" a younger black woman shouts. "I can't believe Diane D's other personality killed a priest this time! First her other personality killed cops and a swat team and caused that little kid Marcus to take his own life, and now her other personality has killed a priest?!"

"Wow! I guess Diane D's other personality doesn't discriminate! It doesn't care WHO you are! You mess with Diane D, her other personality is gonna come after you plain and simple, even if you're a priest!"

"Even if you're a priest?!" the young white male shouts. "But what did the priest do to deserve this?!"

"He came into that hypnosis room with the security guards when the security guards were about to go for Diane D! That's when Diane D's other personality threw and tossed that psychiatrist couch right across the room at them full speed ahead and slam that couch right into those poor souls smashing the couch right into their heads!"

"My God!" the white woman says. "Thank God I wasn't inside that hypnosis room!"

"Well wasn't Diane D's family members inside that hypnosis room when Diane D's other personality went berserk and wild in there?" the young white male asks. "Her family survived! I didn't hear of any of them being hurt, injured, laying in the hospital or even killed!"

"Well that's because that's her family! That's what probably saved them! Look what happened to the poor souls inside that room who WEREN'T her family! You see what happened to them! The ones who are still alive are still laying in the hospital with some of them in comas and others with fractured skulls, broken necks and their heads split opened! They might never come out of that hospital alive like the others didn't! The six victims who already passed away all died right in the hospital, neither one of them ever came out alive!"

"Wow Diane D's other personality did a whole bunch of damage to these people," the black woman says. "That other personality of hers does not play!"

"Wow!" the younger black woman says. "I would never want to cross Diane D, because if you cross her, her original personality might not come after you, but her other personality will!"

"Well that's what happened to that little boy Marcus inside that school hallway! Diane D's original personality didn't beat him up! I heard her original personality refused to beat him up because he was a kid, it was her other personality who did that! So I guess her other personality said 'if she don't beat the hell out of that kid, they're gonna do it', so that's what happened! That other personality took over Diane D's body and wind up beating the crap out of that kid Marcus half killing him!"

"That's why Diane D doesn't remember beating him up, right?"

"Yeah that's why she doesn't remember it."

"Well!" the young white male shouts. "Now that Diane D has killed a priest, there goes her performance career!"

"There goes her performance career?" the younger black woman says. "What do you mean?"

"I mean she might as well say goodbye to it because as we can see, that woman's performance career is over! She is going to be put in prison for life! I'm going to miss that woman's performance! I'm going to miss seeing Diane D performing on stage because she is one hell-of-a performer!"

"She sure is! I'm gonna miss seeing her perform too!"

"Well I guess the only place she can perform now is in the slammer! At least the inmates in there will get to see her perform."

"Wow, I'm gonna miss Diane D. I used to be a big fan of hers! I still am!"

"So am I."

"You two want to be fans of a killer?!" the white woman shouts. "Seriously?! Come on you two, Diane D is a killer! She just killed her sixth victim last night! And you all talking about still wanting to see her on stage and gonna miss her performance?! She's a murderer!"

"But it wasn't her original personality who killed those people!" the young black woman shouts.

"Either or, it was still her body that threw the couch at all those law enforcement officers and authority figures! People lost their loved ones because of her!"

"It wasn't her! It was that OTHER personality who did that!"

"Well whoever! People's lives were still lost thanks to her or her other personality!" The people sadly look at the woman. They then look at the article.

The following day, Margarita, Tomas and Barry are sitting at the long tables in front of the large banquet room at the organization with around two hundred people inside the room facing them. Margarita stands at the podium. There is a microphone at the podium. Everyone turns and faces Margarita. Margarita then speaks to the crowd and says, "Good morning everyone."

"Good morning Miss Margarita," the crowd sadly says.

"This has been a sad time for us," Margarita says with tears in her eyes. "I'm sure we all heard by now what happened a couple of nights ago. I know you all know that the priest has passed away from what happened inside that hypnosis room."

"Auuhh," the crowd says.

"Are you okay Miss Margarita?" Alex asks.

"No Alex," Margarita says. "I don't think I'll ever be okay after everything that has happened. How can my family and I be okay. Lives were lost. I will never be right after this, neither will my family.

355

Our lives has changed forever! All we can try to do, is help the surviving victims and their families. So we're going to have a fundraiser. With all the chaos that happened with Diane that involved the deaths of several law enforcement officers and authority figures with some others left terribly injured, we're going to do a fundraiser to raise money for the victims and their families. We're going to put on a show and sell tickets."

"What kind of show Miss Margarita?" Vivian, a black female staff members, asks.

"We're going to put on an All-Cultural show, where different cultures from around the world will perfrom."

"Will Diane perform in the show Miss Margarita?" Evette, a black female staff member, asks.

"No Diane will not perform in the show. She's not allowed to. She's still on house arrest and probation from that incident."

"Ohhh," the rest of the crowd says.

"But she might come around at the end of the fundraiser with her two probation officers."

"She might come around the end with her probation officers?" Kory, one of the staff members, asks. "How come?"

"Well she wants to come there to support the victims for what happened to them."

"She wants to support the victims for what happened to them? You mean she wants to support the victims for what SHE did?"

"Well as far as she's concerned, she doesn't believe she did anything."

"She still doesn't believe she did any of that stuff?"

"No she doesn't."

"But you were all there when it happened Miss Margarita," Stephanie says. "You all witnessed it first hand! I'm sure you all told Diane she did it!"

"Yes we told her she did it," Tomas says. "We showed her the entire video of what happened inside that hypnosis room, she still doesn't believe it was herself in the video because she claim she would never say stuff like that or do things like that."

"Plus she said she is not that strong or capable to lift up a psychiatrist couch or throw it across a room," Barry says. "She claims things like that are impossible."

"Even though you all and her doctors witnessed her doing that, she stilll doesn't believe she did it?" Kory asks.

"No she still doesn't."

"Wow," the crowd says.

Three days later, there is a funeral for the priest at the Cathedral. There are thousands of other priests, police officers and civilians gathered at the funeral.

Chapter 29

Curious Reporters Approach Nancy About Diane D

Nancy is walking down the street in White Plains, New York as Charlotte, Miranda, Bernice, Lonna and Kelly walk with her surrounding her. Lonna turns to Nancy and says, "So we're not going to participate in the fundraising Nancy?"

"I'm not sure what plans Grandma and Grandpa have for us yet Lonna," Nancy says.

A few local reporters a white male with light brown hair, a white female with dark hair, a big stocky black male and a camera man anxiously approach the Dianettes as the white male reporter says, "Hey Dianettes!" Nancy, Charlotte, Miranda, Bernice, Lonna and Kelly stop and turn around towards the reporters. "Hi!" the white male reporter says. "How are you Dianettes?! How are you all doing?!" Nancy, Charlotte, Miranda, Bernice, Lonna and Kelly puzzled look at the reporters. "Hey Dianettes!" the white male reporter says. "We just want to ask Nancy some questions about her encounter with Diane D's other personality!"

"That's right!" the white female reporter says. "Hey Nancy! Hi Nancy!" Nancy looks at the female reporter as the female reporter says, "So Nancy! What's this we hear about you having an encounter with your cousin Diane D's other personality?! I mean your cousin Diane D's other personality has been all over the headlines lately!"

"It sure has!" the black male reporter says. "Her other personality is the talk of the town! Everybody is fascinated by it! People are curious and want to sort of see your cousin Diane D's other personality, but are afraid to! They said they want to see her other personality from afar and not get close to it! What is your take on it Nancy? We heard that you met your cousin Diane D's other personality first hand! We heard that you accidentally encountered your cousin Diane D's other personality right inside your family's home one night. Is it true? Is it true that you encountered your cousin Diane D's other personality right inside your family's home?" Nancy hesitates as she stares at the reporters.

"What's wrong Nancy? Is it true that you encountered your cousin Diane D's other personality inside your family's house?"

"Yeah it's true," Nancy says.

The reporters gasps as the female reporter says, "It is?"

"Yeah."

"Oh my God Nancy! What happened?! Everybody in town wants to know about it!"

"Yeah Nancy!" the white male reporter says. "Tell us about it!"

"I don't really like to talk about it," Nancy says.

"You don't?"

"No."

"Why not?"

"It was a frightening situation for me! I try not to even think about it!"

"No? We hear that you and your cousin Charlotte didn't want to stay inside the hypnosis room during the second part of your cousin Diane D's hypnosis because you feared encountering her other personality again. Is that true?"

"Yes it's true."

"Why did you fear encountering your cousin Diane D's other personality again during the hypnosis?"

"It was a bad experience for me when I accidentally met it face to face!"

"Wow, that sounds scary!"

"It does," the female reporter says. "Can you at least just tell us about what happened that night Nancy?"

"Yeah," the black male reporter says. "What happened?"

"I can't talk about it," Nancy says. "If I talk about it, it means that I have to relive it, and that's one thing I do not want to relive!"

"Well how do you feel emotionally Nancy?" the white male reporter asks. "How do feel knowing, that your cousin Diane D's other personality injured over twenty authority figures when she threw that psychiatrist couch at them at full speed and took the lives of six of them so far, including a priest this time?"

"I feel real bad for the people who lost their lives! I feel for their families too!"

"You do?"

"Yes I do!"

"We hear that you sort of blame yourself for all of what happened. We hear that you are now sorry for telling your family about the encounter you had with your cousin Diane D's other personality, because you feel that if you had never said anything and kept quiet about it, none of this would have happened. Is that true?"

"Yes it's true."

"Do you feel that you're carrying weight on your shoulders because of it?"

"Yes I do."

"So what would you do, if God forbid you accidentally have another encounter with your cousin Diane D's other personality again? Would you say anything about it?"

"I don't even want to think about meeting that other personality again!"

"Why not?!"

"Because why would I want to meet something that is so cruel and so vicious?!"

"Cruel and vicious?! You mean because of what that other personality did to all those authority figures including the priest?"

"Exactly! That other personality caused my family to be traumatized by the things it said and did during the hypnosis!"

"We heard that your family was traumatized by that whole incident! Are they all okay now?"

"Not quite. But they're trying to pull through."

"Well what did that other personality say during the hypnosis?! I mean we know what it DID during the hypnosis, but what did it say?!"

"I don't know. Charlotte and I left the room when the doctors first brought that other personality out to the surface."

"I heard you two left the room. Why? You two were afraid, weren't you?"

"Of course we were afraid!" Charlotte shouts. "We're still afraid!"

"Wow. Well since you two left the room as soon as the doctors brought that other personality out, did you two watch the video of the hypnosis?"

"No. We were too afraid to look at that."

"Y'all haven't seen the video? Y'all haven't seen the part of the video when Diane D's other personality was admitting to all these things that happened in Diane D's past, like beating up that little boy Marcus, kung fu kicking that stuck storage room door wide open at the hospital she used to work at, fighting correction officers inside a jail cell, then was admitting to things that happened way way in the past before Diane D herself was even born, like killing people in different parts of the world throughout the centuries once every fifty years?"

"No we didn't see that part of the video either. How do you know about that part anyway?"

"People who saw the video inside the courtroom mentioned it. They do talk. What do you think of the part when Doctor Stone had Diane D's second personality sit up on the couch to identify her family, and her second personality just looked right at Diane D's family like they were complete strangers, saying that 'she's seen them before'? Then identifies them by saying 'That's Diane's family', then identifies each of them by saying 'that's Diane's grandma, 'that's Diane's grandfather, 'that's Diane's mom, 'that's Diane's dad, you know, speaking of herself in the third person! What did you think when you heard about that part?"

"I thought wow. How unbelievable, that she saw our family sitting right there watching her, then looked at our own family like they were strangers."

"But it wasn't Diane D's original personality who looked at her family as strangers. It was her other personality who did that."

"We understand that. But it is still strange to know, that Diane's physical body was sitting right there looking at our family, then identifies our family as if they were strangers! I thought it was so weird when I heard about that part!"

"But her other personality did identify each of Diane D's family members correctly!"

"Yeah, but it was like her other personality KNEW OF our family! But didn't know our family on a personal level. It is so sad!"

"It is. Do you two plan to see that video?"

"No we do not want to look at it!"

"I don't blame you. What did the rest of your family think when they saw the video?"

"None of them could look at it too long," Nancy says. "Some of them stopped watching certain parts of the video then left the room."

"They did?"

"Yes. They said they couldn't take it anymore."

"I see. Did Diane D herself watch the video?"

"Yes she looked at it with the rest of our family."

"She did? Did she watch the whole video or some of it?"

"She watched the whole video."

"She did? How did she handle it? How did she handle seeing herself on video like that?"

"She says she doesn't behave like that and would not do things like that."

"That's what she said?"

"Yeah."

"Wow." The white male reporter turns to Miranda, Bernice, Lonna and Kelly and says, "How about the rest of you Dianettes? Have any of you seen the video of Diane D's hypnosis?"

"No," Miranda, Bernice, Lonna and Kelly say.

"You haven't?"

"No."

"Do y'all want to see it?"

"No."

"You don't want to see it either?"

"No."

"Wow." The white male reporter turns back to Nancy and Charlotte and says, "Now Nancy and Charlotte, we heard that you two and your family members actually saw your cousin Diane D's physical body wrapped in chains and chained to the psychiatrist couch while she was unconscious and under hypnosis before the doctors brought her other personality out to the surface, and she wasn't even aware of it! How did you two feel, when you saw your cousin Diane D's body wrapped in chains and chained to the psychiatrist couch while she was under hypnosis and wasn't even aware of it?"

"It was sad!" Nancy says.

"Yeah very sad," Charlotte says.

"It's devastating to see anybody in that condition, especially our own family member, knowing that the doctors feel that they had no choice but to wrap your family member up in chains and have them chained to a couch, because they see your family member's other personality as a total threat and potential danger to their safety!"

"Wow," the black male reporter says. "My goodness! We also heard that the doctors discovered, that your cousin Diane D still had another personality besides her original personality and her second personality. We heard that the doctors discovered, that she had a third personality! Is that true?"

"Yes."

"And the third personality is the one who actually attacked the doctors, the security guards, the priest, the police officers and a swat team with that psychiatrist couch and used that psychiatrist couch as a weapon against them! Right?"

"Right."

"Which personality did you encounter inside your family's home, the personality who admitted to have beat up that little boy Marcus inside the school hallway?"

"Yes."

"Wow. Which of Diane D's other peronalities do you find to be the most vicious and the most cruel, the personality that you had an encouter with which is the same personality who beat up that kid Marcus inside the school hallway and kung fu kicked that stuck storage room door at the hospital wide open and tried to viciously attack the correction officers inside the jail cell, or the third personality who took down the doctors, security guards, a priest, the cops and a swat team?"

"They're both vicious and they're both cruel and I hope I never run into either one of them ever again!"

"Wow," the female reporter says. "That is something! We heard even your own grandmother Miss Margarita had her own encounter with Diane D's other personality right inside Diane D's hospital room late one night! Is that true?"

"Yes it's true."

"It's true?! Oh my God! What happened?! How did your grandmother Miss Margarita have an encounter with Diane D's other personality?!"

"It happened when she stayed with Diane overnight in the hospital."

"I heard it happened even while Diane D was sedated, unconscious and bedridden and hooked to machines and monitors! Is that true?"

"Yes it's true."

"What happened?!"

"Yeah Nancy," the black male reporter says. "Tell us about it."

"My grandma said she and the doctor were in the hospital room looking over Diane," Nancy says. "Then my grandma and the doctor stepped out of the hospital room. After the doctor left, my grandma said when she went back into the room. She said then she closed the door behind herself while her eyes were closed. When she opened her eyes and looked at Diane's hospital bed, Diane was gone."

"What!" the reporters shout.

"Diane D wasn't in the bed?!" the female reporter asks.

"No," Nancy says.

"Well where did she go?!"

"My grandma found her standing in the bathroom facing the mirror."

"What! Your grandmother found Diane D standing in the bathroom facing the mirror?!"

"Yes."

"How in the world, did Diane D wind up getting out of the bed, then go into the bathroom then stand there facing the mirror, when she was supposed to have been sedated, unconscious and bedridden?!" Nancy suspiciously looks at the female reporter. The female reporter then says, "Oh no! Don't tell me, that it was something out of this world! Don't tell me that the other soul, spirit or personality came into Diane D's physical body and had her physical body get out of the bed and go into the bathroom?!"

"You guessed it."

"Oh my God! How did Miss Margarita handle that?! Was she frightened?!"

"Of course my grandma was frightened! She was startled like I was!"

"Oh my God! What did Miss Margarita do or say when she had an encounter with her own granddaughter's other personality?!"

"She said she yelled at the other personality!"

"What! Your grandmother Miss Margarita yelled at Diane D's other personality while Diane D's other personality was in the bathroom?!"

"That's what she said."

"What did your grandmother say to that other personality?!"

"She said she told that other personality to leave Diane alone and not to come back around Diane ever again!"

"What! That's what your grandmother Miss Margarita said to Diane D's other personality?!"

"That's what she said."

"Oh my God! What did the other personality do or say when Miss Margarita told it to stay away from Diane D?! Did that other personality become aggressive towards her? Did it threaten her and attack her like it did to Doctor Stone and the other doctor?!"

"No it didn't."

"It didn't?!"

"No."

"So what did that other personality do or say?!"

"It told my grandma that it will not come around Diane anymore."

"What? That's what that other personality told your grandmother?"

"Yes."

"My God. From hearing that, I'm afraid to come near Diane D myself! I'm afraid I might accidentally get her angry and upset then the next thing I know, that other personality might surface and attack me like it did to those doctors, those security guards, the priest, police officers and a swat team!"

"That's true," the first male reporter says. "Nancy let me ask you. Has Diane D's husband ever had an encounter with her other personality?"

"Not that I know of," Nancy says.

"He hasn't?"

"Well he never mentioned anything about having an encounter with her other personality."

"He never mentioned anything at all?"

"No. I've never heard him talk about it. So I assume that he never had an encounter with her other personality. If he ever did had an encounter with her other personality, I'm sure he would have mentioned it like me and my grandma did."

"Wow." The white male reporter turns to Miranda, Bernice, Lonna and Kelly and says, "What about the rest of you Dianettes? Have any of you ever had an encounter with Diane D's other personality like Nancy and Miss Margarita did?"

"No," Miranda, Bernice, Lonna and Kelly say.

"Never?"

"No."

"Well that's good." The white male reporter turns back to Nancy and says, "Hey Nancy! Is it alright if we also talk to your grandma Miss Margarita about her encounter with Diane D's other personality? We would like to hear it from her point of view. Is it alright if you and her can come on some talk shows and talk about your encounters with Diane D's other personality?"

"Yeah Nancy," the female reporter says. "We would also like to have your family members, who witnessed the entire thing that happened inside the hypnosis room then wind up being traumatized by it, to come on some talk shows too! We would like to hear it from their point of view as well."

"My grandma doesn't really like to talk about it," Nancy says. "And neither do I and neither does the rest of my family who witnessed what happened inside that room! We would really like to try to forget about it! I'm sorry folks, but I cannot talk about it anymore because I'm starting to relive it by just thinking about it!"

"You are?"

"Yes! It was a frightening experience for me!"

"We understand Nancy. In the meantime, we hear that your family's organization is trying to have a fundraiser for the victims' of Diane D's other personality wrath and their families. Is that true?"

"Yes it's true."

"That's nice. What made your family want to do that?"

"My family feel it's the least we can do for the victims and their families, since it WAS Diane's other personality who caused some of their deaths and some of the others' injuries."

"My God!" the white male reporter says. "It seems like your cousin Diane D's other personality have no problem killing people! How does Diane D's original personality feel about that?"

"She doesn't believe she did it."

"I know her original personality doesn't believe she did it. But how does she feel that her other personality did it?"

"She doesn't believe she has another personality!"

"She doesn't?!"

"No! She doesn't believe in split personalities!"

"She doesn't?!"

"No!"

"So who do she think killed all those authority figures?!" the black reporter asks.

"She said she doesn't know WHO killed them! She says all she knows, is that SHE didn't kill them."

"That's what she said?"

"Yeah."

"Okay," the white male reporter says. "Since she doesn't believe that she killed all those authority figures, how does she feel about their deaths anyway?"

"She says she feels real bad about what happened to them."

"She feels bad about it?"

"Yeah."

"My God. So what's happening with your cousin Diane D now, where is she?"

"She's on house arrest."

"Is she?"

"Yeah."

"You mean she's not allowed outside of the house?"

"No she's not allowed outside of the house unless she be at her other grandparents' house in Queens because she's in their custody also."

"She is?"

"Yeah."

"Well which grandparents' house is she staying at right now?"

"She's back at my grandparents' house in Northern Westchester."

"She is? You mean she was just at her other grandparents' house down in Queens, then came back to your grandparents' house in Northern Westchester?"

"Correct."

"I see. So what do you think is going to happen to Diane D in the future? Will she be sent to prison for killing all those authority figures and the priest?"

"No. She's going to be committed back into the state hospital."

"What! She's going to be committed back into the state hospital again?!"

"Yes."

"Wow. For how long?"

"We don't know."

"I see. Well thanks for talking with us Nancy! And try to think about taking up our offer to appear on some talk shows because the public is real fascinated about hearing more and learning more about Diane D's other personalities! Some people have even built a web page about Diane D's other personalities!"

"What!" the Dianettes shout. "A web page?!"

"You got to be kidding," Nancy says.

"No I'm serious Nancy!" the white male reporter says. "People have built a web page dedicated to Diane D's other personalities!"

"Seriously?"

"Seriously Nancy," the female reporter says. "Diane D's other personalities has its own web page! I've seen it!"

"Oh my God."

"Yeah!" the black male reporter says. "Some people commented on the web page talking about Diane D's third personality taking down the cops, the swat team and other authority figures, saying that her third personality became a one person army! Some people labeled her third personality 'The Lone Warrior'!"

"The Lone Warrior?"

"Oh yeah! They say that is one Lone Warrior that they would not want to mess with! And they labeled her second personality 'The Ninja'!"

"The Ninja?"

"Yeah, because they heard the way it kung fu kicked that kid Marcus in the school hallway and heard the way it kung fu kicked that stuck storage room door wide open at the hospital and heard the way it tried to attack those correction officers inside the jail cell! That web page just went up last month and it already has over a million followers!"

"Over a million followers?!"

"Yes, and counting!"

"Oh my God! I don't believe it!"

"It's true Nancy!" the female reporter says. "None of you knew about it?"

"No, I guess we didn't!"

"Nobody in your family knew about it either?"

"No, I guess not!"

"Well what do you think about it?!"

"What do I think about it? I'll tell you what I think about it. I don't think people should be glorifying what those other personalities did! Lives were lost! People lost their loved ones, other victims were seriously injured! A lot of the surviving victims are still laying in the hospital, right now! Some of them are still in comas, some of them have concussions, some of them have fractured skulls, some of them had their heads split wide opened, some of them have broken necks, some of them have brain hemmorhages! Some of them could still be dying! The ones who are still alive so far might wind up being paralyzed for life, if they survive! Families were destroyed, including my family! My family have to lose our loved one too when Diane gets committed and sent away back into the state hospital! That other personality of hers did a lot of destruction that day and caused a whole bunch of chaos! So people should not be glorifying what those other personalities did at all!"

"No Nancy!" the black reporter shouts. "You got it all wrong! I don't think people are glorifying what Diane D's other personality or other personalities did! I think they're just fascinated by it."

"Fascinated by it?"

"Yeah, from afar."

"Wow Nancy," the white male reporter says. "I think you and your grandma Miss Margarita should really think about coming on some talk shows to talk about your eerie encounters with Diane D's other personalities. And I think your family members who witnessed the entire thing that happened inside that hypnosis room, should come on some talk shows too to talk about their frightening encounter with both of Diane D's other personalities inside that hypnosis room! Try to think about you, your grandma and your family members who were inside that hypnosis room to come on some talk shows. I think you all should write a book together about your eerie encounters and frightening experience with both of Diane D's other personalities!"

"Write a book?" Nancy asks.

"Yes! And the title of the book should be called 'Our Eerie And Frightening Encounters With The Other Personalities'. What do you think about that title, huh? Catchy isn't it?"

"I don't know about that. But listen. We have to go now."

"Oh. Okay Nancy. Think about it! We hope to see you and your family on some talk shows soon, and we hope to see that book of yours and your family's soon too!"

"Well, bye."

"Bye Nancy. Bye Dianettes."

Nancy turns and walks away as Charlotte, Miranda, Bernice, Lonna and Kelly turn and follow her. The reporters stand there sadly looking on at Nancy and the rest of the Dianettes.

The next day, Margarita and the rest of Diane D's family are inside the organization office. They are all surrounding Nicolas as Nicolas sits at Margarita's desk looking at the computer screen. They are shocked and stunned to see a web page of Diane D and her other personalities divided into three parts. On the first page, they see a heading that says 'THE ORIGINAL PERSONALITY'. Underneath the heading, they see another heading that says 'THE ORIGINAL'. Underneath that heading, they see photos of Diane D's original personality when she's posing in photo shoots and other photos of her singing and performing on stage with the Dianettes. They see other photos of her smiling with her family and other photos of her posing with Michael.

On the second page, they see a heading that says 'THE SECOND PERSONALITY'. Underneath the heading, they see another heading that says 'THE NINJA'. Underneath that heading, they see a pair of evil eyes that resemble Diane D's eyes with a Ninja mask above and below the eyes. Underneath the eyes, they see sketches, drawings and paintings of Diane D's 'Second Personality' angrily staring down a dark school hallway at a frightened Marcus. They then see sketches, drawings and paintings of Diane D's second personality kung fu kicking a storage room door wide opened inside a dark clinic hallway. They then see sketches, drawings and paintings of Diane D's second personality having an encounter with Nancy in a dark hallway outside bedroom doors. They see sketches, drawings and paintings of Diane D's physical body laying on the psychiatrist couch wrapped in chains and chained to the psychiatrist couch with her eyes closed and hands folded with shackles on her feet. They see sketches, drawings and paintings of two doctors sitting near Diane D's physical body near her head talking to her as she lays on the psychiatrist couch under hypnosis wrapped in chains and chained to the psychiatrist couch with her eyes closed and hands folded. They see sketches, drawings and paintings of Diane D's second personality killing people throughout the centuries. They then see sketches, drawings and paintings of Diane D's second personality having an encounter with Margarita in a dim hospital bathroom.

On the third page, they see a heading that says 'THE THIRD PERSONALITY'. Underneath the heading, they see another heading that says 'THE LONE WARRIOR'. Underneath that heading, they see another pair of evil eyes that resemble Diane D's eyes. Underneath the eyes, they see sketches, drawings and paintings of Diane D's physical body levitating over a stage. Underneath those sketches, drawings and paintings, they see more sketches, drawings and paintings of Diane D's physical body laying on the psychiatrist couch wrapped in chains and chained to the psychiatrist couch with her eyes closed and hands folded with shackles on her feet. They see more sketches, drawings and paintings of two doctors sitting near Diane D's physical body near her head talking to her as she lays on the psychiatrist couch under hypnosis wrapped in chains and chained to the psychiatrist couch with her eyes closed and hands folded. They then see sketches, drawings and paintings of Diane D's third personality breaking loose from chains breaking the chains loose from a psychiatrist couch! They see sketches, drawings and paintings of Diane D's third personality kung fu kicking the two doctors! They see sketches, drawings and paintings of Diane D's third personality holding a psychiatrist couch high up in the air as she spins her body around with the attached chains hanging from her body swirling around with her body as her frightened family and injured authority figures watch in horror from beyond! They see sketches, drawings and paintings of Diane D's third personality throwing the psychiatrist couch right across a large room at security guards as their heads lay bleeding on the floor! They see sketches, drawings and paintings of Diane D's third personality throwing the psychiatrist couch right across a room at police officers as their heads lay bleeding on the floor! They see sketches, drawings and paintings of Diane D's third personality throwing the psychiatrist couch right across the room at swat teams as their heads lay bleeding on the floor!

"My God," Nicolas says. "I can't believe they made a web page of all her personalities! Whoever drew or painted these sketches didn't seem to leave out any details! They didn't leave out any details at all!"

"I know!" Barry shouts. "I can't believe all the followers this page has! Over a million followers!"

"Wow," Tonio says.

On the fourth page, they see a heading that says 'THE 'NINJA' PERSONALITY Vs. THE 'LONE WARRIOR' PERSONALITY: WHO WOULD WIN?: Underneath the heading, they see two pairs of evil eyes that resemble Diane D's eyes. "My God!" Nicolas says. "They even have T-Shirts of all Diane's personalities!"

"T-Shirts!" everyone shockingly shouts.

"People are wearing T-Shirts of Diane's personalities?!" Margarita shouts.

"Yeah Mom!" Tonio says. "Look!"

Margarita and the rest of the family look at photos on the computer monitor. On the bottom of the page, they see people wearing T-shirts dedicated to Diane D's other personalities. Some people are wearing T-shirts that say 'THE SECOND PERSONALITY' holding their thumbs up looking at the camera smiling while other people are wearing T-shirts that say' THE THIRD PERSONALITY' holding their thumbs up looking at the camera smiling. Some people are wearing T-shirts that say 'THE NINJA PERSONALITY' holding their thumbs up looking at the camera smiling while other people are wearing T-shirts that say' THE LONE WARRIOR PERSONALITY' holding their thumbs up looking at the camera smiling. Some people are wearing T-shirts that say 'THE ORIGINAL PERSONALITY' holding their thumbs up looking at the camera smiling while other people are wearing T-shirts that say'

368

THE ORIGINAL' holding their thumbs up looking at the camera smiling. "My God!" Margarita shouts. "These people are sick! Why would they glorify what Diane's other personalities did when lives were lost, other people were injured and families were broken?!"

"I know!" Gracy shouts. "That is terrible!"

"It is," Tomas says as they all continue to look at the web page.

Chapter 30

The Diaz-Davidson Organization Does A Fundraiser

It is one week later, 4:00 Saturday afternoon. The Diaz-Davidson Organization is having a fundraising at the stadium. The stadium is packed full of people. There are around several thousand people at the stadium. Some people in the crowd are wearing T-shirts with horror fonts that say 'THE SECOND PERSONALITY' while other people in the crowd are wearing T-shirts with horror fonts that say 'THE THIRD PERSONALITY'. Other people in the crowd are wearing T-shirts with horror fonts that say 'THE NINJA PERSONALITY' while other people in the crowd are wearing T-shirts with horror fonts that say 'THE LONE WARRIOR PERSONALITY'. Some people in the crowd are wearing T-shirts with regular fonts that say 'THE ORIGINAL PERSONALITY' while other people in the crowd are wearing T-shirts with regular fonts that say 'THE ORIGINAL'.

Some people in the crowd are wearing T-shirts with drawings and paintings of Diane D's physical body laying on the psychiatrist couch wrapped in chains and chained to the psychiatrist couch with her eyes closed and hands folded with shackles on her feet. Other people in the crowd are wearing T-shirts with drawings and paintings of Diane D's physical body levitating over a stage. Some people in the crowd are wearing T-shirts with drawings and paintings of Diane D's third personality breaking loose from chains breaking the chains loose from a psychiatrist couch. Other people in the crowd are wearing T-shirts with drawings and paintings of Diane D's third personality holding a psychiatrist couch high up in the air as she spins her entire body around with the attached chains hanging from her body swirling around with her body as her frightened family and injured authority figures watch in horror.

A white woman in the crowd around her mid fifties approaches some of the people wearing the T-shirts and says, "Excuse me." The people wearing the T-shirts turn to the woman as she says to them, "I just want to ask you, where did you all get these T-shirts from? Is Diane D's family selling these T-shirts?"

"No her family is not selling these T-shirts," a young white male in the crowd says. "Some guys up the street are selling these T-Shirts."

"Some guys up the street?"

"Yeah."

"Well I hope those guys up the street use that money that they're making for a good cause. I hope they donate some of that money to the victims of Diane D's other personality's wrath and their families."

"I think they are gonna donate the money."

"Oh. Okay then. That's good. How much are they charging for the T-shirts?"

"Eight dollars each."

"Eight dollars?"

"Yeah."

"Oh. Okay, thanks."

The crowd turns from the woman and continue to happily where the T-shirts.

There is a stage at the stadium with performers doing a dance routine.

Five minutes later, the performers finish their dance routine. The crowd screams and cheer. A Hispanic male announcer comes out on stage and shouts to the crowd, "Let's give it up for the Essential Dance Crew!" The crowd screams and cheer again. The announcer then shouts, "Okay Ladies and gentlemen, we have another wonderful Diaz-Davidson act about to come out. Ladies and gentlemen, let's hear it for the Techno Band!" The crowd starts to cheer. Five white male band members come out on stage with their guitars and wave to the crowd. The band starts to play the guitar and sing some tunes.

Five minutes later, the announcer is backstage. He turns to two Latin females Carmen, a slim Hispanic woman with long curly hair, and Rachel, a plus-size Hispanic woman with a very short curly hair cut, who both wanted to perform on stage with Diane D two years prior, but wound up having problems with the Dianettes instead. He says to them, "Are you Ladies ready to perform?"

"Yeah we're ready," Carmen says. "As long as we don't have problems with the Dianettes like we did before when we tried to perform with Diane D."

"Well you're not trying to perform with Diane D now are you?"

"No," Rachel says. "Diane D is not allowed to perform."

"Okay then. As long as you're not trying to perform with Diane D, you'll be alright."

"Okay."

"When the Techno Band finshes, I'm gonna get back on stage and announce you guys."

"Okay."

The announcer turns and walks away.

Five minutes later, the Techno Band finish their performance. The crowd cheers. The Techno Band turns and leave the stage. The announcer comes back on stage and shouts, "Alright ladies and gentlemen, give it up one more time for the Techno Band!" The crowd cheers again. The announcer then shouts, "Okay, the next performance is about to come out! Ladies and gentlemen! The Diaz-Davidson Organization presents Carmen and Rachel!" The crowd screams and cheers as Carmen and Rachel come out on stage. Latin music starts to play. Carmen and Rachel start to do a little Latin dance routine as they sway their hips and twist their feet to the music. They then start to sing and perform a Latin duet song.

A few minutes later, Carmen and Rachel finish their song duet. The crowd cheers. Carmen and Rachel turn and leave the stage. The announcer comes back on stage and shouts, "Alright ladies and gentlemen, give it up one more time for Carmen and Rachel!" The crowd cheers again.

Five minutes later, the crowd starts to wonder around the stadium. A large group of a Hispanic family and Hispanic friends walk around the stadium. They are also wearing the different T-shirts that say 'THE NINJA', 'THE LONE WARRIOR' and 'THE ORIGINAL'. They look around the crowd. One of the young men in the group around his early twenties looks in the distance and shouts, "Hey! There goes Diane D! Oh my God, I see Diane D over there!"

"What!" the rest of the family and friends shout.

"You see Diane D?" a young female around her early twenties shouts. "Where?"

"Over there with her family!"

"Oh my God!" The family and friends look and see Diane D way in the distance surrounded by the Dianettes, her family and a bunch of other relatives. They see two probation officers standing near her family and relatives.

"Oh wow!" an older woman in the group says. "I didn't know that Diane D would be here!"

"Well this IS her family's organization's fundraising!" an older man in the group says.

"Yeah but we didn't know that SHE would be here! We heard that she's on house arrest!"

"She is. I think those are her probation officers standing right near her and her family."

"They are?"

"Yeah." The people continue to look at Diane D.

In the distance, Diane D is surrounded by the Dianettes as the Dianettes talk to her. She is leaning against a bench as she holds the 2 year-old Spanish boy who was on her hospital bed by piggyback as the little boy stands on the back of the bench with his arms around Diane D's shoulders. At the same time, Diane D also holds the 2 year-old Spanish girl who was on her hospital bed on her chest with the little girl's arms around her shoulders also. She still has the ankle monitor strapped around her ankle. Her brothers Nicolas and Mickey are there, Michael is there, her aunts Marilyn, Aunt Celeste, Aunt Jean, Aunt Laura are there, her Uncle Willie is there. Tomas is there talking with his look alike brother from the Dominican Republic. Grandpa Mike is talking with his look alike brother from St. Thomas. Margarita's sister Marlena from the Dominican Republic is there. Gracy is there. Diane D's two probation officers are there and tons of her other relatives are there.

Back in the distance, some people continue to look at Diane D as the older woman says, "Wow, I wonder how she feels about all these people out here wearing these T-shirts about all her personalities."

"I don't know if she even notices it," a man in the crowd says. "She's standing in the front not far from the stage. Everybody else in the crowd is behind her. I don't know if she even sees them wearing the T-shirts."

"Wow."

"I wonder which personality of hers is there right now," another woman in the crowd says, "her original personality, her second personality or her third personality.

"I don't know," another man says, "and I wouldn't want to go up to her to find out either! I don't want to run into any of her personalities."

"No? What about her original personality?"

"I don't know. That second or third personality of hers might come out to the surface and strike at any minute if her original personality gets upset or angry."

"I know."

"How can her family and her probation officers be close to her?" the young Hispanic male asks. "Aren't they scared that other personality of hers might come out and kill them like it did to those police officers, swat team members and now a priest?!"

"I know! I'm not stepping foot over there near Diane D!"

"Me neither! She's a cop killer! She killed three police officers and two swat team members and don't even know it! Now she just killed a priest! She's a priest killer now!"

"I know! Ain't that messed up?!"

"It sure is," the older man says. "Several schools had requested for her to visit them around a year ago?"

"They did?"

"Yeah."

"Even though she beat up that kid Marcus?"

"Yeah, but after all that had happened with her other personalities and the authority figures this year, they all cancelled that idea."

"I don't blame them! Nobody wants a killer at their schools, especially with children!"

"I know." The people continue to look at Diane D.

Back in the distance, the little Spanish boy piggybacking on Diane D's back is drinking from a juice bottle. The little girl on Diane D's chest suddenly reaches over Diane D's right shoulder and grabs the juice box drink from the little boy. The little boy starts to holler. Mary approaches the little boy and shouts to him, "Aquí! Usted toma este!" Mary hands the little boy a juice box drink then hands the little girl another juice box drink. The little boy and the little girl both start to drink out of the juice boxes. Diane D looks at the little girl as the little girl drinks the juice box. She then turns her head and looks at the little boy. She turns her head back towards the Dianettes as the Dianettes continue to talk with her.

Back in the distance, the crowd continues to watch Diane D staring at her as the older woman in the crowd says, "I still wonder is that her other personality right there or is it her normal personality?"

"You want to go up to her and find out?" another man in the crowd says.

"Hell no! I'm not stepping foot over there near Diane D!"

"Me neither!"

"How can those two little kids that she's holding be anywhere near her?!" a third woman in the crowd says. "I'm scared for them!"

"I'm scared for them too!" a second man in the crowd says.

"Who are they anyway?"

"I think they're her little relatives from the Dominican Republic."

"Her relatives from the Dominican Republic?"

"Yeah. I heard a whole lot of her relatives came up from the Dominican Republic when they heard what was happening with her."

"Oh yeah?"

"Yeah." Crowd continues to look at Diane D.

Forty-five minutes later, the fundraiser is about over. Margarita comes on the stage. The crowd sees her and starts to cheer. Margarita grabs a microphone. She then speaks into the microphone and shouts to the crowd, "Hello everyone!"

The crowd cheers again as they shout, "Miss Margarita!"

Margarita speaks to the crowd and says, "Okay everyone!" Everyone in the crowd, including Diane D and the rest of the family look at Margarita as Margarita shouts, "I would like to thank each and everyone of you for coming here to this fundraiser!" The crowd cheers again as Margarita shouts, "I would like to thank all of you for supporting this fundraiser event! My family and I really appreciate this from the bottom of our hearts! Thanks to all of you for making this possible! Now as we close the fundraiser, the Techno Band will close the show! Thank you again!" The Techno Band come back on stage as the crowd cheers. Margarita turns and heads towards the side of the stage. She then steps down from the stage.

Margarita turns to Tomas and shouts, "Tomas!" Tomas turns towards Margarita as she shouts to him, "Voy a ir a la cocina y decir a los trabajadores para iniciar la limpieza! Todos mantienen sus ojos en Diane! Estaré de vuelta!"

"Esta bien Margarita!" Tomas shouts.

Margarita turns and heads into the stadium building as the Techno Band start to play their music again.

In the distance, some of the people in the crowd are about to leave, but before the leave, they look in the distance and take another look at Diane D.

In the distance, Barry takes the little boy off Diane D's back. Diane D then takes the little girl off her chest. She gently puts the little girl down. Another little Spanish girl around three-years old holds her arms up to Diane D wanting Diane D to pick her up. Diane D looks down at the little girl and says to her, "Hold on Baby?" Diane D then turns to Barry and says, "Dad. I'm gonna head inside."

"We'll go with you Diane," Barry says.

Diane D turns from everybody and starts to head towards the building as the Dianettes turn and follow her. The rest of Diane D's family and relatives turn and start to follow her. The two probation officers turn and start to follow Diane D and everybody else towards the building.

Ten minutes later, the Dianettes, Diane D's family and relatives are all standing in the building outside the Ladies' Bathroom all chit-chatting as the two probation officers stand aside looking on. Suddenly the Ladies bathroom door opens. Diane D comes right out of the Ladies' bathroom followed by Nancy, Gracy, Aunt Celeste, Aunt Jean and Aunt Laura. The Dianettes turn towards Diane D. They then approach Diane D. Diane D then turns the other way and starts to head down the hallway as the Dianettes walk with her surrounding her. Everybody else turns and follow Diane D as the two probation officers turn and follow also.

Inside the kitchen area, the Diaz-Davidson staff members are putting food away trying to clean up the place as an Asian male stadium worker and a slim dark skinned African female stadium worker around her mid thirties wearing a turban argue with a Hispanic male staff member. Other staff members come between them trying to break up the commotion. Margarita suddenly approaches and shouts, "What the heck is going on here?!" She tries to go between the Asian male, the African woman and the Hispanic male and shouts, "What happened?!"

"I'll tell you what happened Miss Margarita!" the Hispanic male shouts. "Those two stadium workers came right into this kitchen and tried to sneak all that leftover food into their bags! They are stealing food from this area and caused me to drop my plate of food, now they won't clean it up!"

"We didn't make you drop that plate of food!" the Asian male shouts back. "You made your own self drop that plate of food?!"

"Yeah because you two were trying to steal the food?!"

"We weren't trying to steal the food!" the African woman shouts back with an accent. "Maybe if you weren't so high, you would walk straight and see where you're going!"

"Maybe if I wasn't so high?! So you want to start with me?!"

"I should!"

"Don't mess with me!"

"I need to!"

"You keep messing with me, you here?!"

"Don't tempt me!" the African woman shouts as she points her finger at the Hispanic man.

"Excuse me Miss!" Margarita shouts to the African woman. "Can you just go to the side?!"

"You keep messing with me!" the Hispanic male shouts to the African woman.

"I will!" the African woman shouts back. She starts mocking the Hispanic male.

"Alright Miss!" Margarita shouts to the African woman. "That's enough!"

"You keep messing with me!" the Hispanic male shouts to the African woman again.

The African woman continues to mock the Hispanic male as Margarita shouts to her, "Alright Miss, that's enough!"

"Grandma!" Diane D's voice calls out. Diane D suddenly enters the kitchen as the Dianettes and the rest of her family and relatives follow right behind her. They are stunned to see a commotion. They stop and stand a few yards away looking on at the commotion.

"You keep messing with me!" the Hispanic man continues to shout to the African woman. Tomas, Barry and Tonio approach the commotion.

The African woman continues to mock the Hispanic male as Margarita shouts to her, "Alright Miss! I said that's enough!" The African woman still continues to mock the Hispanic male as Margarita shouts to her, "Excuse me Miss! That's enough!" The African woman still continues to mock the Hispanic male. Margarita puzzled looks at the African woman and shouts to her, "Excuse me Miss! Do you hear me?! Miss!" The African woman still continues to mock the Hispanic male. Margarita turns to Tomas and Barry and puzzled looks at them as Diane D and the rest of the crowd look on at the African woman. Mary steps away from the crowd and walks towards the African woman.

Mary approaches the African woman and shouts to her, "Excuse me Miss! But my mom is speaking to you!" The African woman stops and looks at Mary stunned as Mary shouts to her, "My mom does not need this crap, neither does the rest of my family! We already been through a whole lot and we certainly do not need this added drama! Since you didn't seem to hear my mom speaking to you, let me have a word with you! I want to talk to you way in the back of the hallway! Since you seem to be hard of hearing, I'm going to REALLY get loud back there! So let's go to the back of the hallway so I can scream at you! Let's go this way!" Mary grabs the African woman by the arm and starts to lead the African woman away.

The African woman stunned looks at Mary and shouts, "Where're we going?!"

"Come let me talk to you!" Mary continues to take the African woman away.

"Don't be too hard on her Mary," Margarita says.

"I won't Mom!" Mary takes the African woman to the back door as the Asian man turns and follows.

Margarita then approaches Tomas, Barry and Tonio as they stare towards Mary and the African woman watching Mary and the African woman go out the back door. Margarita then turns to Barry and says, "Barry, I think you better keep an eye on Mary."

"You got that right mom," Barry says. Margarita, Tomas and Tonio look towards Barry as he heads towards the back door to follow Mary. They then turn towards each other. They then turn towards Diane D and start to walk towards her. They approach Diane D as everyone starts to surround her.

Chapter 31

Diane D Returns Back To The Mental Institution

Diane D is laying on her bed chest down with her face to the side sadly staring into space as her family and relatives sadly surround her. Margarita then says, "Diane? Are you okay?"

Diane D turns around chest up. She sits up on the bed and says, "No I'm not okay Grandma. I don't want to be committed again and have to leave you all again. Man, I should have never allowed myself to be hypnotized, because look where it's gotten me. Now I have to be committed again and leave home again."

"I know baby. We'll be staying with you at the state hospital."

"I know, but that's not the point Grandma. I still have to leave home and I don't want to. Did Doctor Stone say how long I will be committed?"

"No he didn't say how long Diane," Barry says. "We don't know. But we have to get you going. Doctor Stone is downstairs waiting for you."

"There I go again back into the state hospital." Diane D's family and relatives are in tears as they sadly look at her.

It is fifteen minutes later. There are a few vans outside Margarita and Tomas mansion. Diane D's family and Michael are outside the vans loading Diane D's luggage into the back of the first van which is a 15-seat passenger van as Dr. Stone and Diane D's two probation officers stand aside looking on. Diane D stands outside the van talking with Nancy and Charlotte as Michael turns to her and says, "I got your papers Diane."

"Okay Michael," Diane D says.

Margarita turns to Diane D and says, "Obtener en el interior de la camioneta Diane." Diane D turns and is about to get into the van as Nancy and Charlotte are about to follow her in. Margarita turns to Nancy and Charlotte and says to them, "Wait you two." Diane D,

Nancy and Charlotte stop as Margarita says to Nancy and Charlotte, "Sólo quiero Diane para entrar en la furgoneta por ahora."

"Just me?" Diane D asks.

"Yes just you." Margarita turns back to Nancy and Charlotte and says, "Por el momento, ustedes dos ir y obtén el resto de las pertenencias de Diane."

"Okay Grandma," Nancy and Charlotte say as they turn and walk away from the van.

Margarita turns back to Diane D and says, "Entrar en la camioneta."

"But nobody else is inside the van yet Grandma," Diane D says. "I thought you didn't trust me being anywhere by myself."

"I don't Diane."

"But you trust me being in the van by myself?"

"Yes I trust you being in the van by yourself Diane, you know why? Because I'm going to give you this bible to hold and to read again," Margarita says as she holds a bible up to Diane D. "Instead of you having the urge to meditate, I want you to have the urge to read the bible and I want you to continue reading this bible while we're riding to the state hospital."

"Read the bible while we're riding to the hospital?"

"That's right."

"Do I have to Grandma?"

"Listen Diane, I want you to read this bible the whole entire time we're riding to the state hospital unless you happen to fall asleep, do you understand?"

"But Grandma..."

"Do you understand Diane?!"

Diane D sadly looks at Margarita. She then says, "Yes Grandma."

"Good. Ahora toma la Biblia dentro de la furgoneta y empezar a leerlo." Margarita hands the bible to Diane D. Diane D takes the bible. Margarita then says, "And I want you to sit right there in the middle of the second row seat while you're reading the bible." Diane D turns and gets into the van. Once Diane D gets inside the van, Margarita shouts to her, "Start reading!" Margarita closes the van door. She gives another look towards Diane D. She then turns and walks away from the van and walks towards the rest of her family.

Diane D is inside the van sitting in the middle of the second row seat frustrated and upset as she looks out the window at Margarita. She then turns her head and looks around the van. She sees that she is all alone inside there. She turns her head back forward and looks back out the window angrily looking back at Margarita. She then sighs and looks down at the bible that's in her hands. She opens it and starts to read it.

Outside the van, Dr. Stone brings Margarita, Tomas, Mary and

Barry to the side away from the van. He speaks to them and says, "So how does Diane feel about herself killing people, especially police officers, and now a priest?!"

"She still don't believe she did it Doctor Stone!" Margarita says.

"She doesn't?"

"No!"

"Why not?"

"Because she says she's not a killer!"

"She's still claiming that?"

"Yes Doctor Stone! She says she does not go around killing people!"

"That's the same thing she said about that kid Marcus, that she doesn't believe she beat him up either and claims she does not go around beating up children! It's true that her ORIGINAL soul, spirit and personality doesn't go around beating up children or killing people. Too bad we can't say the same for her other personalities."

"That's true Doctor Stone," Mary says. "So far Diane still believes that she's being punished for something she didn't do!"

"It is true that her original personality is being punished for something her original personality didn't do."

"Doctor Stone," Tomas says. "I'm still worried about while Diane is committed in the mental institution, that other personality will pull her original soul and spirit right out of her physical body again then enter her physical body and take her place again like it did before, and the people in the mental insitution won't even know it. They'll just assume that it's Diane's original soul, spirit and personality!"

"Well it's a good thing that some of you guys are staying in the mental institution with her. That way that other soul, spirit or personality will keep away from her and stay at bay. That other soul, spirit or personality did say that they DO NOT pull Diane's original soul and spirit out of her physical body and enter it while her family is around. It did claim that it does not have an encounter with Diane's family while Diane is in the state hospital, that they leave the family encounter to Diane herself. Have any of you including Nancy and Charlotte ever encountered that other personality again since Diane left the hospital?"

"No," Barry says. "As far as we know, none of us encountered that other personality since Diane left the hospital. We haven't noticed anything strange about her."

"You haven't?"

"No. So far she's been behaving normal."

"She has?"

"As far as we saw, she has."

"What about her facial appearance? Has her facial appearance seem normal or pale?"

"As far as we've seen, we haven't notice anything strange about her facial appearance either."

"You haven't?"

"No."

"Has she been meditating since she left the hospital?"

"As far as we know, she hasn't meditated. We had her watched at all times."

"You have?"

"Yes we have."

"What about Dana? Has she been meditating so far?"

"If Diane is not meditating, you will not find Dana meditating either, so you really don't have to worry about her."

"Oh that's good. Maybe that's why that other soul, spirit or personality hasn't come around, because Diane hasn't been able to meditate again with you all having her be watched. Maybe your method of having Diane be watched at all times worked Miss Margarita."

"I hope so Doctor Stone," Margarita says. "All I can do is hope so, because if that other soul, spirit or personality comes back inside my grandchild's body again, I have more words to say to it!"

"You do?"

"Of course I do!"

"Wow, you have guts Miss Margarita. I don't know if anybody else would want to challenge that other soul, spirit or personality! After what happened inside that hypnosis room whiched so far caused six people to lose their life, I don't dare challenge that other soul, spirit or personality ever again!"

"Well I better have guts Doctor Stone! I have to have guts in order to protect my grandchild!"

"I understand Miss Margarita. But when I tried to challenge that other soul, spirit or personality and told it to stay away from Diane and not to come back around her anymore, we all saw what happened as a result. Her other soul, spirit or personality broke loose from those chains and viciously assaulted me and Doctor Kahn and brutally attacked anybody else who dared to enter that hypnosis room. That soul, spirit and personality has taken the lives of six people from that incident and has even driven Marcus to take his own life! That's seven deaths altogether, so far! But for some reason, that other soul, spirit and personality did not turn on you inside that hospital room bathroom Miss Margarita. It didn't turn on you when YOU told it to stay away from Diane and not to come back around Diane anymore. Instead, it just seemed to respect you and told you that it won't come back around Diane anymore. Why did that other soul, spirit and personality respect YOU Miss Margarita? What's your secret?"

"There is no secret Doctor Stone. That other soul, spirit or personality told me plain and simple, because I'm Diane's family and that Diane loves her family."

"I figured that might be the reason, but you just confirmed to me, that it is."

"That is the reason Doctor Stone, there's no other reason, or secret."

Dr. Stone sadly looks at Margarita. Margarita then says, "Well I guess we better go get Diane settled in at the State Hospital, because after we get her settled in, we're going to come back for Dana."

"Dana? You're going to come back for Dana? Come back for Dana for what?"

"To be committed!"

"What! To be committed?! You want Dana to be committed Miss Margarita?!"

"Of course I do! She needs to get counseling!"

"But she hasn't done anything! She didn't kill anybody so far!"

"That's right she didn't kill anybody, yet! And that's the way I want to keep it! I don't want Dana to get influenced by Diane anymore and wind up meditating with her again! After what that other soul, spirit or personality told me inside that hospital room bathroom, that they were about to use Dana's physical body in an attempted murder and Dana didn't even know about it and wasn't aware of it, that scared me! What also scares me, is the fact that Dana STILL does not know that her own physical body was about to be used in an attempted murder!"

"Oh my God."

"So I said to myself, 'no way'! Dana needs to be committed too and watched whenever she's with Diane! It's bad enough that Diane meditates and now we have to worry about Dana meditating right along with her too?! Especially now that I know the fact that Dana sees absolutely nothing wrong with Diane meditating?! No! She is going to be committed and get counseling to keep her from going along with Diane and meditating again! I'm not gonna let her escape this!"

"But how did you find out that Dana sees nothing wrong with Diane meditating?"

"Nancy and Charlotte told me! They told me that when they were staying at Gracy and Mike's house and Diane left the bedroom and didn't come back, they left the bedroom and told Dana about it! They said Dana told them that Diane went down to the kitchen. They said that they asked Dana could she go down to the kitchen and check on Diane because they were afraid that Diane could be secretly meditating while she's alone down in the kitchen and no one is watching her, and they said that Dana said to them 'So what. What's wrong with her meditating?"

"What's wrong with her meditating?! That's what Dana said to them?"

"That's what Nancy and Charlotte told us! They said to Dana 'doesn't she know that strange things usually occur whenever Diane meditates'! Then they said Dana told them those strange things that occur have nothing to do with Diane meditating, that she thinks they're coincidences."

"Coincidences?! Dana think they're coincidences?!"

"Yeah, according to Nancy and Charlotte! They said they asked

Dana again could she go downstairs to check on Diane because they told her they don't want to run into that other personality just in case that other personality emerges out of Diane again and they said Dana told them 'there's no such thing that she doesn't believe in split personalities that she doesn't believe that another personality caused Diane to attack the doctors, a priest, security guards, police officers and a swat team that she believe Diane's original personality attacked them and got so angry that her original personality forgot she did it'! She believes that Diane's original personality was so angry that she blocked it out and thinks it could happen to anybody."

"That's what Dana thinks, that things like that can happen to anybody?!"

"That's what Nancy and Charlotte said!"

"Things like that don't happen to anybody. As a matter of fact, I don't think things like that happens to other people at all, just Diane!"

"Well Dana certainly doesn't believe that it was another personality involved?"

"Then where does she think Diane get her superhuman strength from when Diane literally broke loose from those chains she was wrapped in and breaking the chains loose from the couch she was chained to then lifting and tossing that heavy couch thirty feet across a room at seventy or eighty miles an hour, faster than most cars?! Where does she think Diane get her superhuman strength from?!"

"She think they're just coincidences too! She doesn't believe in split personalities at all! She's just like Diane because Diane doesn't believe in split personalities either! They both think all these supernatural occurences that happen right after Diane meditates are just plain coincidences! So therefore, after we get Diane settled in, we're coming back for Dana, because she's next! Gracy and Mike will be waiting for us when we come back for Dana."

"They are? So that means they agree with you?"

"Yes they do. They and Dana's parents are planning to ride with us when we come back for Dana."

"You got it Miss Margarita."

"Let's go." Margarita turns and walks away as everyone else turn and follow her.

Margarita shouts to the rest of her family, "Let's get going everybody!" Margarita turns and walks to the van as everyone else turns and follows her.

Inside the van, Diane D is now leaned back against the second row seat with one knee up holding the bible in front of herself leaning it against her lap as she angrily looks at it reading it. She then hears the van door about to open. She looks towards the van door and sees Michael coming into the van. Michael says to her, "Hey Diane, slide over this way. Your mom is gonna sit on the opposite side of you while

I sit on this side of you." Diane D sits up. She then slides over towards Michael. Michael sits down next to Diane D and puts his arm around her shoulders. Michael looks at Diane D and says, "Is everything okay?"

"No everything is not okay Michael," Diane D says. "I'm still being committed."

"It's going to be okay." Michael and Diane D then look outside the van at the rest of the family.

Mary then gets into the opposite side of the van. She sits right next to Diane D's left. Barry then gets into the other side of the van. Charlotte gets into the van followed by Nancy. Mickey gets into the van followed by Nicolas. Margarita gets into the van followed by Tomas. One of the probation officers get into the front passenger seat as Dr. Stone goes around the van to the driver's side. Dr. Stone then gets into the driver's seat.

Uncle Tonio, Aunt Marilyn and other relatives get into a second and third vans. The vans sit there for a minute. Then all the vans' doors closes. The vans then drive off and head down the road following one another.

It is two hours later. The three vans continue to drive as they drive in Upstate New York.

Inside the first van, Dr. Stone continues to drive. Everyone else inside the van has fallen asleep except for one of the probation officers who's sitting in the front passenger seat. Michael, Diane D and Mary are sleeping in the second row seat with Diane D laying on Mary. Tomas, Charlotte and Margarita are sleeping in the third row seat with Charlotte laying on Margarita. Barry, Nancy and Mickey are sleeping in the fourth row seat and Nicolas and the other probation officer are sleeping in the fifth row.

As Dr. Stone continues to drive, he looks in the rearview mirror. He suddenly sees Diane D's other personality sitting there with the eerie pale face and puffy swollen eyes angrily staring at him through the rearview mirror! "Aaaahh!" Dr. Stone screams! He panics and is about to have an accident! Suddenly Diane D's other personality quickly lunges at Dr. Stone and grabs him by the neck! "Aaaahh!" Dr. Stone screams as the van goes off the road and crashes through a rail barrier! The van then goes over a cliff and plunges as Doctor Stone screams, "Aaaaaaaaahhhh!"

PRESENT:

"Aaaaahh!" Dr. Stone screams as he wakes up from a nightmare! He looks around and finds himself sitting in the passenger seat of the van instead of the driver's seat as the van continues driving. He nervously turns his head around and looks towards the back seats and sees Diane D and her family puzzled staring at him with Diane D leaning her back against Mary's chest with Mary's arms wrapped around her.

"What's going on Doctor Stone?!" Margarita shouts from the third row seat.

"Yeah!" Barry shouts from the fourth row seat. "You practically scared us half to death! What happened?!"

Dr. Stone is nervous and sweaty as he puzzled looks towards the back seats. He then looks towards the driver's seat. He sees the probation officer driving the van instead. The probation officer puzzled looks at Dr. Stone and says, "Doctor Stone, are you okay?" Dr. Stone puzzled looks at the probation Officer.

"What happened Stone?!" Margarita shouts.

Dr. Stone turns his head back around towards Margarita and nervously says, "Oh! It was nothing Miss Margarita! It's just that I had a bad dream that's all."

"A bad dream?!"

"Yeah."

"About what?!"

"Yeah Doctor Stone," Michael says. "What happened in your dream that made you scream?"

"Well," Doctor Stone says as Diane D and her family puzzled stare at him. "Oh nothing. It's just that I dreamt we had an accident."

"You dreamt we had an accident?!" Margarita shouts.

"Yeah. I got startled and woke up that's all. I didn't mean to wake you all. I'm sorry." Dr. Stone then turns his head and looks back at the probation officer. He then whispers, "What am I doing in the passenger seat? Wasn't I driving?"

"Yes you were driving Doctor Stone," the probation officer whispers as he continues to drive, "but you kept dozing off at the wheel! We almost had an accident!"

"We ALMOST had an accident?!"

"Almost! So I had to take over the wheel or else we would have actually had an accident!"

"Oh my God! But how did you wind up taking over the wheel while I was driving?"

"I encouraged you to pull over to the side, so you did. Then I got out of the car, came to the driver's side, got you out of the driver's seat and walked you to the passenger seat, sat you down in the passenger seat, closed the passenger door then I went back around and got into the driver's seat. That's when I took over the wheel."

"Oh yeah?"

"Yes."

"I don't remember any of that."

"Well of course you might not remember any of it, you were out of it, that's why you don't remember. You were tired and probably just needed some rest, that's all."

"Oh." Dr. Stone continues to puzzled look at the probation officer. He then turns his head back around again and looks back at Diane D's family who are trying to go back to sleep. Dr. Stone puzzled looks at Diane D. Then he puzzled stares at Diane D.

Diane D has the back of her head and shoulders laid on Mary's lap with her eyes closed, head back and the bible still in her hands while her legs rest on Michael's lap. Mary looks down at Diane D as she strokes and checks the skin on the front of Diane D's neck. Margarita leans forward towards the second row seat and checks on Diane D. Mary turns to Margarita and says, "Ella está bien Mamá. Ella se había secado para arriba polvo en el cuello."

"Ella hizo?" Margarita asks.

"Sí. Tuve cuidado de ello ya."

"Bueno eso es bueno," Margarita smiles and says. Margarita takes one more look at Diane D. She then leans back in her seat as Charlotte leans her head and back against her. Mary looks back down at Diane D. She smiles at Diane D then bends and gives Diane D a loving kiss on the cheek. Diane D feels the kiss and smiles as her eyes remain closed. Mary hugs and holds Diane D more tight. She brings Diane D up a little as she presses her and Diane D's faces against each other. Mary then lays her profile right on top of Diane D's face as she tries to rock Diane D back to sleep.

Dr. Stone continues to puzzled stare at Diane D. He then turns his head and looks back at the probation officer as the probation officer continues to drive. He then turns his head forward and worriedly looks out through the front window.

THE END